D0182412

7 241 343 000

Robert Fabbri read Drama and Theatre at London University and worked in film and TV for twenty-five years. He has a life-long passion for ancient history, which inspired him to write the bestselling Vespasian series and the Alexander's Legacy series. He lives in London and Berlin.

Also by Robert Fabbri

ALEXANDER'S LEGACY

TO THE STRONGEST

THE THREE PARADISES

AN EMPTY THRONE

ARCHIAS THE EXILE-HUNTER

THE ISSOS INCIDENT

THE SIEGE OF TYROS

THE VESPASIAN SERIES

TRIBUNE OF ROME

ROME'S EXECUTIONER

FALSE GOD OF ROME

ROME'S FALLEN EAGLE

MASTERS OF ROME

ROME'S LOST SON

THE FURIES OF ROME

ROME'S SACRED FLAME

EMPEROR OF ROME

MAGNUS AND THE CROSSROADS BROTHERHOOD

THE CROSSROADS BROTHERHOOD

THE RACING FACTIONS

THE DREAMS OF MORPHEUS

THE ALEXANDRIAN EMBASSY

THE IMPERIAL TRIUMPH

THE SUCCESSION

Also

ARMINIUS: LIMITS OF EMPIRE

ALEXANDER'S LEGACY

BABYLON

ROBERT FABBRI

CORVUS

First published in Great Britain in 2022 by Corvus,
an imprint of Atlantic Books Ltd.

10 9 8 7 6 5 4 3 2 1

A CIP catalogue record for this book is available from the British Library.

Hardback ISBN: 978 1 83895 609 7
E-book ISBN: 978 1 83895 611 0

Corvus
An imprint of Atlantic Books Ltd
Ormond House
26–27 Boswell Street
London
WC1N 3JZ

www.corvus-books.co.uk

Printed and bound by CPI Group (UK) Ltd, Croydon CR0 4YY

To my wife, Anja, with all my love.

SELEUKOS
THE BULL-ELEPHANT

ROXANNA
THE WILD-CAT

POLYP...
TH...

MACEDON

THRACE

AMPHIPOLIS
PASSERON PELLA
EPIRUS THESSALONIKE KARDIA BYZANTIUM
PYDNA
THESSALY LEMNOS CIUS
HELLESPONTINE AMISIUS
ERYTHRAE HALYS KAPPADO...
LYDIA PHRYGIA
CORINTH SARDIS
MEGALOPOLIS ATHENS EPHESUS
SPARTA CELAENAE
CARIA PISIDIA CILICIA

RHODOS TARSUS ISSUS ...MES...
RHOSOS
CYPRUS THAPSACU...
MARION SALAMIS TRIPOLIS
PATHOS KITION SYRI...

BERYTOS DAMASC...
TYROS

CYRENE
BARCA
CYRENAICA
NILE DELTA
HIEROSPHYMA
ALEXANDRIA GAZA
PELUSIUM ARAB...
MEMPHIS

EGYPT

Nil

W...

PTOLEMY
THE BASTARD

KASSANDROS
THE JEALOUS

A list of characters can be found on page 477.

SELEUKOS.
THE BULL-ELEPHANT.

'**G**ARROTTED?'

'Yes, sir, I saw the body.'

Seleukos squeezed his throat and winced as he digested the spy's news. 'That it should have come to this: Alexander's generals executing each other as if they were common thieves or murderers.' Rubbing the back of his thick neck, he shook his head; the spy made no comment. *None of us deserve a slow death like that; not even a sly little Greek like Eumenes.*

He walked to the window of his first-floor suite in the palace of Ataxerxes, a royal hunting lodge on the western bank of the Cheaspes River, and gazed across his siege lines towards Susa, on the far bank, set before the magnificence of the Zagros Mountains, verdant with forest and tipped by ice-laden peaks. With cool air and plentiful game, the city had always been a favourite of the old Persian Achaemenid dynasty and, as such, contained a royal treasury full of the bounty of the east. It was because of this fortune that Antigonos the One-Eyed had entrusted the siege of Susa to Seleukos six months previously, with inadequate resources. High were its walls, tall were its towers and bitter was its defence in the able hands of Xenophilus, the garrison commander and warden of the royal treasury. *Curse the old cyclops for leaving me just two thousand men to take a city, knowing full well that it wasn't enough, but what can I do? By executing Eumenes, Antigonos has just sent a loud message to anyone who thinks to stand against him. How can I retain Babylon now?*

And that was the problem in which Seleukos had found himself: he had been set up to fail by the man whose ambition now drove him to possess the empire that Alexander had bequeathed to 'the strongest', neglecting to specify exactly who he meant.

In the aftermath of the great man's death, his former body-guards and senior generals had quickly disagreed upon who should command and stand regent for Alexander's as yet unborn child. Matters had been further complicated by a faction within the army insisting that Alexander's dim-witted half-brother, Philip, be made joint king, causing yet further rift – especially when Roxanna was delivered of a boy named after his father. Perdikkas, the senior bodyguard to whom Alexander had handed the Great Ring of Macedon as he uttered those fateful words, tried but failed to assert his leadership in the name of the kings, and was dead within two years – indeed, Seleukos had been one of the three to wield the assassin's blade.

It had been Eumenes, Alexander's former secretary, a Greek among Macedonians, ever loyal to the Argead royal house, for the favour he had been shown by Alexander and his father, Philip, before him, who had fought to keep the empire entire for their line. The sly little Greek had battled with Antipatros, the eighty-year-old regent of Macedon, as he had attempted to take power on Perdikkas' death. However, during this struggle, Krateros, the darling of the army and Macedon's greatest living general, had been killed; Eumenes had been held responsible, outlawed and condemned to death by the army assembly.

At a conference at The Three Paradises, a royal hunting park in the hills above Berytus in Phoenicia, Antipatros had made a settlement, distributing military commands and satrapies – including making Seleukos the satrap of Babylonia. However, the agreement could be but temporary, for it failed to address just where power lay: was the empire subject to Macedon or was the home-country an equal part of that empire? And, besides, the satrap of Egypt, Ptolemy – reputed to be the bastard half-brother of Alexander – had refused to attend thus signalling that he considered himself independent; the empire had already started to disintegrate.

Antipatros too had died, grieving for his young son, Iollas, killed in a skirmish with Eumenes, leaving Antigonos untrammelled to make his claim for empire; a claim that Seleukos had supported – albeit reluctantly – for he could not bring himself to join with Eumenes and take orders from a Greek. But Eumenes had resisted Antigonos to the last in the name of both the kings and then solely for the young son once Alexander's mother, Olympias, had murdered the fool.

And now Eumenes was dead, defeated in battle and then executed by Antigonos, the satrap of Phrygia whom Alexander had left behind to complete the conquest of Anatolia as he marched on, south and then east, to steal an empire. But the man who had been almost forgotten by all as Alexander had led his army in glory to Egypt, Persis, Media, Bactria and even to India only to die in Babylon after ten years of conquest, had emerged from obscurity to become the main power now within the convulsing empire. Having, with his men, ships and gold, helped Kassandros, Antipatros' eldest son, to install himself as ruler of Macedon, he had chased Eumenes east and there, at the battles of Paraetacene and Gabene, the issue had been decided. Although Seleukos was technically on the winning side he was uneasy: for he had Babylon and he wished to keep it but he suspected that Antigonos would take it from him and would use his failure at Susa as an excuse to do so. Having no army of his own he would be unable to prevent it.

He turned back to his spy, who, although not small, was a head shorter than Seleukos. 'Where is Antigonos now?'

'His army's at Aspadana in Paraetacene. He went back to Media to have the treasury at Ecbatana emptied—'

'Has he left Peithon as the satrap of Media?'

'Yes.'

'Then it was wise to take the money from the treasury to prevent Peithon having another go at rebelling.'

'Yes. Now he's secured the treasury, Antigonos will soon be heading south from Aspadana with an army of sixty thousand – he signed on most of Eumenes' men. He should be in Persepolis in under a moon.' The man, in his mid-thirties and unshaven and unkempt from a month on the road, took a deep breath. 'Antigonos also executed Eudamos, burned his body in a fire-pit and then threw Antigenes in alive.'

Seleukos gaped in alarm at the spy. 'Alive?'

'Yes, sir, I witnessed it; he did not die well.'

'I'm sure he didn't. What did he do with Teutamus, the joint commander of the Silver Shields?'

'It was him who organised the exchange, Eumenes for the Silver Shields' baggage that had been captured during the battle.'

'And so Teutamus bought his life with that of his comrade, did he?'

'It seems so; he's now commanding Antigonos' phalanx along with Pythan, another of Eumenes' officers who was a part of his betrayal.'

It was to be expected, Eumenes' Macedonian officers going against the sly little Greek in the end. 'How did Antigonos kill Eudamos?'

'Beheaded him.'

'Well, at least he gave one fellow satrap the decency of a clean death; but burning Antigenes, Alexander's appointment as commander of the Silver Shields, alive is unforgivable.'

It's abundantly clear that Antigonos is not of a forgiving nature; I think I made a tactical mistake accusing him of dishonourable behaviour.

And that was the crux of Seleukos' problem: he had objected to the way that Antigonos had tried to deceive Eumenes, tricking him into a position whereby he could massacre his entire army. Eumenes had not fallen for it, but for his temerity Seleukos had been sent back to Susa to be made a laughing stock.

He handed the spy a weighty purse, dismissing him with thanks before turning to the only other person in the room, sitting in shadows at the far end on a large divan surrounded by cushions.

'Well, Apama, what do we do?'

His wife, recently arrived from Babylon now that the roads were opening up again after the winter, tapped the cushions next to her. 'Come and sit down, my love; this will need a lot of thought.'

It was with exhausted bodies but clear heads that Seleukos and Apama, curled around each other, bathed in sweat, began to put some thought into the problem a good time later.

'If Antigonos is going to be in Persepolis within the month then he could be here soon after the spring equinox,' Apama, said, stroking her husband's barrel chest, a major part of a physique that could be a model for a statue of Heracles. 'If I understand the military position correctly, there is no way Susa could have fallen by then.'

'On the contrary; it will be stronger.'

She looked up into his dark and intense eyes, either side of a thin but prominent nose bisecting an angular face. 'How so?'

The eyes narrowed as his lips creased into a wry smile. 'Spring is here. Antigonos didn't leave me any cavalry – I specifically asked for five hundred – and without them I can't patrol the surrounding area to catch the foraging parties that Xenophilus sends out at night. My two thousand men cannot seal the whole perimeter. Therefore, as food becomes more abundant Susa will grow in strength. Xenophilus has at least the same numbers as I do, so storming the walls is unrealistic. And even if I were successful, he would fall back on the fortified treasury complex on the acropolis which could hold out for a year or more.'

'Mining?'

'The foundations are very deep. We've sunk a few mines under them and then filled them with fire to burn away the wooden supports, but that's done very little to weaken the walls above, even if we shoot heavy boulders at them all day long.'

'Subterfuge?'

'I don't think they'll fall for a Trojan Horse.' He cupped her head in his bear's paw of a hand; pulling her closer, he nuzzled her raven hair, savouring its scent as he had done since the first time he had experienced it. The daughter of the Sogdian noble Spitamenes, a great foe of Alexander, Apama had been one of the many Asian brides that Alexander had forced his officers to marry, here at Susa, almost eight years previously, in an attempt to meld east with west. Unlike many of his peers, Seleukos had not repudiated his wife upon Alexander's death; he would not and could not for he loved his olive-skinned beauty with a force that was beyond physical. He could never tire of her and now that she had recently given him a second son, Archaeus, a brother for the seven-year-old Antiochus and their five-year-old daughter Apama, his urge to protect his growing family had strengthened. Thus it was imperative that he should find a way through the unfolding events that would secure his position as satrap of Babylonia.

'Bribery?' Apama asked.

Seleukos stirred out of his reverie. 'What? No, I've tried it but Xenophilus has over twenty-five thousand talents in gold, silver and jewels; he's promised that Eumenes will give a handsome reward when he comes to claim the treasure.'

'But Eumenes isn't coming now.'

'No, he isn't. But then Xenophilus will try to make the same promises to his men for when Antigonos comes.' Seleukos rolled over onto his back, one arm behind his head.

Apama caressed his chest once more, pulling herself closer to him. 'Do you think Antigonos will be in the sort of mood to reward the man who, last year, refused him access to the largest treasury in the east?'

'That is just what I was starting to wonder. I was there when Antigonos demanded that Xenophilus open the gates. When he refused, Antigonos shouted that he had just signed his own death warrant.'

'It seems to me that Eumenes' execution could just have put you on the same side.'

'In that we both want to protect ourselves from Antigonos?'

'Yes, and the best way of doing that is?'

'By giving him something he wants, and also turning his attention in another direction.'

'I think you should go and talk to Xenophilus.'

'I think you might be right.'

It was not without trepidation that Seleukos entered the besieged city to parley; his armed guard of eight men was a mere token force, easily overcome should treachery be on Xenophilus' mind. Xenophilus had, unsurprisingly, refused to come out and Seleukos had not wished to shout up at the garrison commander standing upon the walls so that all would hear the very sensitive suggestion he wished to lay before his foe – a suggestion that would, if it came to Antigonos' ears, be rendered obsolete.

The escort that led Seleukos and his guards through the narrow streets, climbing up to the acropolis, were, he noted immediately, smartly dressed, well fed and of a clean appearance; they did not look like men who had suffered a seven-month siege. Indeed, the city itself looked as if nothing was amiss: wooden shutters on windows – one of the first casualties from lack of fuel – were still in place, the local population were not emaciated and he saw a couple of dogs flitting though a side-street; he even noticed some cats sleeping in the sun, completely unafraid of ending the day in a cooking pot. *We will never starve them out as it is and Xenophilus will be perfectly aware of that; he'll believe that he has the upper hand. I think I'll delay the news about Eumenes for a while; I'll let him gloat and then bring him down to reality.*

And it was with this tactic in mind that Seleukos was shown into the audience chamber in Darius' palace on the acropolis; overbearing, with high windows letting in shafts of mote-filled sunlight to reflect off the glazed tiles, of rich blues, yellows and greens, covering both walls and floor. His footsteps, and those of his escort, echoed as he made his way to the solitary man waiting in the centre of the great chamber.

'You need have no fears for your safety, Seleukos,' Xenophilus said, as he greeted him. 'If you are prepared to come here under such circumstances then I can only conclude that what you have to say is worth listening to without threat of violence. Please, sit.' He indicated to a couple of chairs set on either side of a round table laid with wine and pastries.

I have no choice but to trust him. Seleukos turned to the commander of his guard. 'Wait outside.' He took a seat as his men stamped out; a slave poured wine and water into the two cups on the table and then scuttled out without being ordered.

'Good,' Xenophilus said with a smile, 'we're alone now.'

'Eavesdroppers?' Seleukos asked.

'We'll talk in hushed voices, but I think I can trust my people; after all, we're still inside the walls and you are still outside them, as none has seen fit to open the gates to you.'

'A reasonable point.'

'And we're all looking very well; I'll think you'll agree. I had your guide take you on a slightly circuitous route so that you would get a good idea of conditions in the city.' Xenophilus, a balding man in his late forties and running to fat after ten years, since his appointment by Alexander as the garrison commander and warden of the royal treasury, raised his cup with a self-satisfied grin. 'Your good health, Seleukos.'

Enjoy your gloating whilst it lasts. Seleukos returned the toast; the wine was of the finest quality.

'Yes, we have almost everything we need in here,' Xenophilus said, evidently reading the appreciation on his guest's face. 'Now what is it that you wish to say that you believe would tempt me out of this very comfortable billet?'

'It's not for me to tempt you out; it's for you to decide that it would be in your best interests to leave.'

'I agree; but only if I would be saving my own life would it be in my interests to go. At the moment I can't see any threat; especially not from you, Seleukos, without wishing to cause offence.'

Seleukos raised his cup again. 'None taken. No, I was never meant to be a threat to you; Antigonos saw to that by taking away most of my men when he went north. I was just here to

17

keep you inside and then to be used as a scapegoat when he came back.'

'But what if he doesn't come back and Eumenes does?'

'Then that would be a remarkable feat; one that has never been accomplished by a mortal.'

Xenophilus considered the statement for a moment. 'You're saying that the struggle has been decided in Antigonos' favour?'

'Antigonos had Eumenes garrotted over a month ago.'

'Garrotted?'

'I know, nasty, wasn't it?'

Xenophilus put his hand to his throat and winced. 'Very.'

'He also burned Antigenes alive.'

Xenophilus' eyes widened and he swallowed hard and audibly.

Seleukos rolled his cup between his palms. 'Yes, that's roughly how I reacted when I heard the news.'

'Are you sure this is true?'

'I pay my spies very well; they have no reason to lie to me.'

'But you have reason to lie to me.'

'Do I? Really?' Seleukos took a sip of wine, placed his cup on the table and then leaned back in his chair with his hands across his taut belly, fingers locked. 'Look at it from my point of view, Xenophilus. If Eumenes is still alive and has won, my taking Susa wouldn't save me: I wouldn't be able to outrun the men he sent after me and take a significant amount of the treasure with me as well. Result: I lose Babylon and probably my life. So I stay here instead but Eumenes would besiege me and I would be a very rich man unable to go anywhere until I was relieved of my life. The third option would be to voluntarily surrender the treasure to Eumenes, and I'm sure he'd be really grateful, but he would still deprive me of Babylon, even if I might just get to keep my life.'

Xenophilus nodded, pursing his lips as he thought. 'Yes, that would seem a reasonable assessment of the situation and in all those scenarios I get to survive and am handsomely rewarded.'

'Indeed. Now shall we consider the other alternative: that I'm telling the truth about Eumenes having been executed?'

'By all means.'

'Firstly, and I was there on the day he said it, Antigonos told you that in not surrendering the city you had signed your own death warrant.'

'Yes, I remember it well.'

'And I have no reason to think that he would change his mind if he came back to find you still in possession of the treasury; do you?'

'None.'

'So you run, but like me, you wouldn't be able to take a sufficient amount of treasure with you and outrun the pursuit, and I'd catch you because presenting Antigonos with a fugitive might save my life but he would still take Babylon. So, perhaps you decide to travel light – poor, in other words – and have a chance of reaching the sea and taking refuge with Ptolemy without me catching you; but who are you to Ptolemy and what use could a pauper like you be? You would fade and I would still lose Babylon and, no doubt, be executed for letting you get away; unless I too run and throw away Babylon in order to save my life. Have you heard a pleasing outcome yet?'

'I can't say I have.'

'No, nor have I.'

'Do tell me there is one, won't you, Seleukos? I assume that's why you're here?'

Seleukos leaned forward with his elbows on the table, steepling his fingers and pressing them to his lips. 'We give him the money before he comes for it; you take it to him.'

'Me?'

'Yes, you.'

'But surely he'll kill me anyway?'

'Not if you've already been a part of exposing a plot against him.'

Xenophilus smiled. 'And will I have?'

'We both will have.'

'And who will we have denounced?'

'Peithon.'

Xenophilus' smile broadened. 'Someone more deserving would be hard to find. It was he, after all, who started the war out here by deposing the satrap of Parthia and replacing him with his own brother, causing the other eastern satraps to unite against him and defeat him.'

'Thus drawing Eumenes east with the intention of siding with the alliance after Antigonos had captured his fleet—'

'Thus leaving him unable to take his army to Europe to join with Olympias against Kassandros and drawing Antigonos' attention west. Shame, really; we could have been spared all this had Peithon not united the east against himself.'

'Yes, and Antigonos will find our story easy to believe as Peithon had already tried to take twenty-five thousand Greek mercenaries into his army who had deserted their posts in the east just after Alexander's death and were trying to make it back to the sea.'

'Indeed, I remember.'

'Had Perdikkas not sent me there to remind the Macedonian troops of their obligations and made sure that they massacred the deserters to a man, Peithon would have had the power to rebel. Antigonos is well aware of that story, I'm sure.'

'So what are we going to say that Peithon has done this time?'

'No more than I'm sure he's already doing now that Antigonos has left Media and is heading south to Persis, leaving Peithon to his own, dim and slow-witted, devices: sending out feelers for a rebellion in the east once Antigonos goes back west.'

'But how will we prove it?'

'Peithon would need money to rebel but Antigonos took the precaution of emptying the treasury at Ecbatana.'

Xenophilus chuckled in approval. 'He would have to try his luck with me.'

'Which he will think is a certainty seeing as he also heard Antigonos say that you had just signed your own death warrant.'

'A forged letter?'

'Two, actually: one to you asking you for the contents of the Susa treasury in return for making you satrap of Susiana once he's secured the east; and one to me offering troops to take Susa and share the treasury before Antigonos arrives.'

'Ha! A masterstroke: portray Peithon as being duplicitous even in his duplicity.'

'Yes. I think Antigonos will find it difficult not to believe that to be the truth. It's no secret that Peithon isn't overburdened with subtlety – or intelligence, for that matter. I'll send a fast courier to intercept Antigonos with the sad news before he gets to Persepolis.'

'And me?'

'I'll give you half of my men, a thousand to add to your two thousand, to escort you south with the full contents of the treasury – minus a few bits and pieces for our expenses, naturally.'

'Naturally.'

'I think that will be enough men to look like you mean to keep the treasure safe, rather than fight him for it.'

'I should hope so. And what about you?'

'I'll leave five hundred men here as a garrison and take the other five hundred back to Babylon and hope that giving

Antigonos Peithon and the Susa treasure is enough to keep me installed in Babylon when he arrives there. Don't forget, he's already taken Teutamus and Pythan onto his staff because they gave him Eumenes. Let us hope Antigonos will be as accommodating with us.'

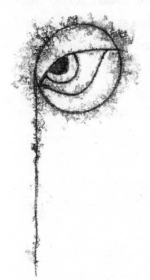

ANTIGONOS.
THE ONE-EYED.

'MY ARSE! MY sweaty arse! The man must be an idiot.' Antigonos was not in the best of moods, nor had he been since physically kicking the courier who had brought Seleukos' despatch back through the tent entrance to sprawl in the mud outside.

'Father, you know he is. Why are you so surprised?' Demetrios, Antigonos' twenty-one-year-old son, struggled to keep a smile from his face, a face that was far more appealing, although dominated by an impressive nose, than the grey-bearded, weather-beaten visage of his one-eyed father. He ran his fingers through his ample curls of black hair, sweeping them back from his forehead. 'Peithon can never be accused of intellectual prowess, and don't claim that knowledge comes as a surprise to you.'

He's right, the young pup; why am I so surprised that Peithon not only tries to rebel but does it in such a cack-handed manner? I should never have left him in position. Antigonos wiped a red-stained tear, oozing out of the ravaged socket of his left eye, and glared with the fully-functioning right at his son. 'The reason I emptied the Ecbatana treasury was to stop him – or anyone else I might have made satrap of Media, for that matter – rebelling; and so he writes to Xenophilus in Susa and tries to get hold of the gold there! My arse!'

Demetrios refused to be outraged. 'Well, for a man of little brain it would have seemed like a shrewd move; after all, he did hear you tell Xenophilus that he had just signed his death warrant when he refused you entry to Susa. Peithon just assumed that Xenophilus would come over to him in order to save his life.'

'But, instead, he contacts Seleukos to warn me and it turns out that Peithon has also made overtures to him too. The man must be an idiot!'

'Father, we've already established that he is. Shall we move on from that point and discuss what to do about the idiot?'

'Are you being flippant?'

Demetrios sucked in a breath. 'No, Father; I just think we should move on from the ranting stage and get to the decision stage.'

'Oh, so now that you're a father again, you think that you have the monopoly on maturity and I'm just a blustering old man who has to be handled with care, do you?'

'No, Father, Phila giving birth to young Stratonice is neither here nor there in this conversation; you've been a grandfather for almost three years now, since young Antigonos was born, so you should have had time to get used to it. Now, what are we going to do about Peithon?'

'Execute him, of course.'

'Good; now we're getting somewhere. How are we going to execute him? Shall we send assassins – although I fear that Archias the Exile-Hunter is too far away to do the job with sufficient haste and I can't think of a more reliable man for the mission – or shall we summon him to us on some pretext?'

Antigonos stopped his pacing around the tent and scratched his grey-flecked beard with vigour. 'I need to resinate myself,' he said, pouring a decent amount of resinated wine into a cup and downing it in one. 'We get him to us; there's too much that can go wrong with an assassination, even with the expertise of someone like Archias, and anyway, the last I heard of him he was with Ptolemy. No, we're fifteen days from Persepolis; we summon him there. If we send a messenger back up to Ecbatana now, Peithon, riding fast, could reach Persepolis at about the same time as us with the army.'

'What would induce him to come?'

'He won't suspect that Seleukos or Xenophilus would have betrayed him as he would have calculated that both of them would have more to gain from him.'

Demetrios frowned. 'Wait a moment, Father, they both have: you've promised to kill Xenophilus and you've made Seleukos look so stupid sitting outside Susa that Peithon's offer of troops would be welcome to help him save face. So why have they come to you with this information?'

Antigonos had no doubts. 'Because they can see that, in the long term, I will be the one with the patronage; Seleukos wants to keep Babylon and Xenophilus wants to keep his life. Ha!'

'If I were you, I would certainly spare Xenophilus.'

'Spare him?'

'Yes, and keep him in his post.' Demetrios put both his hands up as he read the signs of an imminent explosion. 'Listen to me, Father; he may have denied you access to Susa, but he was only acting under the orders of Eumenes who was officially commander of the east as appointed by the then regent, Polyperchon. Had he opened the gates to you I would say that would be a reason for his execution, but because he didn't I can't think of a better man to have looking after the treasury at Susa for us.'

Antigonos poured and downed another cup of wine. 'You're right, curse you for a smug little puppy.' He crunched the cup back down on the table. 'Xenophilus has given me Peithon, and he is bringing the treasury to Persepolis as a precaution against Peithon launching an attack on Susa when he realises that he is not going to cooperate with him. I should reward him in a way that is also advantageous to me.'

'The wine seems to be working, Father.'

Antigonos grunted and poured himself another. 'As for Peithon, I shall order him to Persepolis, hinting that he's about to get what he wants without having to rebel: I'll imply that I'll make him commander of the east free to act with his own authority after I move back west. He'll not be able to resist that.'

Demetrios smiled. 'No, Father, he won't; I think the journey to Persepolis will be his last.'

'Apart from the one to the Ferryman.'

'Ah, yes, there's always the Ferryman.'

It was in a far better mood that Antigonos gazed upon the walls of Persepolis in the eastern foothills of the Zagros Mountains at the end of a seventeen-day march; shining bright in the strengthening sun, they encircled the capital of the satrapy of Persis, built on an artificial platform so that the city itself was level despite the local topography. Partially destroyed by fire by Alexander in a drunken spree, encouraged by Ptolemy's mistress, Thais, it was the seat of the satrap of Persis, Peucestas. Eager to arrive, for it was here that he would finalise his settlement of the east and thus leave himself free to return west to deal first with Seleukos and then Ptolemy, he left the army, under the command of Teutamus and Pythan, to trudge the last few leagues and went ahead with his son and an escort of fifty Companion Cavalry – unshielded lancers.

They were not challenged as they clattered through the east gate; indeed, it was quite the reverse as there awaited them a guard of honour welcoming party and flocks of citizens dressed in their best robes cheering and scattering flowers in their path.

'Peucestas is evidently anxious to ingratiate himself with me,' Antigonos commented to Demetrios as they trotted along the wide thoroughfare that headed to the Tachara, the winter palace of Darius, the first of that name, one of the few structures to totally escape Alexander's arson. With scores of skipping children leading the way and their mothers and fathers cheering from the sides of the street, it was to a holiday atmosphere that Antigonos arrived at the gardens in front of the Tachara; lush they were, laid out with lawns and sprinkled with fountains; pathways and verdant shrubberies bisected them and an air of calm enveloped them.

'I can see why Peucestas is so keen to remain here,' Demetrios observed as they dismounted and walked through the gate guarded by two Macedonians at rigid attention.

Never really having been one to appreciate beauty, Antigonos grunted and stomped towards the multi-coloured building rising tall from nature's bounty. With stairs on either side leading up to a terrace, supported by a wall engraved with life-sized, brightly painted depictions of Apple-Bearers, the tiara-wearing guards of the Great Kings of old, it was a feast of artificial colour. Tall columns behind the terrace supported a high roof that provided the royal skin with respite from the sun or shelter from the rain. Behind and to each side lay the formal rooms, the walls and intricate pattern of many-hued tiles depicting hunting scenes, military triumphs or just abstract formations. To either side of the structure, two mighty, horned bulls stood on giant pedestals of carved marble, whilst on the roof, overlooking each of the sets of steps up to the terrace, two lions perched ever roaring at all who approached.

And it was on the terrace that Peucestas stood, resplendent in the trousers and long tunic of a Persian noble and standing stiff-backed straight for on his head he wore a tiara, tall and unwieldy. His personal guard, Macedonian Hypaspists, stood at attention on the steps; with bronze helmets, breastplates and shields and red cloaks over their shoulders, they provided the one western prospect in an eastern vista.

'If he thinks that he can impress me dressing up as a barbarian, he's going to be bitterly disappointed,' Antigonos growled, quickening his pace. 'No doubt he's been taking it up the arse all morning judging by how he's standing. Nasty eastern habits he's picked up; treachery not being the least of them.'

'The satrapy of Persis welcomes Antigonos, lord of the east, and invites him to a welcoming feast,' Peucestas declaimed, extending his arms towards Antigonos, scrunching his way along the gravelled path. 'And I, as satrap, recently reconfirmed in my position by the lord of the east, do also welcome him and name him the Bear of Macedon.'

The Bear of Macedon, my arse! I'll give him Bear of Macedon. 'Stop all these eastern theatrics, Peucestas,' Antigonos snarled as he reached the bottom of the steps. 'You're meant to be a Macedonian, not some outgrown Persian bum-boy; so try to act and sound like one.' He looked at the guards as he mounted the steps. 'What do you lads think of all this eastern frippery? Makes you laugh, does it? Or have you all succumbed to trousers, buggery and sherbets as well?' The men kept their eyes focused on the mid-distance and their thoughts to themselves, as Demetrios followed him up.

Peucestas turned to face Antigonos as he reached the terrace, a smile just visible beneath a red-hennaed, tightly curled beard that hung to his chest. He extended his arms, but concern showed in his eyes as the pace of his guest failed to slacken.

Antigonos' hand came out but it was not to clasp that of his host; it flashed through the air, open-palmed, and struck the tiara from Peucestas' head. 'Since when do Macedonians wear such effeminate head-gear?'

Peucestas, shocked, his mouth hanging open, blinked as he stared at Antigonos for a few moments, unable to martial his thoughts as the tiara scraped along the tiled floor, cracking into a column. 'But I meant only to welcome you,' he spluttered, 'compliment you.'

'Dressed like that?' Antigonos pulled at the baggy sleeve of Peucestas' tunic and then spat in disgust on the delicate yellow slippers on his feet. 'You think calling me the Bear of Macedon is a compliment?'

Peucestas' eyes flicked left and right but no one was coming to his aid; his guards remained to attention staring straight ahead as if nothing untoward was occurring, let alone their satrap being assaulted. 'Alexander was the Lion of Macedon, so I thought "Bear" would be an appropriate compliment for you.'

'The Resinated Cyclops of Macedon, perhaps, or just that Resinated Cunt, as most of my men call me, but don't try to flatter me with mock-heroic epithets when we both know that I'm a plain-speaking Macedonian and you seem to have lost your way. Now come with me.' He pulled Peucestas by the embroidered collar and dragged him towards a set of double doors standing open at the back of the terrace, leading into the royal garden chamber, where once the King of Kings took his leisure.

'Father!' Demetrios shouted, following. 'That's enough!'

But Antigonos was in no mood to be restrained. 'I'll say when it's enough. You stay there.' Once inside the chamber he threw

Peucestas down onto a couch. 'Did you honestly think that display would impress me?'

Peucestas looked up with hate in his eyes, the shock of the assault now turning to burning resentment. 'My dignity, Antigonos, has been severely compromised.'

'Your dignity dissolved when you pulled on your first pair of trousers. Your dignity was absent when you betrayed Eumenes to me so you could keep Persis. What do you think your men made of you ordering them from the field in Paraetacene? Yes, I was pleased we could have made the arrangement but it gave me no pleasure to deal with such a grasping little traitor, and any respect I may have had for you for old time's sake evaporated as I saw you as you really are. If you had any dignity left, your guards would have come to your aid, but no, what did they do? They stood there and did nothing. Why? Because they knew that I was right; because they, like me, can see what you are. So either give us an enjoyable performance of *The Persians*, by Aeschylus, seeing as you seem to be dressed up as Xerxes, or go and get out of that ridiculous costume and into something more civilised before you host me to, what I imagine will be, an unnecessarily exotic feast.' He did not wait for a reply.

'Feeling better?' Demetrios asked as Antigonos emerged back onto the terrace.

'No.'

'Then why put the man through all that humiliation?'

'Because in making a fool of himself he makes a fool of me if I am seen to condone it.'

'And by condoning it, you mean not slapping him around in public?'

'He's lucky that I only knocked his tiara off. I knew it was bad when I saw his beard after Paraetacene, but at least he was in a Macedonian uniform, albeit with trousers underneath; but

30

what I saw just now was unacceptable in any Macedonian, let alone a satrap, and a satrap who I have reconfirmed in his post. If I wanted a Persian here I would have appointed one. The idea of blending east with west was Alexander's big mistake: it weakens Macedonian blood; but the idea of Macedonians voluntarily taking on the aspects of the east is degrading and will lose us respect.'

'I think you're wrong, Father. If we are to keep the east and take advantage of the wealth that it brings, we must be seen to rule in partnership and not just be their overlords.'

'We do rule in partnership; why else do you think I appointed the Persian, Orobantes, to be the new satrap of Parthia? Why did I confirm all those other easterners in the posts? I'm not stupid. My point is that we need to keep ourselves separate; there are far more easterners than Macedonians, they would easily absorb us out here if Peucestas sets a precedent. I've just let it be known what I, "*the Bear of Macedon*",' he paused to snort at the ludicrousness of the name, 'what I think of people going native. No, if we allow that to happen then the Macedonian empire won't last; instead it will become a hybrid culture. Take Seleukos, for example: he's kept his Persian wife and has now had three half-breed children with her; it's already starting and it mustn't be allowed to go any further.' He looked around the terrace. 'Now, I assume that someone here knows where we are to be quartered. I'll see you at the feast later on.' He stomped off, leaving his son looking after him, deep in thought.

The banquet was as Antigonos had suspected it would be: a prissy affair with the rigid manners of the Persian elite precluding any of the raucous behaviour that should, in his opinion, go with good food and copious drink. Instruments droned on, unseen, in some corner of the banqueting hall, sounding to him like the last lamentation of a wounded beast in dire need of being put out of its misery. Conversation was stilted, with Peucestas, now dressed in Macedonian fashion, being keen to impress his guest but nervous of what his Persian nobles would think of a descent into old-school Macedonian drinking and boasting. And thus, with Peucestas' obvious unease with his own kind, preferring instead to pander to the sensibilities of a conquered race, Antigonos had come to a decision about his future, a decision enforced by the fussiness of the food, picky little plates with nothing substantial to get your teeth into. 'And what am I supposed to make of this?' Antigonos asked, lifting up a tiny spatchcocked gamebird, covered with a deep red spice.

'That is a quail grilled in a coat of sumaqqa,' Peucestas answered, wiping the tips of his fingers with a moist sea-sponge; he might have forgone eastern dress but not eastern manners – or, for that matter, his eastern beard. 'You pull the flesh from the bones and eat it.'

'It hardly seems to be worth the while,' Antigonos muttered, tossing the offending item over his shoulder and looking around the array of dishes on the table before him for something that looked able to satisfy a hearty appetite. 'What's that?' He pointed to a long sausage-like creation covered in small pale seeds.

'That is a loin of pork cooked in honey and rolled in sesame; it's most delicious, especially if you eat it in conjunction with the rice with rosewater, almonds and dried apricots.'

Antigonos grunted and picked up the loin whole, took a bite off one end and began to chew with gusto. Teutamus and Pythan, reclining on couches next to him, laughed at the ill-manners and grabbed at hunks of meat themselves.

Persian nobles, reclining nearby, averted their eyes and whispered to one another.

'Hmm, not bad,' Antigonos said, lobbing the meat to Demetrios across the table from him. 'Give it a go.'

Demetrios caught it in one hand, placed it on his plate and set to it with a knife, causing some murmurs of approval from many of the Persians. They still refrained from looking at Antigonos, however, who was now sucking the honey from one finger at a time, making popping sounds as he finished each one.

'How about something substantial, like a whole roast deer or boar?' Antigonos said, raising his voice so that all two hundred diners in the room could hear. 'I've had enough of theses fripperies.'

'These fripperies, as you call them,' a Persian on the next table said, standing up, 'are some of the finest cuisine known to man. That you fail to appreciate them says more about you than it does about the food.'

The room went silent as the Persian stood, staring at Antigonos.

Antigonos smiled; it was not a pleasant sight. 'My, my, an easterner with spunk. Demetrios, make a note of the date and place; they will never believe us back home. What's your name?'

The Persian was not to be cowed. 'Thespius; my family are originally Greek from Lydia but have lived here in Persepolis for generations. You may have come here to deliberately insult us and our culture but we know that there are some Macedonians with a sense of propriety who manage to show respect for our ways. Peucestas here is one of them and we are grateful to have him as our satrap.'

'Well, then I'm afraid that I'm going to have to disappoint you: I've decided that Peucestas is not a suitable satrap and so I will relieve him of his position and appoint someone with a little more authority.'

Peucestas' eyes widened in horror. 'But you promised!'

'I know; but I've changed my mind.'

'It would be hard for us to support any other satrap,' the Persian said, coming to Peucestas' side.

'Would it now, Thespius?' Antigonos raised his hand. 'Guards!' From the double doors of the chamber, where they had been stationed, came half a dozen men. Antigonos pointed to the Persian. 'Teutamus, take this man and execute him.'

Thespius stared in horror at Antigonos as Teutamus shrugged and got up from his couch. 'You can't do that.'

'Why not? You just said that you did not think you could support another satrap, which means that you must be a traitor and, as *the Bear of Macedon*, I have to keep order here.' Antigonos got to his feet and looked around at the many diners. 'Is there any other man here who feels that they can't support my new choice of satrap, whoever that might be, and would rather join Thespius?'

There was no rush to join the hapless Thespius now being manhandled away by Teutamus and the guards.

'Good; that's settled then.'

Peucestas still stared beseechingly at Antigonos, oblivious to his loyal supporter's fate. 'Antigonos, you promised me when I agreed to take my men from the field at Paraetacene that the reward would be reconfirming my position here in Persis.'

Antigonos reclined back down on his couch, shaking his head in disbelief. 'Surely you must be a canny enough politician to realise that a man who betrays his friends as easily as you did cannot be trusted and therefore any promises made to him are null and void? No? You're not that canny? Never mind; I'll find something for you that will fit with your limited intellect and pumped-up vanity. How about I make you general in command of Asia in place of the little Greek? That sounds important, don't you think?'

'Antigonos, you promised me Persis!'

'General commanding Asia is far more important.'

'I thought that *I* was to be given that role, Antigonos,' a voice said from the door.

Antigonos turned to see Peithon walking into the room. *Ah, good! I am enjoying myself this evening.* 'Peithon! Well, well; the guards are going to be busy this evening. I shall be heading west to settle with Seleukos sooner than I thought.'

SELEUKOS.
THE BULL-ELEPHANT.

AND WEST WAS where Seleukos was headed; west as far as Babylon. And as he saw the distant outer city wall, shimmering golden in the morning sun away across the plain, his relief at arriving unmolested was palpable; for he had travelled the hundred leagues from Susa with his wife, six hundred talents in gold and silver and an escort of just five hundred men, through a land ravaged by Eumenes' advance from the north through to the east of the satrapy just a year previously.

Dire had been the consequences of the sly little Greek dividing his army into three columns so as best to plunder the wealth of Babylonia; villages and towns had been abandoned for lack of food and those inhabitants who had stayed had not yet managed to bring in the first harvest due in a couple of months at midsummer. Gangs of dispossessed and despairing people of all ages roamed the land, malnourished, feral and heeding only the instinct to survive; there had not been a night on the journey when the camp had not been attacked in some form by the ragged column shadowing it, if only to kill a sentry for the contents of his purse. On one night a great troop of the desperate, nearly two hundred in total, attempted to storm the horse-lines to grab as many of the beasts as possible for their cooking fires; many had died in the attempt and no horses had been lost, but it had served as a stark lesson to Seleukos of the damage that war had done to the eastern and northern regions of his satrapy.

Once he had crossed the Tigris the agricultural situation was much improved, for it had been untouched by Eumenes that far south; but this presented its own problems in that the scavengers from the eastern bank would raid their more prosperous western bank neighbours causing resentment and blood feuds.

To regain control he would prioritise some of the money he had taken from the Susa treasury for purchasing grain to distribute throughout the ravaged areas in order to ease the suffering. If he wished to secure his position even more in Babylonia, importing food was as important as importing mercenaries.

There was no welcome as the column clattered through the east gate in the outer city wall, a plain affair of cut stone compared to the brilliance of the blue-tiled inner wall. Through the gardens that thrived between the two defences they progressed, crossing the bridge over the canal before coming to the Marduk Gate decorated still with the figures and beasts of Babylon's past days of glory of Nebuchadnezzar, when it ruled an empire, subject to no man. Passing through the gates into the city's grid-like system of streets, the size of the population became apparent for there was humanity everywhere; buying, selling, discussing, arguing, copulating up side-streets or just sitting, displaying whatever gross deformity that might induce another to drop a small bronze coin in a bowl.

'But at least they seem to be reasonably well fed,' Seleukos said to Apama as the escort cleared the way along the main thoroughfare in the Kullab district, with as much restraint as possible on Seleukos' orders; he did not want the people resenting his return.

Along they went at a slow pace before turning left at the Eridu district onto the Processional Way that led past the Southern Citadel in the Kardingira district to the Ishtar Gate and then on to the Main Citadel beyond which housed the treasury.

'So, Temenos, how much of this year's taxes have you managed to collect?' Seleukos asked the commander of the Babylon garrison, once the six hundred talents had been secured in the treasury.

Temenos, in his mid-thirties with the refined dress and jewellery of one with a taste for eastern luxury, sucked the air through his teeth.

Seleukos did not need him to say more. 'Well down?'

'Yes, lord; because of the famine in the north and east of the satrapy.'

That comes as no surprise. 'How much, would you say?'

'We've collected just over half of what we would normally expect in a good year; this is the lowest I've ever known it since Alexander appointed me commander of the garrison.'

'So the six hundred talents should just about cover the shortfall?'

'Yes, just about.'

'Start buying grain from anyone who has it; I need to stabilise the situation.'

'I will, lord. As a matter of fact, Babrak the Pathak merchant recently arrived here with a proposition along those lines. He has been waiting to see you.'

'Then find him and send him to me.'

'You do me too much honour, great lord, in granting me a private interview.' Leather-skinned, hook-nosed and with sunken dark eyes twinkling out from beneath a white headdress, Babrak bowed, touching his right hand to his forehead.

Seleukos waved the compliment away and sat back in his chair. 'Babrak, we both know that I would be foolish not to see you in private, so don't pretend that this is an unusual occurrence. But first to business.'

Babrak grinned, his red-stained teeth appearing ghoulish in the lamplight of Seleukos' private study in the Main Citadel. Seleukos indicated to the chair at the table opposite him and nodded.

'You rush to business with no preamble, my lord,' Babrak said, seating himself, 'like a travel-weary merchant would to a favoured boy after long absence.'

'Well, I wouldn't put it quite like that myself; but yes, I'm keen to know what you can offer me.'

'What I do is for you and not for personal gain, great lord; I am only pleased to be able to be of service to you.'

'Yes, yes; get on with it, Babrak. What have you got?'

'Grain, lord; five transport ships full of it, moored under heavy guard, you must understand, expensively heavy guard, fifty leagues upstream at the port of Is. I heard about the disgraceful way that the traitor Eumenes abused your satrapy by stripping it bare with three advancing columns and so I decided that I must do what I can to aid you.'

'Very altruistic of you, I'm sure.'

Babrak inclined his head. 'You are too kind, lord.'

'So, how much grain is there?'

'Four hundred talents in three of the ships and five hundred in the other two.'

'Two thousand two hundred talents in all; how much do you want for it?'

Babrak spread his hands, hunching his shoulders. 'Great lord, how can I answer that question? It is like asking a brothel keeper the price of a boy in general without inspecting the wares or ascertaining what each one can do.'

Does everyone have as much difficulty as I do in understanding what he is going on about? 'Meaning?'

'Meaning how much do you want, where do you want it and how soon?'

'What has that got to do with brothel keepers and their boys?' Seleukos put his hand up as Babrak opened his mouth to answer the question. 'Never mind, Babrak. I'm sure it was an apposite simile. I want it all, I want it here and I want it now. How much?'

Babrak heaved a deep breath as if the weight of the question was crushing him. 'My lord asks a great deal.'

'Babrak! Don't play your games with me. I'll give you above the going rate: one silver drachma to the mina of grain.'

'That is sixty drachmae to the talent, which makes...' Babrak did a series of calculations counting knuckles and finger joints and then tallying with his thumbs. 'One hundred and thirty-two thousand drachmae or two hundred and twenty talents of silver, or twenty-two in gold.'

Seleukos' arithmetic was not so advanced. 'I'll have someone check it.'

'That is not much more than what I paid for the grain, lord, and then there is the hire of the shipping and the guards.'

'Which are your responsibilities as without them you wouldn't have got the goods here so as you could make a profit on them by selling them to me.' Seleukos pointed a finger at the Pathak. 'And, by the way, I'm well aware that you are intending to blackmail me by threatening to walk away with something that you know I desperately need, so I say this to you: two hundred and fifty in silver or I'll impound your ships for entering Babylonia without my permission.'

'But I don't need your permission so long as I pay the tax.'

'Times change, Babrak, time's change.'

'Two hundred and sixty in—'

'Babrak!'

'In silver would be too much, great lord; two hundred and fifty it is.'

He spat on his hand and proffered it.

Seleukos took it and clinched the deal. *That will buy me time and it's pleasant to reflect upon the fact that Antigonos is paying for it.* He clapped his hands; slaves appeared with wine, sherbet, and honey and pistachio pastries. 'So, Babrak, help yourself and tell me the news; we have heard nothing of the west since the autumn equinox last year. What of Kassandros?' He unhooked a bulky purse from his belt and casually placed it on the table between them.

Babrak eyed the purse as he poured himself a sherbet. 'He is to marry Thessalonike.'

Seleukos looked at the merchant, astounded. 'Alexander's half-sister?'

'The very same.'

'But surely Olympias will prevent that.'

'Olympias is dead; Thessalonike betrayed her to Kassandros and she was stoned to death by the families of her victims from her time as regent.'

'No!' Seleukos was incredulous. 'Kassandros condemned her to death?'

Babrak wiped some excess froth from his moustache. 'No, lord, I heard he was far more subtle than that. He knew that he would never be able to advance himself in Macedon with the stigma of being the man who condemned and executed the mother of Alexander, so he let the people's assembly do it, only the assembly was made up purely of the relatives of her victims.'

'Very clever, for a pockmarked little toad. So now he is unchallenged in Macedon and has a royal bride.'

'Aristonous still holds out against him in Amphipolis, the last I heard, but that may well have changed by now. King Aeacides

41

in Epirus was deposed and the new regime has signed a peace with Kassandros, so he is safe from the west.'

'And the east?'

'Lysimachus continues to build his fortresses to defend the north against the coming of these barbarians whose name I forget.'

'Keltoi.'

'Yes, something like that. He has also taken advantage of Antigonos' absence to create a presence in Hellespontine Phrygia.'

'Ah, so he claims both banks of the Hellespont; very lucrative.'

Babrak flicked another look at the purse. 'Indeed. And Asander, the satrap of Caria—'

'I know who Asander is.'

'Indeed, forgive my patronising surplus of detail, lord.'

'Go on.'

'Well, Asander has been interfering in Kappadokia since hearing of Eumenes' death; he may well have managed to secure it by now unless Ptolemaios, Antigonos' nephew, reacted swiftly in the absence of his uncle.'

Seleukos chuckled. 'That will infuriate the resinated cyclops when he gets back west. That must be the first interesting thing that Asander has ever done.'

'You are not the first to have made that observation, lord.'

'I'm sure I'm not. And to Kassandros' south, what is happening there?'

'Ah, Aeacides fled with a few of his men to Polyperchon who is in Perrhaebia in north-western Thessaly with a ragtag army of no consequence; they have no power and are irrelevant. Alexandros, Polyperchon's son, continues to hold the northern Peloponnese, but Demetrius of Phaleron's hold on Athens in Kassandros' name is so strong that he is unable to advance into Attica.'

Seleukos pondered the situation for a few moments. 'The question is: now that Kassandros has become a force in his own right, will he show himself to be for Antigonos or against him?'

Babrak shrugged. 'I know only the news, lord, I steer clear of opinions.'

'Very wise. Now tell me of Ptolemy.'

'Ah, well, since Ptolemy seized most of the Syrian coast and Antigonos' navy from another of his nephews, Dioscurides, as soon as the One-Eyed went east, he's been quiet. I was in Egypt last year and he was more concerned with his domestic issues; he seems to have more trouble with his wives than I do and he has fewer; especially having repudiated Artakama whom Alexander forced him to marry at the Susa mass wedding.'

Seleukos smiled. 'He's a fool for doing so, she's a beautiful woman.'

'I have not seen her, lord.'

'She lives here in Babylon and is a close companion of my wife. But Ptolemy only has himself to blame for his woes, marrying Eurydike's cousin so soon after she had given birth; women don't take kindly to that, you know.'

Babrak's expression as he shook his head implied that he knew all about it.

'Although I believe Berenice is a stunning woman.'

'I have only seen her from afar, lord.'

'So Ptolemy is quiet.'

'He still has garrisons in Tyros and on Cyprus and all up the Phoenician coast as well as a few of the cities in Coele-Syria and Palestine, Gaza in particular; but he makes no war. Trade in Egypt is very good and I shall be going back there once I have attended to some business at home; my cousin has recently arrived from there and he tells me that my wives are restless and need to be fertilised.'

'Yes, well, I wish you all the best with that.' Seleukos pushed the purse across to Babrak. 'Have the grain here in ten days and your money will be waiting for you.'

The Pathak stood and touched his fingertips to his forehead and chest. 'The great lord can rely on me.'

'No, Babrak, the great lord can rely on your lust for money.'

'Less than two years, lord,' Naramsin, Seleukos' architect, informed him as they and Apama walked through the building site surrounding the Ziggurat of Bel Marduk at the centre of the Eridu district of the city. 'Around the winter solstice next year would be a reasonable guess. Most of the structure is now safe. We have one more level before we can dedicate the altar to Bel Marduk at the very top, and then the business of beautifying it will commence.'

'Very good, Naramsin,' Seleukos said, looking at the reconstructed Ziggurat rising sixty paces above him. 'Very good.' He beamed at the Babylonian who, in his long, flared-sleeved priestly robes and conical hat, looked more like he should be officiating up at the altar rather than organising its reconstruction. But that was the way with a great many of the priests of Bel Marduk, Seleukos had learned, they did not just confine themselves to the practice of their religion but, rather, explored all branches of knowledge; in Naramsin's case, architecture. And very glad Seleukos was to have him for he had managed to rebuild the Ziggurat at a speed that none would have thought possible having seen the ruin of the original. Initially partially pulled down on Alexander's orders just before his death so that the dilapidated structure could be reconstituted, nothing had happened to the building until Seleukos had taken Babylon and had made its resurrection a priority. And now, there it stood, in the midst of its rebirth, visible to the whole population of Babylon over whom it would once again tower, an ever-present reminder of the piety and deep purse of the satrap; yet another way that Seleukos was buying himself into the hearts of the Babylonians.

Naramsin gestured towards the steep flight of steps that soared up the front of the construction to the second of the successively receding levels. 'Would my lord and his lady care to ascend to inspect the work more closely? The upper levels are accessed by staircases cut on the side of each one. It would not take long.'

Seleukos looked at the dizzying height and knew that his head would spin if he looked down from even the second level; it would be hard enough forcing himself up there, let alone making it all the way to the top. *I'll have to go to the top when the new altar is dedicated; best not to know what to expect before that time comes.* 'Thank you, Naramsin, but I would rather wait until the project is complete.' He winced as he felt Apama elbow him in the ribs.

'As my lord wishes.'

Seleukos looked down at his wife who was evidently suppressing giggles behind her veil, judging by her eyes and the shaking of her shoulders. 'Are you all right?'

Apama squeezed her eyes shut, shaking her head, and waved away his concern with a flick of the hand. He turned back to the architect. 'Now, tell me, Naramsin, how is the rebuilding of your accommodation going?'

'Your lordship is gracious to enquire. That too is almost complete and, thanks to your generosity, it is even more comfortable than before.'

'It was the least that I could do seeing as the divinely set fire that destroyed your buildings also facilitated my entry into Babylon. That Bel Marduk should have seen fit to aid me in such a manner has been one of the great fortunes of my life; it is only right that I ensure the comfort of his followers who were so inconvenienced by the fire.' Neither Seleukos nor Naramsin gave the slightest impression that this complete reworking of history was anything other than the absolute truth; it had been agents of Seleukos who had torched the buildings around the Temple of Bel Marduk, the priests' quarters included, to the south of the Ziggurat. It had been necessary in order to get the main river gate opened on the night that Seleukos had taken Babylon from the usurper Docimus. The modern pumping system employed by the priests to stop the fire spreading to the temple required the hoses to go through the open gates and into the river, thus giving him and his men the opportunity to storm through and take the city. He had made lavish gifts to the priests in order that this far more opportune reading of events – a divine flame aiding the saviour of Babylon – should prevail as the truth. Fortunately it was convenient for both sides to maintain the pretence.

'Is there any other way that I might be of service to you, lord?'

'There is, Naramsin; it is a delicate matter.' He took the priest by the arm and walked him away a few paces from his bodyguards so that none but Apama could overhear. 'I fully intend to stay here in Babylon, as I'm sure you are aware from the effort I've put in to ease the burdens of the ordinary people.' Seleukos glanced around to make sure his bodyguards had not come forward. 'The thing is, Naramsin, that Antigonos has designs on Babylon and I believe he will try to install his own man here; a man who might well be less sympathetic a ruler than I am.'

'I pray that Bel Marduk will keep us safe from that eventuality.'

'Indeed; but should he be unable to, I have taken precautions for my swift departure. You need not know what they are for obvious reasons. However, should I escape to safety I will, some day, wish to return and reclaim what is mine from whoever Antigonos puts in my place.'

'Indeed, lord, and we will long most pitifully for that glorious day.'

They are so prone to exaggeration, these people. 'Yes, well, let's not go too far. The point is that I may need a way back into the city for me and a few hundred men; after all, Bel Marduk can't necessarily be relied upon to start a second fire.'

'The great god is all powerful: should he desire a second fire he can arrange it.'

'Yes, well, I think a tunnel would be easier and less prone to misadventure.'

'A tunnel? From where to where?'

'From the priests' accommodation to come out under the bridge, so that the entrance is masked.'

'Under the walls?'

'I see no other way of doing it. Your buildings almost back onto the inner wall and it cannot be more than a hundred paces to the river. You have plenty of slaves and so the work could be done in two years, three at the most. If anyone questions you too closely about what you're doing, tell them that it is a sewer project to improve the hygiene of the priests' living space. Would a donation of a talent of gold and ten of silver be adequate?'

The greed flicking across Naramsin's eyes amused Seleukos as he looked down at him. 'More than adequate, lord; work will commence immediately.'

'Excellent; just make sure it's wide enough for three men to run abreast and high enough so that they don't hit their heads.'

Naramsin looked up at the great Macedonian towering head and shoulders over him, his eyes widening.

Seleukos smiled. 'No, not me, Naramsin; just an average man.'

'Indeed, great lord; it shall be done.' Bowing, the architect backed away.

'You're being pessimistic,' Apama commented.

'No, just practical; it's one thing escaping but it's another to get back in.'

'Well, if we do have to flee, you won't have to inaugurate the altar of Bel Marduk, right at the very top of that frighteningly high building you're so scared of climbing.'

'Who said I was scared?'

'Oh really, Seleukos; it was so funny watching you come up with a reason not to go up.'

'So that's what you were laughing at?'

'Yes, a big and strong bull-elephant of a man brought low by a tall building.'

'I just don't like heights, that's all; I keep getting the urge to jump off and my knees shake. It's best if that is not observed by the locals.'

'Poor little boy.'

It was Temenos who relieved Seleukos from a position of spousal mockery. 'A message has just been relayed along the Royal Road, lord.'

Seleukos took the tablet, broke the seal and read.

'Well?' Apama asked when he had finished but remained in thought.

'Well, it is from Xenophilus. When he sent this he was two days from Persepolis, so he is probably just arriving by now. Antigonos has ordered him to testify against Peithon; it would seem our plan is working.'

'Yes, and now the question becomes: will Peithon's death make it more or less likely that Antigonos will keep you in position? How many of Alexander's generals can the resinated cyclops be seen to destroy?'

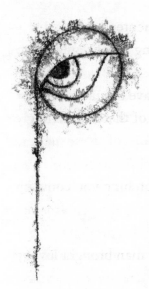

ANTIGONOS.
THE ONE-EYED.

'THE COLUMN IS in sight, Father,' Demetrios informed Antigonos, putting his head around his father's study door. 'It should be here before sundown.'

'Excellent,' Antigonos said, looking up from his desk full of correspondence; his secretary sat opposite him. 'Have Xenophilus report to me as soon as the treasure has been secured in the treasury; I will want him to go through it with me. Just to see how much he and Seleukos have taken for themselves.'

Demetrios nodded and then left his father to his work.

Antigonos settled back down to his correspondence with a feeling of contentment, for he was near completing his settlement of the east and would soon be westward bound. He nodded to his secretary. 'To Sibyrtius, satrap of Arachosia, greetings from Antigonos, commander of the east. Having decided to split up the Silver Shields so that never again will they be a corrosive force on the morale of the army, I shall be sending the last five hundred of them, the hard-core agitators, ostensibly to join your garrison. As they were supporters of Eumenes until they gave him to me in return for the baggage, and as you were a supporter of the sly little Greek until he falsely accused you of betrayal, I feel sure that you will welcome them for being the instrument of Eumenes' demise.' He paused, considering how to phrase the next line so as to get the greatest amount of satisfaction from it. He smiled to himself. 'However, I feel that men who will betray their commander once will easily do it again, so I would recommend that you use them for high-risk operations in which the chances of survival are minimal. I never want to see them in the west again. In obliging me in this matter you will please me, and I will have no cause to replace you.' *And that finally gets rid of the last of the Silver Shields, and very satisfying it feels, too, to have spread them all over the east without any hope of ever getting home.* He rubbed his hands together, pleased with his progress.

Removing Peucestas from his post had also been a satisfying achievement. Once he had seen with his own eyes just how influenced by eastern culture the man had become, he had realised that it would be an act of folly to keep his word and allow Peucestas to retain the satrapy of Persis. No man who embraces a foreign culture to the exclusion of his own could be trusted to rule over that culture with Macedon's interests at heart rather than those of the locals – especially not one who betrays his allies so easily.

But it was Peithon's arrival and subsequent detention that had contented him most, for with that move he had neutralised the greatest threat to his power in the east – not that he expected to keep direct control of events between the Zagros Mountains and the border with India, but he did expect to benefit from a great deal of the tax revenue, which would have dried up had Peithon successfully revolted. And now he had him confined and awaiting the trial that would be convened as soon as the main witness to his perfidy, Xenophilus, was present. It was not that Antigonos had any scruples about executing Peithon summarily, it was just that he felt it would be more politic after his treatment of Eumenes, Antigenes and Eudamos, to dispose of Peithon in a reasonably legal manner – the man had, after all, fought for him very successfully in his previous two battles and Antigonos did not want to seem ungrateful executing him without the benefit of a trial, potentially discouraging others to support him.

And thus it was with a far different demeanour that he welcomed Xenophilus than that with which he had said goodbye to him on the last occasion they had met.

'I did not want the Susa treasure to fall into Peithon's hands, so I brought it south to its rightful owner,' Xenophilus said by way of unnecessary explanation.

'You didn't think that I was the rightful owner last time we met,' Antigonos said, slightly gruffer than he had intended to be at this meeting.

'That's because Eumenes was the general commanding the east with a mandate from the then regent, Polyperchon. Now, with him dead, you are the general in the east and therefore it is my duty as the garrison commander of Susa and warden of the royal treasury to ensure that you receive it in its entirety; and that I couldn't guarantee if it remained at Susa, for it would not have taken Peithon long to march down from Ecbatana whilst you were here all the way south in Persepolis – and he would have far more troops available than you allowed Seleukos.'

He thinks he's a cunning little fox, but I can see through him. However, Demetrios is right: he should keep his post as he seems to have some sense of due process which can be of benefit in an underling. 'I'm grateful to you, Xenophilus; you've discharged your duty creditably, and I'm pleased to reappoint you in your post. Now, before I ask you to bear witness against Peithon, let us take a tour of the treasury so that you can show me just how honest you've been. Antigenes was quite forthcoming about the contents before he was executed.' Antigonos smiled inwardly as he watched Xenophilus blanch. *Not as honest as you should have been, judging by your expression.*

'In the three years since the Three Paradises conference when Antipatros sent Antigenes, Teutamus and their Silver Shields to bring the contents of the Susa treasury west in order to settle the back-pay owed to the army, it has been replenished to the tune of twenty thousand talents,' Antigonos said as he and Demetrios pored over the inventory that Xenophilus had furnished them with, now spread over the study desk. 'Fifteen in treasure and five in coin. Add that to the five thousand that we took from Ecbatana and we've more than enough to afford an army this size for a couple of years without any worry.'

Demetrios let out a soft whistle, shaking his head as he ran his finger down a column listing sacks of gold coinage. 'How accurate do you think this is?'

Antigonos shrugged. 'Well, judging by the tour that Xenophilus has just taken me on, I would say that it's a reasonably good estimation. And even allowing for the fact that he and Seleukos more than likely helped themselves to a goodly amount each, it still represents an impressive return in less than four years.'

'How much do you think they both took?'

'Between three and five hundred talents apiece, I should think.'

'How do you know?'

'Because it's what I would have taken in their place: it's enough to make a difference to their finances but not enough to really be noticed as missing from such a huge amount.'

'Still, it would be nice to get it back.'

'Oh, we will, Demetrios; you can be sure of that. Especially from Seleukos; Xenophilus is a good functionary but our

Titanesque friend has ambitions beyond his station and needs bringing down.' He got to his feet, once more rubbing his hands together. 'But one thing at a time, eh, Son; let's deal with the man who would have taken the lot if he could.'

The satrap of Media's dark eyes, lifeless at the best of times, remained expressionless as they bored into Xenophilus, holding the letter that he, Peithon, was purported to have sent. A man of few words and most of those of minimal syllables, he confined himself to: 'This man lies.'

Antigonos was not surprised by the statement. 'So you deny writing to Xenophilus asking him to join your planned rebellion and to bring the Susa treasury with him.'

The dead eyes now turned on Antigonos. 'I never wrote to him.'

'Ah, so you do not deny that you planned rebellion.'

'Clever talk proves naught, cyclops.'

Antigonos sat back in his chair, raised on a dais in the royal garden chamber, drumming his fingers on the arm and looking down at the serial rebel standing before him, surrounded by four guards; ringed behind him were Demetrios and all the senior officers from the army here to bear witness to Antigonos' sense of justice. *I had better remind them all of his previous history in that respect.* 'First you tried to incorporate nearly twenty-five thousand Greek deserters into your army only to be thwarted when your men were reminded of their duty to kill them all for abandoning their posts.' *No point in mentioning that it was Seleukos who brought the men to their senses; I don't want to complicate things in Babylon by portraying him as a sympathetic character. It's bad enough that I've got to use his supposed loyalty to me against Peithon.* 'Then, two years ago, you deposed the satrap of Parthia and installed your late brother there as you tried, once

53

again, to make a grab for the east. And now, after I reward you for having fought for me against Eumenes by confirming you as satrap of Media, you repay me with rebellion.'

'There was no rebellion.'

'So you keep on insisting and yet Seleukos also reported to me that you had offered him troops to help take Susa.'

'More lies. Why would I do that?'

'As another way of getting hold of the Susa treasury should Xenophilus reject your offer.'

'Idiot!'

'Calling me names is not going to help your cause.'

'My cause is lost; and you talking rubbish like that proves it: why would I give Seleukos troops to take Susa when anyone with sense would see that the first thing he would do with the captured treasury is go straight back to Babylon and hire as many mercenaries as he can, and not come and join me in a rebellion in the east?'

'Ah, so you admit there was a rebellion now, do you?'

The dead eyes closed and the jaw muscles tensed; Peithon took a deep breath, clenching his fists as if restraining himself from violent conduct. 'Get on with it, Antigonos. I've killed enough men in my time to know how easy it is, so I was puzzled why you are having such difficulty killing me; but I think I understand now.'

'You are on trial to ascertain whether you are innocent or guilty.' *This is just making me look stupid in front of the army.*

'No, I'm on trial to ascer- ascer- to see if you can find a good excuse to execute me as I was one of Alexander's bodyguards and am therefore harder to kill than a sly little Greek or an old man like Antigenes. I know what you are up to: I heard how you have removed Peucestas and yet you still keep him alive because he too was also one of the Bodyguard. We are hard to kill

54

because we were Alexander's chosen.' He turned to face the officers. 'We fought at Alexander's side whilst this soaked old cyclops rattled around in Phrygia trying to mop up a few backward mountain tribes. Now he wants to execute me; accusing me of rebellion with lies and forged letters as he has no real evidence. I say, kill me or kill him!'

There was a stir amongst the assembled officers that sent a chill through Antigonos; he glanced at Demetrios, standing within the crowd, and indicated that he should come and speak to him.

'What if those letters are forged?' he whispered in his son's ear.

'What difference would it make?'

Antigonos frowned. 'All the difference; he wouldn't be guilty.'

'Father, Peithon's right in what he said: his guilt is irrelevant; this trial is about having a good reason to execute him because of what he was and still is. You want him to be guilty so guilty he is; now take his head and get it over with because he's rapidly gaining sympathy.'

And then I'll need to take their minds off the matter. Coming to a decision, Antigonos stood, holding his arms out for silence. 'No man, whatever their rank or former position, has the right to rebel; this man has done just that. I am satisfied of his guilt: the letter to Xenophilus, which we have all heard, proves it, and the second letter to Seleukos plus Peithon's previous conduct since Alexander's death freed him from the constraints of loyalty both support that conclusion. Guards, seize him.'

Peithon was restrained, but he made no effort to run. The fur-covered muscles in his arms bulged as they were pulled behind his back and a manacle was clamped to his wrists. Down onto his knees he was forced, his struggles frenetic, his guards resolute.

Antigonos stood over him, imperious, determined to wrest the situation back into his favour. 'For this and the other treasonous actions against the memory and legacy of Alexander, I, Antigonos, the guardian of his memory and general commanding the east, sentence you to death. The sentence is to be carried out immediately. Do you have anything to say?'

Peithon looked up from his enforced kneeling position, his eyes as dead as if the sentence had already been carried out; he spat at the dais. 'You wish to take it all, Antigonos? Well, I will tell you this: I may not be the brightest of men and I am well aware that people tell jokes behind my back about how easy it is to outwit me, but I have always been loyal to Alexander and his memory. When I tried to sign up the Greek mercenaries it was because I thought someone needed to show Perdikkas that he could not just have it all his way; Alexander gave his ring "to the strongest" and I thought: "Why shouldn't that be me?" And then when, after Perdikkas' death and then that of Antipatros, I saw that the strongest two leaders emerging were a Greek and a man we had all forgotten about, of course I tried to form a powerbase here in the east so that I could be the strongest. Me, one of Alexander's chosen; not a forgotten old man or a foreigner. So take me, Antigonos, but I promise you that Macedon will never accept you as king, or whatever you want to call yourself, because the lads all know that you never shared our time with Alexander.'

It was with heart racing and eyes smouldering with hatred that Antigonos stepped down from the dais without reply. His sword was out and in his hand without him even noticing. He strode over to Peithon, who looked at him, his mouth a rictus grin, but he did not struggle.

'You'll never be one of us, Antigonos; and nor will your whelp.' Once more he spat, the globule splattering Antigonos' sandal, before stretching out his neck. 'Make it clean before all these witnesses, old man.'

And there was nothing that Antigonos could say or do that would show him in a better light other than strike the head cleanly from Peithon's shoulders; and strike it off he did. But he could find no pleasure in the deed, for he had been wounded at the last: all present would know that Peithon's parting shots were aimed true.

He looked down at the dead eyes still staring at him as they had done in life and then raised his one eye to his officers. 'Get back to your men,' he growled. 'We march at dawn.'

Passing the site of his defeat by Eumenes at the Coprates River did nothing to improve Antigonos' mood, which had grown ever grimmer in the twenty days since the army had left Persepolis, traversing the Cissia pass and coming down onto the western foothills of the Zagros Mountains. The memory of the aftermath of that failed river crossing caused him great grief: his life-long friend and brother-in-arms, Philotas, had been captured and sentenced to death by Eumenes; Antigonos had insisted that he wield the blade to sever his comrade's head himself, for it was unconscionable that Eumenes, a Greek, should execute Philotas. The image still haunted him and, despite ordering Eumenes' execution by garrotte – a far worse demise – he still grieved for his friend of over fifty years. Indeed, he had not the heart to fight in the front rank of the phalanx any more for he would miss Philotas' shoulder next to his.

With the Coprates behind them and then the Pasitigris crossed a few days later, the army came to Susa. Still Antigonos brooded for he was not unaware of the respect he had lost from some of his officers and many of his men with the execution of Peithon.

'Many of the lads who were in Alexander's army feel that what Peithon said at the last had merit,' Demetrios told him in one of the rare conversations Antigonos had held with his son, as he stood in a high window of Darius' palace looking out over the huge army encamped across the Cheaspes River, smoke rising from the fires of the evening meals. 'In the last few months you've executed Eumenes, Antigenes, Eudamos and Peithon, all of whom were a major part of the conquest. They're starting to wonder if being a part of that army now counts for nothing. They're not stupid, after all; they heard about you helping Kassandros – another who did not take part in the adventure – to defeat Polyperchon and Aristonous, who both did. Also, they haven't failed to notice the Silver Shields have been split up and posted to the arse-end of the empire seemingly to rot. Look at it from their point of view, Father: if the most elite unit in the whole army, a unit that has never been defeated, can be treated so, then where do the rest of the lads stand?'

'They stand with me.' Another cup of wine disappeared down Antigonos' gullet. 'I've fought for Macedon all my life. Just because I wasn't at Gaugamela or the battle of the Hydaspes doesn't make me a lesser man. My arse! I spent ten years subduing the interior of Anatolia.'

'That doesn't count in their eyes compared to taking places like the Sogdian Rock or the march back west through the Gedrosian Desert.'

'So what do they want?'

'Respect.'

'They've got my respect.'

'And yet you help a man who everyone else hates to power in Macedon against men they once fought under; you then execute their generals and exile their most senior comrades.'

'Not all of them: what about Teutamus and Pythan? They were with Alexander and yet I didn't execute them when I defeated Eumenes; they're on my staff now.'

'And what about Antigenes, Eudamos, Peithon and Eumenes himself?'

'They all deserved it.'

'You might think so, but they are used to those kind of decisions being made by the army assembly, not in a high-handed manner by a man they haven't heard of, let alone seen, for ages.'

'My lads have been with me all the way through.'

'It's not your lads who are doing the whispering; it's Alexander's veterans.'

'Then bring me the ringleaders and I'll soon see to it that they won't whisper again.'

'And that is just the kind of thing that will make matters worse. Even Eumenes didn't condemn Philotas out of hand; he had his army assembly do it – you should know, you were there.'

Why do I get the feeling that he may well be right? It's never occurred to me that I was considered irrelevant just because I was busy fighting somewhere else. He reached for the jug on the table; another cupful of wine disappeared. Antigonos looked at his son, grunted and then hurled his cup to smash against the wall. 'So what do you suggest I do?'

'I don't know; but I know what I would suggest you didn't do.'

'What?'

'Don't execute any more officers or men who served with Alexander. Otherwise, it will be deemed that you have a jealous vendetta against them or a sense of inadequacy.'

'I am not inadequate! My arse, I'm not.'

'I didn't say you were; I just said that's how it might look.'

'So don't execute anyone?'

'Yes; at least not for a while.'

'Not even Seleukos?'

'Not even Seleukos.

'What about Ptolemy?'

'Especially not Ptolemy.'

'Kassandros, then?'

'He never served.'

KASSANDROS.
THE JEALOUS.

ANCIENT AND GRIMED were the walls of Amphipolis, the stronghold of Aristonous, the last of the Argead royal house supporters still holding out in Macedon after Olympias' death; but despite their age the walls were still formidable, well founded and towering. Kassandros pulled up his horse, safely out of arrow-range, and surveyed the chaos and filth that was a siege in progress. Trenches and stockades surrounded the town and a pall of smoke had settled over it in the absence of a breeze. Yet for all the scale of the endeavour very little seemed to be occurring: a few soldiers sat around talking in a listless manner as they drank from wineskins as the artillery pieces, all set up and ranged, stood silent.

Having just completed his first successful siege, at Pydna, and despite his relative lack of other military experience, Kassandros' temper was quickly rising. 'Where is Crateuas?' He turned around to the escort of cavalry that had accompanied him in the twenty-league ride from the port of Therma, and indicated to his younger twin brothers, Philip and Pleistarchos. 'Find him!'

As the twins rode away Kassandros gazed around, incredulous, at the lack of purpose or action, his pockmarked, avianesque face with its beak of a nose turning as red as his hair; even his presence had not roused any of the men to a significant level of activity. *I'll have heads for this.* Drawing his sword, he kicked his mount forward and slapped the nearest man on the back of the head with the flat of the blade. 'What do you think you're doing, taking a holiday?'

Now unconscious, stretched out on the ground, the soldier was unable to answer; his mates, however, jumped up and stepped away from the man they now recognised as their general.

'Why aren't you attacking?' Kassandros bellowed. 'Where are your officers?'

The men turned and ran.

'Round them up!' Kassandros ordered his remaining escort. As his men gave chase, he shook his head in disbelief. That the situation was bad in Amphipolis he was already aware, but this bad? No, he could not credit it. Crateuas, who, along with Atarrhias, was one of the two generals commanding the troops and fleet that Antigonos had lent Kassandros to take Greece and Macedon, had originally proved his worth and yet, entrusted with the siege of Amphipolis, he had been a failure.

Kassandros had sent his twin brothers to investigate reports that the siege was not being pressed as vigorously as could be expected, only for them to find Crateuas' men shut in Eion, Amphipolis' coastal port a league to the south, and himself a prisoner after Aristonous had soundly defeated him. With no fleet of his own, Aristonous could not prevent the coming evacuation by sea with the ships that Philip and Pleistarchos requested from Kassandros, and therefore withdrew back to Amphipolis with his captive before the rescue arrived.

After that, Kassandros had no further information as he had travelled directly by sea from Pydna to Therma, across the bay, and thence by horse overland; but that things had grown this slack surprised and infuriated him in equal measure. And now that he came to look at the situation more closely he realised that the reason for the inactivity was that there were in actuality very few men manning the siege lines; indeed, those he had assaulted were some of the only soldiers around, their absence being covered by the smoke. 'Where is everyone?' he yelled, his temper tight within him making his head pound.

It was not long before his men dragged in a couple of the fugitives, throwing them to the ground before his mount.

'Well?' he asked in a voice taut with anger. 'Where is everyone?'

The men shared a look of fear before turning back to Kassandros. 'Gone, sir,' they said in unison.

'Gone? Gone where?'

The elder of the two, greying around the temples and beard, swallowed before answering. 'Back west. They left yesterday morning; a few of us were left behind to make sure that Aristonous keeps to his oath.'

'Keeps to his oath? What oath?'

'That he wouldn't attack Crateuas as he withdrew.'

This was too much for Kassandros; he jumped from his horse and grabbed the man by the tunic, hauling him up. 'Why was Crateuas withdrawing?'

'Aristonous had made him swear an oath not to fight him any more in return for giving him his freedom and allowing him and his men to leave bearing their arms.'

Kassandros' temper could take no more; he slit the man's belly open and left him to drop screaming to the floor clutching at spilling viscera. His mate looked at him, terrified, and then up at Kassandros who, in his haste to get after Crateuas, contented himself with kicking him on the jaw, snapping his head back, rendering him unconscious.

Leaving the gutted man moaning behind him, Kassandros swung up into the saddle and kicked his mount west.

'The column is camped three leagues away,' Pleistarchos reported as he led his scouts back in the following morning.

Kassandros wiped his last hunk of bread around the bowl, soaking up the dregs of the olive oil, popped it in his mouth and chewed, looking deep into the fire. 'Did you speak to Crateuas?'

'Yes.'

'And?'

'And he confirmed that he had indeed made an oath not to fight Aristonous any more.'

'Did he care to explain why?'

'He said he would be only too pleased to give you an explanation when you catch up with him.'

'What! He's not even going to sit there and wait?'

'No; he says he's heading for Pella to join Atarrhias and his men. Now that he has done everything that Antigonos wanted of him he thinks it's time to take their men and ships back to Asia.'

'Does he now?'

'You now hold all of Macedon in Antigonos' name,' Crateuas said, looking sidelong at Kassandros as he rode beside him at the head of the column, ten thousand strong. 'My work is done so I shall be taking my men back to join him, as he ordered and as you agreed.'

Kassandros had never been one to set too much store by agreements but for now it suited him to stick to the deal. 'I did agree, yes, I did. I agreed to let you go once the whole of Macedon had been freed from the supporters of Olympias, which, clearly, it is not as you left Aristonous in possession of Amphipolis.'

Weather-beaten, roughened and old in the ways of war, the experienced general dismissed the detail as trivial with a wave of his hand. 'There is nothing that I can do about that as I've given him my oath not to go against him.'

'In return for him releasing you.'

'Yes.'

'And what sort of commander does that make you, managing to get yourself captured and your men routed to the safety of a town a league away?'

'Aristonous surprised me with a pre-dawn attack; he's a great general and I was fairly beaten just as we beat him fairly when we surprised him in his camp at Alorus with a pre-dawn attack.'

'Fairly beaten! Can't you hear what you're saying? Fairly beaten! Is this some sort of a game to you?'

Crateuas turned on Kassandros in anger. 'We are all Macedonians! There is no need for excessive loss of blood. For Aristonous and I, honours are equal; we can both walk away with heads held high.'

'But I don't want you to walk away. I want you to do what Antigonos promised you would do.'

'What, win your war for you in a way such that you personally never have to strike a blow – unless the man is unarmed – and certainly never get yourself anywhere near the frontline? Is that what you want?'

'How dare you talk to me like that?'

Crateuas shook his head. 'Kassandros, Atarrhias and I have served with you now for almost two years; we are not stupid. We see you for what you are; we know you shied from the fight in Alorus and then blamed a brave officer and had him executed. I have done all that honour requires for a man who has shown very little honour himself. Now, I'm going back to Asia with my men. For me the war in Europe is over; if you want to carry on and remove Aristonous from Amphipolis then go ahead, but do it without me and my lads.'

Kassandros was not quick enough. Crateuas' hand snapped around his wrist as he went for his knife.

Crateuas tutted, shaking his head. 'That is nasty behaviour. Now go, before I decide that you've been too long on this earth without a meeting with the Ferryman. My son Peithon has told me all about you when you were pages together with Alexander; he was in no doubt what sort of a man you were and he is not the quickest, as I freely admit. So don't tempt me, Kassandros. I look forward to sharing the tales I have of you with Peithon, next time I see him.' He twisted the wrist, forcing Kassandros to drop the knife. 'Now go!'

Kassandros felt some of Crateuas' Companions begin to crowd in on him from behind, protecting their general. *The more I order him and the more he refuses me, the more face I'll lose. I'll make him pay for this.* He pulled his horse to the left, away from the column, to join his brothers and his escort. 'Philip, ride on to Pella and make sure that Crateuas has no access to the shipping in the port. Pleistarchos, get to Pydna and do the same and then bring the army north; we may well need to fight Crateuas and Atarrhias.'

The twins looked concerned. 'But they've got just shy of twenty thousand, between them, almost as many as we can field,' Philip said.

'And they are experienced generals,' Pleistarchos added.

Kassandros' eyes narrowed. 'Just get on with it. I'll see you back in Pella.'

'Where are you going?'

'To make Aristonous an offer he'll find hard to reject.'

*

'We have let this go on too long,' Kassandros said as he sat across the table from Aristonous, placed outside the gates of Amphipolis; six guards accompanied each of them. 'Olympias is dead and before she died she wrote to you ordering you to surrender Amphipolis.'

'I agree that it has gone on too long,' Aristonous replied, leaning one arm on the table. 'And perhaps I would have obeyed Olympias' order had you not executed Monimus when he surrendered Pella, also on Olympias' order.'

'It was my younger brothers who did that without my knowledge; they thought it would please me.'

Aristonous' smile was cold on his lined, strong-jawed face; now in his fifties with grey hair he was the oldest of Alexander's former bodyguards; a man steeped in war and a respecter of tradition. 'It comes so easy to you, the lie, does it not, Kassandros; and you feel no shame. I know it was you who ordered Monimus' death. Don't insult me.'

Kassandros shrugged. 'Have it your own way.' *He'll not get an admission of guilt out of me.* 'How many men do you have inside?' He indicated with his head to the gates. 'Six thousand? Seven thousand? Enough to beat the thousand in a pre-dawn attack, but not enough to fight your way back to your estates in the west.'

'Your point is?'

'My point is that you are stuck here.'

'I could always go east to Lysimachus in Thrace.'

It was Kassandros' turn for a cold smile. 'You have nothing there; all your land is here and from what I know of Lysimachus he's using all the money he gets to build his fortresses to keep out the northern tribes so I doubt you'll get much charity from him. Face it, Aristonous, you either stay here until you starve because I'll bring my army up to finish the siege—'

'What's left of your army now that Crateuas and Atarrhias are taking their men back to Asia.'

'You let *me* worry about that. Whatever happens, there will be men here sealing off the town entirely. I've just done that at Pydna; I can do it again.'

'Or?'

'Or I guarantee you safe passage to your estates where you can live out the rest of your life in retirement, as you always wished to do after Alexander's death, in return for handing your men over to me.'

'Thus making you unassailable in Macedon.'

'I think I already am; but either way I will get your men.'

'It just depends what condition they're in when you do.'

'Exactly.'

'And what about the king and his mother?'

'I am the king's regent; I will ensure his safety.'

'Will you, though? It seems to me that if you're marrying Thessalonike, the king becomes an inconvenience.'

As are your questions, old man. 'I could not be seen to be responsible for the death of the son of Alexander.'

'No, but somehow you could be seen to be not responsible for the child's death, much like you distanced yourself from that of Olympias.'

'Olympias had many enemies, Alexander doesn't.' *Only me.*

Aristonous studied Kassandros for a few moments, while Kassandros did his best not to flinch under such scrutiny.

'Very well,' Aristonous said eventually. 'How can I trust you?'

'I'll swear an oath.'

Aristonous gave a grim chuckle. 'You expect me to believe that you, a man of no honour, a man who is reputed to be a coward, would hold to an oath? No, Kassandros, take your oath by all means, but if my life and the life of the rightful heir to the throne are to hang on an oath, let it be that of someone I trust and who has a hold on you. Let it be your future wife Thessalonike's oath.'

THESSALONIKE.
THE HALF-SISTER.

'I SWEAR BY GAIA, the Earth Mother, that I will ensure the safety of Aristonous' life during his journey from Amphipolis to his estates and thereafter; and I further swear to be the guardian of the life of Alexander, the fourth of that name to be king of Macedon. Whilst I live neither shall come to any harm.' So did Thessalonike swear on the altar to Gaia in the goddess's temple just within the walls of Amphipolis. She had not baulked at making the oath, for she had always liked Aristonous and would happily ensure his safety in return for his retirement and troops; as for Alexander, well, who would take the very life that gave her future husband his legitimate power as regent? It was, therefore, with a clear conscience that she dipped her fingers in the blood of a white goose and touched them to her forehead.

The priestesses began a chant whilst striking together small cymbals on their middle fingers and thumbs as the goose's liver was examined by the leader of their order.

'The goddess accepts the oath,' the high priestess announced from behind her veil, 'and will hold you to account should you break it.'

Thessalonike bowed her head in acknowledgement of the goddess's power. *I will not break it.*

Aristonous, standing next to Kassandros behind Thessalonike, stepped forward. 'I am satisfied with your oath, Thessalonike. I'm now prepared to hand my men over to Kassandros and retire to my estates, never again to involve myself in the politics of Macedon or her empire.' He looked to Kassandros. 'Leave me in peace, Kassandros; and let the boy grow to manhood. If you do that then perhaps the world will think better of you. I leave my men in your charge and will take only my kinsmen and the men from my estates home with me.'

'You are free to go, Aristonous.' Kassandros' face betrayed no emotion.

Thessalonike studied her future husband. *He's hiding his thoughts; this might well prove to have been a farce.*

Aristonous turned to Thessalonike, walked her away from Kassandros and lowered his voice. 'I've always liked you, Thessalonike, and despite your betrayal of Olympias, I wish you no harm; but I promise you this: if you have children with this man and he breaks his oath, their lives will be cursed. The Earth Mother will see to that.' With a curt nod, he turned on his heel and strode from the temple.

Thessalonike glanced at her husband-to-be. *The question is, Kassandros, will you risk breaking your oath and, if you do, what will I think of you?*

And that was the question which Thessalonike was always asking herself about the man she had consented, much to everyone's shock and surprise, to marry: what did she actually think of him? She could come up with as many different answers as there were hours in a day. She knew his many weaknesses: his jealousy, probable cowardice – although she had not witnessed that at first hand – his cruelty, his maliciousness and vengefulness and his dishonesty, just to name a few. But she also knew that he was so deeply in love with her that she could bind him to her will with little effort. No, he was not a good-looking man, tall, lanky, thin and slightly stooping because of the limp that had afflicted him since his leg was gouged in a failed boar-hunt. And yes, he still had to sit upright at the table like a small child for he had not won the right to recline like other men who had speared a boar in the hunt without the use of a net; but the way he dealt with what must be a humiliation at each meal she had come to admire. And so, what did she think of the man whom she was very soon to marry?

The truth of the matter, she found herself admitting, was that she was ambivalent towards him. To her, Kassandros was but a route to power, and her personal feelings, one way or the other, did not signify so long as he treated her person with the appropriate respect. How considerate a lover he could be was something that she would only find out on her wedding night, having pushed away all pre-nuptial advances, uneager to welcome the spindly frame of her intended into her bed before she was obliged to. But aside from his unappealing physical aspects – which she would just have to ignore as he mounted her – there was very little that she either objected to or admired. He was just a tool with which she would gain the power that her late adoptive mother, Olympias, had craved and in doing so she would avenge herself upon the murderer of her birth mother. Thessalonike had accepted Olympias as her mother – even after she had guessed how that had come to pass – until Olympias had humiliated her by slapping her across the face in public. It had been an insult that Thessalonike had never been able to forget or forgive and had been the catalyst that led to her betrayal of Olympias and her decision to marry Kassandros. The knowledge that Olympias died – stoned to death by the families of her victims – knowing that she would be the most powerful woman in Macedon had given Thessalonike great pleasure, for that was the one thing that her adoptive mother had always craved and had so briefly tasted.

Thessalonike looked once more at her husband-to-be; he met her gaze with wide-eyed appreciation and what passed for a smile on his birdlike face. *That he is completely and utterly in love with me is something I couldn't have wished for in my most ambitious dreams. It makes handling him so much easier.* She reached out her hand and he took it, a rare hint of colour without anger coming to his cheeks. 'It's time we returned to Pella, Kassandros. Now we have made peace with Aristonous and taken command of his men we should neutralise Crateuas and Atarrhias and then do the most important thing we have yet to do.'

'Get married?'

Thessalonike smiled. 'No, Kassandros, although that is important, I grant you; but what I have in mind for after the marriage is far more important: it is what kings of Macedon have traditionally done throughout our history.'

Kassandros looked at her with a quizzical frown. 'You mean bury their predecessors?'

'I do indeed.'

'It's too early to think about taking the crown.'

'I agree; but it's never too early to begin our preparations. You and I, the regent of Macedon and his Argead wife, burying Philip, my half-brother, in the royal burial ground at Aegae sends a strong message. However, to prevent the people thinking that we are overreaching ourselves, we shall also have the young Alexander present; that way we make the statement but are still able to cloak it with a veil of legitimacy.'

Kassandros' leer was that of a man who sees his way to his dream of power become that much easier. He reached out and cupped Thessalonike's chin with a gentle hand. 'You and I make a formidable team.'

Thessalonike stroked the back of his hand. 'We'll be even more formidable once we're married.' She enjoyed the misty look of love that floated across his eyes. 'Come, Kassandros; we go to Pella, defeat our enemies, marry and then bury the dead.'

'But we don't know where Philip is buried.'

'*You* don't know, but I do as I was there when Olympias had them secretly interred with no ceremony whatsoever. We shall change that and bring tears to the eyes of every Macedonian who witnesses it.'

'There,' Thessalonike said, pointing to the corner of a little-used courtyard in the heart of the palace at Pella. 'Dig there.'

The four soldiers crunched their shovels into the gravelled ground, pressing down on the metal blades with their feet, and began the dig, overseen by their officer.

'How deep are they?' Kassandros asked.

'Deep enough, but it won't take long.' Thessalonike settled down in a chair to wait; Kassandros hovered by the excavation, his impatience obvious to all. Indeed, on the three-day journey from Amphipolis to Pella he had urged haste and had talked of little else for he had realised the true value of what Thessalonike was presenting him with. She had concealed her delight in her future husband's excitement as it put him deeply in her debt and she was certain that she would be calling in a favour very soon. For the present, she was happy for him to make plans which, other than burying her half-brother Philip, included the apprehension of Crateuas and his men before they joined with Atarrhias.

Having left Philip and Pleistarchos at the port of Therma to ferry Aristonous' former men across to Pydna, where the rest of

Kassandros' army was still based after the siege, Kassandros and Thessalonike headed at speed to Pella. Here, Kassandros gave orders to ready the garrison to follow Crateuas south as he attempted to join with Atarrhias, planning to crush the two between himself and the twins as they brought their newly strengthened army up from Pydna. And now, as the Pella garrison prepared to march, they hunted for a dead king.

'That looks to be a thumb,' Kassandros said as the soldiers stood waist deep in the hole, scraping loose earth from the centre of it.

The officer jumped down, and began to worry at the earth around the digit with his fingers. 'It's an arm,' he called, lifting the partly decomposed limb; leathery skin clung to the bone and the stench of putrefaction rose from the ground.

'Just pull the body out,' Thessalonike ordered. 'It's one of the four slaves who dug the pit and threw the bodies in. They were silenced. Philip's wife, Adea, should be the fifth body you come to; she was lying face up on her husband.'

'Here she is,' the officer called up sometime later over the piles of bones, clinging flesh, scraps of clothing and matted hair that now surrounded the grave.

Kassandros looked into the hole and then back at Thessalonike. 'It seems like her.'

Thessalonike placed a cloth over her nose as she rose from her chair and looked down at the body. 'Yes, that's her; that's how I remember her lying.' And it was unmistakably Adea: her wide shoulders still had some dried muscle covering the bone, and her face, a mummified rictus grin drawn over it, still had the aspect of the Illyrian amazon despite it being more than a year since she had hanged herself.

Thessalonike turned away from the sight as in death Olympias had provided Adea with no dignity; naked she lay on her decomposing husband, her legs spread and what was left of her shrivelled loins free to view. 'Treat her and her husband with respect as you get them out. Try not to let the bodies fall apart.' She pointed to the two biers waiting close by. 'Get them both onto them and then take the bodies to the cellars to keep cool.' She turned to Kassandros. 'Come, my dear; I have need of a drink.' She took her husband-to-be by the arm and walked away.

'What should we do with the bones of the slaves?' the officer called after her.

Thessalonike waved a dismissive hand over her shoulders. 'Just throw them back in the hole before you fill it in.'

'We will be ready to march by mid-afternoon, sir,' Prepelaus, the commander of the Pella garrison, five thousand strong, informed Kassandros and Thessalonike as they entered the great hall of the palace whose wide doors looked south through the heart of the grid-planned city to the river port in the distance. 'With the reserves that have been mustered we have a total of just over seven thousand infantry, mainly heavy, plus just over five hundred cavalry.'

Kassandros grinned, clapped his hands together and rubbed them. 'Excellent; that number combined with what my brothers now have down at Pydna should mean we outnumber them by a good four or five thousand.'

Thessalonike suppressed a smile. *I have never seen him so full of goodwill; he didn't even attempt to find something to criticise. If only he were always so amenable, people might be more willing to give him their wholehearted support.*

'Will you be coming with me, Thessalonike?' Kassandros asked, a look of hope in his eyes.

'Of course, my dear; a wife should always support her husband.'

'A wife? Does that mean we can…' He let the sentence fade.

'When we are married; I just used the term figuratively.' *The disappointment on his face is almost too much.* 'Once Crateuas and Atarrhias are defeated we shall marry and then we can…'

'Eight or nine days at the most.'

'Let us hope you are right.' *And I'm very much interested in watching how you act in the field; don't think that I haven't noticed you've given the twins the more dangerous job of taking the enemy straight on whilst you stab him in the back.*

It was only until the following morning, when they were less than four leagues from Pella, that Thessalonike had to wait to see the quality of the man with whom she would share her life; and it came as no shock to her.

'What do you mean, Crateuas has joined up with Atarrhias and they have turned and are heading back north towards us?'

Prepelaus shrugged. 'Just that, sir: they must have turned about yesterday evening and then carried on this morning retracing their steps. The scouts report that they are a couple of leagues away; probably a lot less by now.'

The look of terror in Kassandros' eyes was well concealed but Thessalonike glimpsed it nevertheless. 'Do we have an accurate estimation of their numbers?' she asked Prepelaus, causing Kassandros to glare at her.

'According to the scouts, just under twenty thousand.'

'Nearly three to one, Kassandros; Alexander faced much worse in his time.'

Kassandros' face went the colour of his hair. 'I am not Alexander!'

'No, you are not, my dear; which is why I recommend that we should pull back to Pella and endure a siege until the twins manage to bring their army up to relieve us. I suggest you get a message down to Pydna by sea as soon as you like.'

The relief on his face was pitiful. *He's pathetically grateful that I've not suggested standing and facing them but, rather, bravely running away to hide behind walls until help comes. Oh, well, I can't say that I hadn't been warned of his cowardice.*

It had been a hasty retreat, and Thessalonike had sensed that Kassandros was always no more than a moment away from suggesting that she and he ride on ahead to Pella, leaving Prepelaus to bring the army as quickly as he could. Grateful though she was that he managed to hold onto his dignity and resisted making such a humiliating suggestion, she could not help but picture him doing so as if it had really occurred. *I must put the image from my mind*, she thought as she stood in the highest tower of the palace, looking south at the approaching host; all around the city the garrison of Pella manned the walls in a strong show of defiance.

Thessalonike frowned as she watched the army halt and still remain in column. *Why do they not move to surround the city? They have the men.*

It was not long until the reason became obvious: from just behind the vanguard a group of horsemen appeared under a branch of truce. Up they rode to the south gate and became lost to her view, but she could tell from the activity there that a parley was in progress. She turned and descended the stairs to be with Kassandros as he received the message that was sure to come. *Now is not the time to let him make any rash decisions out of malice or a desire for vengeance.*

'Crateuas and Atarrhias want to speak with me in person?' Kassandros was astounded at what the herald from the two generals had said. 'Only if they come before me on their knees.'

Thessalonike reached out and touched her future husband's arm and leaned towards him. 'Let's not be ungenerous,' she whispered in his ear. 'We don't know what they wish to discuss. If you put conditions like that on the talks, their dignity will preclude them from coming.'

Kassandros stiffened; he turned to glare at her.

Thessalonike bestowed her warmest smile upon him, filled with promise.

Relaxing, he turned back to the herald. 'Very well, they may enter the town and travel here unmolested.'

The herald cleared his throat. 'They have said that they will not enter the city. The parley is to take place at the gates, which are to be left open.'

Thessalonike grabbed Kassandros' arm again as he tensed for an explosion. 'Control yourself, my dear; that is only to be expected. Would you go into their camp?'

'But they are implying that they don't trust me.'

'Would you trust you?'

Kassandros grunted and then stroked Thessalonike's hand. 'Very well, tell Crateuas and Atarrhias to meet me there in one hour. Six bodyguards for each side.'

'Agreed.'

'And one final condition: only one gate will be open; the other will remain closed in case it is just a ruse to try and storm in whilst they're both open.'

The herald thought for a moment. 'I think my masters can agree to that.'

'There is also one other issue,' Thessalonike said. 'And that is I shall also be sitting down at the table.' With a nod she dismissed the open-mouthed herald. She turned to Kassandros who was equally open-mouthed. 'Well, come on then. I for one am going to change. We should look our finest.'

*

And it was a spectacular sight that Thessalonike made as she walked through the gate on the arm of Kassandros: her golden hair was piled high and secured with pins of silver with jewelled heads; two ringlets hung down by either ear, framing a milk-pale face with sapphire eyes. Feet invisible beneath a long gown of saffron linen, she glided next to her husband-to-be who faded into insignificance in comparison, despite his shining breast-plate, high helm and blood-red cloak. All eyes were fixed upon her as she took her seat at the round table and then with a graceful gesture of her hand indicated that the others too might sit.

'Crateuas and Atarrhias, you are welcome,' Thessalonike said once all were seated.

Atarrhias, of an age with Kassandros, but everything he was not – broad, dark and rugged, a life-long natural soldier – was the first to overcome his surprise at a woman hijacking the parley. 'It is good to see you again, Thessalonike; especially looking so radiant.'

She inclined her head at the compliment, enjoying the bris-tling she felt emanate from Kassandros next to her. *So, you get jealous even when I'm paid a compliment, do you? That will be very useful.* 'You are too kind, Atarrhias.'

Crateuas, older and more grizzled than his colleague, grunted his greetings, evidently in no mood for small talk and courtesies.

'What is it that we can do for you two gentlemen?'

'I can no longer go back to Asia,' Crateuas said.

'What he means is,' Atarrhias interjected before Thessalonike or Kassandros could respond to the blunt statement, 'is that he can longer go back to Asia unless he is part of an army big enough to defeat Antigonos.'

Kassandros leaned forward, his attention immediately grabbed. 'So you are saying that you want to stay here in Macedon?'

'Yes.'

'With your men?'

'Yes.'

'And you, Atarrhias?' Thessalonike asked, keeping the excitement from her face in a way that Kassandros could not.

'I will not go back and serve a man capable of such disloyalty such as the resinated cyclops.'

Thessalonike nodded as if it was an accepted fact that Antigonos had no loyalty. 'What has he done this time?'

Crateuas lifted his head and looked at her for the first time; there were tears in his eyes. 'He has executed my son. Atarrhias had a message from his younger brother serving out in the east.'

Atarrhias shook his head in regret, his eyes sombre. 'There can be no doubting it; it was my brother Drakon's letter and he has no reason to tell me a lie.'

Tears now rolled down Crateuas' lined and stubbled cheeks. 'He cut Peithon's head off himself. My son! My son executed by him after I had served him for more than ten years since Alexander left him to subdue Anatolia. I fought his battles for him, endured hardships, froze in the mountains and thirsted in the sun for him. When he told me to come to Europe to help you, I did not argue and fought hard for you.'

'As we will both attest to,' Thessalonike said, her most understanding and sympathetic look on display. 'You have shown remarkable loyalty to us.'

'Apart from striking a deal with Aristonous,' Kassandros reminded everyone. 'That is something that I find hard to forgive.'

'My dear, I don't think you should be so hard on the man; after all, you now have Aristonous' men.'

'And he still has his life; which I find inconvenient.'

81

Crateuas shook his head. 'I did it because I wanted to return to Asia to go back to soldiering with a man who I thought was my friend.'

'Meaning I'm not,' Kassandros said in a harsh tone.

'We have a professional relationship and I would be very pleased to carry that on. The way I see it is that if I help you secure all of Greece, including defeating Alexandros down in the Peloponnese, then you would be strong enough to negotiate an alliance with Ptolemy and, perhaps, Lysimachus, against Antigonos. From now on that is all I have to live for. Peithon's younger brother was killed after he was foolishly installed as satrap of Parthia – neither of my sons were ever very bright and should have kept out of politics as I did – so there is nothing left for me now but revenge. I intend to kill Antigonos on the battle-field for how he has repaid my loyalty to him.'

The cyclops must be a worse political operator than I thought to have alienated such a man in so final a way. 'And you wish to stay too, Atarrhias? What will become of your brother when Antigonos finds out that you have deserted him? It doesn't sound like he's against executing the nearest and dearest of people who are loyal, let alone those who have betrayed him.'

'I have already sent a message to him to leave Antigonos as soon as he is able.'

'You seem confident that I am going to accept your services,' Kassandros said, surprising everyone.

Again Thessalonike laid a soothing hand on his arm. 'I think we should be grateful that they are bringing us their men.' She looked across to the two generals. 'And ships?'

'And ships,' Atarrhias confirmed.

'I was always going to keep the men and the ships,' Kassandros snapped, 'the only difference now is that they expect to keep their lives.' He stood, his fists leaning on the table. 'How do I trust you, Crateuas? You made a deal with one of my enemies once; what's to say that you won't do it again?'

Crateuas looked up with bloodshot eyes. 'You keep my men and I will show you my loyalty. I believe that you are getting married soon.'

Thessalonike smiled. 'We are.'

'Tomorrow, now that I have your men.'

'Perhaps not that soon, my dear. In four or five days, I should think, as we have got to get Alexander and his eastern wild-cat of a mother up from Pydna; it is essential that the boy is present at the wedding and then at the funeral of Philip and Adea.'

Crateuas wiped his face with the back of his hand. 'Then I will bring you a wedding gift that will bind me to you. Until then you can rely on Atarrhias to begin the process of having the men swear loyalty to you, Kassandros.'

'And to me,' Thessalonike said.

'Indeed, Thessalonike – and to you.'

Thessalonike rose. 'Good, our business is done. Come, Kassandros, we have wedding plans to make and the first thing we need to do is send Prepelaus to Pydna to fetch Roxanna and her son. They still have a use.'

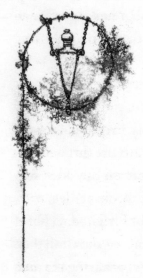

ROXANNA.
THE WILD-CAT.

THAT A QUEEN should be treated thus was intolerable. Roxanna hurled yet another cushion at the locked door which kept her and her son prisoner. And that was her main point of contention: it was just her and her son; gone were her slaves and the boy's nurse, leaving her, a queen, the wife of the great Alexander himself, to tend to her own needs as well as those of her son. If her father, Oxyartes, could see her now, he would die of shame as he watched her wash and dress the seven-year-old Alexander, the fourth of that name to be king of Macedon. But these menial tasks had to be performed for, despite the humiliation, it was vital that the boy be kept looking his best as surely there would soon come a time when the people of Macedon would be able to see him. *And when they do they will recognise him as their rightful monarch and I will be treated with the respect that I deserve.*

But until that moment came she was a captive in a small set of rooms in the highest tower of the royal palace of Pydna. Through her east-facing window, chill, salt-tanged winds blew in from the sea, sparkling azure in the morning sun; it was an alien smell to her, used, as she was, to the dry high-desert winds of her native Bactria. She looked at the young Alexander, sitting at the window gazing out to sea as he did most of the empty days, and seethed at her restraint. Why had her husband died at such a young age, leaving her unprotected as his followers scrabbled for the power that should, rightly, be her son's? Why did no one recognise the injustice of the situation? Why, now that the witch Olympias had killed the man-child and his man-woman of a wife before being so pleasingly executed herself, was there any question about her son's right to the throne?

Thessalonike! It must be her doing. She spat on the floor and shrieked, causing Alexander to turn and look at her with vacant eyes, before returning to his maritime vigil with not a word. *I should have cultivated her as a friend, but how was I to know when I met her that she wasn't Olympias' servant but Alexander's half-sister?* Again she cursed herself for her haughty attitude to Thessalonike, coming as close as she ever could to admitting a mistake of her own making rather than it being the fault of another.

It was the sound of the bar on the other side of the doors being removed that brought her out of her introspection – it was too early for their midday meal to arrive. She stood, ready to face whatever was to come through; Alexander did not react to the movement, fixed, as he was, on the far horizon.

The doors swung open to reveal a Macedonian officer. 'Pack your things and be ready to leave in an hour.'

'Who are you to give orders to a queen in such a manner?'

The officer opened his mouth to reply but then turned on his heel and walked away, the doors closing behind him, a hurled vase smashing against them as they did.

How to pack? It was something that she had never attempted. There was a wooden trunk in the sleeping quarters, it would have to do. 'Alexander, come and help. We're leaving.'

The boy gave no indication that he had heard.

'Alexander!'

Slowly he turned his head to face her.

'Alexander, we're packing. We're finally leaving here.'

It took a moment to digest this news. 'Where are we going?'

'Does it matter? Anywhere but here.'

'Will I be able to see the sea?'

'Does it matter?'

'I like the sea.'

'Come and pack your things; we'll put everything in that wooden trunk.'

'I don't have anything.'

'What about your tunics and sandals?'

'What about them?' He turned back to studying the sea.

Stamping her foot, Roxanna stomped off to chuck her limited wardrobe into the trunk; much had been lost during the siege.

The Macedonian returned at the allotted time with slaves for their meagre luggage and guards for their safety – or to prevent escape. But where was there to run to? During the siege of Pydna she had tried to flee with Aristonous but he had betrayed her and given her back to Olympias, causing her such grief for she had thought he desired her. *Curse him to the very bones.* Even if she were to escape her guards there was no one she could turn to; she was alone in the world and a thousand leagues from home.

'Where are we going?' she asked the officer as he led the party down towards the main hall.

He did not reply at first but then decided there could be no harm in her knowing. 'Pella.'

Pella; she had been a virtual captive of the man-woman and her fool for months in Pella, but Aristonous had rescued her. Her belly contracted at the thought of the man she had hoped would keep her safe; the man she had dreamed of bedding, relieving the sexual tension that mounted with each passing moon. *Curse him! Curse him to the very bones.*

The officer was no more forthcoming as they walked through the palace. Waiting at the foot of the steps down from the main doors was a covered wagon drawn by a team of four horses. Inside it seemed comfortable enough, furnished with plump cushions spread on thick carpets from her homeland.

'This will take us down to the port where a trireme is waiting to sail to Pella,' the officer said, indicating that she should get in with her son. She lifted Alexander up; he offered no resistance and little help. Before she stepped up into the carriage she turned to the Macedonian. 'Why am I going to Pella?'

Again he seemed minded not to reply but decided that she may as well know the reason. 'Alexander is to attend the wedding of Kassandros and Thessalonike and then the funeral of King Philip.'

Her heart leaped as she climbed into the wagon. *A royal wedding and a royal funeral; public occasions that we shall be visible at. The people of Macedon will see that my son is growing; I shall try to get him close to them.*

'Your son will ride behind Kassandros and I as we parade through the streets after the marriage ceremony,' Thessalonike informed Roxanna. 'He may wear a purple-bordered chiton and a purple cloak in respect of his rank. He may also wear a silver diadem.'

Despite her fury at being made to wait over two hours for her audience with Thessalonike upon her arrival in Pella and then the humiliation of being made to stay standing as Thessalonike addressed her, sitting raised above her, Roxanna was almost grateful to hear this. *His position is being recognised in public, finally; even though it is only a silver diadem.* 'Who will ride next to him?'

Thessalonike looked down at her, her smile cold. 'He will ride between two of Kassandros' Companion Cavalry officers; he will be well attended to.'

'But not visible; he'll be dwarfed by them,' Roxanna replied. 'The people won't notice him and that is why you've brought us here, is it not? You want the people to see the boy who gives Kassandros his legitimacy. Put him in as much purple as you like and place ten diadems of gold, not silver, about his head, but if he's between two huge troopers you might just as well not have him there. The people have never seen him close up; he's been locked away ever since he arrived in Macedon for almost the whole time. The only occasion in which he appeared in public was at his betrothal to Deidamia and then he was only seen at the top of the palace steps from afar. No one knows what he looks like.'

Thessalonike's eyes bored into Roxanna as she assessed the situation. 'And what will make him more recognisable?'

'Me riding next to him.'

'You?'

'Yes; then there will be no question that he is the real Alexander when they see his eastern mother next to him.' *That I should have to present myself as an oddity is so undignified; but if it achieves my purpose then so be it.*

Again Thessalonike scrutinised her as she weighed matters in her mind. 'You have a point: why have Alexander there if no one knows who he is? Yes, it would be meaningless. Very well, Roxanna, you may ride next to your son; your outlandish eastern appearance will confirm what the people have all suspected in their minds.'

'That I am a barbarian?'

'Exactly.'

Making Kassandros' position as the regent legitimate in their eyes; just keep on thinking that, bitch, whilst I show you how a child of Bactria can turn the scales on an arrogant westerner like yourself.

Thessalonike flicked her hand. 'You may go.'

Tight did the population of Pella pack the sides of the main thoroughfare running from the palace to the agora at the city's heart; and loud did they cheer as Kassandros and his bride drove in a chariot to the Temple of Zeus to give sacrifice, and petition the god to bless their marriage.

Roxanna followed the newly-wed couple, riding next to her son who wore a kingly diadem upon his head for the first time – be it only of silver. Behind them rode the might of Macedon; five thousand troopers clattering over the paved road, their bronze burning bright in the sunlight and their smiles wide as they held their lances, decorated with fronds, up to the crowd.

Looking out of the corner of her eyes from beneath her veil, she could see that the people were genuinely enthusiastic for Kassandros and Thessalonike, but after what she had heard of Olympias' excesses it did not surprise her that the commoners would enthuse about her successors; not that she cared for the common people, so long as they took to her son. And so she began to do something that she had always thought to be beneath her dignity: she played to the crowd; for it was in order to do so that she had manoeuvred herself into this position. No longer could she afford to conduct herself by the customs of the land of her birth where the ruled did not question the rulers and they in turn had no practical need of their subjects other than to provide the tax and labour to keep them in comfort. But Roxanna had witnessed all too closely how Adea had manipulated her way to power by relying on the common people, in her case the army. *Now I shall try the same trick with the citizens of Pella*. Leaning over to Alexander, she took him by the hand, lifted it and displayed him first to the left and then to the right and then back again as the procession progressed through the city. And loud was her reward for the people cheered their king; the blood of their great Alexander flowed in his veins and they loved the child for it.

New to receiving, for the first time, the plaudits of people so far beneath her – and finding herself enjoying the experience – Roxanna continued to display her son to them, a smile on her face, hidden beneath her veil, as she turned him from side to side, moving her hand to the back of his head to better manipulate him. But Alexander did not share his mother's enjoyment; for him, so used to solitude in the recent months, the proximity of such a crush of people was overawing and, had she bothered to look at her son's face, Roxanna would have seen tears rolling, from fearful eyes, down his cheeks. But he said nothing and maintained what dignity he could for he knew what he was and he knew much was expected of him – and he was already well aware that he could be killed at any moment. His life had been thus since he could first remember and, by now, he had learned to live with it; gazing out to sea cleared his mind of the fear, but being surrounded by so many brought it vividly back. Nonetheless, he allowed his mother to show him off, controlling the rising panic within, for what difference did it make?

And the cheers feted them to the Temple of Zeus where Roxanna and Alexander dismounted and followed Kassandros and Thessalonike up the steps to an altar set at their head. Here a white bull and a swan waited with the priests of the order and a band of acolytes playing pipes and lyres to the slow beat of a drum.

Roxanna took a position at the top of the steps to the right of the altar, far enough away not to be impinging on the action around it, but close enough to be very noticeable to all those watching. She stood facing the vast crowds on either side of the eight-trooper-wide column of cavalry, filling the entire agora, and put her arm around her son's shoulder, drawing him close to her. 'Wave at them, Alexander.'

The boy did as he was told and, once again, the crowd cheered him.

She risked a quick sideways glance; it was enough to see Thessalonike was resenting the attention being drawn away from her. *If I overdo it, she will prevent us from going to the funeral.* 'That's enough.' But it had, indeed, been enough; she now knew that the citizens of Pella had a positive feeling for their young king and that was something she would be able to exploit; one step at a time.

With the sacrifices made and the auspices taken – all of which were positive, for how could they not be at the marriage of an Argead princess to the regent of Macedon? – Kassandros turned to the crowd. 'Citizens of Pella!' His voice was pitched high to carry across the masses and was surprisingly strong considering his weak chest. 'Soldiers and people of Macedon, I stand before you as your regent with my new wife, Thessalonike, the sister of Alexander!'

Half-sister.

The crowd cared not for the details and cheered until Roxanna's ears rang.

Kassandros signalled for silence that was slow in manifesting. 'Today is the beginning of a new age in Macedon; the age of a new king.' He pointed at Alexander.

Roxanna tapped her son on the shoulder. 'Wave, Alexander.'

The boy obeyed his mother again and was rewarded with another ovation.

Thessalonike could not help a scowl.

'To begin his reign as is proper, tomorrow he shall accompany Thessalonike and I to Aegae as we take the bodies of King Philip, the third of that name, and his queen, who were both so foully murdered, for sacred burial.' This announcement brought the loudest roar of the event. 'Alexander shall witness the interment of his predecessor as is tradition in the Argead royal house.'

Kassandros extended his arms to the crowd as they cheered him, ignoring the inconvenient fact that Philip and Alexander were joint kings but everyone understood the symbolism and continued to applaud with vigour.

Roxanna smiled once more beneath her veil, for now that Kassandros had confirmed in public that Alexander, her son, would definitely be present at the funeral she knew that the second part of her scheme was possible.

It was in an atmosphere charged with emotion verging on religious awe that Kassandros and Thessalonike, humbly on foot and with heads covered, led the funeral cortège of King Philip and his wife Adea, who had taken the title Queen Eurydike. The funeral column was as long as their marriage procession had been, but this time the cavalrymen were on foot, and they were joined by an equal number of infantry.

A sonorous dirge of horns and measured drumbeats accompanied the slow-stepping march as the two bodies, covered and laid out on their funeral biers carried on ox-drawn carriages decked with flowers, began their two-day journey to Aegae; thousands looked on, a wail rising from them.

Tears streamed down the face of many in the crowds, tears that Roxanna could not understand for Philip had been a fool whose greatest joy was to play with his toy elephant; a man-child who should never have been made king. And yet, the people of Pella mourned for him in a way that was beyond reason.

But failing to understand the grief was one thing, exploiting it was another. 'Cry, Alexander; cry like your life depended on it.' *And it does; as does mine.*

Being overwhelmed once more by the sheer size of the crowd, Alexander had no trouble crying; indeed, he was already doing so as he envisaged the natural simplicity of the open sea to help defend himself from the overcrowded reality of the present. And so the tears fell as he followed the cortège, and all who saw them felt for the boy-king and cried out to him that he must now bear the burden on his own, making Roxanna's heart race with joy as she wailed and rent her clothes. On they travelled, once more, down to the agora, but there they turned right and headed for the western gate and the road to Aegae, seven leagues distant.

At the slow pace of the oxen and the beat of the drums, they walked on, west along the road. At each town and village the entire population turned out to witness the last journey of their king and then to see the young king for the first time. Excitement grew as the rumour went ahead that the blood of Alexander was present in the form of his son. Soon Alexander became more of the focus of interest than his mentally challenged late half-uncle, or even Kassandros and his new bride taking the prime positions at the head of the cortège.

Roxanna felt the triumph of victory surge within her as the blessings of the crowd rained down upon her son, trudging forward, eyes downcast and tears on his cheeks. *They love him; they're accepting him as their rightful king.*

And so, the following day, as the pyres raged and the mourning hymns were sung whilst the organs of the sacrificed beasts lay sizzling upon altar fires, Roxanna, veiled and wrapped in a long cloak against the cold, knew the time had come to make her bid for public recognition. She had coached Alexander in what he should do and, despite his fear of crowds and his desire for nothing more than the tranquillity of a sea vista, he had mastered his part. But first she had to perform hers.

With their heads bowed, Kassandros and Thessalonike opened the door of the newest tomb along the long line of the royal resting places, half excavated into the rock, which housed the remains of the Argead dynasty since the first king, Caranus, had come from Argos to found his kingdom five hundred years previously. Built by Kassandros' father, Antipatros, on the orders of Perdikkas, so that he could inter Alexander's body upon his return from Babylon, it was sumptuous in the detail of the carving covering the only wall visible. Ptolemy, however, had hijacked Alexander's funeral cortège and taken it to Egypt, refusing ever to return the body, thus rendering the tomb obsolete – until now.

And as the door swung open, a line of nobles, each bearing gifts of great value, magnificent armour, precious cups and fine weaponry, lined up before it. Into the tomb they filed, one by one, depositing their treasures around the walls, decorated with the great feats of the one who should have been interred within. When the last man had delivered his gift, Kassandros and Thessalonike stepped forward, she with the royal sceptre of Macedon and he with the kingly ceremonial sword.

In they went, disappearing into the lamp-lit interior to pay false homage to the fool.

Roxanna slipped the cloak from her shoulders to reveal a gown of Macedonian simplicity, and then took the veil from her face as she pushed her son forward. 'Now, Alexander; go now and, as they come out, turn to the crowd and do as I said.'

'I will,' the boy whispered, a tremor in his voice.

With a dignity that belied his age, the seven-year-old king approached the tomb. A murmur went around the crowd, a murmur of approval; the shaking of his body through nervousness mistaken for sobbing emotion. Alexander stopped a few paces short of the door and turned to the assembled witnesses. He put his hands to his temples and raised the silver diadem from his head, holding it aloft for all to see. As Kassandros and Thessalonike emerged from the tomb their faces froze in horror as the young king displayed his gift, left and then right, and then turned and walked between them into the tomb; they could do naught to stop him for he was a king honouring another and to stop him doing so in such a public way would be to court a propaganda disaster – and this Roxanna had realised upon hearing that Alexander would attend the ceremony. It was with genuine pride that Roxanna, dressed as a Macedonian, watched her son, holding his diadem in both hands, turn at the doorway and once more display his gift to the multitude.

Into the tomb the child went to lay his gift for his erstwhile co-king and when he emerged the crowd erupted in cheers. Kassandros' and Thessalonike's faces fixed into cold smiles as they each placed a hand upon his shoulders in an attempt to share the ovation. But the look they reserved for Roxanna was icy death; however, she cared not, for her objective had been achieved. *My son was the last to honour the dead king and you can never take that away, Kassandros. The people witnessed it and cheered him for it. He is now a part of their lives and I have shown that I am not just some barbarian princess but a queen of Macedon.*

The pyres had cooled. The ashes had been scooped into two urns and placed within the tomb and the door had been sealed upon the king with the mind of an eight-year-old and the wife whose ambition had led him to his final resting place. It was in good heart that Roxanna had left her mortal enemies encased for ever in a cold tomb, never again to challenge her son for the positon that was rightfully his. It was with even greater cheer that she travelled back to Pella, for more than a few of the escorting soldiers made efforts to get close to the boy and smile upon him, calling out blessings upon him as the true heir to Alexander and upon her as his mother.

'I fought with you father, sire,' one veteran said, having come forward during a break in the march, mid-afternoon, 'and you have his eyes and bearing, if I might say.' His mates nodded and grunted their agreement.

'Thank you,' Alexander replied, keeping to the prescribed short answers his mother had instilled in him.

'We admired the way you honoured King Philip, despite his, well, you know...' another said, mumbling in his nervousness at addressing the king. 'It was something that your father would have done and we honour you for that.'

'Thank you,' Alexander said, this time with the hint of a smile.

And so it went on all the way back to Pella and, despite herself, Roxanna encouraged the men in their forwardness, not caring that a king and a queen should not be so importuned by the lowly. She had seen her enemy Adea gather such power through this method and, desperate as she now was, it did not take much for her to hold her nose and garner support; sometimes she even deigned to reply to the coarse compliments that she and her son received and encouraged Alexander to smile at the men and expand his answers to 'Thank you; I do my duty', and other such words to the same effect.

It therefore came as no surprise to Roxanna to receive a summons to the audience chamber in the palace upon their return to Pella – in fact, it was what she had desired for now was her chance to establish the rules.

'It makes a change to be able to see your face,' Thessalonike remarked as Roxanna stood before her dressed in the Macedonian style, 'although I can't admit to it being a pleasant one. Change, that is.' She paused. 'And the face.'

'Save your caustic remarks for others, Thessalonike; I think that we have both now realised that we need one another.'

'Have we? I didn't notice.'

Roxanna ignored the rebuff. *I must stay strong in my course and apologise although it makes me the supplicant.* 'I admit that I made a mistake when we first met and treated you in a manner that was not becoming; it was wrong of me and I apologise.'

'Well, that is something that I never thought I would hear from you.'

'It is meant as a peace offering. You are the wife of the regent and also the aunt of my son; it is fitting that we should be on good terms.'

'Fitting? Fitting after the tricks that you just pulled? You used a solemn occasion to forward the position of your son and yourself.'

This was too much for Roxanna's fragile dignity. 'How dare you accuse me of pulling tricks when you were simply using my son, the king, to give your husband a vestige of legitimacy as he tried to perform the ceremony that only a king should do. My son did no more than was expected of the king.'

'Your son stole my husband's position.'

'My son is seven; your husband is in his thirties.'

'And you,' Thessalonike spat, pointing a finger at Roxanna, 'what do you think you are doing dressing as if you are a Macedonian and not the barbarian that you are?'

'I have given birth to the true King of Macedon and so therefore I shall become a Macedonian. The men accepted me on the journey back from Aegae and accepted my son; they have seen him now and they love him for what he is.'

'Ha! That can be easily changed.'

'But can it, Thessalonike? I know that you swore an oath to protect my son and ensure that no harm comes to him.'

Thessalonike's smile was slow and cold, her eyes slits. 'That is so; and you will also know that I swore an oath to protect the life of Aristonous.'

Roxanna felt a chill at the mention of the man who had so betrayed her. 'I know you did.'

'Does that mean that Aristonous still lives?'

Now the chill deepened. 'What do you mean?'

'I mean that just because I swore an oath doesn't mean that I can protect that life. I can't be everywhere at once all the time.' She flicked her fingers. 'Find Crateuas and tell him to bring the wedding present he has just given Kassandros.'

The wait was uncomfortable for there was no question of small talk as Thessalonike was enjoying the iciness of the situation.

It was the smell that first heralded Crateuas' coming. 'You sent for me, my lady?'

'I did, Crateuas; I wanted to thank you for the very considerate present that you had waiting for Kassandros and me upon our return.'

'I'm glad that it pleased you.'

'It did; and it also bought our forgiveness and secures you in our service as we make our break from Antigonos.'

Crateuas bowed his head. 'For this I thank you, my lady.'

'Show Roxanna just what you gave us.'

Roxanna had no need to see the gift for she had seen the size and shape of the box in Crateuas' hands and smelt the putrefaction emanating from it. And so it was with a slow inevitability that the lid was opened to reveal the head of the man whom she had hoped to bed. The blank eyes of the man with whom she had wanted to flee, the man who had betrayed her, stared at her and she knew that she had lost.

'You see, Roxanna, just because I swear to preserve a life doesn't mean that others can't take it without my knowledge. My conscience is clear; I did not ask Crateuas to kill Aristonous and nor did Kassandros. We both stuck to our oaths. But as to my oath to your son: how can I be sure that the same thing does not happen to him?' Again her smile was of ice. 'Well, my dear, you shouldn't worry yourself on that account as I have already considered the matter. I will keep him and you safe; safe from the outside world so that my oath will hold true. Alexander is already waiting in a covered wagon in the courtyard so that his new legions of admirers don't see him as he travels to Amphipolis. Crateuas will take you to join him. Amphipolis should be a safe place for you both to see out your days. Take her!'

It was, at first, a silent scream that formed in Roxanna's gorge as the heavy doors of her luxurious prison in the royal residence of Amphipolis were closed; as she fell to her knees, a sound trilled from her before firming into a piercing shriek that echoed around the bare walls of the chamber. She tore at her cheeks and ripped clumps from her hair, lamenting her life for surely it was now done. But it was another scream that cut through her grief, a scream even more piercing than her own; it silenced her as she looked for the only possible source: Alexander stood by the window. She staggered to her feet and went to him; it took but a moment to realise what was wrong: there was no sea. The view was of rough hills and coniferous forest; duns and greens and finite. Alexander writhed as she tried to still him; writhed and screamed as if something within him had broken and he no longer had control of body or faculties. And it was infectious for Roxanna felt herself weaken and then succumb to the full despair that had hit her son. Together they fell to the floor and lay there in abject misery. *Who will come now? What friend do I have left? None. But I never had any in the first place as I assumed that a queen was above needing them; how wrong I was. And now we will rot here until we die, whilst Kassandros takes Alexander's place and Thessalonike takes mine as they face Antigonos and fight for my son's rightful inheritance.*

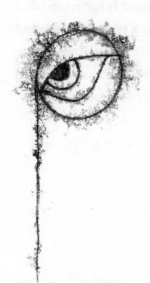

ANTIGONOS.
THE ONE-EYED.

'YOU ARE A most generous lord,' Babrak the Pathak merchant said, touching his fingertips to his forehead as he bowed.

Antigonos tossed him a weighty purse. 'No more generous than the other lords who pay you well for your news, Babrak.'

'A boy with an interesting skill will have many admirers reaching for their purse.'

'Yes, I'm sure you're right; now get out of here. Oh, and good luck with impregnating your wives.'

Babrak looked pained. 'A man has many duties; most are onerous and none makes one richer.'

'Then it's just as well that you got all that silver and gold from Seleukos for the grain you sold him.'

The red-stained teeth flashed in a smile. 'That is true; I have the finances to buy good stock for next year's caravan. I shall look for you upon my return.' He bowed again and left the tent.

Antigonos turned to his son. 'So, Seleukos has managed to stem the famine in Babylonia with grain bought with money he clearly stole from Susa.'

'It would seem that way,' Demetrios replied, replenishing his cup of wine. 'How else could he have afforded to do it with the tax levy from the greater part of the satrapy almost non-existent after Eumenes ravaged the place?'

'Quite; and we took most of his reserves of coinage when we passed through shortly after that.' Antigonos rubbed his hands together, grinning. 'I've got him.' Getting to his feet, he stuck his head out of the tent. 'Get Aristodemus here at once,' he ordered one of the guards.

'Aristodemus?' Demetrios questioned.

'Yes,' Antigonos said, sitting back down and looking at the list of transactions that Babrak had given him.

'Why?'

Antigonos looked at his son with exaggerated disappointment. 'If you can't guess, you'll just have to wait until he arrives.'

It was not long before he appeared, and Demetrios was none the wiser when he did.

'Sit down, and pour yourself a drink,' Antigonos said, his voice as genial as it could be after so many years of barking orders.

A tall but slender, balding man with cunning, quick eyes and thin lips, Aristodemus made a graceful acknowledgement with his head and one hand before sitting in the chair indicated and helping himself to the wine pitcher. 'How can I be of service, sir?'

'By getting me Babylon.'

The seeming magnitude of the task did not faze Aristodemus. 'And how would you suggest that I do that?'

'I need you to go there immediately; I should arrive with the army shortly after the summer solstice in ten days. I will supply you with a warrant to show Seleukos, giving you the right to go through the satrapy's accounts.'

'Ah!' Enthusiasm kindled in Aristodemus' eyes. 'An audit.'

'An audit, my arse; it will be much more than just an audit. It's going to be so thorough and you'll dig so deep into Seleukos' affairs in Babylon that you'll reach the foundations of the city and maybe break through into whatever Babylonians call Hades.'

'I see. You want to know everything.'

'I want to know things that even Seleukos or his deputy, Temenos, don't even know. I want you to make things so uncomfortable for Seleukos that when I arrive and get around to asking him a certain question he will be terrified of either lying to me or telling me the truth.'

'I understand, Antigonos; thorough it shall be.'

Antigonos handed Babrak's list of transactions to Aristo-demus. 'Take this and see how or whether it fits into what you find in the treasury there. You will leave tomorrow at dawn with an escort; Teutamus and Pythan will join you. I'll have my secretary draw up the document by this evening. You had better go and pack.'

'You're going to do a thorough audit?' Demetrios said once Aristodemus had gone. 'What good will that do?'

'You advised me not to execute any more of the men who travelled with Alexander in case it began to smell of jealousy, did you not?'

'I did.'

'Well, if I can't execute Seleukos what's the next best thing?'

Demetrios considered the matter for a few moments. 'Make him think that you will.'

His father's one eye glinted with mischief. 'Just the threat of it will be enough to remove him from Babylon and then it will be mine without anybody being able to criticise me, as all I did was have his accounts looked through. A few drops of ink, perhaps, but no drops of blood. And then I can demonstrate my forgiving nature to the world by making Pythan the new satrap and placing Teutamus in command of the garrison.'

Demetrios smiled in approval and toasted his father.

Babylon had impressed Antigonos on the first occasion he set eyes on it and this second time it seemed no less imposing. Larger than any other city he had seen, it struck him with its sense of permanence and power – the two things that he quested after. *It's probably geographically not the best place to make my capital but as a symbol it is by far the most potent. And it's the gateway to the east; whoever holds Babylon controls the east.*

It was in buoyant mood that Antigonos entered the city with his son and an escort of a hundred cavalry, leaving the army to camp on the open ground outside the walls to the south, downstream so as not to foul the city's water supply.

Through the city they clattered, drawing no more than cursory glances for the population were, by now, well used to soldiery.

It came as no surprise to Antigonos to see Seleukos waiting to greet him in person as his party approached the Main Citadel on the northern side of the Ishtar Gate. 'I hope you're not going to spout any nonsense about the Bear of Macedon,' he shouted to Seleukos, before pointing to Peucestas, commanding his escort, 'like this idiot did.'

Peucestas, already humiliated by his lowly position, reddened and looked to the ground.

'I heard about that,' Seleukos said, coming forward as Antigonos pulled up his mount. 'The Cyclops of Macedon perhaps, or even the Resinated Cyclops of Macedon, but never the Bear of Macedon.'

'That Cunt of Macedon is how my men think of me but that's far too coarse for Peucestas' Persian manners.' He looked at the object of his derision. 'But surely you can shed those now that you've managed to shed the trousers?'

Peucestas' reply was inaudible.

'Speak up, man, I can't hear you.'

Peucestas shook his head. 'It was nothing.'

'That doesn't surprise me.' Antigonos swung his right leg behind him and jumped to the ground.

It was a friendly greeting that he and Seleukos shared; friendly in the way that two enemies, neither of whom wanted the other to know the depths of their mistrust, would greet one another.

'Baths are prepared for you and Demetrios,' Seleukos said, breaking from the embrace, 'and then we shall feast.'

'Feast?' Antigonos looked puzzled. 'I'm surprised that you can afford to throw a feast after what the sly little Greek did to your satrapy. You must be doing better than I thought.'

'We make do with what we have,' Seleukos replied with an attempt at a light laugh that was as phoney as the smile on his face.

This is going to be an entertaining evening.

And so it proved to be, but not in the way that Antigonos had expected. The meal far surpassed anything that Antigonos had seen since coming to the east for it consisted mainly of the grilled and roasted meats that formed the central part of Macedon's unpretentious cuisine, but was supported with the more substantial dishes from the various cuisines of the east.

'It's because Babylon is such a melting-pot of cultures,' Seleukos explained, his conversation lubricated by Macedonian quantities of wine of un-Macedonian quality. 'Here we have food from all over the world.' He picked up a skewer of tender cubes of lamb grilled over an open fire. 'But nothing compares with lamb the way my grandmother used to do it.'

Feeling the geniality of much wine, Antigonos raised his cup. 'To grandmothers.'

'To grandmothers!' the assembled diners, over a hundred in number, chorused.

'And all who ride them!' Antigonos shouted as he downed his cup, bringing raucous laughter from all and much spillage of wine.

The feast went on in true Macedonian style in the very Babylonian surroundings of the lesser dining room in the summer palace. Situated among verdant gardens, to the north of the main city but still within the outer walls, Seleukos had taken the beautiful antique building as his main residence.

And very comfortable it is too; if slightly garish and eastern for my taste.

And as the sun dipped, the diners raised their pitch with drinking competitions, boasts and spontaneous wrestling matches as the slaves scurried around with rags and buckets of water, trying to limit the amount of wine and vomit on the floor for their betters to slip on.

Antigonos was content to drink himself into oblivion for he had a harder head than most and rarely suffered from a hangover, especially with the delicate vintages of the east. It was just as he was about to pass out on his couch that he turned to Seleukos. 'How are you getting on with Aristodemus?'

Seleukos looked at him with unfocusing eyes. 'That arsehole? He's an arsehole, as are his two little friends, Teutamus and Pythan.'

'Good. I noticed that you had not invited them this evening. Aristodemus must be doing an excellent job; we will find out tomorrow. I'm meeting him at the treasury; you would do well to be there.'

*

Cold water on the ears and the back of the neck was all Antigonos needed to forget the debauchery of the evening before. Feeling refreshed and greatly looking forward to the day, he sat down to the substantial breakfast of cold meats, bread and fruit that had been laid out on the terrace of his east-facing suite.

Washing down a mouthful of olives with a draught of well-watered wine, he clicked his fingers at his body-slave waiting upon him just inside the room. 'Go and see what's keeping my son.'

Picking up a duck leg he tore into it, enjoying watching the sun rise and strengthen, and relishing the cool breeze coming off the extensive gardens now bursting into spring life. *This will suit me very well.* He turned to look back inside. *Where is that boy?* Taking another mouthful of duck he heard the door to his suite open, but it was his slave who came out onto the terrace, alone.

'The young master's slave tells me that he has a hangover and doesn't wish to be disturbed.'

Lightweight. Chuckling, Antigonos carried on with his breakfast, considering what his wife, Stratonice, would think of being removed from Sardis to come to live in Babylon – if she was still speaking to him after an absence of two years and very few letters. *The gardens will do it for her; they seem to be the sort of thing that women like.* Never having been one to appreciate beauty and therefore able to grade it, he came to an uncertain conclusion as he rinsed the grease from his hands in a bowl of warmed water.

'Send a message to Seleukos,' he said to his slave as he took the cloak he held up for him, 'telling him to meet me at the treasury in the Main Citadel at midday. And tell Demetrios to meet me there as soon as his hangover permits him.' Draping the cloak over his shoulders and fastening it with a golden brooch, he strode from his suite and stepped out into a wide corridor with columns punctuating a balustrade along the opposite side that opened out onto a formal staircase. Doors were interspersed along the wall and from the suite next to his scurried a girl; a very attractive and young girl. Chuckling again to himself in a proud, paternal manner, he made for the stairs and took them two at a time.

It was, therefore, in an extremely good mood that Antigonos greeted Aristodemus as he walked through the gates of the Main Citadel. 'You must be doing something right: Seleukos thinks you're an arsehole.'

Aristodemus laughed, his thin lips tight along his teeth. 'Seleukos has done all that he can to hide the fact that he arrived here from Susa with six hundred talents unaccounted for.'

'Six hundred? I didn't think that he would risk more than five.' He put his arm around Aristodemus' shoulders and led him towards the treasury door. 'Come, show me.'

Preferring to leave arithmetic to the experts, it was a struggle to follow Aristodemus' reasoning as he flicked the beads on the abacus whilst detailing tax revenues and expenditure that a slave read from a series of lists. What was certain, however, was that it was impossible to have paid Babrak what he had done for his huge delivery of grain out of what had accrued in the treasury since Antigonos had last emptied it two years previously.

Aristodemus looked up from his work and indicated to the heavy doors of the three strong rooms off the counting hall in which they were sitting. 'And even with what is still left locked up in here there are still fifty talents unaccounted for.'

'Well, that's not such a large amount.'

'You said that you wanted to know everything about what was going on here financially.'

'You're right; here, give me those.' Antigonos took a look at the lists the slave had been referring to.

'I'm sorry I'm late,' Demetrios said, coming into the room. 'I had a dreadful hangover.'

'Yes, I heard,' Antigonos said, not looking up.

'But it's gone now.'

'Yes, I know; I saw it leave your suite.' Not daring to look at his son's expression for fear he would collapse in mirth, Antigonos continued to study Aristodemus' workings with a growing warm feeling in his stomach. *I've got you now, my Titanesque friend.* He put the lists back down on the table. 'Well, I think we have a few questions to ask Seleukos.'

SELEUKOS.
THE BULL-ELEPHANT.

BUT IT WAS Seleukos who was currently asking the questions. 'You say that Eumenes wanted you to get to me, Artonis?'

'He did; he said that I would be safe with you.'

Seleukos studied the woman standing before him, wondering what she looked like behind her veil; her body, however, seemed shapely enough beneath a gown of indifferent quality. *She's slightly on the short side; but Alexander did choose her for the smallest of his friends. I imagine she and Eumenes were a good match, size wise.* 'And yet you travelled with Antigonos' army.'

'I told him I wanted to take my husband's ashes to his native Kardia; he gave me permission to join the baggage train as the army moved back west and then I think that he forgot about me.'

'What would he say if he knew that you had sneaked away to come to see me?'

Artonis shrugged. 'That depends upon what I persuade you to do.'

Seleukos was intrigued. 'Persuade me to do? What do you have in mind?'

'How do you stand with Antigonos?'

Seleukos considered the question then got to his feet and stepped down from the audience chair, indicating to a round table in the corner of the chamber. 'Come and sit with me, Artonis.' He clapped his hands; a slave appeared. 'Sherbet for the lady.' Bowing, the slave backed away.

'Now,' Seleukos said once they were comfortably settled opposite each other, 'why do you wish to know what the relationship is between Antigonos and me?'

Artonis looked him straight in the eye. 'I want only to avenge my husband; my life has no meaning other than that. But I cannot do that by myself and nor, indeed, could you.'

'And why would I want to be avenged on him?'

'My husband told me that even though you sided with Antigonos in the last war it would not be enough for you to keep Babylon.'

And it looks as though he was right, judging by what that arse-hole Aristodemus is doing. 'Are you implying that we may have a common cause?' He held his hand up to prevent any further talk as the slave brought in the sherbet. Once he had gone he indicated for her to carry on.

'Eumenes predicted that you would be forced to flee Babylon and he said that I should travel with you to Ptolemy so that I could tell him – as I will tell you – what Antigonos offered Eumenes in return for his life.'

'And what was that?'

'Antigonos wanted Eumenes to support Kassandros and Thessalonike's claim once they were married and so unite the families who have always supported Kassandros and those who have supported Alexander's son.'

'And Eumenes refused?'

A look of sadness crossed Artonis' dark eyes. 'Yes; and I agreed with him when he told me his reasons.'

'Which were?'

'He said…' She squeezed her eyes shut, trying to remember. 'I can't recall his exact words but it was something like this. "It leaves Antigonos free to deal with Ptolemy without having to worry about Kassandros. If he sends me to Macedon to support Kassandros and Thessalonike and declare them the rightful Argead heirs, he places Kassandros deep in his debt. Meanwhile, Kassandros will spend a good couple of years securing his position with his new wife, and having children. Once he has a son he will kill Alexander, whilst Antigonos is leagues away in the south and is thus completely innocent of that crime; the one crime that even he would not dare to commit but needs to if he is ultimately to rule the empire. If he manages to defeat Ptolemy – and that's a big if – he will then be so strong that he will come back north, brush Kassandros aside and have it all. If he doesn't defeat Ptolemy, he'll come to a peace accord with him whereby they both head north and brush Kassandros aside together; a state of affairs that will last for a while until they decide to go to war again to see if they can settle the matter. But either way, Kassandros gets brushed aside after having killed the only legitimate male heir to Alexander: his son. Antigonos can rightly claim his innocence but I will have been seen as being part of the conspiracy: the ultimate traitor to the Argead cause." Or something like that; but, anyway, it makes sense.'

Seleukos contemplated the analysis, rubbing the back of his neck. 'It does make sense. So Eumenes wanted you to share that with me, Ptolemy and Kassandros in the hope that it would unite us all against Antigonos?'

'And Lysimachus, yes.'

'And I'm to be the one who facilitates this having been forced to flee from Babylon rather than face execution as Eumenes predicted I would?'

'Yes.'

'The sly little Greek is still up to his tricks from beyond the grave.'

Artonis' eyes smiled with a look of love remembered. 'Yes.'

'And why should I fit into this great scheme?'

'He said that you would flee to Ptolemy and no doubt fight for him, as defeating Antigonos was the only way you could regain Babylon. And that is all that motivates you.'

'But Ptolemy might not want to fight Antigonos if he doesn't attack him first.'

Again Artonis' eyes smiled but this time it was with pride. 'Exactly.'

Of course; he was *a sly little Greek.* 'Which is why he sent you and didn't just let the situation develop by itself; you can bear witness to Antigonos' offer for your husband's life and his thinking in rejecting it. Ptolemy will take notice and Kassandros will take fright thus propelling them together into an unlikely alliance that will stand a very good chance of defeating Eumenes' executioner; especially if they persuade Lysimachus to join them. Vengeance from beyond the grave. Brilliant.'

'Yes.'

Seleukos paused to appreciate the beauty of it and then nodded. 'But first, I need to find out the answer to your question.'

'Which one?'

'How do I stand with Antigonos? And there is only one way to find out. Where is your baggage?'

'With the army.'

'I'll organise to have it brought to you. You stay here; I'll have my wife, Apama, look after you whilst I go to see Antigonos and talk about the satrapy's accounts. When I come back we'll either be travelling west together or I'll send you off on your own.

Either way, I think Ptolemy has been far too comfortable for far too long. He needs to be goaded into action.'

'You four, come with me,' Seleukos ordered, pointing to the front rank of his escort, as he slipped from the saddle outside the gate of the Main Citadel. 'Temenos, stay here with the rest of your lads.' He adjusted his helmet, straightening it. 'And be ready for a quick departure.'

'Yes, lord.'

Seleukos looked towards the Ishtar Gate, just across the bridge over the canal that encircled the eastern half of the city. 'And, as a precaution, tell the guards to close the gate and not to let anyone out of the city until I say so.'

Leaving Temenos to his orders, Seleukos passed through the gates and crossed the empty main courtyard of the fortress, curious that Antigonos had not brought any men with him. *He must suppose that he already has me cornered and doesn't want to spook me; so despite what Demetrios told me last night, I am in danger.*

It had been an interesting conversation he had had with Antigonos' son after the old man had passed out; yes, he was pleased to hear that Demetrios had warned his father against executing more of Alexander's generals but was unconvinced that the cyclops would necessarily take the advice to heart. *And anyway, what was Demetrios' motivation for telling me that? Perhaps it was just the alcohol.* Seleukos had sent one of the girls he kept for pleasuring his more important guests to Demetrios as an acknowledgement of his friendly gesture; but he still suspected that there was more to Demetrios' actions than just drunken friendship.

It was with this warning in his head that, leaving his guards outside, he opened the door to the treasury and stepped into the counting hall.

'Ah, our host!' Antigonos cried with exaggerated affability, setting down a scroll. 'Come, come and sit down.'

Seleukos gave his warmest smile and nodded to Demetrios. 'Pleasant night?'

'Yes, thank you.'

'She's one of the best in the city.'

Demetrios gave his father an embarrassed look.

Antigonos looked surprised. 'She seemed rather young to be that.'

Seleukos kept his face straight. 'Why don't you try her tonight and judge for yourself?'

'I might just do that.'

The idea of his father following him did not go down well with Demetrios, judging by his pained expression.

'So what can I do for you, gentlemen?' Seleukos asked, looking through to one of the strong rooms where Aristodemus could be seen weighing silver on a set of big scales. Teutamus and Pythan leaned against the wall next to him, grinning at Seleukos.

Antigonos followed his glance. 'Ah, yes; you know Aristodemus; he was that arsehole we spoke of last night. The arsehole who has been checking the satrapy's accounts. And those two arseholes next to him are here... well, we'll find out why they're here once we've had a look at the full audit.'

So, they're here to replace me; it's time to go. 'Which reminds me, Antigonos: by what right do you send someone to check up on my satrapy's accounts?' Seleukos spoke lightly in a tone that conveyed genuine interest.

'Don't give me that. I hold the east and I will do exactly as I please.'

Now we have it out in the open. 'And, saying that I accept that, what have I done to warrant this investigation?'

'I had a very interesting conversation with Babrak who I ran into on the way here.'

'Did you? I assume he told you that he sold me a lot of grain; grain that I badly needed to relieve the famine that Eumenes caused.'

'Grain you badly needed but grain you could not afford.'

'Of course I could afford it, I paid for it. Did Babrak claim I cheated him?'

'Of course not. Babrak always tells the truth without prejudice; that's why we all tolerate him. No, he told me exactly how much you paid and we've worked out that you couldn't have afforded it from the tax revenues from here so you must have stolen it from Susa. You stole from me!'

'I didn't steal from you; I just took back the money that I lent you when you came through chasing Eumenes.'

Antigonos slammed his palm down on the table. 'You didn't lend it to me, I took it.'

'You stole it, you mean.'

'I can't steal what's mine.'

I'm not going to win this argument. 'All right, so I took the money; so what?'

'So, can I trust you?'

'I fought for you against Eumenes.'

'But you also took Ptolemy's offer of men to take back Babylon, deserting me.'

'That was three years ago. You wouldn't give me the troops to take what was mine. And, I'll remind you, I chased out Docimus and Polemon from here who had been Perdikkas' allies.'

'Both of whom were irrelevant to the war against Eumenes at the time. No, Seleukos, don't try to pretend that you used Ptolemy's largesse to take Babylon for yourself for altruistic reasons; to help me. So, I ask you again: can I trust you?'

'Of course you can trust me.'

'Then why has Aristodemus told me that you did everything possible to obstruct his audit and that you even went so far as to threaten him with imprisonment?'

'That's a lie. I told him that if he insisted on going through everything without me or Temenos present then I would confine him to his quarters.'

'Imprison him.'

'Confine him to his quarters.'

'Either way, you were trying to punish my representative for doing a job that I had requested he do.'

Seleukos took a deep breath to rein in his temper. 'Where is this going?'

'You tell me.'

'I will be loyal to you.'

Antigonos' cyclopic eye burned into Seleukos but he stood firm. 'Will you?' Still the eye burned but still he did not flinch. 'Very well. I will talk to my son and make a decision; you can go. Teutamus and Pythan will see you out.'

Seleukos glanced at Demetrios, whose expression gave nothing away, and then turned on his heel and left without another word, ignoring Teutamus and Pythan following on his shoulders.

'We'll be watching all the gates, Seleukos,' Teutamus growled in his ear as they walked out the door. 'Antigonos has promised Babylon to us and we'll not risk you escaping, just to collect an army and come back to threaten us.'

'No,' Pythan said. 'You're a dead man as soon as the result of the audit is out.'

Seleukos turned and faced the two men as he reached his escort. 'And you are both too stupid to hold Babylon with loose talk like that. Peithon had more sense than the two of you put together.'

Teutamus went for his sword.

'Oh, really?' Seleukos questioned as his escort's blades hissed from their scabbards. 'Here, now, so public and so outnumbered? You're more stupid than I realised. Now piss off and go and gloat to someone else about your little plans.'

Teutamus loosened his grip on his weapon. 'Another time, Seleukos.'

'I get the feeling it's inevitable.'

Pythan gave him a cold leer as they both turned away.

Seleukos sighed and shook his head, his mind made up. 'Back to the palace,' he said to Temenos as he heaved himself up into the saddle.

'There is someone wanting to see you,' Temenos said, pointing to a priest sitting on an ass a little way off. 'He came through the Ishtar Gate just before it was closed.'

'Naramsin! What do you want?'

'A word in private, lord, concerning the wisdom of Bel Marduk.'

'Are you sure that is what the prophecy will say?' Seleukos asked Naramsin in the privacy of his chambers.

'Yes, lord.'

'But how?'

'Because we have already cast the prophecy, we just have not told Antigonos yet. We are delaying it until you are safe. He sent to us upon his arrival to ask what the god thought of his taking Babylon. The god was quick in his response.'

'That if Antigonos takes Babylon but lets me escape then I will come back and retake it and then go on to be the cause of his downfall and eventual death?'

'You have it, lord.'

'Leaving him no choice but to execute me.' *Or, at least,*

allowing Teutamus and Pythan to murder me and thus escape most
of the blame. That changes matters.

'I think not. You should flee; we won't tell him the prophecy until you are gone. We will say that the god is still deliberating such is our gratitude for all you have done for us.'

'Thank you, Naramsin. I should leave immediately.'

'It would be best; we cannot delay the god's answer indefinitely.'

'Of course not.'

'You need to be gone before dawn tomorrow.'

I won't wait that long. 'Go, get back to the temple. Have you started the tunnel to the bridge?'

'We have, lord.'

'Well, it would seem that I'm going to need it.'

'But it is not nearly finished.'

'Not to get out, Naramsin; that I do from here. It's to get back in when I return, and I *will* return. Bel Marduk has foretold it.'

'Indeed he has, lord; and I rejoice at the thought.'

Seleukos turned to the door. 'Temenos!'

The door opened.

'Temenos, see Naramsin out and then get ready to leave within the hour. Tell my wife to be ready and find Artonis, she should be with her.'

ARTONIS.
THE WIDOW.

IT HAD BEEN eight moons – eight moons and six days to be accurate – since Antigonos had taken her husband from Artonis; still she burned with desire for him and cried with rage and sorrow alone in the dark. There was not a moment in the day in which she was unaware of her loss and so there was no moment when she was not thirsting for the vengeance that Eumenes' plan would bring. But burn and thirst as she might, Artonis knew that it was not a short road that she had embarked upon: to utterly destroy the man who had taken love from her would require years of persistence, for Antigonos was strong and the men she needed to suborn to her will were equal to him if acting in concert, but men could rarely act thus, as her late husband had found to his ultimate cost.

Hard it had been at first to travel with the baggage train of her foe's army, being always so close to him, even seeing him now and again, but soon she had learned to focus on the past – the love of her husband – and the future – his revenge from beyond the grave – and leave the present to take care of itself. *Let Antigonos be,* she had told herself. *I must ignore him and concentrate on the things that will make me strong. I must disappear until my time comes.*

To that end she had forsaken her fine wardrobe, choosing instead clothes of a homespun variety to blend in with the main body of the camp-followers and better to fade from Antigonos' view as she did not want him to be reminded of her and perhaps reflect upon the wisdom of allowing her liberty. South to Persepolis and then north to Susa and west to Babylon she had travelled with the army, unnoticed, attended by her two slaves, and now finally she had come to the city where her mission was to begin in earnest.

She was walking in a private garden in the shade of the western wall of the royal palace with Apama, Seleukos' Sogdian wife, talking and waiting for the woman she had not seen since the mass wedding at Susa all those years ago. Fountains cooled the air baked by a merciless summer sun.

'I am ready to go at a moment's notice,' Apama said, indicating to her masculine trousers and riding boots. 'Seleukos told me to dress like this all the time now; I've been out riding every day getting used to the saddle again. It's been many years since the long rides of my youth.' They were speaking in Greek as Apama was Sogdian and Artonis was from Hellespontine Phrygia. 'I don't think Seleukos will be sending you off on your own; we'll be coming with you if I know Antigonos.'

Artonis caressed the flower she had been admiring and then stooped to catch its scent. 'Yes, I think you will too. Perhaps you might lend me some suitable clothes if we are to be riding.'

'I have already asked one of my bedchamber women to find some for you.' Apama, a head taller than Artonis, looked down at her. 'Although I'm afraid they might be a little baggy for you.'

'As long as I can ride.' Artonis moved on to another flowering shrub, savouring the beauty after so long in the squalid and crowded confines of the baggage train. 'What will you do with your children? They can't ride, surely?'

Apama smiled. 'We've already sent them north; they are waiting for us at the port of Is. Seleukos is not a man to risk being blackmailed for the lives of his children.'

Artonis felt a stab of jealousy as she heard the love in Apama's voice as she spoke of her husband. *I must keep that feeling, no matter how it pains me, as it will keep me focused on what I must do.* 'You're lucky to have such a man.'

'I know; and I'm sorry for your loss.'

'As am I, Sister.'

Artonis turned to see Artakama, her younger sibling, walking towards her. They ran to each other's arms. Tight they held one another, for many a racing heartbeat, having been so long parted.

Artonis stepped back and held her sister at arm's length to better study her. 'Eight years, Artakama; eight years. You are a beautiful woman now.'

'Rather than the pubescent runt given to Ptolemy as a plaything.'

Artonis paused, remembering the tears in her sister's eyes as she described the things that Ptolemy had made her do and endure on their wedding night. 'Yes, you were too young to be married.'

'I was just thirteen and had barely had my first moon. I knew nothing of what a man and a woman could do other than the basics and then after all I went through, everything I did to satisfy him, he leaves me here, discarded and forgotten.'

Artonis held her sister close. 'Not forgotten, I'm sure; never forgotten.'

Artakama smiled. 'Well, we'll soon find out; I'm coming with you to Egypt. Apama has persuaded Seleukos to take me as well.'

Artonis tried to keep the smile on her face from slipping. *Coming before Ptolemy in the company of his scorned wife is not going to be the best way to induce him to do what I wish.* 'It will be like when we were young again, riding out into the hills; I'm looking forward to it.' She hugged Artakama again, realising that there was nothing she could do to prevent her sister joining her; she stroked her hair and kissed it.

But the reunion was brought to a sudden close with the arrival of Temenos. 'Ladies, prepare yourselves; we're leaving.'

That it had been well planned in advance was evident by the smoothness of their departure. Quick they ran to Apama's rooms where her slave had suitable riding apparel ready for both Artonis and Artakama; her baggage, including the urn containing her husband's ashes, was also waiting. Once changed, and the essentials packed, Apama led them down into the cellars, where more people joined them, and then on to a small door in the northern wall. Guarded by half a dozen men, it was open; through it Artonis went with her companions to find herself in a stable containing many horses.

'We have all you need,' Seleukos said, taking his wife's hand and leading them towards the open doors at the far end where six horses awaited held by grooms. 'Two mounts each,' Seleukos explained, 'so that we can alternate horses and keep going as fast as possible.'

Artonis took the reins offered her and stroked her mare's neck, examining the creature. 'She's in fine shape.' She checked the saddle cloth and then examined the two saddlebags hanging to either side. 'They're heavy; what's in them?'

Seleukos grinned. 'Don't lose them; they are our travelling expenses. Each horse is carrying half a talent in silver or gold as well as bread and dried meat. Mount up and be ready to leave.'

Around them Seleukos' Companions fastened small packs to their second horse, checked tack and swung up into the saddle, their voices low in the manner of men about to embark upon a mission fraught with danger.

Artonis strapped her bag containing Eumenes' ashes and the few clothes that had fitted around it on the spare horse, mounted the other and then kicked it forward, through the gates of the stable into the dry heat of the afternoon sun. As Apama and Artakama joined her, she looked back at the building and saw to her surprise that it was a temporary structure, built against the walls of the palace.

'Seleukos had it built as soon as he got back from Susa,' Apama explained. 'He wanted a way to leave the city without opening any of the gates, so he knocked a hole in the wall instead and built somewhere to keep the horses ever ready.'

'With luck we shall get away unnoticed,' Seleukos said, pulling on the reins to control his skittish mount as he turned to check that his men were ready, formed up in column.

Temenos came up to him on foot. 'All is set, lord.'

'Well done, Temenos. You know what to do?'

'Wait three hours and then inform Antigonos of your escape.'

'Good man; let's hope that is enough for him to take you into his service.'

'I hope so, lord; if so, I shall be waiting for your call when you return. Good luck.'

'And to you, my friend.' Seleukos leaned down and clasped the proffered forearm. 'I'll keep in contact through the priests of Bel Marduk.'

'I shall become a devotee of the god.'

Smiling, Seleukos sat tall in his saddle, raised his arm and signalled for the column to move off. As Apama took her place next to her husband, Artonis and her sister moved in behind her, their spare mounts' reins held in their left hands. Raising much dust with the speed of their acceleration, the fugitives from

Babylon raced north following the well-worn road along the eastern bank of the Euphrates.

With her head forward over her mare's neck, Artonis felt the power of the beast surging beneath her; to either side of her, her spare mount and that of her sister kept easy pace tossing their heads and snorting, nostrils flaring, as the excitement of the sudden rush communicated its way through the equine members of the column. The sense now of urgency came to Artonis; finally after months of progressing at the slow pace of the oxen in the baggage train, she was moving forward with a speed that was suited to her purpose.

It was with an image of Eumenes fixed in her mind that Artonis let the leagues pass beneath her, conversation being impossible over the thunder of the hooves, and too tiresome during the short breaks to change and water the horses.

And so it was upon her dead husband that Artonis concentrated in order to keep her mind from the growing pain in her body as it clung to the horse. It was the difference between him and the other invaders of her country that first attracted her to Eumenes. The brash, arrogant uncultured Macedonians whom her father, Artabazos, had resisted right up until Darius' death were the antithesis of the people she had grown up amongst – she had been born after her father's return to the Persian empire from his exile in Pella. Yes, Alexander and his Companions had been educated by Aristotle and took pleasure in some of the finer things in life: the poetry, for example, that her mother, a Greek from Pergamum, had instilled in her; but they also destroyed: the burning of Persepolis was a crime that she could never forgive. Despite this sin, Alexander had triumphed and Darius had been defeated and then murdered, leaving her father a fugitive. But Alexander had pardoned Artabazos, taken his eldest daughter, Barsine, as his mistress. Thus, at the mass weddings at

Susa with their half-sister Barsine installed in Alexander's bed – and having already given him a bastard son, Heracles – Artonis and Artakama found themselves to be prized gifts.

And her terror at being given to a Macedonian had been great, for small in stature as she was the thought of being given to a huge brute of a man was terrifying; it was therefore with relief that she stood before her husband-to-be and only had to raise her eyes slightly to meet his. And then to find that he was a Greek from Kardia and Alexander's secretary caused relief to flow through her and for her to smile at Eumenes with an openness that, she hoped, would attract him; and on their wedding night, and those subsequent, she found herself not disappointed. Despite their being apart for almost five years after the death of Alexander, she remained his wife for he did not repudiate her as so many of the Macedonians had done.

Artonis choked with emotion as she remembered their reunion in Susa and the passion that she had felt for her husband; she forgave the long absence for it was due to his determination to fight for Alexander's heirs against a one-eyed brute who would steal all for himself. And now the one-eyed brute had triumphed and her husband was no more but she was to be the instrument that would fashion Eumenes' revenge and the destruction of Antigonos.

It was in good heart that Artonis rode north.

On and on they rode through the lessening heat of the afternoon; the beasts settled into a steady canter, sweating beneath the saddle-cloths.

It was a cry from the rear that was relayed up the column which caused Seleukos to slow and look behind. Artonis followed his gaze. Distant it was, but unmistakable as the westering sun picked it out, rising in the air: dust; dust from many horses travelling at speed.

'So Antigonos would rather not let me go,' Seleukos said to Apama. 'And that is before Naramsin has told him of the prophecy. We were right not to wait.' He turned and urged his mount forward, his followers surging after him; now that the possibility of capture had found space in a corner of their minds, they pushed their horses as hard as they dared for none had any doubt as to what the orders of the pursuers would be or the size of their number.

The light began to soften and as the heat lessened so their pace increased having changed mounts once again. Golden glowed the desert all around as the sun drew close to the western horizon but Seleukos showed no sign of relenting the pace. Chancing a glance over her right shoulder, Artonis could see the dust cloud glow red in the distance but it seemed to be no further away. *If anything, it might have gained; they will keep going and so must we.*

And so they did; and as the sun faded and dusk brought with it a light dew and a cooling breeze their pace slackened, but they pressed on for it was forty leagues between Babylon and Is and they still had the majority of them to go.

Long through the night they rode, keeping the Euphrates within earshot, to their left, until the moon rose and gave them a degree of clarity. Sleep fought a losing battle with Artonis for she was determined not to be the first to succumb and fall from her horse. At midnight, Seleukos called a halt, more for the sake of the exhausted beasts than his fatigued followers. Water was distributed to the grateful mounts and then nosebags were attached, allowing them to feed with contented snorts, swishing tails and the stamping of hooves; the harnesses, however, remained on. When she had taken care of her horses – for there was no one to do it for her – Artonis took a loaf from her saddlebag and sat next to her sister on a rug; breaking the bread, she handed a hunk to Artakama who grunted her thanks, took a small mouthful and then lay back, closed her eyes and fell to sleep, bread still clutched. With a smile, Artonis could fight no more; lying down, she wrapped an arm around Artakama and pulled her close. Dawn was the next thing that she was aware of; dawn and a great pang of hunger.

The bread was quickly consumed by the sisters as they saw to their horses, watering them again and tightening any tack that had loosened. Having taken it in turns, with Apama joining them, to hold the blanket up so that each could ease themselves in relative privacy, they mounted and were ready before the main column had completely formed. Artonis shared a smile with her sister, relieved not to be seen as the slowest element.

And then they were off again. The sores from yesterday, still raw, burned and chaffed and the aching muscles cried out for reprieve; but none came as the leagues passed for they could not pause or even slow as the dust cloud following them was closer than before; much closer.

'They must have stopped for half the time that we did in the night,' Artonis shouted at her sister. Artakama did not respond, her eyes squeezed tight with pain. Artonis could tell that beneath her veil her sister's teeth would be gritted.

Urgency transmitted through the column and the speed increased to a level that the horses could just bear, but for how long Artonis could only guess. Speed was becoming a cause for worry to her now as she considered the possibility of being overtaken by the pursuit. *What would Antigonos make of me trying to escape with Seleukos? It would certainly arouse his suspicions. I could hardly say that I wanted to get to Kardia quickly to bury my husband when it is obvious that Seleukos would run to Ptolemy.*

But there was naught that she could do to change the situation and so she concentrated on blocking the pain from her mind; pain that was coming close to being unendurable.

A quick pause at midday to change horses and grab a hunk of bread and a strip of dried meat was all Seleukos allowed, but it was enough for Artonis to see the blood stains coming through her trousers on the inside of her thighs.

As she hauled herself back into the saddle, she looked behind to see the chasing dust cloud was less than a league away and the shadow of the riders beneath was now visible. 'Don't they ever stop?' she said more to herself than anyone else.

'It's less than five leagues to go,' Seleukos shouted to give heart to the men. 'I sent a messenger on last night to warn the garrison at Is that we are hard-pressed; let's hope he was not delayed.' Again he raised his arm and flung it forward, kicking his mount into action as he did.

And on they went, the slow-moving Euphrates ever to their left, two hundred paces wide, flowing past them back to Babylon; it was for this reason that they had not taken ship earlier, for rowing against the current would have been slower than the speed of a horse. However, that was becoming more irrelevant now that the pursuit was drawing so close: what was the point in transferring to ships at Is, if their pursuers could outpace them? If that were to happen, Antigonos' allies to the north would be alerted in time to block the river and they would be trapped.

Looking back over her shoulder she could now make out the mass of horses following them and thought that sometimes individual riders could be discerned; indeed, many of her comrades felt the same and an attempt to quicken the pace was made. The first horse stumbled. Down the beast went, sending its rider tumbling to the ground to disappear beneath the hooves of those following with a curtailed scream. A groan rose from the column as the realisation of the inevitability now of being caught hit home: the horses could go no faster and must therefore soon slow unless they stopped completely to change mounts.

But surely they must have to stop to switch horses as well. And then, as she looked back again she saw what had given their pursuers the edge over them: each had a second mount but they did not pause to change, they leaped from one to the other as she watched. It was then that she realised that it was not Macedonians chasing them but, rather, tribesmen from the east; men born to the saddle and deadly with the bow: Bactrians or Sogdians or maybe Arachosians. *Sogdians, let them be Sogdians.* 'Apama,' she shouted, 'Apama!' Urging her horse closer to Seleukos' wife, she pointed back to the pursuit. 'Apama, can you recognise where they are from?'

Apama looked back for as long as she dared and then turned to Artonis, shaking her head. 'Horse-archers, but who I don't know. Antigonos must have incorporated them from Eumenes' army.'

'Exactly; they were loyal to my husband, and if they are Sogdian they would have been loyal to your father too.'

The relevance of that observation was not lost on Apama who immediately passed it on to Seleukos.

And the race continued, although it was with a flicker of hope now that Artonis rode; hope that, although Antigonos had chosen the right men to outpace Seleukos and his Macedonians, he may have chosen the wrong men to stay loyal to him. *We shall soon find out.*

It was as the first arrows landed amongst the column that Seleukos realised that further flight was impractical; their numbers would just be whittled down slowly but inevitably. It was time to try to fight. He held up his hand, palm forward and then signalled to the right to wheel the column. Around they went, his men taking their lances from their holsters. Into line they formed as arrows rained down on them, taking a couple down and a few horses.

Artonis knew little of war, but she could see that the situation was hopeless: unshielded lance-armed cavalry at a standstill were useless against fast-moving horse-archers. Even if they charged, the best that they could hope for was to chase the lighter cavalry off for they surely would not wish for contact.

There was nothing else for it but to gamble. 'Come, Apama, it's down to us to save our lives.' She made sure her veil was secured as she did not want to cause offence by showing her face and then pushed her horse forward, breaking the line with Apama following; pressing their horses into a canter, they each held a hand in the air signalling to the enemy to stop losing arrows. She felt her mare buck at the quivering thump of a hit to its rump but with a sharp tug on the reins managed to get the beast under control, the skills of her youth coming back to her. 'Stop! Stop shooting; we come to parley.'

Apama then shouted in her native Sogdian; it had immediate effect: the horsemen slowed and lowered their bows. 'They *are* Sogdians,' Apama said, a look of relief on her face.

At least three hundred of them, I should guess. We won't stand a chance should this fail. They rode up to the warriors until they were no more than ten paces away from the chieftain; he had an arrow nocked but the bow was not drawn. Dark eyes stared at them over the rim of a scarf drawn over his face against the dust.

'Why do you chase us?' Artonis asked in Greek.

'Why do you flee?' the chieftain answered.

Apama took the lead. 'I am Apama, daughter of your former lord and master, Spitamenes.'

This seemed to impress the chieftain. 'Spitamenes was a great man; I followed him until his defeat and then murder by his wife. She sent his head to Alexander.' He looked directly at Apama. 'But then you know that. I remember you as a little girl, Apama; I wonder what you have grown into: your father or his treacherous wife?'

'I am my own woman; but first and foremost, I am a Sogdian. Why do you threaten a fellow Sogdian?'

'I serve Antigonos now that Eumenes is dead; and he bids me chase Seleukos.' He indicated that they could pass. 'You are free to go.'

'We all go or none go.'

'You served Eumenes?' Artonis asked.

'I did.'

'Then would you serve his wife? I am Artonis, the wife of Eumenes.'

The chieftain looked hard at her eyes, her only visible feature. 'You are really she?'

'I am.'

'Then what is my name?' He unwound the scarf, exposing his face.

And it was with joy that Artonis recognised him from Eumenes' dinner table for he had dined regularly with her husband. 'Azanes.'

Azanes bowed his head. 'I am yours to command, lady, for the sake of your husband.'

'That pleases me, but first, tell me, why did you join with Antigonos?'

'A man must fight for someone.'

'But now you fight for me.'

Azanes turned to his men and addressed them in Sogdian, gesticulating to Artonis and then Apama. A cheer erupted from them at the end; Azanes punched the air with his bow and his men followed his lead.

'I think we can take a more leisurely attitude to the rest of our journey to Is,' Artonis commented as Azanes continued the rhythmical cheering.

By the time they reached Is the horses had partially recovered from their ordeal and were docile as they were loaded onto the transport ships awaiting them on the eastern bank to ferry them over to the river port itself which lay on the west bank. Three trips were necessary to bring the Macedonians and the Sogdians across.

Seleukos looked at the Sogdians as they disembarked. 'Bel Marduk must really be holding his hands over me that Antigonos should make such a mistake in sending Eumenes' men after us.'

Artonis smiled up at him. 'He didn't make a mistake as far as he was concerned at the time. He didn't know I was with you; he might well have chosen differently had he done so.'

'Well, that will give him quite a puzzle to solve when he hears that the Sogdians deserted to me. He'll know it wasn't for money because I've hardly got any and he has more than enough.'

'Let him wonder; by the time he finds out we'll be safely with Ptolemy.'

PTOLEMY.
THE BASTARD.

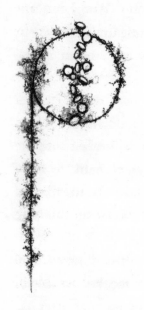

I T SEEMED TO Ptolemy that life had become an endless stream of children: aside from the three he had with his long-term mistress, Thais, he had also two sons with his second wife, Eurydike, and now another daughter with his new wife, Berenice – not to mention the three children from Berenice's first marriage whom he had inherited when he had married her. It was only his first wife, Artakama, who had failed to provide him with any – but then he had not made much effort to impregnate her, preferring instead to satisfy his other needs during their brief time together; needs that would never result in pregnancy. But the rest of his women had proven very fertile.

It was all very well, as he would need as many children as possible to secure marriages, create alliances and to hold the thrones of client kingdoms that would ensure the birth and survival of his dynasty. Each would be of use according to their status: the children he had with Thais, as well as the step-children from Berenice, would do for marrying petty kings and princesses; those of Eurydike would be suited for the offspring of Macedonian generals; and the children he would have with Berenice, who was of royal blood, would be for dynastic matches; powerful marriages that would secure his family's position in the world for generations to come. And he meant generations, for Ptolemy had grabbed Egypt and intended to stay, creating a dynasty that would be the envy of all. Thus, children were necessary; but was it really necessary for him to take an interest in them until they at least could hold a conversation? *I can't see either of my wives without them being worried about the latest infant,* he reflected as he looked out over the Great Harbour of Alexandria to the Heptastadion, the huge mole, nearing completion, joining the Pharos Island to the mainland and dividing the port into commercial on this side and military on the far.

'How do you keep your children from disturbing us?' he asked Thais, who was reclining in the shade, on a leather couch, behind him.

'*Our* children, you mean.'

'You know what I mean.'

Thais looked up from her reading – a new comedy by Menander, a young Athenian playwright whose work was proving popular in Alexandria's new theatre. 'Do I? It sounded for a moment like you were abdicating all responsibility for them.'

'What I mean is that Eurydike has two children and each time I visit her I'm expected to take some sort of an interest in the brutes despite the eldest, my namesake's, temperamental and spiteful behaviour and the youngest being nothing more than a wailing, milk-guzzling bundle. Berenice, who I thought was reasonably sensible, also has one, a daughter, I believe, who is only two months old and I'm meant to find the creature interesting.'

'Thank the gods that she doesn't force your step-children onto you.'

'Yes, I suppose that's something to be thankful for. You, however, never force me into the nursery.'

'Which just proves how little you know about our children: Lagus is thirteen, Leontiscus is ten and Eirene is eight; all of them are far too old to be in the nursery.'

'Well, wherever it is that they spend their days, then; you know what I mean.'

'You keep on saying that I know what you mean and I keep on denying it. But, seeing as you've brought the subject up, it was something that I've been intending to talk to you about.' Thais put the scroll down and sat up upon the couch. 'Lagus is now of an age where he might well have become interesting in your terms so I was thinking that you should spend more time with him.'

Ptolemy turned to face his mistress, a scowl on his face. 'I ask you how come you never let your children disturb us and the answer I get is that you are just about to start allowing them to.'

'*Our* children.' Thais smiled her sweetest smile, the smile that had made her the most highly paid courtesan in the world – albeit now with only one client. 'Now, Ptolemy, it's about time you got to know Lagus as a man: wrestle naked together or hit one another with wooden swords or whatever it is that men do with each other. I don't know what you all get up to but it's time you started doing it with your oldest son.'

Ptolemy grunted and turned back to his admiration of his construction work. 'Thank Serapis that you stopped at three children.'

'*We* stopped; you somehow fail to grasp that it takes two to have a child. And it was nothing to do with Serapis.'

Ptolemy waved away the criticism; he was not in the mood to be lectured. He had only brought up the subject of children in order to divert his attention from the pressing problem irking him: now that matters seemed to have been settled in the east in

Antigonos' favour and with Eumenes dead – *garrotted! You didn't deserve that, you sly little Greek* – should he make approaches to Kassandros for an alliance against the resinated cyclops who would emerge, stronger than ever, from the depths of the east? *If I were him, my first reaction would be to refuse my offer and attempt to remain Antigonos' ally thus isolating me; but then I – if I were Kassandros – would wonder what would happen to my position in Macedonia if Antigonos managed to take Egypt – not that he will, but hypothetically.*

'You'll just appear weak if you approach Kassandros,' Thais said, surprising him. 'It will look like you don't have the confidence that you could repulse an attack on Egypt and want to make an alliance with your brother-in-law – whom you hate, as he is well aware – in order to divert Antigonos' attention away from you onto him.'

Ptolemy turned to Thais. 'How did you know what I was thinking?'

She smiled, her tongue – the bringer of so many pleasures – moistening her top lip. 'Why else have you spent so much time with Eurydike since hearing from Seleukos the news of Eumenes' death and Antigonos' victory? It wasn't to see the baby as you have just admitted, and you can't bear young Ptolemy; nor does she satisfy your needs as your constant complaint about her abilities in bed is that she just endures not enjoys.' Thais shrugged. 'I can therefore only assume that you are trying to persuade her to take a letter to her brother because it's certainly not to learn how to change a nappy – not that she would know how to anyway.'

Ptolemy stared at Thais, her eyes sparkling with amusement. Her face, cream skinned, framed by red-gold hair, piled high and cascading down to her shoulder in ringlet-falls, was the most beautiful he had ever seen and always took his breath away; it was the thing that he prized most about her with perhaps one exception: her mind. Her analysis of any situation was always the most pertinent and he had come to rely upon her. 'I was going to talk to you about it as soon as I had considered the matter further.'

'As soon as you've come to the wrong decision, in other words.'

'Not necessarily.'

'Well, if you were trying to persuade Eurydike to go north to see her brother, then I would say you already had.'

'I was trying to persuade her to be willing to go to Macedon should the need arise in the future.'

'And?'

'And she refused me.'

'Sensible girl.'

'Insubordinate girl.'

'No, she's preventing you from making a tactical error.'

'Namely?'

'Namely, if you want an alliance with Kassandros then you have to wait for him to come to you, begging for it.'

'And what will make him do that?'

Before she could reply, Lycortas, Ptolemy's steward, glided onto the terrace, his feet, obscured beneath his long, loose-fitting, white linen robe, seemingly motionless and irrelevant to his propulsion. He bowed, his bald head pudgy and shining in the sun, his arms crossed and his hands hidden up his sleeves. 'The Jewish delegation is here to see you, lord.'

'Again?' Ptolemy sighed. 'Tell me, Lycortas: what do you think would induce Kassandros to beg me for an alliance?'

'A direct threat to his position and life, lord.'

'Obviously; but what form would that take for him to react to it?'

Lycortas pursed his lips. 'Alas, lord, I am unable to supply the direct threat myself, a failing that causes me deep regret and compounds my sense of inadequacy in your service, for I know that you despise the "pockmarked toad" – as you so colourfully refer to him – with a vigour that surpasses almost, but not quite, your ability to enjoy yourself.'

Ptolemy frowned at Thais as she stifled an explosive laugh. 'Thank you, Lycortas, for your profound and insightful observation. I shall be down shortly.'

It was another two hours before Lycortas announced Ptolemy's arrival in the audience chamber, two hours that had been very well spent with Thais in proving the veracity of Lycortas' profound and insightful observation. And Ptolemy thanked himself for having used the time so well, for his sense of well-being fortified him against the endless speeches of the Jewish elders.

'And that is the basis of our case, Lord Ptolemy,' the leader, a grey-beard of many summers, standing before him in a domed hat and a black and white mantle about his shoulders, said having summed up.

Ptolemy took a few moments to return from the pleasant part of his mind in which he had been residing whilst each of the dozen-strong members of the delegation had all made speeches of unnecessary floweriness. 'Hmmph. Yes; so let me recap on the points that you have made in the last couple of hours.' He struck his right forefinger with his left. 'Firstly, you want to have one of your own to collect taxes from the Jews here in Alexandria.' He then struck his middle finger. 'Secondly…' He made a show of thinking, looking puzzled. 'Secondly? Remind me what your second point was, would you, Matthias? I seem to have lost it amongst all the arguments.'

Matthias looked confused. 'There was no second point, Lord Ptolemy. It was just that we request a Jewish tax collector to collect Jewish taxes; that was all.'

'And you took two hours to do that? Two hours of my time?'

'Well, the arguments needed to be made.'

'The arguments, or argument I should say, was that you wish your people to have as little contact as possible with what you call gentiles; which is just about everyone with a foreskin, am I right? That's the argument, yes?'

'Well, it's not that simple.'

'Yes, it is. That is the crux of it, is it not?'

'Well... er...'

'I am a patient man, and reasonably forgiving, Matthias, as my sitting through the last two hours has proven. Is that or is that not the crux of your argument? Yes or no.'

'Yes.'

'Good, we're getting somewhere, finally. And so, this official, or Alabarch as you would choose to call him, should I decide to appoint one, will, for a small commission naturally, pass on the revenue to my treasury. Is that correct?'

'Yes, Lord Ptolemy.'

'And that is it?'

Matthias looked at the ground, suddenly finding his sandals of great interest. 'Yes, Lord Ptolemy.'

'It seems to me to be a perfectly sensible and workable solution. I can see no objection to it: you get the degree of autonomy that you want and I get my coinage.'

'So you are minded to grant the request.'

Ptolemy paused and looked at the grey-bearded delegation with mischief in his eyes. 'On one condition: that you never waste my time with useless chatter again. I am a Macedonian not a Greek; we don't have time for all that sort of thing. Now, go away and resolve who shall be your first Alabarch and then send him to me and I will decide if he is suitable. And I promise you, if he should say more than ten unnecessary words in answer to my questions then he'll end up in the harbour as an integral part of the Heptastadion.' He pointed over his shoulder to the construction work through the open window behind him. 'Now, get out and next time you have a request only one of you need speak.'

The delegation stood motionless, their mouths opening and closing.

'Go!'

Matthias stepped back and then straightened himself up, pulling back his shoulders. 'There is also the question of my men still held in captivity since you took our land.'

Ptolemy took a deep breath. 'Then perhaps you should have used some of the time to address that issue rather than making the same point endlessly.'

'But—'

'No!' Ptolemy held up both hands. 'No! I've freed many of your people; so many that you now want an Alabarch because your community is thriving. I still need slaves to build the city.'

'But what about my men, my personal men who followed me into battle, what about them?'

'They are young and fit and making a great contribution to the construction of the city; I might yet free them if I were to find another use for them. Now go, before I lose my temper.'

'If you freed them now—'

'Go! Or you'll all be joining them.' Ptolemy stood and glared down at the delegation.

As one they turned and scampered to the doors, forgetting their dignity.

'Masterful, master,' Lycortas said, with genuine admiration in his voice. 'A masterclass in how to thoroughly enjoy oneself; I shall be ever grateful.'

'Yes, well, let's not take it too far, Lycortas. It served its own purpose in that I hope it will get around that, if anyone wants something from me, it's best not to waste my time with endless rhetoric.'

'Ah! That is advice which I shall take to heart when I ask you for more generous remuneration tomorrow.' He glanced through the window to a trireme moored in the royal harbour – the small, private dock next to the royal palace. 'Your ship is ready and waiting.'

One of Ptolemy's pleasures in life – and he had many – was to admire his navy, for it was upon sea-power that he relied to keep Egypt safe. Any army coming south through Syria and then west from Gaza in Palestine needed control of the sea, else their lines of communication would be compromised at the very least or, at the very worst, an army could be landed behind them; and so Ptolemy had spent much time and gold building four separate fleets – either through construction or stealing them from Antigonos' nephew, Dioscurides, who had been left in command along the Syrian coast. Taking great interest in the minutiae of their organisation, he visited the military harbour often.

Thais was already aboard when Ptolemy stepped onto the trireme waiting for him in the royal harbour. That did not surprise him, for she appreciated his inspection visits as much as he did; what did surprise him, though, was Lagus sitting under the awning, next to her. *A good-looking boy; but then how could he fail to be, with Thais as his mother?* 'So you're coming to learn about the Alexandria fleet, are you, Lagus?'

Lagus got to his feet. 'Yes, Father; I often go down to the military port with my weapons tutor and I enjoy the visits; that's why I was so pleased to get your invitation to join you and Mother today.'

Thais' smile was all innocence.

Ptolemy managed to refrain from raising an eyebrow. 'Yes, well, I thought it was time that we started doing a few more things together. I'm going to inspect the ships that we've captured so far this season.'

'Twenty-seven,' Lagus said.

'Twenty-seven? How do you know?'

'Every time our ships bring in their prizes, my weapons tutor takes me down to look at them. There are eighteen triremes, three Fours, a Five and the rest are *lembi*. Then, on top of that we've captured thirty-nine cargo ships.'

Ptolemy was impressed. 'Very good.'

But Lagus was not finished. 'If you add that score to the hundred and twenty-one naval vessels and ninety-six cargo ships that we captured from Antigonos last year, it is fair to assume that when he gets back from the east Antigonos won't have a navy waiting for him.'

Ptolemy steadied himself against the rail as the ship cast off with a stream of nautical orders from the triarchos. 'Now, who said that the ships originally belonged to Antigonos? I am not at war with Antigonos and so have no reason to act aggressively towards his fleet.'

'I know, Father; these were all ships suspected of being involved in piracy; all the crews have admitted so and have been only too pleased to sign on with you for wages that exceed those they earned as a pirate. It's just a shame that so many of them operated out of ports loyal to Antigonos that you have recently, since his venture east, seen fit to occupy. All of them in fact, I believe.'

Ptolemy grinned and ruffled his son's hair; Lagus went to snatch away the hand and then thought better of it. *He thinks he's too old to have his hair ruffled. Well, perhaps he's going to be a little more interesting than I thought. And he has a nice turn of phrase.*

And it was an interesting afternoon, for Ptolemy found that his eldest son was very knowledgeable on all things naval from ship-building to ship-sinking; what was more, he thoroughly enjoyed displaying his knowledge to his father in intelligent and sometimes witty language. 'Theoretically there is no reason why you could not build a Twelve with three rows of oars each operated by four men. Obviously it would be the biggest ship ever seen and probably of little practical use other than as a Nile Cruiser, but it would be an interesting project to undertake.'

Ptolemy contemplated the notion as they walked down the ship's gangway onto the quay in the military port, having first come via the construction site in order to inspect the progress of the Heptastadion. 'That's twenty oars on each row, that's one hundred and twenty, making it four hundred and eighty rowers.'

'I think it would be more, because the hull would have to be much taller to accommodate three rows of four oarsmen as their seats would have to be ascending so that they could all get good purchase on their sweeps. Therefore the ship would also need to be longer to make up for that extra height, otherwise it would be ungainly and prone to capsizing in the slightest of squalls.'

Ptolemy looked down at Lagus; his face was serious concentration as he worked through the problem, his eyebrows knitted in a frown.

'So I would say you would have to make it a quarter as big again, which would give it twenty-five oars in each of the three rows thus making a total of six hundred oarsmen.'

Ptolemy did some quick mental arithmetic. 'It would be almost a hundred paces long.'

'Yes, Father; quite a thing, eh? I think it's possible.'

'But if it would be of little practical use, why bother?'

'Because you can, Father; because you can.' Lagus pointed to the Heptastadion. 'Look at that; it's almost finished but why did we go to the bother of doing it? Why does the Pharos Island need to be joined to the mainland? Why does the harbour need to be physically divided in two? It doesn't really serve a practical purpose as the harbour is already protected by the sea walls. You're just doing it because you can.'

'That is the first time that you have been wrong, Lagus. Alexander ordered the mole to be constructed.'

'But you didn't cancel it when you came to Egypt seven years ago; you are carrying on with the project purely because you can.'

'No, Lagus. I'm carrying on with the project because it will lead to another grander construction which will see my name immortalised.'

Both Thais and Lagus looked at him, waiting for him to enlighten them as to what he had in mind.

'Ah, no, not yet,' Ptolemy said as the harbourmaster approached. 'Not until the idea is firm in my mind and it has been properly designed and costed.' *Although I don't suppose I'll live to see it completed.*

'You are the most infuriating man,' Thais said, never having appreciated not being a part of a secret. 'Now I'm going to spend all my time guessing.'

'Guess as much as you like; I won't tell you until I'm ready.' With an expression of finality, Ptolemy turned his attention to the list that the harbourmaster gave him. He scanned down it and then looked at Lagus. 'You were absolutely right with your figures. I'm impressed.' He felt Lagus glow in the warmth of his praise and enjoyed the sensation of making the boy happy. *Yes,*

Thais is right: I must do this sort of thing more often with the lad. He carried on along the quay, checking the list and tallying it up, with reference to the harbourmaster, with the ships moored alongside, feeling pride in his ever-expanding navy.

'You look to be a man gloating,' a voice said, pulling him out of his naval concentration.

Ptolemy did not need to turn to see who it was. 'I was wondering how long it would be until you came scuttling to me, Seleukos.'

'I didn't scuttle, I rode.'

Ptolemy turned, pleased to see his old comrade. 'As it turns out, you've come just at the right time: I have a job for you; two to be precise.'

'How many ships?' Seleukos asked as he and Ptolemy strolled past the warehouses and chandleries lining the dockside of the commercial harbour. Thais and Lagus had been sent on ahead in the trireme so that they could talk in private together as Ptolemy had always found Seleukos to be more forthcoming alone.

'A hundred should be sufficient,' Ptolemy replied, acknowledging the salute of a party of marines loading bundles of javelins onto a trireme.

'And men?'

'That will depend on just how far Antigonos advances south through Phoenicia, Coele-Syria and Palestine. But let's assume that he comes all the way south to my border and I have to withdraw all my garrisons, then it will be in the region of ten thousand.'

'And I will be in sole command?'

'Not of the army but of the navy, yes; unless you feel that your lack of experience in naval matters means that you require assistance.'

'I'm fine with ships and you know it.'

Ptolemy looked at his new guest as their escort cleared a path through a crowd of oarsmen waiting to embark onto a huge Five. 'I hope so, because when Antigonos gets back to the coast the first thing he will do is try to reassemble a navy, as I've spent the past two years stealing what ships he left on the Syrian coast. When he gets here next spring he'll try to use the shipyards in Cilicia, Phoenicia, Syria and Palestine for construction; it will be your job to frustrate his plans as much as possible in Phoenicia and Cilicia, which will prove difficult as he will use ports all along the coast, making it almost impossible to locate each one.'

'What about Syria and Palestine?'

'The fleet based at Tyros will see to them. My brother, Menelaus, is in command; he'll do his share of raiding and burning, and also keep Tyros from Antigonos for as long as possible.'

'It's a massive area to cover.'

'Yes, and eventually Antigonos will get a navy of a reasonable size; we can only delay that time by destroying his ships faster than he can launch them for as long as we can. But my ultimate objective is to keep Cyprus within my sphere of influence. With a navy Antigonos can invade the island, but if it is firmly under my control and with a large garrison present, he will find it impossible to take.'

'And Cyprus is my second job?'

Ptolemy feigned surprise. 'How did you guess?'

'It must have been something you said. Very well, I'll do it.'

You seem very confident, my friend, for a man who has limited naval experience; but still, at least you have military sense and so you're the best I can get at the moment. 'I knew you would.'

'But in return I want you to help me retake Babylon.'

'Naturally. Nothing would please me better than for you to be safely reinstalled as my neighbour; Antigonos is a threat to us all.'

'And what about Kassandros?'

Ptolemy smiled. 'That, my friend, is the problem that I've been wrestling with: how to make Kassandros want to be on our side.'

Seleukos shared the smile. 'I think I have something that could help you there.'

It was the expression that greeted him on Thais' face that warned Ptolemy something was amiss; he was certain that when he found out what it was his mistress would be greatly amused. 'What is it?'

Thais shrugged, her eyes alight with mischief; glancing at Seleukos, who refused to meet her look, she composed herself. 'Nothing, Ptolemy; nothing that you can't cope with, seeing as you have so much experience in that particular field. Lycortas has organised Artonis' accommodation; he will bring her to see you when you're ready.' She walked away, leaving Ptolemy none the wiser as to the cause of her mirth.

He turned to Seleukos who also seemed to be trying to hide his amusement. 'What is so funny about Artonis coming to see me? She was Eumenes' wife, after all, and knows that her late husband's enemy is also mine.'

'Quite,' Seleukos said. 'And what she has to say will be of great use.'

Ptolemy sat, mulling over Artonis' words as he contemplated her, sitting, veiled, before him with her head lowered and eyes staring at the floor. *So Eumenes faced the garrotte rather than betray the Argead cause to Antigonos. I never would have taken the sly little Greek to be a man of principle; he could easily have gone along with Antigonos and then slipped away at a later time. And now he's trying to release his vengeance from beyond the grave.*

Clever as well as honourable. Well, well. He turned to Seleukos. 'The way he treated you in Babylon can leave no room for doubt: Antigonos is after it all.'

'Yes, and he's in no rush. He will do things slowly and methodically; he will get to Kassandros eventually.'

Ptolemy nodded, pleased with the thought. *It's a direct threat to his position and his life; that can't be denied. It will send him running to me for an alliance as soon as he hears of it. The question is: when should he hear about it? This will be all about timing.* He turned his attention back to Artonis. *Who do those eyes remind me of?* 'I'm grateful to you, Artonis. With what you can vouch for, we will be able to build a coalition against Antigonos and you will eventually have the revenge that you require.'

Artonis lifted her face, her dark eyes levelled at his. 'So you will get me to Kassandros?'

'I will.'

'After which I can go to Kardia to inter my husband. I have brought his ashes with me.'

'Indeed; and see Lysimachus, who will be fascinated by what you have to say. But I have to decide upon the timing. Even if Antigonos set out the day after you left Babylon, travelling with an army so large he would not come to Thapsacus, which is the closest point that the Euphrates comes to the sea, before the autumn equinox; there will be no further campaigning this year. I imagine he will go into winter camp there, where the Euphrates can supply his vast army with all the water it needs, and then cross the desert to Syria in early spring. For Kassandros to take this seriously he needs to see Antigonos come back west, preparing for war; they both need to be goaded.'

'So I am to be here for the winter?'

'Yes, whilst I set the ground. I shall make you as comfortable as possible.'

'In that case I have two requests.'

'Name them.'

'Firstly, I have an escort of three hundred Sogdian light cavalry; I would be grateful if you would take them into your service.'

Horse-archers; very useful. 'Consider it done.'

'And then I would ask that you accept my sister back as she has nowhere else to go.'

'Your sister? Back?' He looked again at Artonis' eyes and then the cause of Thais' amusement became clear. *Of course! Artonis is Artakama's sister. You bastard, Seleukos, you knew.* He looked at Seleukos who, again, would not meet his eye, and then back at Artonis. 'Is she here?'

'She is.'

The coming horror of Eurydike's reaction when she heard of another new rival's presence shrieked around his head. *And Berenice won't take kindly to this new addition. And, as Artakama was, no, is, my first wife, she might try to assert her seniority over the others.* His heart sank, disappearing into his bowels. 'Why?'

Artonis looked at him as if he were a recalcitrant child. 'Why? Because she is your wife and she did not want to fall into the hands of Antigonos. That's why.' Artonis turned and called towards the door. 'Come, Artakama.'

And as the woman he had not seen for eight years since he had left her in Babylon walked into the room, Ptolemy would have given almost anything for her to have been in Antigonos' hands.

'Why didn't you warn me?' Ptolemy glared at Seleukos.

'I thought it would be a nice surprise for you; after all, you haven't seen Artakama for seven years.'

'Eight! And yes, there's a reason for that: I didn't want her as a wife. Alexander forced her upon me. That's why I left her in

Babylon.' He stared up into Seleukos' eyes and detected well-disguised mirth. 'You knew full well what my reaction would be and you did it on purpose, didn't you?'

Seleukos raised both his palms. 'I genuinely thought you would be pleased to keep her safe from Antigonos. Apama said—'

'Apama! So that's it, is it? You do everything that Apama tells you to do, do you? That means it's your cock that's doing the thinking as it listens to everything that your wife says. What about your brain, Seleukos? Doesn't that get a look in nowadays? So what did Apama say, eh?'

'She said that if Antigonos got hold of Artakama then he would have leverage over you.'

'Did she, now? And did you pause to consider whether that was true or did your cock just agree blindly with her and then carry on with an agenda of its own?'

'But Antigonos—'

'Even if Antigonos had done what he liked with her, it would have been nothing to me. But we don't make war on women.'

'You executed Perdikkas' sister, Atalanta.'

Ptolemy opened his mouth and then closed it; his eyes narrowed and he shook his head at the memory. *That is always going to haunt me, although the deed did have its uses.* 'That was different. She had been condemned by the army assembly and had I not carried out its will I would have lost face.'

Seleukos wagged his forefinger. 'It was more than that, Ptolemy, and you know it. In killing Atalanta you made it personal with Eumenes and all of Perdikkas' followers; you took us past the point of no return. I saw your expression change from reluctance to a realisation that this death could be useful to you and so you went through with it. Apama was right to persuade me to bring Artakama with us; if he got hold of her and killed her then it would cease to be business with Antigonos and become personal; and that is something that we all want to avoid.'

Ptolemy grunted. 'For as long as possible.'

'Yes, for as long as possible.'

'Perhaps you're right.' Ptolemy pursed his lips and looked out over the Great Harbour. 'Well, seeing as it is just business, I've got some for you to do before the sailing season closes.'

'Name it.'

'Go to see Lysimachus, Asander and Kassandros and tell them that I'm going to send a delegation to congratulate Antigonos on his great victory when he arrives back in Syria in the spring; if they wish, they can send their own representatives. We'll remind him that we all had a part to play in it and are looking forward to receiving our share of the rewards: namely, the contents of the treasuries at Susa, Ecbatana and Cyinda and then, of course, territory; I will take Phoenicia, Coele-Syria and Palestine. They can choose what they want. They'll all want to be a part of that even though they'll be aware Antigonos will not be able to accept our demands. And then we shall watch what he does and send Artonis to Kassandros at the right time.'

KASSANDROS.
THE JEALOUS.

'THESSALONIKE, OF COURSE; what else could I call it?' Kassandros' pinched, pale and pockmarked visage wore an expression of complete love and devotion – a combination that did not sit well on such a countenance – as he held his wife's face in both hands and kissed her on the lips. 'And it shall be the greatest city in Macedon, if not the whole of Greece.'

Thessalonike responded to his kiss with more enthusiasm than he had previously experienced; he risked pressing his tongue past her lips, an act that she had always resisted, even after he had entered her. This time she allowed it and even pressed her belly against his groin and slowly rubbed against his arousal. *She's coming around to me.*

And it was a blissful thought for he truly loved Thessalonike and had done so since the moment he had first beheld her as an adult. However, he had been under no illusions that the marriage was but an alliance of convenience for Thessalonike; he knew only too well that women found him unattractive for his life had been a series of rebuffs if he had tried to take any through seduction rather than by force. Thessalonike had been the first to genuinely allow him to penetrate her without scratching and biting thus forcing him into more extreme violence. Perhaps now, with this kiss, the tide of her affection was turning and he would feel the genuine love of his wife when he next came to her bed.

He broke off the kiss, reluctant though he was to do so, as his twin younger half-brothers stood adjacent and cleared their throats, looking in any direction but his. He stroked Thessalonike's cheek; she almost gave him a smile but turned away at the last moment to look out over the long bay below them in which nestled the small port of Therma.

'What gave you the idea to found a city on this place?' Thessalonike asked, disengaging from him.

'Pella's port is small and more than two leagues up an inlet and Pydna is in the south of the country and is also not as large as we will soon need. So when I saw this place whilst travelling to Amphipolis I started to conceive large plans because I now feel safe enough to trust that we have the time to see them to fruition.'

And Kassandros had had a good couple of years since he had, at the beginning of last year, indicated his intentions towards the throne of Macedon by presiding over the funeral of Philip the fool, admittedly with the young King Alexander present; but it was Kassandros and Thessalonike, not the young Alexander, who acted the part traditionally played by the new king in burying his predecessor. Having already taken in marriage an Argead princess, Thessalonike, he had further given a clear signal of his desire for the crown by founding a city and naming it Kassandreia after himself, a deed that in the past had only ever been the prerogative of the King of Macedon.

However, he had a problem: unfortunately, the child Alexander still lived – albeit under house-arrest in Amphipolis – and Kassandros knew that he could not be seen to get rid of the boy, until he had enough support to ensure that he could survive the quiet assassination of the heir to the throne before he came of age. And so in the summer of the previous year, whilst Antigonos, with Eumenes defeated, tarried in the east, making a settlement that suited him, Kassandros had taken an army south. Moving swiftly, he had surprised and defeated the Aetolians who were holding the Pass of Thermopylae at the instigation of Polyperchon and the exiled King of Epirus, Aeacides, who had both finally crawled out of their hideaway in Perrhaebia. With his rear secured, he had then moved into Boeotia where he had again asserted the prerogative of a king and re-founded Thebes, destroyed by Alexander twenty years before. He had had the entire surviving population reassembled and set in motion the reconstruction project, to which Greek colonies from all around the sea and even in far off Italia had contributed. Raised from the dead, its walls repaired and its temples and public buildings reconstructed, Thebes had given Kassandros a second client-base in Greece, after Athens, held for him by Demetrius of Phaleron. Citizens of the newly rebuilt city now owed him their allegiance and all the colonies contributing to the rebuilding fund had also implicitly sided with him.

With Boeotia secured he had chased Polyperchon and Aeacides back up to Perrhaebia, settled with the Aetolians, and then moved against Polyperchon's son, Alexandros, who was dug in across the Isthmus of Corinth. Unable to dislodge him, he outflanked him by taking his army across the Saronic Gulf to Epidaurus and then on to Argos, securing its support and that of the surrounding cities. Leaving a couple of thousand men to keep Alexandros cooped up in his fortifications, he marched back to Macedon the undisputed master of Greece north of the Peloponnese.

With his hold over Pella and Pydna firm and most of the surviving nobility, who had not fled to Antigonos, Lysimachus or Ptolemy, supporting him and with all the new citizens of Kassandreia owing him allegiance, he would now be adding a huge new city whose people would also be loyal to him. Soon he would have the confidence to take the final step. Until then he would play a patient game, for Thessalonike had counselled that to rush matters was to leave oneself exposed to miscalculation; he had complete confidence in his wife's advice.

Pleased with all he had achieved since the death of Olympias and delighted by Thessalonike's reaction to having a city named after her, he took another look at the bay that would soon become the commercial heart of Macedon before mounting his horse and leading his party down to the small port of Therma to embark on the ship waiting to take them back to Pella.

The news that Seleukos awaited him in the palace took Kassandros by surprise as he disembarked in Pella. 'When did he come west?' he mused as he and Thessalonike took a small carriage north through the town, along a thoroughfare as straight as an arrow.

'The more interesting question is: what is he doing here?' Thessalonike said, acknowledging the cheers of the citizens to whom the sight of her was so much better than that of her despised adoptive mother, Olympias. 'Antigonos has obviously, and inevitably, chased him from Babylon and taken it for himself in his increasingly naked power grab; so is Seleukos here to ask you for help in regaining his satrapy? I would suggest it is very unlikely since he can't abide you.'

'But then very few people can, my love.'

Thessalonike looked at him, her eyes widening at his blunt honesty. 'True; however, there are very few people whom *you* can abide, so I would say that the score is even. But, whether you are the best of friends or not, Seleukos is anything but stupid; he knows that there is very little you can do to help him in his current predicament; but Ptolemy is far better placed to do so. My guess is that he's here on your dear brother-in-law's business, so I think we should listen very carefully to what he has to say because I've never known Ptolemy offer anything that is what it seems to be at face value. We should be prepared for a trap.'

'He'll never agree to share the contents of the treasuries,' Thessalonike said after hearing Seleukos out. 'And Ptolemy knows that.'

'Indeed he does,' Seleukos replied, hiding his surprise that it should be Thessalonike who responded and not her husband. 'But I don't think that is really what interests him: he's far more concerned with his reaction to the demand for more territory. Ptolemy needs at least Coele-Syria and Palestine as buffer states and so he will ask for Phoenicia as well to give himself room to compromise.'

Kassandros tapped his finger on the arm of his chair, shaking his head. 'Even so, I don't see the point of it.' *At least I'm not going to admit I do to you.*

Thessalonike immediately illuminated him with a hint of irritation in her voice. 'Ptolemy's testing Antigonos as to what his eventual goal is: if he agrees to Ptolemy's territorial demands then that would show he has no ultimate desire to take the whole empire for himself. If he doesn't... well, it would suggest that we all have the same problem and its name is Antigonos.'

Kassandros continued his pretence of being unconvinced. *Thessalonike is just going to have to think me obtuse for the moment until I get Seleukos to spell out exactly what he has been sent here to say.* 'We don't all have the same problem; maybe they do in Asia but not here in Europe.'

Seleukos leaned forward in his chair, adopting an expression of earnest interest. 'And what makes you think that, Kassandros?'

'Because Antigonos has no interest in Europe; I hold it for him.' *At least, that is what I'd have him believe.*

'Do you? Do you really? Does that mean that if he asks for Greece and Macedon, you will give them to him?'

Kassandros was about to reply and then made a show of thinking better of it.

'No, of course not; and why should you?'

'But why should he ask for them?'

'An excellent question.' Seleukos then looked at Thessalonike to provide the answer.

She obliged but in a tone that implied she had understood Kassandros' game. 'If we refused to recognise his authority over the whole empire, he would certainly seek to take control of what we hold – in his name, of course.'

Good woman; that's another reason why I love you: you understand me. Kassandros played confused. 'But why would he ask me to do that? He has Asia, Ptolemy has Egypt, Lysimachus has Thrace and I... *we* have Macedon and Greece. Ptolemy and Lysimachus each have one of my sisters as does Antigonos' son, Demetrios.' He shrugged. 'Where's the problem?'

'The problem is his ambition,' Seleukos said. 'He will try to make himself master of all and in that scenario there is no place for you just as there is no place for me, as my being here demonstrates admirably.'

'I still think that he will be better placed keeping things as they are.'

Seleukos turned to Thessalonike. 'And what do you think?'

Thessalonike gave nothing of her real feelings away. 'I think we have to wait and see.'

'Then would you indulge me with a bit of speculation? Do you have a map of the lands around the sea?'

'It would seem to me,' Seleukos said as he smoothed out a rudimentary map of the Aegean Sea, Greece, Thrace and Anatolia that had been quickly sketched by Thessalonike's secretary, 'that to gain control of all the land around the sea – which, for the sake of this exercise, we will assume is Antigonos' goal – he has to first find some allies. Now, given that you, Kassandros – or should I say, you both, Kassandros and Thessalonike – will either refuse to join with him, or, even more worrying from your point of view, aren't even asked as his plans do not involve you, then that leaves him few choices. Now, assuming that Lysimachus is sensible and either stays neutral, or even becomes hostile to Antigonos, then there are only two possible candidates.' He pointed first to Thessaly. 'Polyperchon here.' His finger then went south to the isthmus of the Peloponnese. 'And his son, Alexandros, here.' He looked around his audience to make sure that he had their full attention. Satisfied, he proceeded. 'Now, Polyperchon you have dealt with and he is no more of a threat militarily; however, politically he is still useful as he is, technically, still the regent of Macedon.'

Kassandros held up the Great Ring of Macedon on his forefinger. 'I hold the ring.'

'But that does not necessarily give you legitimacy because your father gave the ring to Polyperchon.' Seleukos waved a hand to still Kassandros' protests. 'It doesn't matter what arguments you put forward, Antigonos will use the one that suits him and ignore the fact that actually Antipatros didn't have the right to pass on the regency.' Seleukos again pointed to where Alexandros was dug in across the isthmus. 'If Antigonos makes advances towards Alexandros, reinforcing him, and offers to

159

restore Polyperchon to the regency, *then* will you believe his true intentions?'

I think it's now becoming clear just what Ptolemy wants. Kassandros looked to Thessalonike. 'What do you think?'

'I think that this is the beginnings of Ptolemy trying to form an alliance against Antigonos which if we were to join would definitely make us Antigonos' enemy. I said we should beware of a trap and this is it. Do you deny it, Seleukos?'

'An alliance against him would be a good thing.'

'For whom? You for one because it would help you get Babylon back as Antigonos' eye will be drawn away from the east; and Ptolemy for another, for it would spread Antigonos' attentions and keep him from focusing all his time on taking Egypt, which is a far richer prize than Macedon and Greece. Who else have you contacted?'

'After this I go on to Lysimachus in Thrace and then Asander in Caria before returning to Alexandria.'

Thessalonike nodded. 'Both Asander and Lysimachus have cause to be worried about our one-eyed friend: Asander because his satrapy borders Phrygia, and Lysimachus because he has crossed the Hellespont and taken Hellespontine Phrygia, something that, no doubt, Antigonos considers should be his by rights as it too borders his satrapy. No, Seleukos, we want none of this; we won't bait the boar and turn him against us unnecessarily. Antigonos is no threat to us, whatever you may think.'

Seleukos smiled. 'Eumenes, Antigenes, Eudamos, Alketas and Peithon are all dead and Peucestas and I removed from our satrapies; very well then, believe what you will, but remember, this is business, not personal, so put aside what you may feel for Ptolemy and what you may think he thinks of you, and when Antigonos threatens you Ptolemy will be only too pleased to bring you into the alliance because that's the only way we're going to stop the resinated cyclops.'

Kassandros smiled at his wife after Seleukos had been shown out. 'Did you really believe that I could be so obtuse?'

Thessalonike looked at him not unkindly. 'I'm sorry, I misunderstood at first and patronised you; but in the end it was better for the pretence because Seleukos heard genuine irritation in my voice whilst explaining the basics to you.'

Kassandros took her hand. 'Next time I'll warn you; but to tell the truth it only occurred to me to play slow on the uptake after you said that we should watch for the trap.'

Thessalonike squeezed his fingers and gave him a look that sped his heart. 'Yes, you made him admit that Ptolemy wants an alliance, which implies that Ptolemy is not feeling as strong as perhaps we thought. What we've learned is that we should wait and see: we might well be better off settling our differences with Antigonos and joining with him.'

'We'll wait to see how he responds to Ptolemy's delegation.'

'I think I know exactly how Antigonos will react.'

Feeling encouraged by his wife's warmth towards him, Kassandros leaned down to kiss her; she responded. 'I have an excellent idea of how to pass the time waiting for the cyclops' next move in the spring.' He led her towards their living quarters; she followed willingly.

Antigonos.
The One-Eyed.

I T WAS GOOD to be next to the sea again, to smell it and hear it break upon the rocks and crash against the harbour wall far below. It was good to be in Rhosos again, almost three years since he had last been here before he chased Eumenes out east; it was especially good as the Ptolemaic garrison had withdrawn before him, leaving the city open for his men to enjoy after the twelve-day march across the desert from their winter camp at Thapsacus on the Euphrates. Antigonos stood on a terrace, admiring his regained possession from on high, secure in the knowledge that the east was now under his sway, settled to his satisfaction and profit. The great cities of Susa, Ecbatana and Persepolis, and their entire wealth, were his, but the key to them all was Babylon. *And she is mine and no man will take her from me.* With his senior commanders, and his agents from Cyprus, Rhodos and Tyros, freshly arrived at their master's bidding, Antigonos was enjoying the elation of control.

The sound of his men's carousing drifted up from the streets and bazaars surrounding the harbour; he felt a warmth within as he recalled the debauchery of youth and then a twinge of regret that his stamina was now – although still great – not what it had been. He had allowed a few days' furlough for the men as soon as they had arrived on the coast as he planned to keep them very busy now that the cold months of the year were at an end.

'Make sure they're all back in camp by sunset tomorrow,' Antigonos said to Peucestas, pointing to the sprawling array of tents to the south of the city walls.

'The orders have already been given,' Peucestas replied, his expression blank.

'Now, now, cheer up, Peucestas. You're commander of the armies of Asia, you've got a decent black Macedonian beard again and you're not wearing trousers. What's there to be so glum about?'

'I never thought that I would come west again.'

'You had better get used to it, if you wish to stay alive.' *How he can behave with such a lack of dignity is beyond me; to think that he used to be one of Alexander's seven bodyguards.*

He turned to Agesilaos, tall, chiselled-featured, with striking blue eyes, richly attired and oozing the wealth that flowed through his hands to buy his master's will in Cyprus. 'How is your work coming along?'

Agesilaos opened his hands and inclined his head a fraction in a gesture of 'so far so good'. 'Of the twelve petty kingdoms on the island, King Nikokreon of Salamis is totally unmoved by my overtures and remains entirely Ptolemy's creature.'

'And he is the one we need most as he rules the eastern coast. I imagine he realises how strategic his kingdom will be in the coming struggle and is holding out for more.'

Again Agesilaos inclined his head, this time in acknowledgement of his master's understanding. 'Indeed, lord.'

'Offer him more, then.'

'It will be done. In better news, just to the south of Salamis, King Pygmalion of Kition will, I believe, come over to us should you take Phoenicia, he and his subjects being of Phoenician descent.'

'That is the plan.'

'Indeed it is, lord.'

'And what of the west of the island?'

'Alas, Pathos is totally for Ptolemy; Menelaus, Ptolemy's brother and his governor on the island, has made it his seat and the king is completely in his thrall. However, King Stasoikos of Marion, just to the north of Pathos, has agreed to support you, giving us a base on the west coast.'

'Very good. And what of the eight other kingdoms?'

This time the open-handed gesture included a slight shrug indicating, along with the sharp intake of breath through the teeth, a tricky and finely balanced set of negotiations. 'I believe that both Lapithos and Keryneia on the north coast will follow Marion. However, Stoli to the east of Marion, between it and Lapithos, still seems to be pro-Ptolemy. As to the rest, it will become easier as you reassert your power in Phoenicia and further south and the quicker you achieve that the more convincing my arguments to the Cypriot kings will become.'

Antigonos looked south and mentally listed the strategic ports from Rhosos to Gaza on the Egyptian border. He turned to Aristodemus. 'What news from the south?'

'It is as we had expected from the reports we received at Thapsacus: Ptolemy has occupied Phoenicia, Coele-Syria and Palestine whilst you were away; he has garrisons in all the major towns and ports and has left you without a navy.'

'Dioscurides,' he growled, looking at his nephew, 'how did you allow that to happen?'

Dioscurides, in his early thirties, the son of Antigonos' sister and thus of a considerable family likeness, was not intimidated by his uncle. 'I did not allow that to happen, Uncle; *you* did by leaving me without the resources to protect the fleet against far superior forces.'

And I can't deny that; I won't argue. 'And his fleets are where?'

Dioscurides relaxed. 'Cyrene, Salamis on Cyprus, Alexandria – although we think that was the one seen heading north to the Aegean early this year; where it is now we haven't heard yet. The other one is still based in Tyros.'

Antigonos turned to Moschion, his agent in that city. 'How strong is the garrison in Tyros?'

'It's the largest outside Egypt; at present it numbers two thousand one hundred and thirty-six fit for active service.'

'Enough to man the walls. Is the mole joining the city to the mainland still intact?'

'Yes; the idiots have done nothing about it. I myself have been using my influence on the council to leave it intact, arguing that the expense of dismantling it would be crippling and that it would be better instead to spend the money on rebuilding the walls, which are still in a state of disrepair after Alexander's siege. Needless to say we cannot decide upon anything.'

Antigonos rubbed his hands together. 'Excellent; it would seem that Tyros doesn't want to make it too difficult for me, but it will give the lads something to get stuck into. Alexander took seven months to break Tyros; let's see if we can do it in six, seeing as we don't have to go to all the trouble that he did with his mole.' He turned to his son. 'Demetrios, have orders drawn up for ten thousand of the lads to move on Tyros in four days after they've had their furlough sweated out of them; that should be enough to seal off the city from the mainland. You can take command of the siege until I arrive.'

Demetrios looked less than pleased with his assignment.

'You'll do as I say; you learned the basics of siege-craft at Susa, before I had to take you away, so now let's see if you can remember

165

the lessons. No, don't argue. With the rest of the lads I'll evict all Ptolemy's garrisons along the coast and then we'll build enough ships over the summer so that I can seal off the port in the autumn and so by next spring it will be mine. Dioscurides, you go along the coast of Cilicia to all the small ship-builders there. I want vessels from every one of them, or their yards will be burned. Understand?'

'Very well, Uncle.'

'Aristodemus, I need you to go with Idomeneus to Rhodos and explain to them exactly what it will mean if they decide not to support me and start building me ships; you'll take adequate gold with you to make a very convincing case.'

'I'm sure they won't need too much convincing.'

'They're Greeks, remember.'

'So am I.'

'But you hide it so well.'

'Only when I'm with you; I'll get you Rhodos.'

'You do that; with Rhodos and Tyros, Cyprus will follow. And then we must plan for afterwards; I'll need your powers of persuasion in Greece. I imagine that Demetrius of Phaleron will keep Athens loyal to Kassandros as he has always been his creature, but I want to know where Polyperchon's son Alexandros stands; he has no love for Kassandros but does that mean that they would remain neutral if – or when – I move against the pockmarked little toad, or could I count on him? And find out where Polyperchon is hiding. Despite my feelings for the lacklustre nonentity, he can still claim to be officially the regent of Macedon; politically it would be useful to have him on my side. Offer him a high-sounding title but not too much responsibility. You'll have a thousand talents; hire a mercenary army and tell Alexandros and his father that it can either be used against them or they can use it for me. Make it clear to them that I will have Greece with or without them.'

Aristodemus smiled. 'With or without them. And without Kassandros?'

Antigonos' one eye gleamed with ambition. 'I think so; but how I get Macedon is a question for the future.' *And then, Ptolemy, you will soon be running to me to swear your allegiance. You will be mine or you will be dead.* Again he rubbed his hands with vigour; it was all coming together. Now that he had the biggest army in the world and the time to use it to construct the largest navy in the world in a region where the timber supply was optimal, it would not be long before all were seeking terms with him. He did not need to fight constant battles; he did not need to fight *any* battle; he just needed his enemies to know that he could and that he could keep on going for longer than they could. This time he would do it without a war. *At least, not too much.*

It was therefore with great interest that he admitted messengers from Ptolemy, Asander the satrap of Caria and Lysimachus of Thrace into his presence the following day. *Do they want to come to terms before we've even started?*

It was the messenger from Ptolemy, a curious-looking bald, pudgy man in a long, white linen robe, who seemed to take control of the other three. *So this has been organised by Ptolemy; interesting.*

'Lord Antigonos, my name is Lycortas, steward to Ptolemy; I thank you for making the time to see us.' Lycortas bowed, his arms folded across his belly, hands hidden in the flared sleeves of his robe.

Antigonos grunted and waved a hand to indicate that he should come straight to the point. 'I'm a busy man.'

'Indeed you are, lord; and have been exceptionally busy for the past three years. Ptolemy, my master, sends his congratulations on the superb campaign against Eumenes; a masterclass in strategy, he called it.'

'How does he know, he wasn't there?'

'Ah, but Seleukos was and since he arrived in Egypt last summer he now works – shall we say – for Ptolemy.'

'So that's where the thieving bastard ran to; I thought as much. My arse, he had better not come near me for his sake.' Antigonos glowered at Lycortas with his one eye, only to be disappointed in the steward's lack of reaction. 'Get on with it; what does everyone want?' He looked at the jug of wine on the table next to him but resisted the temptation.

'No more than is fair, lord,' Lycortas replied, his voice honeyed with reason. 'Now that the war is over the empire can settle down to a long period of peace. To show his good faith in the matter, Ptolemy is prepared to withdraw all his garrisons from Phoenicia.'

Antigonos was unimpressed. 'Including Tyros?'

'Apart from Tyros.'

'Then it is an empty gesture.'

'Indeed not, lord; it is at the behest of the Tyrians themselves that he keeps the garrison there.'

'My flabby arse it is. I know perfectly well why he wants to keep his garrison there: it's so that he can keep his fleet in those waters and control the passage to Cyprus seeing as he has another fleet in Salamis.'

'Well, Ptolemy hopes that when you hear what is being suggested you will see that the garrison still being in Tyros is of no consequence.'

I'll be the judge of that. 'Just get on with it!'

'Indeed, lord. Ptolemy has a proposal, as do Asander and Lysimachus, and it is fortuitous that the three delegations should arrive with you at the same time.'

'Don't treat me as stupid, fat man, or I might rethink your status as a messenger come to parley.'

'Your forbearance in the matter would be greatly appreciated.' Lycortas bowed again.

The man is intolerable; no wonder Ptolemy sent him. 'Get on with it!'

'Indeed, lord. So, to get to the point: Ptolemy feels that to settle everything to everyone's satisfaction, the wealth of the east, which you have brought back with you, should be fairly distributed through the satrapies.'

Antigonos choked.

'And that to make matters between you and him agreeable, on a personal level, Ptolemy feels that he should have the right to bring Palestine, Phoenicia and Coele-Syria officially under his authority as well as recognising his right to Cyprus as granted by Antipatros.'

Antigonos grabbed the jug of resinated wine, poured a cupful and quaffed it back, getting his choking under control. Tears rolled from both of his eye sockets, one red-tinged, the other clear, as he looked back at the fat man in the white robe who seemed totally unmoved by what he had just said. 'Is that it?'

'No. Seleukos must be restored to his satrapy of Babylonia.'

'What!' Another cup of wine went down. Incredulous, he looked at the faces of the other two messengers; neither seemed to register the slightest hint of outrage. 'And what are your two masters' demands?' he managed to say after a few deep breaths.

Lysimachus' envoy, a full-bearded man in the uniform of a Macedonian senior officer, stepped forward, blocking the more effete messenger from Asander. 'Lysimachus agrees that the wealth of the east should be shared equally and, furthermore, he wishes that his right to Hellespontine Phrygia and Bithynia should be recognised.'

'Does he now?' Antigonos drank straight from the jug this

time but decided to hear the final outrageous demand, if only to say he had done. 'And what does Asander say?'

The effete delegate stepped forward, scent wafting from him. 'The same, lord: that the wealth should be pooled and also that he should bring not only Lycia but also Kappadokia under his control; to that end he will send an expedition to Amisus, on the northern coast of Kappadokia, to secure it as well as the mouth of the Halys River in the Euxine Sea and enter the satrapy from the north so as not to encroach on your territory in Phrygia.'

Antigonos slammed the jug back down on the table. 'Kappadokia! Kappadokia, my arse! Since I defeated Eumenes, I am the satrap of Kappadokia. Asander can't ask for Kappadokia!' Antigonos got to his feet, his fists clenched. 'I should...' But what he should do he did not say as another fit of choking overcame him.

Lycortas glided to the table and poured another full cup of wine, handing it to Antigonos.

'Get out,' Antigonos whispered through a rasping throat, having downed his drink. 'Get out and don't come back, unless it is to bear me an apology from your masters for their arrogance and a promise that they will submit to my will and recognise me as the supreme satrap in all the empire, master of both west and east and subject to none. Now go!'

'They're forcing me into a war,' Antigonos said to Demetrios after he had calmed down enough to be capable of measured speech. 'It's Ptolemy's doing; only *he* would have come up with such outrageous demands. Asander has been virtually irrelevant since he failed to defeat Alketas and Attalus back in Antipatros' time; he's getting old, he wouldn't have the balls to ask for Kappadokia.'

'He's younger than you; you're seventy, he's fifty-three.'

Antigonos dismissed the statement as a mere trifle. 'Nevertheless, that would have been Ptolemy's idea. And then as to demanding that I share the wealth of the east with them, that was certainly Ptolemy.'

'Lysimachus needs a lot of gold to build his fortresses up on the northern border; he could well have suggested it.'

'Maybe. But it was certainly Ptolemy who said that Seleukos should be returned to Babylon; Seleukos himself hasn't the power to make that demand now that he's nothing more than a mercenary in Ptolemy's service.' Antigonos shook his head. 'I was going to do this step by step, slowly and quietly. Why does he want to force me into a war?'

'Does he, or is he just seeing how far he can go?'

Antigonos thumped the table with his fist, spilling the jug. 'No; he's setting me up to appear the tyrant and therefore unite everyone against me for what will be the final struggle for the empire. It's me against all of them.'

'I notice Kassandros didn't send any demands.'

'No, he didn't, did he.'

'Do you think he refused or did Ptolemy purposely not ask him to join the delegation?'

Antigonos looked at his son, impressed. *That is a very pertinent question; the boy is coming on well.* 'If Kassandros refused, that tells me that he remains loyal to me in as much as Kassandros can be loyal, which means that he doesn't think that if he joined an alliance against me it would have the strength to beat me. But if Ptolemy deliberately left him out, what does that tell us?'

Demetrios smiled, enjoying unravelling the scheming and politics with his father. 'It shows one of two things: either Ptolemy doesn't trust Kassandros enough to go into an alliance with him without some hold over him that he has yet to find; or he has found that hold over him but is waiting to use it to make Kassandros jump into his camp when the war begins.'

'Exactly; which is why he's pushing me into that war: for him to get Kassandros I have got to be seen as the belligerent. But even then, Kassandros knows that should he join with me, he will be sure to end up on the winning side.'

'But you will kill him anyway, once it is over. You can't afford to let Kassandros live.'

'No, but he doesn't know that; he can only guess.'

'So what if Ptolemy has some proof that you will kill Kassandros whatever happens?'

'What proof could he have?' But as he asked the question, the image of the sly little Greek came to his mind and he groaned. 'Eumenes!'

Demetrios frowned. 'What?'

'Eumenes. I sent his wife Artonis to him with what I'd demand from him in return for his life; he must have worked out why I wanted him to support Kassandros and Thessalonike's claim; to give the pockmarked little toad a false sense of security. Of course he did; the sly little Greek was the canniest of us all. He must have told his wife and made her promise to get to Ptolemy so that she could bear witness to the fact that I intend to take it all, including Macedonia. Artonis asked my permission to join the baggage train on the march west, telling me that she wanted to take her husband's remains back to Kardia; but I can see now that it was just a ploy to travel in relative safety until it was time for her to make for Egypt. She's going to be heading south.' Antigonos got to his feet. 'Quick, Demetrios, send men to the camp to apprehend her. If she's gone, send a party looking for her on the road south; she can only have a couple of days' start at the very most.'

'Unless she left at the first opportunity.'

'What do you mean?'

'Seleukos.'

And as Demetrios said the name Antigonos knew it to be true: Artonis left Babylon with Seleukos and she was already in Egypt; she had already done her worst and Eumenes was in the process of organising his revenge from beyond the grave. *Once I start the war Ptolemy will get Artonis to Kassandros and that will convince him to side against me.* But then a darker thought entered his mind: the prophecy of the priests of Bel Marduk. *If Seleukos should escape from Babylon then he will come·back and be the cause of my downfall and eventual death.* 'No, that's rubbish to scare old women with.'

Demetrios frowned at his father. 'What?'

'Nothing; I was just muttering to myself.' He clapped his hands with resolve. 'Right, if Ptolemy wants a war, I'll give him one. Send your cousin Ptolemaios to the treasury at Cynda; I want the entire contents here as soon as he can. We've got ships to build and cities to take; we shall take this war that Ptolemy wanted to him and then we shall see his quality.'

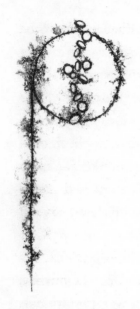

PTOLEMY.
THE BASTARD.

'I WANT HIM TO come here,' Ptolemy said to the garrison commander of Gaza, standing next to him on the battlements, as he looked up at the huge man-made hill overlooking the northern wall of the city. 'He's doing exactly what I hoped he would, which means that he should arrive before the end of the summer; that is why I don't want you to get rid of Alexander's siege hill.'

The commander, newly appointed, in his late thirties and clean shaven in the style of Alexander, took off his helmet and rubbed the sweat from the back of his head, roasting in the blazing summer sun. 'But he'll get his artillery up there and will be able to keep my men off the walls; if he does that then the city will fall.'

'The city will fall not because Antigonos gets his artillery on that hill, Polycleitus, it'll fall because he will bring such numbers here that it would be foolish to oppose him. No, I want that hill left there so that I can get *my* artillery on it when I come back.'

'Provided Antigonos doesn't knock it down himself.'

Ptolemy shrugged. 'That's something I can't control; if he does, he does and it'll just make it slightly harder for me to recapture the place. But it's pointless wasting time thinking about what I can't control.'

Polycleitus gave Ptolemy a nervous look. 'What about me and my men?'

Ptolemy granted the commander his most benevolent smile. 'And that is precisely why I'm here; and it is precisely why I chose you for this job at the beginning of the year.' He looked out to the sprawling camp to the south of the fortified harbour, bristling with the masts of many ships, a quarter of a league away from the city. A defensive ditch filled with sharpened stakes connected Gaza with its port. 'I estimate that you must have in the region of nine thousand lads here, now that all the garrisons north of Tyros have come in since Antigonos has launched his attack against me. I want you to take all your men on a journey, bar the two hundred least reliable; men we can afford to lose. I've brought another couple of hundred no-hopers with me to add to them. When Antigonos gets here I don't want it to seem that I've completely abandoned the city and harbour; there has to be some sort of a garrison to surrender to him.'

Polycleitus nodded. 'And where should I take the rest – back to Alexandria?'

'No, you'll be embarking them onto a fleet of transport ships within the next few days.'

'Might I know where we'll be sailing to, lord?'

'Cyprus; you'll be under the command of my brother, Menelaus. I want the island secured before Antigonos gets himself a navy. Menelaus is in the harbour, get down there and report to him; he's making an inventory of all the ships, deciding what can be used as a troop transport and what as escorts. Tell him I'll come to see him shortly.'

With a brief nod, Ptolemy dismissed Polycleitus and gazed out over an azure sea, sparkling with thousands of reflections of the afternoon sun. He breathed deep of the salt-tanged air and congratulated himself on having come up with an excellent excuse to absent himself from the poisonous atmosphere of the palace after Artakama had been installed – albeit, temporarily – in a suite of rooms that had just been completed in the new east wing. Naturally it had caused Eurydike to erupt in a vicious bout of jealousy, assuming, wrongly, that as the suite was newer than hers it would follow that it was more spacious and luxurious. Berenice had simply refused to talk to him. Only Thais had remained her normal calm self and that was why he had brought her on this inspection of the border defences – and, besides, her advice was ever valued.

'How long before the rest of the transports get here?' Thais asked, walking up from behind him and linking her arm through his.

His gaze went west; he shaded his eyes. 'Two days at the most; Lycortas promised me they would be here by the full moon. I believe that we're still in good time. Antigonos might have taken the main ports in Phoenicia and set about besieging Tyros, but he has captured no more than a couple of dozen ships, nothing to threaten a well-protected convoy heading north to Cyprus.'

'Then once it has gone you'll have no more excuses to be absenting yourself from Alexandria and facing up to your rather complicated domestic situation. If you really want to see some fun, you should get Artakama pregnant and then step back and watch Eurydike's and Berenice's reactions.'

Ptolemy laughed, throwing his head back. 'That would be too great a risk to my health. No, I won't be facing up to the situation as I've already dealt with it. Now Antigonos can be plainly seen to be on the offensive, even though he is yet to draw blood – a state of affairs I shall soon force him to change – it's time to send Artonis north to Kassandros. Artakama can go with her; they'll be arriving with the transports from Alexandria.'

'Where's she going to go? Not with Artonis to Macedon, surely?'

'They're going to travel with the fleet as far as Cyprus and then Seleukos will arrange for Artonis to go on from there to Macedon via Caria and Thrace. The Exile-Hunter will escort them and drop Artakama off on the way with her half-sister Barsine in Pergamum. It would be fascinating to have a spy in the house of Alexander's bastard; the older Heracles gets – he's almost thirteen now – the more interesting he will become, especially as Kassandros has virtually imprisoned the young Alexander and his mother.'

'Why send Artonis on such a roundabout route? Why not have them travel separately?'

'I want Artonis to speak to Asander; it might do him good to hear at first hand what Eumenes was offered for his life. Seeing that he had the courage to join Lysimachus and my delegation to Antigonos, perhaps I can tip him into rebellion against the cyclops by frightening him and then offering to lend him these troops once they have done their job in Cyprus. Artonis can then go on to Lysimachus in Thrace and finally to Kassandros in Macedon.'

Thais looked thoughtful. 'Do you think that Asander would be up to the task? He didn't do well against Attalus and Alketas.'

As ever, Thais was right: Asander had been ordered by Antipatros to deal with Alketas and Attalus whilst they were consolidating their forces in Pisidia; he had failed and the task had been dealt with by Antigonos himself. Alketas had been killed and Attalus and their two lieutenants, Docimus and Polemon, had been imprisoned in a mountain fortress. 'I often wonder the same thing, but then I remind myself that it doesn't matter if he's not up to it. The fact that I'm going to offer to send him an army of nine thousand to add to the fifteen thousand that he already has in Caria will be enough of a threat to force Antigonos to take at least the equivalent amount of his men to neutralise it; I'll make sure that he hears of it from a reliable source.'

'But what happens if Asander refuses the offer?'

Ptolemy tapped the side of his nose and winked at her. 'That won't matter as I'll make sure that Antigonos' reliable source believes he's going to accept the offer, no matter what. The last thing that Antigonos would want to happen is for Asander to move into Phrygia, his personal satrapy; he would lose so much face should he allow that to happen. He'll have no choice but to react.' He squeezed Thais' hand and walked her on around the battlements. 'Using the nine thousand garrison troops who've withdrawn from all the towns that Antigonos has taken over the past few months to secure Cyprus and then bolster Asander is a far better usage of manpower than having them cooped up under siege in various citadels. It'll mean that the army I end up facing here will be that much smaller and, therefore, far more beatable.' He stopped and leaned down to kiss her. 'And winning, my dear, is, as you well know, the only object of the exercise.'

'And you do it so well.'

Ptolemy put his forefinger to his lips and widened his eyes in mock-horror. 'Hush, don't tempt the gods; there is still a long way to go and they have an exceedingly dark sense of humour.'

Thais spat, clutched her thumb between her fingers to ward off the evil eye and then poked her tongue out at Ptolemy with a giggle. He stroked her cheek and kissed her again. 'Why can't my wives behave as you do?'

'Because they have high ambitions for their children and therefore jealously guard their positions, and that involves fighting each other and complaining to you about the others.'

'Whereas you accept things the way they are.'

'I'd be foolish not to; after all, it's far easier to rid oneself of a mistress than it is of a wife, as Artakama just proved by coming all the way from Babylon to Alexandria to upset your equilibrium.'

'Well, that is almost over now.' Ptolemy took Thais' arm and linked it through his. 'Come, my dear, let us go to see how Menelaus is doing over in the harbour.'

'This would have been sufficient to escort the transport convoy to Cyprus, Brother,' Menelaus said as they inspected the scratch fleet cobbled together from the various squadrons of the Phoenician coast. 'But things have become more dangerous now that Rhodos has declared for Antigonos.'

Ptolemy was alarmed. 'They have? When?'

'I found out two days before I left Cyprus.'

'Do you know where Seleukos is? Have you heard from him?'

'It was he who sent me the message; he's been securing the Kyklades islands and destroying Antigonos' shipyards along the Pamphylian and Cilician coasts.'

'Then get back to Cyprus as fast as you can and send a message to him to bring his strength south immediately and not to wait until the convoy arrives in Salamis. I want him to cover the northern coast to prevent the Rhodians sailing around and intercepting it. Send me a message as soon as you know he is on his way and I'll let the convoy go. If it's delayed here whilst we wait for him, so be it. The most important thing is that it arrives in Cyprus safely. If we don't secure the island then my whole strategy is destroyed and the war against Antigonos will be lost before it has properly begun.'

Menelaus looked pained. 'I've only just arrived, and besides, who will command the convoy in my place?'

'Polycleitus is quite capable.'

'Then send *him* to Cyprus to get in contact with Seleukos.'

Ptolemy shook his head. 'I can only trust a brother to do such a vital task.'

Menelaus sighed and gave in. 'All right, I'll leave straight away.'

Ptolemy put his hand on his brother's shoulder. 'It's times like this that I thank Serapis for a brother upon whom I can rely.'

'I don't know whether to take that as a compliment or not, seeing as you have, as far as I can make out, made up the whole concept of Serapis.'

Ptolemy grinned. 'And a very useful concept it is too: an amalgamation of Greek and Egyptian in one body; exactly what I need to be if I wish to retain Egypt.' He slapped the shoulder again. 'But tell me, how is Cyprus? How did the kings take the call for troops?'

'Many of the city-kingdoms wanted to charge far too high a price for the provisioning of their men; King Stasoikos of Marion refused outright to supply me with any and Pygmalion of the only Phoenician kingdom on the island, Kition, promised a thousand, charging a very high price for their upkeep and then promptly welcomed Antigonos' representative, Agesilaos. Whether he has made a formal alliance with him yet my spies cannot tell me as Pygmalion found out who they were, cut out their tongues and eyes and relieved them of their hands. Only King Nikokreon of Salamis agreed to give his contribution of one thousand five hundred infantry and five hundred cavalry free of charge; he's proved to be a good friend, but the rest are starting to look east to Antigonos' progress through Phoenicia and are wondering if they have chosen the right side. I fear that when he takes Tyros many will be covertly changing sides.'

Ptolemy sighed with exasperation. 'These petty kings are so tiresome. They think that just because a few thousand people in some backward little town, with some scraggy fields attached to

it, bow to them and call them king, they can start playing politics and plotting against the present power on their island.
Cyprus is mine and it's not for a cluster of nonentities whose
great-great-grandfathers came down from the hills, chopped a
few people's heads off and decided to crown themselves, to start
intriguing with the resinated cyclops so that he can take what
belongs to me. We'll just have to show them the true meaning of
loyalty by demonstrating to them our strength.'

'That sort of threat should make the bastards come crawling
back for forgiveness.'

'Oh, they need more than just a threat; they need a lesson.
Take Marion; execute the king and let the lads have their fun
teaching the population the meaning of loyalty.'

Menelaus grinned. 'King Stasoikos is a nasty piece of work
whose gullet I shall enjoy slitting myself, very slowly.'

'Well, I'm pleased that I've given you something to look
forward to when you return, to make up for all the inconvenience. It should also bring Pygmalion back into line. Now go and
get a message to Seleukos; if all goes well and the transports
arrive in the next couple of days, which will be followed by
another day or two of loading stores and equipment, we could be
ready to embark the lads in five days. With luck, Polycleitus will
be ready to sail to Salamis in six, weather permitting; it's just
possible that I'll have received your message by then. So hurry, I
don't want to delay too long because at the rate Antigonos is
advancing south he will be here before the new moon, despite
the little show of defiance that I've planned for him.'

ANTIGONOS.
THE ONE-EYED.

DOWN THE COAST of Phoenicia, Antigonos had led fifty thousand men, whilst Demetrios had taken a flying column of ten thousand inland, following the path of the Orontes to the east of the coastal mountains, unseen by the patrols of the Ptolemaic garrisons; thus he had come to Tyros unlooked for, catching the town unprepared for a siege with much of its agricultural produce still in barns in the surrounding country.

One by one the garrisons had withdrawn before Antigonos' might: Ramitha, Tripolis, Byblus, Berytus and then Sidon, the small naval squadrons based in each harbour sailing the men south to rejoin, Antigonos assumed, the main fleet at Tyros and to strengthen the garrison there.

Unopposed, Antigonos had filled the ports, and the small shipyards between them, with timber and men, employing the best shipwrights in Phoenicia, the ancient heart of shipping.

By midsummer, when he had arrived finally at Tyros, the sound of saw, adze, hammer and chisel echoed from the coastal hills and the scent of sawdust from the felled trees blended with the resin of the living pines and cedars.

'Not bad, Son, not bad at all,' Antigonos said, admiring the four great siege towers nearing completion on the mainland end of Alexander's mole, 'although I hope we can take the city without a fight; I don't want to be accused of being the first one to draw blood.' Eight hundred paces long and twenty wide, the mole joined the island city to the mainland. Along its length was a road, with many men working to just beyond bowshot of the walls.

'We've been working on the road, Father. It's just about level enough; a couple more days and we'll try to wheel one of the towers along it.'

Antigonos shaded his eyes. 'What about the last couple of hundred paces?'

'We do the section within range of the walls at night; it's as smooth as the rest. At the far end, Alexander built a platform that can take all four of the towers.'

'And when one gets destroyed?'

'As soon as these are completed, we'll start on another four; we'll be ready before your navy. How is that going?'

Antigonos looked around relishing the activity of the siege lines: every man fully occupied and putting their all into the allotted tasks. 'Much the same as here and all up the coast: busy. We have just over sixty completed that we've managed to save from Seleukos' fleet in the north; not enough yet to challenge the Tyros fleet but it won't be long. Most of those were constructed out of timber that had already been seasoned in the past couple of years but now we're forced to build with fresher wood and the shipwrights don't like that. I told them to get on with it. I need ships now; if they start to fall apart in a couple of years, what do I care?' He gazed at the high walls of Tyros, shaded as the sun dropped towards the west, studded with towers and lined with men. 'That's what I want: Tyros. If it means that the ships we produce in the effort aren't of the best quality then too bad, because at least they'll outnumber the enemy vessels here, especially as Ptolemy has been reinforcing the fleet and garrison all the time.'

Demetrios looked at his father, frowning. 'What do you mean, reinforcing the fleet and garrison?'

'With all the ships that we chased out of the northern ports; they came south.'

'We watched all the naval squadrons sail straight past here; I had cavalry scouts follow them south and they all pulled into Gaza.'

'Gaza? So he's fortifying that too, is he? But why split his forces?' Antigonos shook his head, bemused. 'Well, it just makes it easier for us to get Tyros – particularly if our agent, Moschion, can save us the trouble of an assault and have the gates opened for us – and when we do, now that Aristodemus and Idomeneus have secured an alliance with Rhodos, then Ptolemy cannot long hold Cyprus – especially with Agesilaos intriguing on my behalf with most of the petty kings. And when it falls, that will then mean that Seleukos' fleet which Ptolemy sent up north will be cut off and ready for capture or sinking.' Antigonos' eye sparkled with the promise of victory and he rubbed his palms together with more vigour than was usual. 'Now's the time to press my advantage; you keep up the pressure here, Demetrios; I'm heading south with Ptolemaios and the lads and I don't intend to be gone too long.'

Swift was Antigonos' descent upon Joppa. Giving the coastal town no time to pull in all its surrounding farmers and stock, Antigonos galloped south with five thousand cavalry allowing the infantry and siege train to follow at their own pace. Sturdy and tall stood the walls, their ochre stone shimmering in the midsummer sun as Antigonos laid a cordon around the port from its northern coast to the southern. Ships fled its harbour as the access by land was cut off; a few figures appeared upon the battlements but not nearly enough to imply that the town was taking its defence seriously. 'They have no heart left in them,' Antigonos observed to his nephew, Ptolemaios, sitting on his horse next to him. 'They're running before we've even started; excellent. Another town regained without a fight.' Pleased, as he still had not spilled a single drop of blood in his retaking of the whole coast and so therefore could not be accused of wanton aggression, he slapped his thigh with his reins and then pushed his horse forward at a walk, towards the main gates.

A branch of truce, cut from an ancient olive tree, was handed to him as he came within range of the few archers upon the walls. Holding it up, he raised his voice. 'I have come to parley.' He waited for a response, his eyes fixed at the bowmen aiming their shafts towards him. Silence. 'I have come to parley,' he shouted once more. Silence followed still, broken only by the stamping of his horse and the stiff sea breeze tugging at his cloak. Another hundred heartbeats he waited, his patience wearing thinner with each one, until, vowing to repay the discourtesy with harsh terms when they came to surrender, he pulled on the reins and turned his mount's neck.

'I hear you, Antigonos,' came a shout from the walls. 'What do you wish to talk about?'

Cursing under his breath, Antigonos turned back to see an older, grey-bearded officer standing above the gate, his high-plumed helmet glowing upon his head, flashing the occasional shaft of sun. 'With whom am I speaking? Do you have the authority to treat with me?'

'My name, Antigonos, is Matthias; I am the commander of the garrison. I am here to warn you that this town is under the protection of Ptolemy, satrap of Egypt and Cyrenaica. What business do you have here?'

This was too much for Antigonos, who let loose a bellow of laughter. 'What business do I have here? My arse! It's me that should be asking: what business do *you still* have here? You have an hour to collect your belongings and march out of the gate. You may keep your weapons and either enlist with me or head south back to Ptolemy. But if you do the latter, you had better run, for if I come across you as I head south to Gaza I will either take your surrender or your lives. I will be your choice. Now, there is no need for anyone to die so go and talk to your lads.' Without waiting for a reply, Antigonos turned his mount and cantered back to his lines.

'They haven't moved,' Ptolemaios said, looking at the archers on the walls, as Antigonos pulled up his mount. A clean-shaven, two-eyed version of Antigonos, and, like his brother, Dioscurides, in his early thirties, Ptolemaios and his brother had been with Antigonos all through his time as satrap of Phrygia as Alexander headed east.

'They'll move off soon,' Antigonos assured his nephew. 'What have they got to stay for? Their ships have already left taking the majority of the garrison with them, I should guess.' He gestured to the farmsteads dotted around the town. 'And we surprised them just as we did with Tyros: most of their harvest is still to be gathered and what has already been brought in remains on the farms. They won't want to enter into a siege. And besides, how many of them really care whether they're fighting for me or Ptolemy?'

Ptolemaios shaded his eyes and peered towards the walls. 'Their commander does, it would seem.'

Antigonos swung round, following the direction in which Ptolemaios was pointing. 'My puckered arse! The man must be a fool.'

'He may be a fool; but I would guess that he's a very well-paid fool. Would you like me to go and negotiate to see if I can beat the price that Ptolemy is paying him to resist?'

Antigonos watched as yet more troops swarmed up onto Joppa's walls until their thousand-pace length was covered with about the same number of men. Interspersed along the line, bolt-shooters were raised up, their crews ratcheting back the arms with rolling shoulders and slotting bolts into housings. 'No, Ptolemaios; something tells me that Matthias is not the sort of man who can be bought until he has had a bit of fun and can accept the bribe with a clear conscience. In which case I think we should start amusing him as soon as possible. Bring up the siege train the instant it arrives and have the lads start cutting down trees; we're going to need a lot of timber.'

'How long before it's ready?' Antigonos asked his nephew as they inspected the huge battering ram suspended by many ropes on a wheeled frame covered by a leather roof.

Ptolemaios looked pleased with himself. 'The leather needs to soak for a couple more nights in the cool air to make it as fire-resistant as possible so we could try the day after tomorrow.'

Antigonos grunted; he had already spent more time than he had hoped before the walls of Joppa; twelve days more, to be precise, as he had hoped that it would do exactly what all the other towns had done on this campaign: open their gates once the garrison had fled by sea. But the garrison had not fled and nor had Matthias been susceptible to bribery, even after Antigonos, cursing the garrison commander for forcing him to be the first to draw blood, had sent in a couple of small assaults more for show than in earnest so that the defenders could leave with honour intact. A reconnaissance by a couple of strong swimmers on the first night of the siege had confirmed that there were still a dozen vessels tied up in the harbour – enough to evacuate all the men manning the walls – and yet they still persisted. *Why are they still there? Why am I still here, come to that?* But he knew the answer to that question: if both Joppa and Tyros remained defiant behind him as he moved south then his supply lines would be threatened for the planned invasion of Egypt. And yet what grasp had Ptolemy over these relatively few men that made them want to hold out against the odds? No, Joppa had to fall and if it was to be with an excessive amount of blood, so be it; he had no time for niceties any more.

'Very well, Ptolemaios, an hour before dawn in two days; I'll lead the attack myself.' *Still, at least it's a chance for the lads to enjoy themselves; they could do with the exercise and so could I.*

It was, therefore, with an eager sense of anticipation that Antigonos drained his second cup of barely watered resinated wine and chewed on a hunk of oil-soaked bread and a raw onion, two hours before dawn on the morning of the attack. A couple of lamps flickered in the gloom of his tent as he placed his right foot on a low stool for his body-slave to attach a greave, and held out his cup for another slave to refill. 'Have Ptolemaios report to me as soon as the lads have formed up,' he ordered the officer commanding his personal guard, 'and get the commander of the battering ram here immediately.' Feeling impatient to be getting on, he slapped the head of his body-slave to encourage him to more haste. 'Get a move on.'

With both greaves fastened and his cloak slung over his shoulders and clipped in place with a gold brooch of the sixteen-point sun-burst of Macedon, Antigonos swallowed the rest of his breakfast as the officer in charge of the ram was shown in. 'How's the roof, Argaeus?'

'We're still pouring water over it; it dried out quite a bit in the heat yesterday even though we kept it shaded. But we should be fine, it's still very damp.'

'And the sun won't be burning it off.'

Argaeus grinned, revealing what few teeth he had to be brown and chipped. 'Not at this time of day, sir.'

'Good man. Straight at the gates, don't stop for anything; the assault troops will cover you and the artillery should keep theirs occupied.' He slapped his subordinate's shoulder and dismissed him. Outside he could hear the fall of many feet and the harsh whispers of officers as the men were formed up in the dark; no torches burned in the camp and the exercise was carried out in complete darkness.

Before long, Ptolemaios appeared with a sheen of sweat on his face despite the pre-dawn coastal chill. 'The lads are ready, Uncle, and keen to get it done.'

So, we finally come to a serious blood-letting, Ptolemy; you've forced me into it so I might as well enjoy it. Antigonos clapped his hands together and rubbed them hard as he walked out of the tent into the gloom of the early morn. 'So am I, Ptolemaios, so am I. Come.' *Gods, this will be good; I haven't taken part in an assault for years. First one to the top of the wall; that's what I'll be.*

There was an expectant hush over the dim ranks of soldiery whose outlines could just be discerned as Antigonos passed through the formation, eight deep and armed with javelins and shields; every fifth file carried a ladder the height of five men. In front of them, Antigonos knew, although he could not see them, were the archers and slingers whose job it would be to shoot blind at the top of the walls, along with the artillery, situated behind them, who had sighted their weapons at their targets in the evening light the day before. At the middle of the shadowed host stood the ram, ready to trundle forward on its many wheels, the great trunk of a local cedar swinging on its rigging, safe from fire beneath a soaked roof; it was surrounded by eighty men trained to work as a team to pound the gates to splinters.

Antigonos saw no reason to procrastinate as he and Ptolemaios took their positions at the centre of the unit to the right of the ram; he raised his fist and the clear call of a horn rang out, fracturing the silence as the first glow of dawn lightened the sky behind them.

Forward Antigonos led the assault as the light troops loped across the ground before them, eyes straining to make out the shaded top of the wall. And it did not take long for the first shouts to emerge from behind that wall, for even if the call of the horn had not alerted the watchers within, the crunch of thousands of feet marching in time would have.

Antigonos raised his shield as he heard the hiss of an arrow pass over his head; a moment later he felt the wind of one to his left; a hollow, wet thud, a brief cry and a man was down, his comrade, following, tripping over him with a curse. 'Keep it tight,' Antigonos growled as a shaft juddered into his shield.

More arrows flicked in as the crack of artillery release echoed about; bolts unseen whistled overhead into the defences; the shrieks of a couple of wounded attesting to their accuracy. And now the light infantry released their first volley, a sigh breathed upon the cool air, soon broken by the staccato clatter of many iron heads hitting stone.

By instinct, Antigonos ducked; a great weight soared above him, stopping with an abrupt and hideous butcher's sound. Exclamations of shock were followed by wails of pain as the artillery missile hit home, taking the head off a fifth ranker before skewering the two men behind him together to fall writhing to the ground, limbs thrashing, coupled in agony.

More of the unseen hail hissed in, reaping lives, but the attack did not falter; indeed, Antigonos felt a new resolve flow through his men as they cursed the defenders who were holding out so needlessly. Slowly the wall became a tangible objective whose distance could be measured by eye. *A hundred paces, or so. Any moment now.* Antigonos could make out the faint silhouettes of scores of defenders as the first glimmers of dawn strengthened in the sky above; the light troops kept up their volleys but the defenders remained, returning as good as they received.

Seventy paces. Another arrow slammed into his shield, vibrating with the impact, straining the muscles in his arm, as hits to the left and right of him kept up a constant, irregular pounding, in stark contrast to the steady crunch of marching feet, all of which was blanketed by the constant dissonance of men's pain and anguish.

Fifty paces. 'Now!' he shouted to the trumpeter behind him.

Ascending notes blared out and Antigonos broke into a jog; his men followed, keeping as much to formation as possible over the rough ground. But Antigonos cared not for military rigidity now, for it was not a standing enemy facing them in line but a wall; and the objective was to get to the top of that wall in as little time as possible.

With one last volley the archers and slingers turned and filed back through the gaps of the advancing assault troops who broke into a sprint as they cleared, leaving their path free. With shields held high by their comrades around them, the ladder men heaved up their wooden appliances in arcs to thump against solid stone with reports lost in the mounting din.

Down came the heated sand; up went the howls of unbearable agony as scalding particles seared faces and inveigled their way under clothes onto naked skin, but still Antigonos and his men rushed on. With one foot on the first rung of the ladder,

Antigonos hurled his javelin up its length to slam into the face of the defender trying to dislodge it. Up Antigonos leaped, his shield raised above his head, as the man arched back with a cry. Taking the rungs two at a time, and feeling the weight of his comrades joining behind, he pumped his thighs and pulled hard with his free hand. Whipping his sword out at the last moment, he exploded off the second to last rung of the ladder, the weight of the men behind keeping it wedged against the wall, and threw himself, with an inchoate cry, over the parapet onto the walkway behind. He stepped forward with his right foot to keep his balance as he landed, brought his shield to his front and squatted with his sword tensed over its rim, eyes searching the gloom for a target to strike. But no blow came towards him and none could he give for there was no enemy there but the dead and the dying, and very few there were of them.

With speed, the walkway filled with his men, each breathing hard from the exertion and each blinking fast in the half-light as they sought the enemy that had somehow disappeared. Antigonos relaxed and stood straight as the first hollow boom of the ram striking the gate registered over the descending calm; he looked to the left and right but nothing could he see except his men clambering onto the defences; and then, as the noise of the attack dulled, a new sound caught his ear between the slow, rhythmic pounding of the ram: the clatter of many feet on paved stone.

At once he knew that he had been played by Ptolemy; toyed with and forced into being seen as the aggressor with blood on his hands. With a shake of the head and a wry smile in the growing light, he turned to Ptolemaios as the ram thumped on. 'Go and tell them to stop making that awful noise and open the gate for them. And then find a wounded defender who can talk and join me down at the harbour.'

Leaving his nephew to his orders, Antigonos held his sword in the air and shouted for quiet. 'All officers to me!'

Without waiting for his staff to join him, he walked to the nearest steps leading down from the walls. As he reached the bottom he heard the sound of his tetrarchs following. 'Have your men form up and then send patrols out through the town. Tell them not to be too hard on the populace; I don't envisage any resistance. The defenders have gone.'

'Where?' a voice asked.

'Back to Egypt, I should guess. Their orders were only to make us attack and then as soon as we started to climb the walls they fucked off, fast, down to the harbour and onto the dozen ships that were waiting down there. I imagine that when I get there I'll just see the last one clearing the harbour walls.'

In fact, he was down on the waterfront a little earlier than he had envisaged and it was the third to last vessel that was rowing out into the open sea with the last two making time behind it. Yes, he could have strafed them with arrows, if he had his light infantry with him, but what would have been the point other than to act as a sop to his injured pride? Ptolemy had forced him into drawing the first blood and there was nothing that he could do about it now; it had been well done. *But what hold did Ptolemy have over them to make them stay and resist my offer doubling what Ptolemy was paying? Indeed, why did Matthias apparently laugh at the proposal?*

He did not have long to wait until Ptolemaios found him; with him he had brought a man, bloodied from an arrow wedged in his midriff, lying on a pallet borne by four soldiers.

Antigonos looked down at the man as he was placed on the ground. 'Well?'

The wounded soldier looked up at him, his face contorted with pain.

'What made you stay? I offered Matthias money to leave and yet you waited until scores of you had been killed or injured before doing what you could have done twelve days ago and no one would have been hurt.'

'Money?' the man croaked. He spat a globule of blood; he would not last long. 'We weren't fighting for money. We're slaves; Jews who Ptolemy took back to Alexandria to work on the building sites. We served Matthias before and he negotiated our freedom with Ptolemy in return for us delaying you here and making you fight.'

Of course; Ptolemy, you know how to use people to your advantage, I have to grant you that. He turned to Ptolemaios. 'Put him out of his misery and then get the men back to camp and ready to march south as soon as possible. Ptolemy wanted me delayed; I want to get to Gaza as soon as possible to find out why.'

PTOLEMY.
THE BASTARD.

'SO, JOPPA FELL yesterday morning,' Ptolemy mused.

'Yes, lord,' Matthias answered.

'You did well to delay him for fourteen days and force him to shed blood. You've kept your side of the bargain; now I shall keep mine.'

'Thank you, lord.'

Ptolemy dismissed the thanks with a wave, his mind elsewhere. 'So, you sailed here in one day, which means that Antigonos will take four days to cover the distance on foot, or two if he thrashes his horses and lets the infantry follow on.' He turned to Polycleitus, standing next to him on Gaza's harbour wall. 'That means that we could see an advance party tomorrow and still no news from Menelaus.'

Polycleitus shook his head. 'No, sir, none. Should you now consider embarking the lads today and sailing tomorrow, whether Menelaus' message arrives or not?'

'It is a course that I have to weigh up.' Ptolemy sighed and turned back to Matthias. 'How many men did you lose?' It was obvious from the tone of his voice that he did not really care about the answer.

'Eighty-four, lord,' Matthias replied. 'Although how many of those were only wounded and were taken captive I don't know; but that's how many didn't make it back to the ships.'

'Good, good; excellent.' Ptolemy's mood had been marginally improved by Matthias' news; indeed, it was a vast improvement on how it had been, since, eight days after Menelaus' departure, he had still not received confirmation that Seleukos had been tracked down. It was not knowing whether there was a force now preventing the Rhodian fleet from threatening his convoy to Cyprus that weighed heavily on Ptolemy's mind; his whole strategy was under threat and yet delay could also bring danger. And even as he spoke to Matthias, his gaze continued to wander north in the hopes of spying the ship that would bring that message; and then it wandered south to the convoy beached along the strand that stretched into the heat-hazed distance. He had ordered all stores and equipment to be loaded as soon as the ships arrived and had then had them hauled out of the water for safety. *I need to move soon otherwise I risk having the convoy caught on the beach.* His mind almost made up, he turned back to Matthias. 'Take your men back to Alexandria; Lycortas will organise their manumission and the money each will receive to invest in whatever business they wish; I expect them all to add greatly to the economy.'

'They will, lord; my people have always understood hard work reaps rewards.'

'Which is why they make such appalling slaves.'

Matthias' eyes twinkled with amusement. 'Speaking of which, there are at least twelve thousand other Jews still in captivity in Egypt.'

Ptolemy's countenance clouded. 'No, Matthias; if I were to free them all, building would come to a standstill.'

'But you said yourself that they are appalling slaves, and

196

imagine what a boost to the economy another twelve thousand hard-working Jews would be.'

'I need them to build. Appalling slaves they may be, always making demands and refusing to work every seventh day, but with a will and a whip we get reasonably satisfactory results. Now go, before I change my mind about your own men.'

Matthias saw the resolution in Ptolemy's eyes, bowed and turned away, leaving Ptolemy to contemplate the decision he could no longer put off: should he risk letting the convoy sail without knowing for sure that the threat from the Rhodian fleet had been dealt with? If he did not, he risked Antigonos catching him on the beach. *I don't have the numbers here to face him should he arrive; and even if I did I would be foolish to do so before I drew a good portion of his strength north.* He contemplated the beached ships and the military camp close by them. *Withdraw it all to Pelusium? Hmmm.* 'Tell me, Polycleitus: what's the fastest you could embark the lads, do you think?'

Polycleitus had no hesitation in responding. 'Seeing as all the stores and equipment are already on board, from the moment we started to refloat the ships to when we would be ready to sail is six hours.'

'And if the ships were already in the sea, moored?'

'Just over an hour.'

Ptolemy looked at the sky: it was a deep summer blue. 'I'll risk the weather. Get the ships in the water first thing in the morning and have the lads on standby to embark.' With a flick of his hand he dismissed Polycleitus and again looked north. *Menelaus, what is keeping you?*

'You have no choice, Ptolemy,' Thais said, picking the flesh off the bone of a grilled red mullet in a way that Ptolemy, to his surprise, found very sensual. 'If you don't secure Cyprus soon,

Antigonos will have sufficient ships to beat you to it; and if he beats you to it then you'll never get the troops to Asander to cause a diversion in the north. You can bet Antigonos' agents are going around the island stirring up trouble and lacing the petty kings with large bribes; every day they will be getting closer to joining with him. You have to go soon, with or without word from Menelaus; you must not risk losing Cyprus as you'll be cut off from all your potential allies, Lysimachus, Asander and, dare I say it, Kassandros. And should that happen… well, need I mention it?'

Ptolemy took his mind off Thais' fingers. 'I know; if I'm cut off then Antigonos will double his diplomatic efforts to get them onto his side and I'll end up facing an alliance of everyone. You're right, I should delay no longer.'

But it was Polycleitus, running into the dining room, that firmed up Ptolemy's resolve. 'Sir, I've just received word from our scouts to the north: Antigonos' cavalry will be here by midday tomorrow.'

It was as if a huge weight had been lifted from his shoulders; the decision had been made for him and it came with added urgency. 'Start refloating the ships now; we'll embark the lads at dawn. But keep the cavalry back; they may have to form a screen in case Antigonos tries to harry the embarkation.'

It would have been a sight to warm Ptolemy's heart and ambition as he stood, with Thais and his commanders, on the sea wall of Gaza's harbour, looking south along the beach, had it not been for the urgency of the situation: over a hundred transport ships, at thirty-pace intervals, stretching into the dim distance, hauling in their anchors to edge closer to the shore where each had a line of a hundred men trailing out through the shallows of a calm sea and onto the beach waiting for the embarkation to begin. Mounted officers rode up and down overseeing the operation; their shouts, and those of the officers in the water and on the ships, rose over the cries of the gulls heralding the new day, as they urged their men into more haste in the face of Antigonos' swift advance. Small units of light-horse – helmets and spear-points glowing in the dawn – patrolled to the north of the town, beyond the defensive ditch, keeping in constant contact with the main body of cavalry positioned to the east of the city, ready to delay Antigonos with their sacrifice should he make for the beach.

Ptolemy turned to the Athenian mercenary general he had placed in command of the infantry. 'Myrmidon, emphasise to Seleukos that I want quick results; he's to crush Marion and secure the rest of the island leaving Menelaus in command. He's then to have you and the majority of the men over with Asander in Caria before the end of the sailing season.'

Bull-necked, tanned and scarred, the mercenary grunted, his eyes squinting into the sun. 'I've fought in Cyprus before; they have no stamina. If the force of the initial charge pushes them back, they run. They won't last long if they decide to face us on the field.'

'Make sure they don't. And then when you get to Asander, tell him that in return for these troops, I want him to keep Antigonos busy on the borders of Phrygia. I also expect his attack on Amisius on the northern Kappadokian coast on the Euxine Sea to go ahead; I don't envisage it to be successful but I do expect it to draw a considerable number of Antigonos' troops away to deal with it.'

'I know Asander of old; I'll make sure he does as he's told.'

'Remind him that what he takes from Antigonos, he keeps.'

The mercenary grimaced a smile. 'That always does the trick.' With a nod, he walked away bow-legged along the wall to a set of steps at the far end, leading down to his men along the beach, the first of whom, now neck-deep in the sea, had just begun boarding by hauling themselves up ropes in the stern of the vessel, their shields and kit-bags hanging on their backs, dripping.

Ptolemy turned to Polycleitus, who had overall charge of the expedition until they reached Cyprus. 'Once you've landed the army, your fleet will work to Seleukos' orders as he best understands the naval situation in those waters. When the campaign is complete, if Seleukos decides that you should take Myrmidon and his men to Caria, don't let Asander try to delay you there by pleading that he hasn't got the vessels to get to Amisius and needs to borrow some or all of yours; he has plenty, according to my spies. I'm overstretching myself enough without giving away a fleet; I need you to make yourself busy with Antigonos' ship-building, which is progressing far too well.'

'The fleet will be safe with me.'

'Make sure it is. Good luck.'

Polycleitus snapped a salute and made his way towards his flagship moored next to Ptolemy's personal vessel on the opposite side of the harbour as the escort squadron began to cast off, preparing to leave now that the troops had begun embarkation.

Ptolemy returned his concentration to the embarkation, his eyes ever straying back to the north, past Alexander's great siege hill, searching for the shadow that would herald Antigonos' arrival; with relief, he saw nothing other than his own patrols ranging out in the growing light. *If the estimate of midday is still correct and provided the weather holds, we'll easily win this race.* He looked up to the few high-altitude clouds catching the beauty of the new day. 'Should I be thanking Poseidon or Serapis for the calm conditions?' he wondered aloud to Thais.

'Both will be very happy to take the credit, I'm sure.'

'A white bull apiece, then.'

'More than generous.'

Ptolemy's sense of well-being increased even more as he saw a familiar figure striding along the sea wall towards him, followed by seven Thracians escorting two women and their domestic retinues. 'Archias, it always gives me great pleasure to see you as it usually portends a profitable move on my part and good fortune for both of us.'

Archias' round, boyish face broke into a broad smile whose innocence belied the deadly calling of the middle-aged actor turned assassin. '"It is a joy to share good fortune with a friend."'

'I'm sure we all agree with Euripides on that point. And you've brought *your* little friends along with you; how nice.' Ptolemy gave a genial smile to the seven foul-smelling killers who aided Archias in his lucrative work. 'Welcome, gentlemen. I trust you've had plenty of leisure time with the money I paid you for that bit of business in Hierosolyma last year. You will receive double that this time as it is a far longer job; payment will be on the safe return of Artonis to Egypt.'

'It is always a pleasure to take your money, Lord Ptolemy,' Archias said. 'In fact, it's almost as much of a pleasure as escorting your women; at least, what we can see of them.' He turned and gave a theatrical bow to Artonis and Artakama whose expressions, as far as Ptolemy could make out for only their eyes showed over their veils, indicated that they had long been used to the stench that emanated from the Thracians' fox-fur hats and undyed woollen tunics and cloaks. '"Display to me the beauty of your eyes."'

'Indeed.' *Who wrote that?* He handed Archias a small scroll no larger than his little finger. 'Here's the name of Antigonos' agent in Tyros.'

'Tyros? I know the city well.' Archias opened the scroll, looked at it and nodded. '"Death is a debt which every one of us must pay."' He crumbled the scroll and threw it into the water.

'Again, payment on your return.'

'I am such a trusting fellow.'

I can't help but like the man. 'And don't forget that I am looking after the rest of your wealth in Egypt just to encourage you to come back and not sell Artonis to Antigonos – or anyone else for that matter.'

'"Not only gold and silver be your currency; virtue is the hardest currency worldwide, be not afraid to use it."'

'I couldn't have put it better myself. Euripides always did have a way with words.'

'Which is why he was a playwright.'

'Quite.' Ptolemy turned his attention to Artonis, who was clutching the urn of her husband's ashes. 'I trust that you have both been comfortable here for the last few days whilst awaiting the convoy's departure; the delay was not my wish.'

'Most comfortable, thank you. Might I ask what will happen to the Sogdian cavalry who escorted us here? Why did they not return to Alexandria?'

'I have very few cavalry here so I kept them here until we're gone. They're covering the embarkation; once the convoy has left, they will make their way back to Alexandria. They are in my pay, as you requested, and I will look after them and keep them busy.' He indicated to the urn. 'Raise a tomb worthy of such a great man.'

'I thought he was your enemy.'

'He was also my friend.'

Artonis nodded and then addressed Thais. 'I am grateful for the courteous way that you have treated me and my sister during our stay in Egypt.'

Thais inclined her head. 'Civility between women helps balance the bellicose nature of our men.'

That's the first time I've heard of that concept.

'And yet what I'm about to do is to stoke that bellicosity.'

'In revenge for your man, my dear; a noble act. Are you ready for a long journey?'

'I am; but my sister is not.' Artonis' eyes hardened; she turned back to Ptolemy. 'Why do you send her away a second time?'

Ptolemy's good mood began to evaporate. 'I don't have to justify anything to you – or indeed, my wife.'

'Ah, so you acknowledge her as such, do you?'

'I have never denied it.'

'But you deny Artakama her rights as such; her rights, moreover, as your first wife.'

The gods save me from meddlesome women. 'My domestic arrangements are of no concern of yours, Artonis. If Artakama has an issue with me then let her speak for herself. You should keep your mind on avenging your husband.'

'As any true wife should. Consider that, Ptolemy, and then consider the proper behaviour of a true husband.' She held his gaze for a few moments before walking past him towards a ship that Polycleitus had ordered fitted out with a small pavilion for the women's comfort in the bow.

Ptolemy looked at Artakama. 'Well, are you displeased by going to your half-sister Barsine?'

'My place is here with you, even if you don't come to my bed as I have prayed you would each night I've been here; I always prepare myself for you. But I will do as you command as I am a true wife.'

Gods, the brutes know how to labour a point. 'You will be helping me greatly by providing me with letters detailing the progress of Heracles.'

'Yes, it will be a pleasure to help you in any way I can. He is a very valuable young man now that he is soon to be thirteen.'

'You understand well.' Ptolemy smiled and took her hand. 'I'm sorry, Artakama, the gods have not been kind to you and I have not helped. You go with your sister and, please, take what pleasure you can from life; I would not deny you that.'

Artakama lowered her eyes. 'I am always yours, my lord. I will wait until you have need of me and call me to your side.' She bowed her head and walked after her sister.

Ptolemy watched her go, shaking his head, regretting that he had made her life meaningless and so lacking in joy. *But it was ever thus for some women; I shall, no doubt, condemn one of my daughters to such a life if it suits my political needs at the time.*

'Don't feel sorry for her,' Thais said, linking her arm with his. 'She has made the decision to stay faithful and deprive herself of life's foremost pleasure.'

Ptolemy's sigh caught in his throat; his stomach sank.

'What is it?' Thais asked, alarmed at his expression; she turned to follow his gaze. 'Ah!'

'Ah, indeed; Antigonos must have force-marched through the night to get so close,' Ptolemy said as he watched the northern cavalry patrols racing back across the scrubland pursued by a host of cavalry, dark against the dun earth, at least two thousand strong, suddenly visible as they appeared from behind the siege hill now that the sun had cleared the eastern hills. 'They're no more than half a league away.' He looked back at the progress of the embarkation; it had barely begun. 'This will be a very close-run thing.'

Grabbing Thais by the wrist, he raced along the harbour wall towards the beach where most of the men had still to embark. 'Get to sea as soon as you can, Polycleitus!' he yelled over to the flagship. 'Get all the ships out of the harbour and stand-off the beach waiting for the convoy to finish loading, ready to use your artillery should Antigonos break through.'

The reply was indistinct but Ptolemy trusted the man to do what was best; not that he had any choice in the matter for he needed to warn the beach operation. He pointed to his personal vessel on the other side of the harbour. 'Get on board, Thais, and have the triarchos bring the ship over to here and wait for me.' He did not wait for a response. Along the length of the wall he ran, to the southern end where it once more met land; down stone steps, two at a time, he pelted, his feet hitting the soft sand at the bottom. 'Antigonos is approaching the north walls!' he shouted at the officers and men of the nearest ship, knee- to neck-deep in the sea. 'Our cavalry are not numerous enough to hold him for long.'

The news was enough to speed up their boarding for they knew that should they be caught in the water by cavalry many would find themselves guests of Poseidon before even half of the hour was up.

Military precision and order faded as the men doubled their efforts to wade out and clamber up the ropes whilst others scrambled up the sides of the ship to grasp hands reaching down to haul them in.

The news spread from ship to ship relayed by the mounted officers. Ptolemy grabbed a horse from one, once satisfied that everything possible was being done to speed the departure.

Kicking the beast into a canter, before accelerating into a gallop, he headed from the beach over to the city, racing around the walls; dust clung to his skin, now filmed with sweat despite the cool of the morn.

The cavalry, numbering not more than seven hundred, had formed up with their left flank hard against the city's east gate which remained wide open. *They don't intend to stand; but who can blame them, outnumbered four to one?* But then it came to him: delay could be achieved without sacrifice and he had the perfect tool at his disposal. 'Azanes! Azanes!' He pulled his horse to the right, riding along the rear of the cavalry formation looking for the Sogdian horse-archers. The Greek cavalry commander either knew his business because he had placed them on the extreme right of the formation, or he had decided that they were the most expendable, being barbarians. 'Azanes!' Ptolemy shouted as he reached the easterners mounted on their shaggy ponies, three hundred of them. Two files parted; the Sogdian chieftain pushed his horse through as Ptolemy came to a skidding halt. Ptolemy looked through the gap: Antigonos' force was no more than eight hundred paces away. The last of the scouts galloped back in, their sense of fear unsettling their comrades as they were absorbed into their ranks.

'How many?' Ptolemy asked the dark-eyed and brown-skinned easterner chewing at an unhurried pace on a wad of herbs.

Azanes spat, the brown fluid slopping onto a stone. 'Two thousand two hundred, my scouts say.' He looked with scorn at the mercenary light cavalry that formed the other half of the unit and pointed at them. 'Although they estimate it to be twice that number.'

'We need half an hour; we can do it. We attack; that'll surprise them.'

Azanes grinned, his teeth stained brown, his eyes wide with delight. 'That is always best.'

'Your normal tactics?'

'We know no others.'

'Excellent.' Ptolemy pushed his horse through to the front of the formation and Azanes followed, taking up his place at the centre of his men. Riding out to the front, Ptolemy turned to address all of the cavalry. 'We need time to get the infantry embarked! I need time! I won't ask you to do anything that I won't do.' He pointed to the mercenary cavalry officer. 'Solon, take your men into the town and wait for us to lead the bastards past the gate and then take their rear. You don't need to engage for long, just enough to make them worried that they've fallen into a trap, then get back into the town, close the gates and man the walls with the rest of the garrison. Have you got that?'

Solon saluted and turned to his men. Ptolemy nodded to Azanes as the mercenaries began to file through the gate. The Sogdian raised his voice and shouted in his own language; whatever it was he said, it did the trick for his men cheered him, rearing up their ponies in their enthusiasm before following him forward at the trot. Ptolemy took his place next to the chieftain, unsure of what use he would be but determined to stay with the Sogdians to ensure they played their crucial role; looking left and right at their fearsome faces he had little doubt that they would.

And with a yell they broke into a canter three hundred paces from the oncoming foe; pulling their bows from their holsters with their left hands they clung to their mounts with just their thighs and knees, letting go of the reins to whip an arrow from the quiver, nock it and then draw in one continuous movement; the release was at extreme range, but there was nothing to lose by trying. Their second volley was already flying as a dozen or so enemy troopers fell to the first. And into the gallop the Sogdians went and again they plucked, nocked, drew and released, the elevation coming down as the two forces converged.

Ptolemy was a mere observer but observe he did and was amazed by how each man managed to keep his head level as if he were standing still and not charging across rough ground on the back of a galloping pony. Ululating cries now rose from their throats as their volleys started taking their toll; scores of men and beasts crashed to the ground bringing down those behind or forcing them to slow and negotiate the obstacle, crashing into the troopers next to them. Disorder spread through the enemy – light, javelin-armed cavalry, as Ptolemy could now see – so that when the seventh volley, now delivered at the horizontal, thrashed into the leading ranks, the carnage was great, although Ptolemy had only the merest glimpse of it for at that moment the Sogdians wheeled away, and he was hard put to stay mounted during that brief but critical manoeuvre. Back they now raced towards the east gate, turning in their saddles to deliver one and then two more volleys at the chasing foe, whose taste for the fight was beginning to sour as more of their number were punched from their seats, arms flailing up and a feathered shaft vibrating in their chest or face.

Putting their heads low over their mounts' flying manes, the Sogdians urged them into greater pace in which would lie their safety for they stood not a chance should contact be established.

On they thundered, never allowing their speed to wane for there were no more than thirty paces between the last of them and the front rank of the enemy. But the sturdy ponies of the Sogdian uplands had great hearts and deep chests and never once did one falter; as they passed the east gate the distance between the two units had increased to forty paces.

Now, Solon, now. Ptolemy looked over his right shoulder but, unable to get a line of sight to the gate through the galloping tribesmen, he turned back and worked his mount. Round the walls they raced so that now, in the distance, the far ships were visible; around them there could still be seen men in the water.

Where's Solon? Again Ptolemy glanced back and again he could see nothing. To the front more of the convoy came into view as the city walls veered away, opening up the coast. With the nearest of the vessels no more than a thousand paces away,

Ptolemy knew that they would have little chance of fending off Antigonos' attack before they reached the shore; disaster would ensue as the ships would be forced to cast off leaving hundreds of men in the water, drastically weakening the army and reducing its chances of success in Cyprus and, at the very best, delaying its arrival in Caria.

It was but a faint yell at first, rising above the rumble of thousands of hooves, that told Ptolemy that something was occurring. Again he turned around, but still his vision was blocked; he did, however, detect a faltering of the pace of pursuit and then a change in the tone of the pursuers' shouts. Sensing that his orders had been carried out, he shouted over to Azanes: 'Ready to wheel!'

With a brown-toothed grin the Sogdian agreed; Ptolemy allowed them to rush off for another fifty racing heartbeats before raising his arm. 'Now!'

And around they veered; loosing arrows as they went, Azanes led his men to their right to gallop across the line of the foe who had now slowed, their confidence even more shattered by hostile troops to their rear. And then away did Azanes lead his men, away towards the beach, their pace never slacking so that soon they were two hundred paces distant from the pursuit. In his own tongue Azanes bellowed and as one his men responded, turning upon the foe and, raising the pitch of the ululations, they thundered towards the slowing enemy, releasing barb after barb as they went. Thick was the iron hail that clattered into the disorganised formation now rife with men who knew not in which direction to turn; many were struck down with an arrow in their back as they tried to face the enemy hacking at them from behind. In swooped the Sogdians, releasing shaft after shaft with a speed that amazed Ptolemy, into the meandering mass of cavalry who had now ceased all forward motion. At the last moment they turned away, felling many with their farewell point-blank strafing.

With the sea breeze burning his eyes, Ptolemy felt relief surge through him as he saw the final dozen or so men from each ship scrambling up the sides of their vessel as they began to raise sails and push away from the strand with long poles as the escort triremes waited for them hove-to not far out to sea.

'Ride!' Ptolemy shouted to Azanes, pointing in the direction of Egypt. 'Go before they reorganise themselves.' A glance back to their erstwhile pursuers, five hundred paces away, told them that they would be some time re-forming their ranks but it was safe to assume that once they did vengeance would be on their minds. 'I'll see you back in Alexandria and will reward you and your men for what you did today.'

Without waiting for a reply, Ptolemy turned his mount towards the harbour, urging it to expend its last few drops of energy. Coming to the steps, he leaped from the exhausted beast and pounded up them and onto the harbour wall. Thais waved at him from the rail of his trireme; two sailors stood on dry ground at either end holding the cables that kept the vessel static. As Ptolemy ran up the gangway the sailors jumped aboard and the ship swung out into the now-empty harbour. Out spread the oars that dipped into the water on the first toot of the stroke-master's flute; the great beast of the sea's timbers groaned as it got under way. Through the harbour mouth it powered as the garrison of misfits in Gaza, realising that they had been deserted, abandoned the walls and opened the gate. But Ptolemy did not care for the loss; it would be temporary. As his ship turned west towards Alexandria his hopes lay both in the convoy that was now sailing under escort north to Tyros, whence it would make the crossing to Salamis on Cyprus transporting the army that would force Antigonos to spread his great resources out across many satrapies, weakening him, and in the woman who would help to build the alliance that would one day destroy the cyclops.

Ptolemy stood at the rail in the stern of his ship with his arm around Thais and the sense that he had done all he could in preparing for the war that had just begun; he smiled as he recognised that it was his one-time friend, the sly little Greek, Eumenes, who was his staunchest ally, for, even from beyond the grave, he was still influencing events in the form of his wife Artonis.

Artonis.
The Widow.

To die would be bliss; even without her husband avenged. Artonis groaned and leaned over to the receptacle beside her cot and heaved again; dry and painful it was for there was naught left within her to join the glutinous bile at the bottom of the bowl. Once more she groaned and rolled onto her back, looking up at the leather roof of the pavilion that had been erected on the deck, fore of the mast of the ship, to provide privacy for herself and Artakama. And privacy she did need. Again she wished for death's release as she let pass a rancid burp bearing witness to her troubled insides cursed by Poseidon.

How could the god torment her thus? What had she done to merit such punishment? Clutching at her belly, she squeezed her eyes shut, trying to block out the new wave of nausea that washed over her like the waves crashing into the bow of the ship as it laboured its way north. Nothing had prepared her for this; the short cruise up the Euphrates had been a pleasant affair: days of sitting on deck, sipping juices and nibbling delicacies, watching the landscape go by as the ship was gently rowed up the calm-flowing river. The very image of a delicacy made her retch and the thought of fruit juice was a torment that she could hardly bear for she had such thirst but yet was unable to keep any fluid down at all.

'Rest, Sister,' Artakama said, dabbing at her forehead with a damp cloth. 'Rest and it will soon be over.'

'It won't,' Artonis moaned. 'It never will whilst I remain on this ship – or any ship.' And that she knew to be the truth; yes, she would have to suffer all the way to Cyprus and beyond to Caria, but after that she would never set foot on a ship again, apart from crossing the Hellespont to Kardia. No, the rest of the journey, there and back again, would be on land no matter how long it took and what dangers she would be forced to pass through. But for now she would endure in order not to fail her unavenged husband.

Another convulsion and another dry retch brought tears to her eyes and the desire for oblivion to her heart.

'It won't be long now,' Artakama assured her, 'this is our second day out from Tyros. Archias assures me that we will see the coast by late this afternoon and should be able to shelter in a cove tonight, or even in a port if we're lucky.'

Artonis groaned once more, although her sister's words and her fortitude in Poseidon's realm had given her some comfort. The second night of their journey from Gaza had been spent in Tyros, Antigonos' blockade being only of the land approaches, not the sea – and here at least, she had been able to sleep the night in a solid bed in a house. But by then she had already been so tormented by the sea that, although she had managed to sleep, it had not been a regenerating experience and she had re-embarked feeling fragile and miserable, albeit having eaten a decent breakfast of bread, cheese and olive oil, and kept it down.

And then they had had to wait on board for a couple of hours, bobbing on the swell of the harbour waters, which, though gentle, felt to Artonis in her weakened condition as if Poseidon was venting his wrath; eventually, Archias, her escort, and his seven Thracians reappeared from wherever they had been in the city. She had called him to her and rebuked him for his tardiness that had forced her to suffer more than was necessary; he had responded only with a literary quote, a boyish grin and an extravagant bow. Her anger had been forgotten the instant the fleet left the harbour. If the previous couple of days' misery had seemed bad at the time as they had followed the coast north, it was soon eclipsed by the crossing from the mainland to Cyprus over the open sea. With no coastal protection the waves bucked the trireme as the wind buffeted it without let up, causing Artonis to despair for her life as the contents of her stomach exploded from her in a dozen violent bursts.

But now she felt as if she were no more than the husk of herself, light enough to be blown away on a soft breeze, and she found herself caring not should that happen – indeed, she would welcome it; and it was with this thought in mind that she felt the swell lessen and the ship calm before fitful sleep finally took her.

It was with great relief that she awoke to find herself on dry land; the bed she lay upon was soft and deep and the pillow comforting.

'Rest, Artonis.'

Artonis opened her eyes to see Artakama looking down at her whilst she stroked her brow with a gentle hand. 'Where are we?'

'Salamis, on Cyprus. We will be here for a few days waiting for Seleukos' escort ships to arrive. Menelaus, Ptolemy's brother, was waiting for us; he's just had a message that they should be here in a couple of days or so after Seleukos' main fleet has caught and destroyed a Rhodian squadron that has slipped past his blockade. You've time to recover before we start the next stage of the voyage to Pathos on the west coast. However, I'm afraid that, according to our triarchos, the journey is almost as far as the one we've just completed.'

Artonis closed her eyes; she was beyond caring about the future and lived only in her weakened present.

Sleep took her once more until she felt the cool brush of a moistened cloth wipe the sweat from her face. Again she opened her eyes and again she beheld her sister in the soft light of a lamp, smiling down as she held her hand. 'Go back to sleep,' Artakama said, 'it's the middle of the night. Seleukos has arrived this evening. Sleep now.' Feeling better than she had for days, Artonis found oblivion without a problem. Long did she sleep and pleasant and full of light were her dreams, in palatial chambers with soft furnishings and floors that remained rooted in one place, until she awoke once more with the sun long past its zenith the following day. Again Artakama smiled at her but this time with the round and jovial face of the Exile-Hunter behind her, gazing down with a bemused look.

"'If you are quiet and keep a brave heart, your illness will be easier to bear,"' Archias said. 'I hope you'll recover soon.'

'I think I am recovered,' Artonis replied, surprised by the fact that she actually meant it.

'I'm pleased to hear it. My question is simple: do you wish us to stay here whilst the fleet travels on to Pathos and resume the journey when you have had a chance to eat well and regain your strength, or will you be all right to sail the day after tomorrow seeing as you are already feeling fitter? If it were possible, I would recommend that we go by land, but that is out of the question as we would have to pass through regions that are hostile to Ptolemy.'

I didn't mark him down as a man who would consult me and worry about my health and feelings. She sighed. 'What do you recommend?'

'There is always safety in numbers. And besides, you will no doubt suffer just as badly on the next leg; worse, probably, as it is normally a two-day voyage along the coast. But since the squadron of the Rhodian fleet that Seleukos was chasing has slipped into Kition and made it their base, we have to show caution, I'm told.' He shook his head at the very idea that he should be a party to such a tactic. 'To have the best chance of going undetected, we shall pass a long way to the south of the port and then head west to Pathos adding an extra day to the journey, so you might as well just get it over and done with.'

'I agree.'

Thus the fleet set sail, south, passing way out to sea before turning west towards Pathos on the morning of the second day after Seleukos' arrival. Artonis was unable to rise from her bed once they had passed Salamis' harbour walls. Long did she suffer as the oarsmen heaved on their sweeps, their groans of exertion echoing hers of pain. She had refused Seleukos' offer of transferring to his ship at Salamis as her misery would be the same wherever she was and the fewer people who witnessed it, the better. In and out of consciousness she slipped, her body void, her mind blank; her only sensation when waking was of acute discomfort and the sound of straining rowers below, mixed with the wooden creaking of the ship as it rode the heavy swell, and the wind whistling through taut rigging. Gone was all memory of her brief recovery at Salamis. All through the ordeal Artakama tended to her needs, which were few beyond mopping the sweat from her face and keeping her hair from her eyes as she tossed and turned.

On this went throughout the day and through the night as the fleet hove-to, just off the Cypriot coast, in shallow, dark waters with lookouts posted. Dawn brought no respite as the rowers set to once more, pulling the ship, now west over a choppy sea, towards Cape Gatos, the most southerly point of the island, and still she felt no easing of her affliction. Thus the day passed until night forced the fleet into another heave-to so as to wait out the hours of darkness in relative safety in the lee of the cape.

It was faint at first; a sound that hardly made it through her clouded mind and she paid it no heed. And even as it grew, the sound, or sounds, did not register at all as being a thing of import. It was Artakama who brought Artonis back to the reality of the world. 'Get up! Up, Sister, up!'

Artonis opened her eyes to see a blurred image of Artakama's face leaning over her as she shook her by the shoulders. 'What?' Her voice was weak and dry.

'Up, Sister,' Artakama urged again. 'You must get up.'

Artonis allowed her eyes to focus; as they did they widened for Artakama's head was silhouetted in golden light.

'Up! I don't care how sick you feel; get up! Now!'

The urgency in her sister's voice battered through Artonis' dulled brain and she looked beyond her to the entrance of the shelter. *Fire!* And then her ears processed the dirge of noise surrounding her. *Screams! A fight? Some way off.* She sat up, her senses clearing.

'Fire-boats!' Artakama shouted. 'They've sent fire-boats into the fleet under the cover of darkness. Quick, we need to be on deck in case we have to abandon the ship.'

'I won't be a moment.' All vestiges of Poseidon's curse had fled; her heart had gathered pace. She flung on clothes of the practical, travelling kind, wrapping a cloak about her shoulders and tying on a sturdy pair of sandals before covering her head with a scarf and clipping on her veil. She retrieved her husband's urn and left the pavilion; nothing else did she take for it would only encumber her in the water should the worse come to the worst. Out into the night she followed her sister to be accosted by a prospect of fire and smoke as ships all around burned in the darkness; the last of the oarsmen who had been sleeping on the deck disappeared down the fore and aft companionways to their stations at the oars.

'What happened?' Artonis, wide-eyed, demanded of Archias as he and his Thracians formed a protective ring about the two women.

'We were sitting having a drink on deck when suddenly a ship exploded into flame in the distance and then another and another until—' He shrugged and gestured to the sight before them. 'Until that.'

At least half a dozen fires blazed on the sea as the shouts of men battling to extinguish them rose in the air. Artonis looked down towards the surface of the water, glistering in golds and reds, to see the shapes of two small boats, no more than dark patches in a dim distance but boats nonetheless, heading towards the trireme. 'There!' She pointed at the threat.

Archias leaned forward over the rail, his eyes, unlike those of Artonis, less used to darkness. 'You're right.' He turned to the triarchos, standing between the two steering oars. 'Over there; two boats! They're coming towards us.'

The triarchos took a few moments but then sprang into action; he stamped on the deck and bent to call down the companionway before him. 'Stroke-master, get those lazy bastards moving!' He took another glance towards the shadows. 'Marines, archers, larboard!' A rush of feet thundered across the deck as the ship's company of hoplites trained to fight at sea ran to the side and formed a defensive shield-wall for the ship's archers to form up behind; peering through the gaps they tried to spot the targets. And the targets were becoming more visible with every heartbeat for they were travelling at a good speed under lateen sails with the wind almost behind them.

'Sitalces,' Archias said to the hulking Thracian next to him, 'send a couple of the lads down to the oar deck; we need four oars.'

A barked order in Thracian and a look that brooked no delay sent two of Sitalces' lads down below.

On the boats came, adjusting course so they were ever aimed amidships; neither was more than ten paces in length and both were crammed full of tall jars with wads of cloth stuffed into their tops. Beyond them another of the convoy burst into flames.

'Oil,' Archias muttered. '"Oil quickens a flame."'

The hiss of loosed arrows rose from the archers, their aim more in hope than certainty for all suspected that there was only one man aboard each of the small boats: one man was all that was needed to steer the craft and to ignite it at the last moment. One man on each boat to cause such damage; granted he had a small chance of survival, but what slave promised his freedom and wealth should the gods favour him would turn down such an opportunity?

With no responding volley from the vessel confirming their assumption, the archers changed ranks with the marines whose presence now was superfluous. Arrow after arrow thumped into the wooden vessels and through the leather sails but still they remained on course; their helmsmen, well protected behind specially built wooden screens, were impervious to the strafing.

Artonis looked with growing fear at the oncoming doom. She turned to Archias. 'I can't swim; nor can Artakama.'

Archias did not seem too perturbed. 'Then it looks like I'll be giving you your first lesson very soon, unless we can ward off these boats.' He turned back to the marines now standing in the middle of the deck, unsure of what to do as there was no enemy to face. 'Buckets! Get buckets on ropes! Now!' The force of the command sent the marines pounding away; their footsteps like drumbeats adding to the din that now enveloped the entire fleet for it had been wholly infiltrated by scores of the small terrors. Now many of the transports were heaving up their sails, risking a night voyage just to get away from the danger. Triremes marshalled their rowers and the stroke-masters' pipes sounded, the great beasts awaking from their slumber as the sweeps pulled them away into the night. With relief, Artonis heard the first groans of exertion from below as the trireme's oarsmen put their backs into the initial few strokes and the ship got under way.

Arrows continued to fly but still the boats came on, their shapes solidifying as they passed out of the shadows, rocking on the swell stirred by the stiff breeze.

'Sitalces, take three of the lads to the bow,' Archias ordered as the four oars arrived. 'Take two of the oars and Artakama. Look after her if the ship starts to founder.'

'She'll be fine,' Sitalces growled in his guttural accent.

'Let's hope so; she can't swim.'

Sitalces' reply in Thracian was an expletive of some force as he stomped off to obey his orders, grabbing Artakama by the arm.

'Just do as he says,' Artonis called after her sister as she was hauled away.

If Artakama replied, Artonis missed it as the boat now aimed at the stern of the trireme burst into flame with a series of whumps, the fire spreading from cloth to cloth, igniting the oil within the jars, the heat hitting her face moments later.

Shouts from the oar deck echoed beneath her as the rowers realised the exact extent of their danger. Their oars clattered down; all attempt to get the ship under way faltered and the vessel listed to starboard as the larboard oarsmen rushed across, distancing themselves from the threat. The trireme slowed and skewed to starboard. The boats changed direction to compensate as they came on.

'There!' Archias shouted at the archers, pointing to a figure diving for the stern of the approaching boat. 'The helmsman is swimming away.'

Bowstrings hummed; arrows whipped into the night, speckling the water with splashes as they strafed the area around the man. A scream and an arm thrown up in the air was but a small victory compared to the menace he had delivered. Artonis cast a glance to the bow; the other boat now exploded into flame.

Blazing, the boats drew nearer, their momentum carrying them on despite the sails disintegrating in the infernos.

Archias took one of the oars with the help of a Thracian, whilst the other two took the second, reaching out and leaning down to catch the boat on each side of its fiery bows. On it came as Archias and his men braced themselves for impact, the heat burning their faces. Artonis lent her weight to Archias' back as marines ran in to aid the operation as well.

The jolt was sudden, the weight of it transferring up the oars to push Archias and the Thracians back, sending Artonis stumbling to the deck. As she hit it, the ship shuddered and creaked; smoke wafted over the rail, back-lit by flame, glowing orange and swirling with menace. Cries came from the oar deck as men surged up the companionway, trampling comrades in their haste. Many more slithered from the starboard oar-ports taking their sweeps with them in the hopes that they would preserve their lives as they tried to make it to as yet untouched vessels, all of which were now straining their oars in a desperate attempt to distance themselves from the tiny craft as bigger beasts will flee from a swarm of bees.

And the flames grew, taking hold of the side of the ship and flicking in through the oar-ports to lick the rowers' benches, heating them until they combusted, for there was no one left down there with the will to fight the fire; those few remaining were focused solely upon escape, preferring to chance drowning rather than the certainty of death by fire.

And that was the choice that Artonis faced for she could see that the ship would not swim for long, such was the ferocity with which the flames had spread. She felt her heart sink for she would be unable to keep her promise. She looked at the urn in her hands. *Eumenes, my love, I have failed you; your death shall go unavenged.*

'Come,' Archias said, grabbing her arm and leading her to the starboard side, away from the flames. 'Take your cloak off; it's time you learned how to swim. There's a good chance that we can get picked up by another ship as they row away; to remain here means the chance of death becomes more certain by the moment.'

'But my husband!'

'He's already dead. Leave the urn here, it goes to Poseidon whatever happens and it would be best if it didn't take you too.'

She knew that he was right; there was nothing else for it. Tears slipped down her cheeks as she lay Eumenes on the deck. She unclipped her cloak and let it fall, understanding that its heavy cloth would only serve to drag her under. She looked down the length of the ship and saw her sister being prepared for the jump in the same fashion. She bent down and placed a fold of her cloak over the urn and nodded, steeling herself. 'I'm ready.'

'If she dies we don't get paid,' Archias told his three comrades. 'And we'd struggle to get what we left behind in Egypt back from Ptolemy even if we did decide to risk going back there.'

Artonis could forgive the mercenary aspect of the speech; they would be risking their lives trying to keep her afloat in amongst the chaos of burning ships.

'Hold onto me,' Archias said as two of his men whipped their long curved two-handed blades, rhomphaia, from the sheaths on their backs. Down they slashed, the sleek iron into the rail cutting through the smoothed wood as if it were no more than an outstretched arm. With a couple of kicks they removed the posts supporting it, creating a gap through which they could jump.

'Ready,' Archias shouted, his arm tight around her. 'They'll get you if I lose you. And Rhomesces will be right behind us. Go!'

It was pointless to think about it; she ran and jumped, her hair flying behind her. With a shock of cold, she hit the water and felt hands clamp her wrists.

'Relax,' Archias hissed in her ear. 'It will help you to float.'

Against all nature she went still, fighting the terror of the water lapping around her mouth and up her nose as Rhomesces splashed in next to them.

'Head back!' Archias shouted, adjusting his grip so that he had his arm about her chest, under each armpit, so that she lay on her back.

The grips on her wrists were released and she felt hands trailing down her body, along her legs to seize her by the ankles as another put an arm under the small of her back.

'Pull together, lads,' Archias shouted. 'Now!'

Artonis felt the force of the stroke as the four men securing her pulled their free arms through the water; up the length of the ship they swam to where they had last seen her sister and the four Thracians accompanying her. Archias led, with the two Thracians supporting her legs as they struggled through a swelling sea, up and down wave and trough.

Still and relaxed she stayed, her fear allaying as the comfort of strong men holding her gave her hope that she might survive this unplanned excursion into a foreign element. On, her saviours swam, as fire grew on the trireme and silhouetted figures hurled themselves into the water with little hope of survival, for the confident swimmers had long since abandoned ship.

'Sitalces!' Archias shouted as they approached the bow. 'Sitalces!'

'Here!'

Artonis' relief was great; she suppressed the urge to call her sister's name.

'This way, Archias!'

She felt Archias change direction away from the ship, crossing the line of the swell at an angle, changing the motion of her body; to her surprise, she found herself marvelling that no sense of sickness afflicted her – indeed, apart from the cold, she felt well.

'Artonis!' Artakama shouted in the gloom.

'Relax, woman,' Sitalces barked, 'or you'll take us all down.'

Artonis had heard the panic in her sister's voice. 'Stay still, Artakama. Still!'

'I see you, Sitalces,' Archias called, stretching out another one-armed stroke.

Within a few pulls the two parties were united but there was no time, nor cause, for congratulation. 'Stay still!' Artonis, Archias and Sitalces all shouted as Artakama tried to get to her sister's arms, terror visible in the dim light of her eyes.

Artonis could do nothing to comfort her. 'Lay back, Sister; you will be fine.' But even as she said it she knew that was not necessarily the case for they were adrift in the midst of nautical chaos in the darkest hour of the night with hundreds of other desperate men close by. And it was as she realised the true horror of this thought that the reality of it hit and hands grabbed Sitalces and another of the Thracians from below.

Down they went as the drowning men, trying to save themselves, climbed up their bodies. In the struggle, as they tried to

224

kick away their assailants, their grip on Artakama was released; terror took her and she kicked and floundered as her remaining two helpers struggled to keep her head above water.

'Do nothing but float,' Archias hissed in Artonis' ear, letting go of his grip. Suddenly she found her head unsupported as Archias dived below and the struggle continued beneath the waves, breaking the surface with flaying limbs. Gold glowed the water, spraying up from the thrashing violence, as the great trireme, not a hundred paces away, succumbed to engulfing flames. Artonis squeezed her eyes shut, praying for her sister to cease her struggles as their fate was being decided in the depths, the violence increasing with desperation as the Thracians left on the surface struggled to keep the two sisters afloat.

The shriek, as she felt her robe tugged, was curtailed by water flooding into her mouth; under she went and all thought of relaxation fled with her breath. The hold on her garment remained and the force of it dragged her under as the Thracians with her kicked their legs to stay afloat and heaved at her to bring her back to the surface. And now panic took her for she swirled around and knew not what was up or down; all she could feel was the thrash of limbs all about as bubbles burst this way and that in fire-tinted sea.

And then a dark cloud rose in the water, a spray in slow motion, and the struggle eased. She felt a strong arm around her and then a hand grabbed her hair and pulled. Breaking the surface she sucked in wheezing lungfuls of air, her chest heaving and her throat tight. Hands and arms steadied her; she felt her body calm.

'How is she?' Archias asked.

'Not good,' was the reply. 'She's not breathing.'

But I am; I can feel it.

'Leave her; it's Artonis who we have to get back to Egypt.'

And then Artonis realised what was being discussed. 'No! No, give her to me.' Once more she thrashed, not caring for her safety, wanting only to reach her sister. 'Give her to me!' She felt the body, limp and lifeless, being pushed against her and she knew it to be true: Artakama was dead, drowned in the struggle. Drowned on a journey that she had not needed to make; a journey that her faithless husband had forced her into. Ptolemy had as good as sent her to her death. Artonis held her tight and screamed silently to the sky as the Thracians surrounded her, treading water.

'We must leave her,' Archias insisted. 'She will drag us down.'

Despite her knowing that it was the truth Artonis could not allow that to happen. 'If you leave her, I shall make sure I go down with her and then where will your reward be? I've already lost my husband's ashes to the sea, I'll not lose my sister's body. You take her as best you can.'

And as she spoke they heard the sound of massed men rowing, groaning with each stroke, and a war-galley hove into view lit by the raging fire of their trireme.

Archias and Sitalces waved, shouting their presence as the vessel grew closer.

'I have Ptolemy's wife and Eumenes' widow,' Archias called. 'Ptolemy's wife and Eumenes' widow!'

A figure leaned over the rail looking down into the water. 'Back stroke!' he ordered, peering at the struggling survivors. The oars bit the water in reverse and the ship slowed.

'Who are you?' the figure asked.

'I am Archias the Exile-Hunter, and I have here Artakama, the wife of Ptolemy, and Artonis, Eumenes' widow. Bring us aboard.'

Ropes were thrown over the side; Archias and the Thracians struggled towards them dragging the two women, one dead and one alive, behind them. Up they climbed, Artonis with them, before lowering two ropes to secure Artakama's body. As it was laid down on deck, Artonis fell to her knees and held her sister's limp head in her hands, kissing her as she sobbed, oblivious to what was going on around her whilst Archias spoke with the triarchos of the vessel and the marine officer with him.

Eventually she controlled her grief and looked up at Archias. 'I will bury her in Pathos. How far is it?'

Archias looked down and shook his head, his eyes hard. 'We won't be going to Pathos.' He indicated to the ship and to the sailors around them. 'This is a Kition vessel. They will be taking us back to King Pygmalion of Kition.' He knelt and, grabbing her arms, whispered: 'Trust me.' Looking back at the triarchos he smiled. 'Antigonos and King Pygmalion will reward us both handsomely for this pretty thing and the body of the other one.' He stood, hauling Artonis up with him. 'Take me to the resinated cyclops.'

The triarchos smiled; it was the last thing he did. The smile remained on his face as his severed head hit the deck. Sitalces' rhomphaia continued in an arc to take the right arm of the marine officer as he went for his sword. With a scream and clutching at the spurting newly hewn stump, the man went down onto his knees, staring in horror at the limb lying beside him. Archias' knife stilled his noise.

Alerted by the officer's screams, his men rushed to his aid. The Thracians spread across the deck, giving themselves room to wield their deadly weapons. Flashing in the firelight, the blades – long, sleek iron with a curve at the end, attached to a leather-bound handle, an arm's length – whirred in their hands as the shielded, spear-armed marines rushed them. But they did not realise the danger they hurtled towards for none had faced a Thracian in combat before. Safe, they believed, behind their shields, they formed a wall, with spears spiking over its top.

On they came with confidence, outnumbering their foe five or six to one; but their foe did not cower under such odds. Indeed, they came forward, standing tall as their blades flashed, held two-handed over their right shoulders with taut-muscled arms. The marines stamped their left legs forward, holding their shields firm before them as they punched with their spears at the Thracians' throats; but the Thracians ducked low, sweeping their blades below the shields and taking a harvest of left feet, a couple each, before jumping back as the shield-wall collapsed to the ground spouting blood and shrieking their agony. And then the Thracians pounced as the remaining marines looked down at their comrades in shock. So swift did their blades hiss through the air that Artonis' eyes could not keep up with them; all she could see were body parts slopping to the deck. Those who were beyond the reach of the mortal scythes turned and ran. But on a vessel there are few places to run to; the Thracians hunted down the fugitives in short order, taking their surrender, lives or a limb depending on their whim.

'Come with me,' Archias said, beckoning to Artonis. 'Leave Artakama there, she won't be going anywhere.'

With a glance down at her dead sister, Artonis followed the Exile-Hunter towards the stern of the ship where Sitalces and a comrade now held the two steersmen, their eyes riveted to the curved blades, dripping blood, just before their faces.

'Thank you, Sitalces,' Archias said as if he had just passed him a cup of wine. 'Nip down and bring the stroke-master up here, would you please?' Archias turned to the steersmen. 'Do you wish to return to Kition?' His tone was conversational. They both nodded. 'Good; then you both shall as soon as you've seen us safely back to our fleet.'

'Here he is,' Sitalces said, thrusting the stroke-master at Archias, his hand clamped about his neck.

'Ah, good; excellent, Sitalces.' Archias contemplated the man for a few moments. 'I assume the rowers are all mercenaries; am I correct?'

'Yes; most of them.' The reply was surly, his accent that of Cyprus.

'In that case most of them won't care who is paying their wages. Tell them that if they row, no one will get hurt. Once we rejoin the fleet and get to Pathos, any of you who wish to return to Kition will be free to do so; those who would rather sign on with Ptolemy's navy under Seleukos' command will be welcome. Is that fair?'

The stroke-master muttered his agreement.

'Go with him with a couple of the lads, Sitalces, and make sure that he behaves himself.'

It was with relief that Artonis felt the ship surge forward as the stroke restarted; relief and surprise, for she suddenly realised that her sickness had gone, lost beneath the grief and fear of the past hour. She walked forward and knelt by her sister's body as the Thracians put the maimed marines out of their misery and then cast the bodies overboard. She cupped Artakama's face in her hands and kissed her lips; they were cold; salt water spilled from them. *Ptolemy will pay for his treatment of you, Artakama; but not until he has served his purpose in avenging my husband.* Again she kissed her and then folded the cold arms over her chest.

In silence she stayed, contemplating how she would make Ptolemy pay for her sister's death until an arrow, juddering in the deck a couple of paces to her left, sent her scurrying, heart in mouth, to the rail for some degree of shelter. More of the iron hail thumped into the wood with staccato reports; she looked through a gap to see the dark shapes of the rearmost ships of Seleukos' fleet picked out by the dawn, now glowing behind her, low in the eastern sky. Down the arrows came as the fleet tried to fend off what was assumed to be an enemy vessel. But little harm they did for the deck was mostly clear and the Thracians were using captured shields to protect Archias and the steersmen. There was nothing that she could do other than keep down and hope that Seleukos would soon realise his mistake and they would come safely back into his fleet.

SELEUKOS.
THE BULL-ELEPHANT.

S ELEUKOS CURSED HIMSELF and
his overconfidence for he knew
only too well that the infiltration
of the convoy and its protective fleet
by fire-boats was down to him and his
assumption that the passage so far to the south of Kition would
be safe from the Rhodian squadron based there. But how had the
fire-boat flotilla known where to be and when? It was the loss of
Artonis' ship that would hurt Ptolemy's plans the most: armed
with Eumenes' message from beyond the grave, she would have
been the difference between Kassandros definitely joining the
alliance against Antigonos and him choosing what he would see
as the stronger side without realising the personal danger in the
choice. But it was not just Ptolemy's plans that would suffer at
Artonis' death: it was Seleukos' dream of returning to Babylon
as well. Without Kassandros there was little hope of defeating
the resinated cyclops and therefore little hope of his, Seleukos',
prize. *But at least we didn't lose too many of the convoy. There
remain enough men to do what I need in Cyprus and then help
Asander make enough of a nuisance to force Antigonos to spend men
countering him. But to lose Artonis and Artakama; Apama and the
children will be heartbroken.*

231

Not wishing to think how he would break the news to his wife of her friends' demise, he stood on the deck of his flagship and looked at the convoy of transport ships ahead in the pale dawn light, trying to count the sails but failing to get an accurate result in the gloom. *There are seven missing; that's seven hundred men plus the crews. Rhodos and King Pygmalion will pay dearly for this, one day.* But it would not be this day, but one day soon, and so he breathed deep of the salt air and tried to focus his mind on the task of getting the rest of the convoy to Pathos.

He shook his head and cursed again, reflecting that it had been the first setback he had experienced since Ptolemy had sent him with a fleet into the Aegean; in truth, he had been almost totally unopposed at sea and had been able to establish bases throughout the Kyklades islands. From the Greek mainland to the coast of Anatolia his ships ruled the southern Aegean Sea; only Rhodos could oppose him but they had remained neutral – until recently. And it had been the speed with which they had turned into an aggressive force that had taken him by surprise, hence his failure to post sufficient lookouts as they hove-to for the night in the lee of Cape Gatos. That was a mistake he would never make again now that the war had begun in earnest.

Up until now it had been a question of Ptolemy and Antigonos manoeuvring politically to encourage allies to join either one of them; but now the first blow at sea had been struck and he had been on the wrong end of it. Again he cursed and shook his head; Babylon seemed to be as far away as ever; a vision of the city's tall walls and towers, decorated with ceramic tiles of deep blue, interspersed with figures of men and beasts in yellows and reds, filled his mind and he hungered for the glories of the east.

A shout from the ship' marines' commander drew him back to the west. 'A Rhodian ship is coming up on us from the rear, sir!'

Seleukos turned and followed the direction of the man's pointing finger; through the gloom of dawn he could make out a trireme, its oars pulling at full stroke, chasing the last ship of the fleet as it strafed it with arrows. *What is the triarchos trying to do?* He frowned because it made no sense. There were no other Rhodian vessels in support; indeed, this was the first Rhodian ship of any size he had seen all night other than the small fire-boats, although he had assumed that there were some, escorting the fire-boats, out in the night, but not enough to threaten the fleet otherwise they surely would have done. And as he contemplated the puzzle a smile gradually spread across his face. 'Slow the vessel,' he called to the triarchos, 'and try to get a message to that ship to cease shooting at the Rhodian! It's no threat.'

A stream of nauticalese issued from within the depths of the naval officer's full and bristling beard; the stroke-master's flute slowed its rhythm in steady stages and the vessel slowed as the rest of the fleet pressed on at the pace of the transport convoy keeping it surrounded.

Hailing the rear vessel through a speaking horn, the triarchos convinced it that the Rhodian was no danger to it. The arrow storm ceased and the ship rowed by. Seleukos watched the Rhodian do exactly as he expected: it slowed and gently came to a halt alongside his flagship. Oars were drawn in and the two vessels settled side by side.

Seleukos recognised the round boyish face, surrounded by luxuriant curled locks, smiling at him as he approached the rail amidships. 'I thought it must be you; only you and your Thracians could take an enemy ship without support, Archias. How many of your little friends did you lose? None, I suspect.'

Archias' smile grew even wider. 'Sitalces nearly drowned, but Poseidon refused to have him and rightly so.'

Seleukos hardly dared to ask the question. 'And Artonis?'

Archias pointed to a figure kneeling, plucking arrows from a body laid out upon the deck. 'She is well, but Artakama drowned. Poseidon was far keener on her – and again, rightly so.'

Seleukos nodded, relief flooding through him. 'Bring them over.' *I can't help but like the man even though his sense of humour is questionable. Apama will be devastated; but Artonis! Thank the gods. I'll not let her leave my sight until I've got her to Kassandros. I didn't fully understand it before but she is now crucial to my retaking Babylon.*

And thus it was with two different sets of emotions that Seleukos took Artonis and her dead sister onto his ship and headed the last few leagues into Pathos.

'You missed that Rhodian squadron, I hear; and it is now going to harry our supply line between here and Salamis.' Menelaus' voice had more than a hint of accusation in it. 'My brother won't be at all impressed when I tell him.'

'Then perhaps you should refrain from doing so,' Seleukos said, a smile fixed on his face, surprised by the greeting that awaited him as he came ashore in Pathos having supervised the disembarkation of the army on the beach just south of the city.

'Just like I should refrain from telling him that you lost seven ships and almost a tenth of the army because you *refrained* from setting proper lookouts last night.'

Seleukos rounded on Ptolemy's brother, using his height to look down at him. 'Listen, Menelaus, if you feel it would be helpful to go sneaking to your brother at every opportunity then piss off and do it. Yes, I understand your jealousy that he should have given me overall command of both the fleet and the army but it's you that he wants to rule Cyprus in his name once I have secured it. Once that's done, I'm gone, but you'll stay and be in complete control of the island.'

Menelaus' dark eyes narrowed. 'Jealousy? You think I'm jealous of you because you've got lots of boats to play with and hundreds of men to line up in ranks? No, Seleukos; don't be so naive. I'm not jealous. I'm just worried that you are going to fuck the whole thing up; two mistakes in almost as many days and we haven't even started the campaign yet? But the main thing I'm worried about is your loyalty: why did you take so long to respond to my summons to come and protect the convoy from the Rhodian fleet? It could have been here ten days ago had you come as soon as you were ordered. I sent five ships out looking for you. Were you holding back on purpose? How much has Antigonos paid you to delay and then let the Rhodians sail around the island and support Kition?'

'Don't make out that you're more stupid than you are, Menelaus; I came as soon as I got your message and, no, Antigonos hasn't paid me. My forces were spread out from here to the Greek mainland, securing the entrance to the Aegean with a series of bases; planning for the future, Menelaus. Once we've finished here in Cyprus I've got to get the army to Caria and that involves travelling past Rhodos.'

'Why Ptolemy gave you, a man with no naval experience, the fleet as well as the army, I just cannot comprehend.'

'Then that just goes to show how little you understand of politics. You are a younger brother who is nothing without his older brother's support and has no experience of large commands. I, on the other hand, have been having independent commands since before Alexander died; I know how to think big. Also, and more to the point, I have lost everything to Antigonos and so need Ptolemy to win to have the smallest chance of getting back what is mine. So tell me, who is the most desperate to succeed out of the two of us? And who is the most likely to succeed? I'd say, objectively, that they are one and the same person: me. Now, let's not waste our time squaring up to each other, comparing the size of our balls; instead, let's get on and do what you brother has asked of us, otherwise you'll find me just as capable of telling tales as you are. And, in passing, judging by our relative heights, my balls are far weightier than yours.'

'We shall see. My brother wants King Stasoikos dead and the population taught what it means to betray him; let's judge who has the weightier set by our actions when we take the city.'

The two men stood eye to eye for a few, quick heartbeats; with a slight nod of the head and a sneer, Menelaus turned on his heel and walked away.

'What was that all about?' Seleukos muttered to himself, surprised by the suddenness of the outburst. *A younger brother and not a very tall one at that; not a great combination. I shall clearly have to watch my back with him around.* It was with a puzzled frown that Seleukos went to address an assembly of his senior officers, readying them for the campaign ahead.

And it was with focus and motivation that Seleukos drilled the disembarked army for five days to shake off the fatigue of a long voyage and return them to the peak of fitness, for he had now not one but two targets to make examples of before he would release the army to Asander; Kition would pay for its support of Antigonos as soon as he had dealt with Marion.

'Have the fleet ready to sail at dawn, Polycleitus,' Seleukos ordered as he and his second-in-command watched Myrmidon put the army through the final manoeuvres of the fifth day's training. 'I want Marion sealed off by sea before I arrive with the army; I'll be there in two days.'

Polycleitus rubbed the back of his leathern neck, contemplating the situation for a few moments. 'If the Rhodian squadron remains to our east in Kition—'

'And the main Rhodian fleet is still to our west in Rhodos,' Seleukos interrupted, 'then you are in danger of being surrounded as you blockade Marion, I know.'

Polycleitus looked at Seleukos, waiting for his thoughts upon the subject. 'And?'

'And I mean to take Marion before they can coordinate their attack. But in case there is a hitch, the King of Pathos has agreed to use his small navy to scout for the Rhodians coming west from Kition; we will know of their arrival before they get to Marion.'

'And the main fleet coming from Rhodos?'

'Is your concern. You will need to keep an eye out for that. Now, get going and have the fleet ready. I'll see you in Marion.'

Polycleitus made to give an opinion but thought better of it; with a salute he headed back into the town in the direction of the harbour.

I can't afford to let anything slip after the fiasco with the fire-boats. This had better be a success, otherwise Menelaus will have a lot to write to his brother about.

'The lads look to be keen, Myrmidon,' Seleukos observed as he and the mercenary general inspected the army at the end of the training.

'They've been retreating ever since Antigonos swept down the Phoenician and Syrian coast; not of their own volition, I might add, but on Ptolemy's orders. They're anxious to prove to the rest of Ptolemy's army that they can do more than just fall back in the face of the enemy.'

'Well, that is something that I can help them with.'

'I hope so, sir; in fact, you had better do so quickly as Ptolemy told me to stress to you that he expects swift results, and he did so in a tone that implied great disappointment if he was disappointed, if you see what I mean.'

'I do.' *Pressure from all sides, it seems. I wouldn't think that Myrmidon's got any reason to want to undermine my confidence.* Seleukos studied Myrmidon's profile as he barked out a series of orders, bringing the parade to attention before dismissing it. *He's not the ambitious type either, so he has no incentive to want me to fail so they must be Ptolemy's words; in which case Ptolemy is saying the longer I take in doing this the less inclined he'll feel to help me regain Babylon. I had better get going.* 'We march north at dawn.'

'The officers are waiting for your briefing,' Myrmidon reported to Ptolemy as he appeared through the thick smoke emanating from the fires raging from several huge piles of driftwood – built during the night – set fifty paces out along the curved line of the tall and formidable landward wall of Marion. Semi-circular, the height of four men and made of stone carved with such skill that there was hardly a crack between each block, the half-a-league-long wall had resisted a heavy artillery bombardment over the first couple of days of the siege. It was now clear that it would have to succumb to an assault if the town was to be taken in good time. 'And the wind is in our favour; the defenders won't see us coming until the last moment.'

Seleukos nodded to the two central fires. 'Are the hay bales ready?'

'They are; each one with a rope through it and soaked in oil.'

'Good. I'm right with you.' Seleukos loosened his sword in its scabbard, feeling the familiar rush of excitement engendered by the imminent prospect of battle. All around groups of men talked in hushed voices as they checked their equipment and tested the strength of the assault ladders that would bear their weight to the top of the wall. Their pikes had been replaced by javelins so that they could fully control their shields rather than have them slung from their shoulder. Bets were being made and boasts bruited as to who would be the first of each unit to scale the wall and still be able to stand and fight.

Following Myrmidon to the command tent, Seleukos fought to contain his excitement; despite what he had claimed to Menelaus about having had independent commands, none had ever been this big. Previously his siege of Susa, which had been so deftly sabotaged by Antigonos, had been the largest command he had held on his own. That it had failed and he had been forced to end it by a diplomatic move, aimed against Antigonos, by coming to an agreement with the garrison commander, Xenophilus, had been not of his making; he would have much preferred to have taken the city and with it the treasury. Perhaps had he done so he would not now be in Cyprus fighting for Ptolemy. But that was all in the past now and here, before the gates of Marion, he intended to make a show of his first time commanding an assault and gain a reputation with the men as a fighting general who could win, with minimal loss of life and maximum booty. That would be a reputation that would help him to regain Babylon and then attract the men there to boost his army and secure his position.

And so it was with precise clarity that he spelled out his plan to his senior officers for the first time having not wished to do it earlier for fear of a whisper of it coming to the enemy's ear. The look on Menelaus' face when he had finished was enough to tell Seleukos that his plan had merit. 'Let us get to it, gentlemen.'

And soon all was set and the volunteers and archers he needed for his plan had been briefed. Seleukos, standing at the centre of the central phalanx of the formation, opposite the city gates in the south-facing section of the wall, looked left and right along the curved ranks of assault troops staring towards the walls, hidden beyond the smoke. He signalled with a white flag to Menelaus, commanding the right flank phalanx opposite the eastern section of the wall, and then to Myrmidon, opposite the western section, before stepping forward. Without shouts or calls of the horn, the army followed him. On they marched, their footsteps crunching on the hard ground, nine thousand men determined to vanquish after months of retreat. Seleukos, at their head, felt proud that he should be leading them, for, standing a head taller than most men, he looked like a hero of old, and he knew it, and today he would act the part of one.

Closer they came to the line of fires, the smoke thickening with each forward step, catching in throats and causing many of the men to cough. Just before the line of fires, he signalled a halt; no missile had yet flicked through the curtain, indicating the defenders had yet to detect the beginnings of the attack.

Before him were four huge bales of hay, tightly packed and rounded with ropes coming out of either end. Seleukos took the end of one as seven of the volunteers each took those remaining, discarding their javelins but keeping their shields, transferring them to their right hands if necessary.

'Open ranks!' Seleukos shouted.

Every other man in the central phalanx stepped behind his comrade to the right, creating passages down which scores of archers ran, sprinting out through the smoke and on towards the gates.

'Now!' Seleukos shouted as the last of the archers cleared. With a mighty heave and help from the rest of the volunteers pushing behind, he and his partner got their bale rolling forward; as soon as it gained momentum a brand was thrust into it. Fire caught, slow at first as the bale was revolving, trundling along the flat ground with Seleukos and his partner running ahead, pulling on the rope, taking care to keep it level so that the bale would run straight. Gradually the flames took hold on all four bales as, before them, the archers ran, loosing arrows as they went at the defenders manning the walls above the gate in the south-facing wall.

On Seleukos pushed himself, ignoring the growing heat, dragging at the rope so that the bale did not lose momentum as it now burst into full flame with thirty paces to go to the target. Keeping his shield up, it was rocked by a couple of arrow hits in swift succession, pushing him off balance for a terrifying moment until he managed to get his feet underneath him again. A scream from close by, on the right, and a man went down with an arrow in his chest; another to the left fell, this time clutching at a shaft in his eye. Their places were immediately taken by the volunteers running behind so that the burning bales thundered on towards the gates without pause.

'Keep going!' Seleukos shouted, rather unnecessarily as none of his men were going to stop for that would have been suicide. All around arrows whipped in; off his helmet one clanged, setting his ears ringing and further racing his heart as the nearness of death became only too apparent.

And still they ran as the archers strafed the tops of the wall punching many a defender back only to be replaced by others, for the attack was on the gate alone and was drawing men from either side, east and west to strengthen the south-facing wall. Now so close, Seleukos raised his shield further above his head for he was almost below the defenders whose arrows and now javelins rained down upon him and his men; but they did not falter as they heaved their burning burdens on, slamming them up against the gate, one after the other, piling up a wall of flame against the dry wood. It was as he turned to retreat that his partner arched back, a javelin in his neck, to fall into the fire; his screams carried above the din of the defence and then suddenly silenced as an explosion of flame engulfed him. As Seleukos ran for his life he almost laughed at the stupidity of the defenders having, in their panic, emptied a cauldron of heated oil onto the already raging inferno. *I imagine whoever did that has already been thrown off the wall so that he can examine his handiwork at first hand.*

With the fire at the gates raging behind them, Seleukos and the surviving volunteers pelted back to the central phalanx, which had now covered half of the distance to the walls; of the left and right phalanxes there was no sign, still hidden as they were by the smoke. But that was Seleukos' wish.

Taking up his position in the front rank, breathing deeply from the exertion, Seleukos gave a grim smile as he watched defenders from the west wall to the left and east wall to the right rush to the burning gates to bulk up the defence against the attack that was aimed directly at them. Many still came; their heads and shoulders could be seen speeding along behind the parapet.

On the phalanx lumbered, two thousand pairs of booted feet stamping down in unison, left right, left right, each footfall harder and louder than normal as the men obeyed their orders to make as much noise as possible as they closed on their target; now they cried out their battle challenges, full-throated, as missiles lashed in at them from the walls above, thumping into the upturned shields, the impacts adding to the cacophony that now filled the whole field before Marion.

And at twenty paces out from the gates the phalanx halted, hurling their javelins up at the defenders and then crouching down under their shields making a virtually impregnable roof at which the defenders shot with little success and increasing frustration and bemusement. Shaft after shaft rattled into the leather-covered boards with only the occasional lucky shot finding a gap and a way through to flesh. But Seleukos could afford the odd casualty for this was but a diversion that would save countless lives of his men. Thus as the defenders concentrated their attention on the seeming threat before the inferno that was the gates, the left and right phalanxes rushed through the screen of smoke, sprinting towards the west and east walls respectively; with no concern for formation they ran pell-mell to their target now almost devoid of defenders drawn away by the diversion. It was a few score heartbeats before the two real attacks came to the notice of the defenders on the gates so that they began to rush back to their abandoned positions; but even had they noticed earlier it would still have been too late, for Seleukos had ordered the swiftest men in the army to make up the front ranks of the two-pronged attack. With their ladders carried above their heads they hurtled to their objectives, crashing then against the walls and leaping up their length before they could be dislodged. Up they streamed, in their hundreds, swarming over the parapet onto the fighting platform behind, pushing aside the thin defence, gutting them and hurling them down onto the street running alongside the wall to lie broken and eviscerated on blood-smeared stone.

Along from the east and west walls the twin attacks pressed, Myrmidon leading one, Menelaus the other, around the southern section, their momentum gathering pace with each enemy death, rolling the defence up from either direction with cruel determination, so that soon all were fleeing in the face of such wrath.

The hail of shafts onto the central phalanx faltered and then ceased, allowing Seleukos and his comrades to stand and watch the walls above the gates fall to the assault. With cheers for their mates upon the wall they waited for the burning gates to be pushed down from inside, their charred timbers collapsing and thrust aside by men with long spears, creating a narrow, smoking corridor through which Seleukos led his men.

'Clean it out!' Seleukos shouted as they emerged through the smoke into the town. 'Enjoy yourselves; make an example of them all. And bring me King Stasoikos.'

No second invitation was needed for soldiers who had spent the past year retreating, and a cry went up throughout the city as the rampage began and the men were unleashed.

'How many did we lose?' Seleukos asked Myrmidon and Menelaus as they made their way through the corpse-strewn streets, heading for the palace; the cloying stench of burning flesh lingered in their nostrils. Men, women and children lay tangled together, butchered without pity for Seleukos intended this massacre to be an act that would prevent the repetition of such an event in any other city of Cyprus.

'Less than two score,' Myrmidon replied, 'and nearly half of those were from your initial attack and the supporting light infantry. It was a good plan and it saved many lives.'

'Thank you,' Seleukos said whilst looking out of the corner of his eye at Menelaus; Ptolemy's brother kept his thoughts to himself. But that was fine by Seleukos as it was not Menelaus he had set out to impress with his diversionary attack: it had been the men, for he knew that news of this would spread through the empire and his stock would rise; all preferred to follow a talented general, one who was careful with his men's lives and, since the flames were fed by the defenders' own oil, thus making the diversion even more intense, a lucky one.

Thus it was with an air of satisfaction that Seleukos arrived at the palace, echoing with the cries of the king's women and their female slaves as they endured rape upon rape, and was presented with King Stasoikos by some of the steadier members of his army.

The king, full-bearded and dark-eyed with long, oiled ring-lets cascading to his shoulders, stood tall and erect, with a defiant countenance. Although his hands were bound before him and with the carnage unfolding throughout his city, King Stasoikos managed to convey the impression that he was still in power and was greeting Seleukos' arrival at his palace.

'Control your men, Seleukos,' Stasoikos said. 'They are behaving like animals; my women are being defiled.'

Seleukos snorted. 'I don't think that you are in any position to tell me what to do. As to your women, perhaps you should have thought about them before making deals with Antigonos.'

'He's the coming power, Seleukos; and you would be wise to recognise that fact.'

The slap that rocked the king's head to one side was one of swift, blurred motion; a slap not a punch, as if it were dealt out to an erring wife or a displeasing slave or child. The weight of the insult hurt more than the blow itself and Stasoikos staggered back more in shock than through force. He lifted his head and wiped his lips with the back of a bound hand. 'You will pay for that, Seleukos.'

'Really? I find that highly unlikely seeing as you are going to find yourself dead very soon.'

Stasoikos stared at his captor and, seeing resolution, understood now the futility of his position; no longer could he hope to bargain his way out of the situation as he had assumed. 'And my family?'

'There will be no exceptions.' Seleukos turned to Menelaus. 'It's time to test the weight of your balls. Round up his women and children, pull the lads off them first and then bring them here; he can watch them die before I slit his throat. That should prove to be a salutary lesson for King Pygmalion and anyone else thinking of joining Antigonos.'

'*I* will slit his throat,' Menelaus said in a tone that brooked no contradiction. 'Ptolemy promised it to me.'

Seleukos shrugged. 'As you wish; it's nothing to me.'

'You think that acting in such a barbarous manner will scare people away from Antigonos?' Stasoikos asked Seleukos as Menelaus issued the orders that would wipe out his entire family. 'The money that his agents are spreading around will keep Pygmalion and the others on his side.'

'Yes, I hear that Agesilaos has been busy in Cyprus; but I'll catch up with him soon.'

'Agesilaos? Ha!' Stasoikos spat a globule of blood. 'It's more than just Agesilaos and Cyprus. What about Rhodos? That was Aristodemus and Idomeneus; they turned the Rhodians with the untold wealth that Antigonos has brought back from the east. Every day more of that wealth drips down to secure a new ally for Antigonos. Forget it, Seleukos, Ptolemy is a lost cause. I go to my death knowing I made the right decision but you will soon go to yours realising that you made the wrong one. Antigonos now has Phoenicia, Coele-Syria and Palestine, he has Cilicia and soon he will deal with Asander in Caria. And even now Aristodemus is in the Peloponnese using his money to encourage Polyperchon and his son Alexandros into Antigonos' camp and that will bring in Kassandros if he doesn't wish to be destroyed. You lost before you even started, Seleukos, and you're soon to be dead.'

'Not if I can help it,' Seleukos said, losing his patience; his knife ripped through the king's throat.

Down went Stasoikos, blood spurting from the wound but a look of triumph in his fading eyes and a snarl on his lips.

He taunted me into killing him before he saw his family die. But I need to find out if what he said is true or just bluff. Surely Antigonos has not misread the political situation so and made a deal with Alexandros and Polyperchon? 'Get Polycleitus here,' he ordered Stasoikos' redundant guards, 'I have a job for him.' *He can go across to Greece and find out just what is happening with Polyperchon and his son; this could be too good to be true.*

POLYPERCHON.
THE GREY.

H OW HAD IT come to this: that he and his son Alexandros should be caught in the middle of two opposing forces that were hostile to them both? Having been, against his will and better judgement, named by Antipatros as his successor as regent of Macedon upon the old man's death, Polyperchon had incurred the jealousy of the dead regent's passed-over son, Kassandros, and the enmity of Antigonos who felt that, as the most powerful of the rising warlords, he should have been sent the Great Ring of Macedon. And thus Kassandros and Antigonos had been drawn into an alliance that resulted in Kassandros' invasion of Greece with troops and ships provided by Antigonos.

With the regency of two kings, the child Alexander and the fool Philip, Polyperchon had a degree of legitimacy, but when Philip's ambitious wife Adea took her simple husband over to Kassandros, that legitimacy was halved. Despite Antipatros' dying words warning him never to let a woman rule in Macedon, Polyperchon felt compelled to invite Olympias, Alexander's mother and, therefore, grandmother to the young king of the same name, back from exile in Epirus, to add strength to his position. Never had he made such a dangerous mistake:

Olympias returned with decades of grievance and a burning lust for redress; having defeated and murdered Adea and Philip, Olympias let loose her malice. Realising that he had unleashed a force beyond his power to control, he had voluntarily surrendered the Great Ring of Macedon to her before she would murder him for it. Thus he had become once more the thing that he was most suited to in life: a second-in-command. But at least second-in-command was a position; one to be respected. However, he was second-in-command to the most despised of rulers, for Olympias' cruelty and belief that, as the mother of Alexander, she was entitled to do as she would had alienated the very people he had hoped to please by inviting her back.

And so he had deserted her and fled to his son Alexandros in the south.

But with Olympias' inevitable defeat by Kassandros, backed by the power of Antigonos, and her subsequent execution by the families of her victims, Polyperchon and his son had found themselves more isolated than ever. It had been Kassandros' foray south that had caused him to seek out the aid of the Aetolians. And it had been during this time that he had been joined by the exiled King of Epirus, Aeacides, and a pathetic couple did they make for both had fallen from high places and both were inadequate for the task of clawing their way back up; Aeacides because of his alcoholism and Polyperchon... well, Polyperchon was very aware of his failings, the inability to issue orders being the gravest for he was only comfortable following not leading and yet he craved the dignity of position. And thus it was proven when the Aetolians, who he had persuaded to man the Pass at Thermopylae against Kassandros as he pushed south, were thrust aside under his inadequate leadership. Cut off now from his son entrenched across the isthmus in the Peloponnese, Polyperchon was forced to go into hiding in

Perrhaebia, in north-western Thessaly. And here he remained with an alcoholic for company and the memories of failure to torment him. His confidence was shattered.

But now, perhaps, things were turning his way. *The question is: can I trust him?* He looked again at the messenger who stood before him in what passed for his audience chamber in the upland town of Phaloria, in the shadow of Mount Cercetius that marked the border with Epirus. 'Repeat the message again, word for word as he told it to you.'

The man took a deep breath and launched into the missive for the fourth time. 'Aristodemus asked me to say: "I have arrived in the Peloponnese, with a large purse, on Antigonos' orders, and with Sparta's help I am recruiting a mercenary army. Antigonos needs a man of standing and authority to be his commander-in-chief in Europe. Would you be that man? I await your answer in Corinth."' The man looked at Polyperchon, wondering if he would have to repeat himself for the fifth time.

Commander-in-chief in Europe? But what would my orders be? 'Did he say what he would be expecting me to achieve?'

'Sir, he did not confide in me. He only gave me this message and said that I should either bring your negative answer verbally or escort you to Corinth so that you could answer him in person. That is all I know.'

Polyperchon waved his hand in dismissal. 'Quarters will be found for you whilst I contemplate my position.'

Vacillation is the curse of men who need to be told what to do and yet have no one to do so; for two days Polyperchon was prey to indecision: a champion of hesitancy, drowning in his own irresolution. 'What if Antigonos doesn't send the reinforcements I need when Kassandros comes south?' he asked. The question was aimed at Aeacides but he was too busy worshipping at the feet of Bacchus to be able to provide a coherent, or indeed relevant, reply. 'What if he doesn't manage to rebuild his fleet in time?'

And that was his main concern: that he should declare for the power that was furthest away from him only to be let down by Antigonos' lack of sea-power and then defeated by Kassandros who had no need of a fleet to get to him.

Polyperchon pondered the conundrum once again but found he could come no nearer to a resolution. But then, once again, his face brightened. 'But commander-in-chief in Europe does sound important.' He held out his cup for a slave to refill – Aeacides had long since dispensed with this method, preferring instead to hold the jug in one hand and his cup in the other – although the cup soon became superfluous. Polyperchon had long ceased to notice his ally's drinking and carried on his one-sided conversation. 'It would be a return to the dignity I once had.' *And it would be a return to having to act upon my own initiative if Antigonos makes my command independent.* Perplexed, he took a sip of wine; it was as he savoured the vintage that the solution to his problem presented itself. 'Alexandros! Of course!'

Aeacides looked over to him with unfocused, bleary eyes. 'Whass about shim?'

'From his position dug in across the isthmus at Corinth he'll manage the campaign whilst I will undertake all of the ceremonial functions of the position and take charge of all the administration.'

Aeacides stared at him, his face blotched and flabby, and then fell back onto his couch spilling both jug and cup over himself.

But Polyperchon did not notice for he was toasting himself on the subtlety of his plan. When his cup was empty he clapped his hands for his steward. 'Bring Aristodemus' messenger to me

250

and then organise my luggage; we're going south tomorrow and I intend to stay there for a long time.'

'Eight thousand?' Polyperchon found it hard to believe what he had just heard. 'Eight thousand mercenaries? Is that all you've got for me?'

'Along with your son Alexandros' ten thousand Macedonians, that should be more than adequate to force Kassandros to claim allegiance to Antigonos or to come south and waste time on a futile campaign against you in the Peloponnese.'

'But he could well bring an army of thirty thousand south with him and then call upon Athens and now Thebes to boost his numbers. I could be overwhelmed.'

Aristodemus smiled in a patient and long-suffering manner. 'Not if you keep dug in across the isthmus as your son has managed to do for the last five years. It's an impregnable position even if the enemy sail around and come from the south; and in staying here you will be doing Antigonos a great service as his commander-in-chief in Europe; he'll not forget that, I guarantee you.'

'It will be fine, Father,' Alexandros said, laying a hand upon his shoulder. 'My defences all across the isthmus are solid; nothing can move us. All we need do is sit here and make threatening noises in the direction of Thebes and Athens and then wait and see what Kassandros decides to do.'

Polyperchon looked out over the west-facing harbour at Corinth to the ship that had brought him along the Gulf from Chalcis, in Aetolia, thus avoiding travelling too close to Kassandros' new stronghold of Thebes, with the small escort that, humiliatingly, was all he could muster. He fought the urge to get straight back on board and make the return journey, knowing that should he do so he would be evermore condemned to a life of obscurity, for no one would ever make him an offer like this again; even if it was less than what he would have wished. But the presence of his son soothed him and boosted the confidence that had been so lacking since his humiliation by Kassandros, firstly at Pydna and then again at Thermopylae. No, he needed to feel the importance of command again; he needed the respect and deference that came with it and, sheltered by Alexandros, he would have that. 'Very well, Aristodemus,' Polyperchon said, without, for once during the meeting, a sense of hesitancy in his voice, 'I will do it. I will be Antigonos' commander-in-chief in Europe.'

The Greek smiled, his face all teeth and beard. 'That is a great relief to Antigonos and myself; a strong and decisive man representing his interests here is what he needs so that he can concentrate on taking Tyros and then securing Anatolia. After that your reward will be judged upon the service that you have done him. However, I will give you one word of warning: I have set in motion a series of diplomatic initiatives in the Peloponnese stitching together a coalition of cities that have traditionally been enemies; when I tell you that Sparta is a part of this as well as Argos, Olynthioas, Paracetos and many more then you will understand the precariousness of the alliance.' The Greek's smile widened even further so that he resembled a comedic theatrical mask. 'Therefore I would urge you not to make any *diplomatic initiatives* of your own that might upset the delicate balance I have struck.'

Polyperchon bristled at being told what to do by a Greek. 'But as Antigonos' commander-in-chief in Europe I should have the right to engage with my allies and make new ones.'

'Of course you should,' Aristodemus crooned, 'and you do have that right; indeed you do. But you just won't use it, will you?'

Polyperchon made no reply, his thoughts on the subject clear on his face.

'Will you, Polyperchon?' Aristodemus pressed.

Polyperchon swallowed. 'I will use my initiative.'

'And I will help him in the decisions,' Alexandros put in. 'I understand the work that has been put into an alliance in Antigonos' favour and we won't upset Sparta or any other of the cities.'

Aristodemus looked from son to father and then back to the son again. 'That would be all very well, if you were always to be here; but you won't, Alexandros.'

Polyperchon looked at Aristodemus, worry written in his frown. 'What do you mean?'

'I mean that I have a couple more things to attend to here, people to see and exchange views with, before I head back to Tyros in half a moon, perhaps slightly more. Because of the nature of our respective geographical positions, Antigonos feels that it would be advantageous to have a face to face meeting as soon as possible, at which time we will ask the army assembly to recognise the alliance and to decide what to do with whoever might refuse to join us. So I will take you with me when I go, Alexandros. Your father will just have to manage as best he can for the four or five months or so whilst you're gone.'

'Four or five months?'

'Yes, you won't get back before the sailing season ends, so you'll have to wait until next spring. So, with those circumstances in mind, I shall ask you again, Polyperchon, whether you will refrain from using your right as commander-in-chief in Europe to engage with your allies in diplomatic talks until your son, who understands far better the position in the Peloponnese, has returned.' Again the Greek smiled. 'It's a take it or leave it situation. I'm sure the Epiriot border will get less and less agreeable now that the summer is coming to a close.'

It's an affront to my dignity but all I can do is agree. 'I'll refrain.'

'Good. We have an agreement, gentlemen.'

But if I deem it necessary then, as commander-in-chief in Europe, I shall be obliged to make some diplomatic moves.

Once more it was invigorating to get back into military life on campaign. In the few days he had with Alexandros before his departure for Tyros, Polyperchon inspected each and every fortified position, camp and supply depot; and there was much that he found to criticise: the standard of the men's appearance left a lot to be desired almost everywhere he went, and as for the state of their accommodation, be it tentage or billets, that was some of the untidiest he had ever seen, even during his time in the east before he had fallen foul of Alexander and been forced to return to the west. But it was the discipline of the troops, especially the newly employed mercenaries, which really offended his strict military code: hard fighters they might be but they had no idea of how to parade in straight lines or, indeed, of the importance of standing firmly and smartly to attention.

'They're worse than marines,' Polyperchon said to his son on the evening before the latter's departure. 'This is the fourth unit of mercenaries I've inspected and none of them looks like a soldier.'

Alexandros sighed; he was used to his father's martinet approach to soldiering. 'They might not look like soldiers to you, Father, but to me they look like hardened killers who would as soon slit their grandmother's throat for another handful of coinage as they would yours if you start to give them extra drill.'

Polyperchon indicated to the four units of mercenary peltasts and two of heavy hoplites chatting amongst themselves as they stood in a series of rough rectangular blocks. 'But they can't even form up correctly.'

'They are not paid to form up correctly; they are paid to die having killed at least two of their opposite numbers. That is how we win battles, Father, it's not by seeing who can stand up straightest, doing the best impression of having a spear shaft up their arse.'

The young these days have no idea of pride in appearance. 'I'll knock some military pride into them whilst you're away and then you'll be surprised by their morale when you come back.'

'I'll be surprised if they are still here when I come back, not by the state of their morale as I know what that will be like, should you attempt to do that, so don't. That's how you lost over half of your army in desertions to Kassandros before he drove you into Pydna; they were all on fatigues by the time you were two days out from Pella from what I heard.'

'A smart, well-drilled army is an efficient army.'

'No, Father, it's not; it's a hive of misery and mutiny. My lads have been with me for almost seven years now and we have got to know one another very well. I don't make life too tough for them and they die for me, if it's required. If you start changing their conditions then they will change theirs too in the quickest way they know how by swapping sides at the first opportunity. As for these mercenaries, at the moment they're very pleased to have a billet, but as the war spreads we will look like a very bad option if they're spending most of their spare time cleaning the latrine just because they had a stain on their tunic. Kassandros and Ptolemy don't care for such niceties and can probably match Antigonos' pay; he, if I need to remind you, is the real employer of these men.'

'But I'm his commander-in-chief in Europe and therefore responsible for the state of his troops.'

'Father! No more; you will do nothing to alter the regimes that I have in place here, be it for the eight thousand new mercenaries or my veteran ten thousand Macedonians. Do I make myself clear?'

Polyperchon glared at the offending soldiery.

'If I come back and find that the lads have got complaints about how they have been treated whilst I've been away, I'll not forgive you. And I'll know whether you have been mistreating them because Penelope is not coming with me.'

'What does your wife know of soldiers or military discipline?'

'She has been with the lads as long as I have and they love her; she'll give me a fair account if they come to me with grievances. Do I make myself clear?'

Everyone is trying to undermine my position, even my son. What's the point in having a position if no one respects it?

'Father?'

'Very well.'

'Good, we understand each other.'

But I'll tighten things up around here nevertheless.

And so the route marches and inspections began the moment that Alexandros' ship had sailed from the port of Cenchreae, on the east coast of the isthmus, for Polyperchon was determined to prove his son wrong and had the winter in which to do it. It was gruelling work but Polyperchon put his heart into it and it was not long before he had a very satisfactory long list of men on fatigues; nor was it long before he started to notice a marked improvement in the men's appearance if not their demeanour, which, if anything, was considerably worse.

But that was of no concern to Polyperchon as he toured his command; what did concern him, though, was a message from a man by the name of Polycleitus saying how he wished to come and parley under a branch of truce. 'Who is he?' he demanded of the messenger.

'One of Ptolemy's naval commanders who is currently a part of Seleukos' command in Cyprus,' was the reply.

'What does he want?'

'To parley.'

'Yes, I know, but what about?'

The man looked confused. 'How should I know? I'm just the herald organising the parley.'

What if it's an ultimatum? What if I've chosen the wrong side? But I have no choice; if I send him away, I alienate Ptolemy and Seleukos without even knowing what they wanted of me. 'Very well; I shall meet him at Cenchreae this evening.'

'It's simple, really,' Polycleitus said as they sat at a dockside tavern with a bowl of grilled squid and a jug of resinated wine on the table before them. 'Seleukos wants to know who you are fighting for if you are fighting at all.'

Polyperchon dipped a tentacle into a bowl of olive oil and crunched upon it. 'I would have thought that a little more respect is my due; you should address me as "sir".'

'Oh, should I? I'm sorry, I didn't know. I thought that you were no longer the regent of Macedon.'

'I'm not. I'm commander-in-chief in Europe.'

'Really? And who appointed you that?'

'Antigonos.'

'Did he now? Well, Ptolemy will be fascinated to find that out, as I'm sure Seleukos will very soon after I've reported it to him too.'

Polyperchon smiled an empty smile and washed down his tentacle with a gulp of wine, realising that he had made a mistake by revealing his new position and allegiance before he had ascertained just what Polycleitus had come for. *I can't have the man killed as he came under a branch of truce and there are too many witnesses; I would be shunned for the rest of my life. I just have to trust that I've chosen the right side and that Antigonos can protect me from Ptolemy and Seleukos.*

SELEUKOS.
THE BULL-ELEPHANT.

HALICARNASSUS, WITH THE great tomb of Mausolus dominating the city, shone in the morning sun. To either side of a crowded, waterside agora, filled with fishermen selling their catch, the quays and warehouses of the busy port bustled with activity; ships already docked were hastily prepared to leave their berths to rest at anchor beyond the harbour walls in order to make room for the incoming fleet. Past the Royal Island, to the right of the harbour, Seleukos' ship glided, its oars dipping in slow time, sails furled, his fleet following. Behind it, the transport ships turned to starboard and sailed to the other side of the island to disembark the troops along the shoreline of what had been Alexander's camp during his siege of the city almost twenty tears previously.

And the scars of that siege remained everywhere for the Persians had burned the city as they fled and many of the buildings were yet to be restored to their former glory. But the Tomb of Mausolus, built upon a huge platform, the height of twenty men, engraved with many reliefs celebrating the life of the former King of Caria – albeit under the dominion of Darius, the King of Kings – was in the condition it had been in upon its completion just thirty-six years previously. The tomb itself, surrounded by thirty-six columns and topped with a statue of a quadriga, had been restored; its lush paintwork, deep reds and purples offset by bright blues and yellows, shimmered in the growing heat of the day, inspiring awe in all arriving in the port. That such a thing could be built amazed most people, thus making it one of the wonders of the world; but Seleukos had seen Babylon and for him it was but a shadow of the greatness of the Ziggurat of Bel Marduk. *I wonder if my replacement, Pythan, has continued with my rebuilding of it.* The thought added yet more urgency in his desire to return to the city he considered his own. He felt almost a sexual jealousy at the thought of Pythan and Teutamus enjoying her fruits.

It had been this growing urgency ever since hostilities had started again with Antigonos that had fuelled Seleukos' rapid subjection of the wavering cities on Cyprus – that and the cruelty that he displayed at Marion. The entire family of King Stasoikos had been executed in front of a cowed population and an oligarchy installed. The shockwave had shaken every king on the island, and all who had been thinking about going over to Antigonos suddenly became very eager to profess just how much they respected Ptolemy; treaties had been signed and hostages given by all the remaining kings except one, Pygmalion. But the King of Kition had made a fatal miscalculation: he had counted on the support of the Rhodian navy. However, the Rhodian navy had not come, and so Pygmalion had looked to Antigonos in the east, but all that came from that direction was the Ptolemaic fleet based at Tyros. The king had been left with no alternative but to throw himself on Seleukos' mercy and hope that handing over the Rhodian squadron along with the heads of all the triarchoi would incline him to mercy; and it had, for Seleukos had realised that should all rebellious kings be treated as Stasoikos was then none would ever surrender again. Pygmalion was allowed to keep his throne and swore many oaths of loyalty in thanks.

Thus Seleukos had left Menelaus in command of an island entirely loyal to the Ptolemaic cause and with very little doubt as to Seleukos' resolve or the weightiness of his testicles. With the autumn equinox come and gone, Seleukos took his fleet and the army to Caria before the winter closed the sea-lanes, sending Polycleitus, upon his return from the interesting parley with Polyperchon, on a diversionary cruise along the coasts of Cilicia, Pamphylia and Lycia.

And so with the Rhodians tracking the diversion, Seleukos had come to Halicarnassus safely, with his army and navy both blooded and eager for more; but whether the army would be used to its best effect was the worry that played on Seleukos' mind as his ship berthed. *Much rests on you, Asander; it's time for you to show your quality.* It was of no surprise to Seleukos to see Asander himself waiting on the quay as he descended the gangway. Running to fat and balding, the once martial satrap looked more like a well-to-do merchant than a former general in the army of Macedon. 'Ptolemy sends his greetings,' Seleukos said, allowing himself to be enfolded in a soft embrace, leaning forward, for Asander was more than a head shorter than he.

'My dear fellow, my gratitude to Ptolemy will be expressed in the amount of inconvenience I cause for Antigonos,' Asander said as he released Seleukos and held him by the shoulders at arm's length, looking up at him.

'Inconvenience is, I hope, an understatement.' Seleukos lifted the hands from his shoulders, looking directly into Asander's bloodshot eyes, in no mood now to be polite after such a half-hearted boast. 'We all expect you to be much more than an inconvenience, Asander. An inconvenience is something that causes mild annoyance forcing you perhaps to tut or purse your lips: piles and suchlike. No, Asander, you are going to be a major threat to him; do you understand? A threat; something he fears and is forced to react to, thus weakening his strength in other parts of the conflict.'

Asander took a step back at the vehemence in Seleukos' tone, his eyes widening in surprise. 'Of course that is what I shall be.'

'Well then, say it; say it and mean it.'

'I shall be a threat to Antigonos; a direct threat both by occupying Lycia to the south and by taking Celaenae, his capital in Phrygia.'

'And sending the expedition to Amisius?'

'That has already departed under the command of my brother, Agathon.'

Seleukos slapped him on the shoulder. 'That's better; why didn't you put it that way before rather than just say that you will be a dose of piles?'

'My dear fellow, I have never been one given to hyperbole, quite the opposite in fact as you have surely noticed. I know as well as you that unless Antigonos is stopped, my comfort and well-being are under threat as I was appointed by Alexander and then supported Antipatros, so there is no need to get all aggressive with me about my choice of words; I know what my task is.' His eyes went past Seleukos, looking up the gangway to Artonis who was walking down accompanied by Archias and his Thracians. 'And who is that?' he asked, unable to keep the interest out of his voice.

'That's Archias the Exile-Hunter,' Seleukos replied, deliberately misunderstanding.

'I know who that is, I've availed myself of his services a couple of times. No, who's the girl?'

'Oh, the girl? That is Eumenes' widow, Artonis; and she is not for you so you can forget about looking behind her veil, or any other item of her clothing for that matter. I'm taking her to Kassandros so that she can bear witness to Antigonos' plan to rid himself of the pockmarked little toad, with a view to encouraging him onto our side in this war.'

'Stiffen his resolve, as it were? I'm sure she will do that.' Asander cast Artonis another lecherous look. 'But I wonder whether Kassandros wants his resolve stiffened. From all accounts, Kassandros is very much taken with his new wife. Rumour has it that he is completely in love with the woman and would do anything for her; he's even named his new city after her. I'm told that he plans for it eventually to be the greatest city in Macedon so perhaps it's to Thessalonike to whom you should take the girl. But come, we have much to discuss – and much to eat and drink.'

It was the latter two activities that took precedence over the former, but Asander would do nothing until he had taken his midday meal in the citadel on the Royal Island. Seleukos restrained himself from hurrying on to business, despite his desire to push matters forward, not wishing to display bad manners to a host who was also an important ally. But eventually the meal was cleared away and he joined Asander in his study, overlooking, from a great height, the harbour to the west and, to the east, the disembarkation of the troops, under Myrmidon, along the beach on Alexander's old camp to the east.

'So, Alexandros and his less than whelming father have sided with Antigonos, have they?' Asander mused, taking a seat by the window so that he could cast an eye now and again over his new army assembling on the beach. 'That would seem rather a rash move to me, Antigonos still being hard-pushed for ships and his new allies, the Rhodians, having little interest or desire to interfere in mainland Greece. It would seem that they are setting themselves up for a drubbing from you.'

'Or from Kassandros.'

'Kassandros? I hardly think so; why would he want to effectively declare war on Antigonos when the war is clearly being fought on this side of the Aegean? If I were Kassandros, I would wait and see how things play out over here before I made my move. Just because a has-been and his son with a few thousand men in a ditch somewhere on the isthmus have decided to become chums with our resinated cyclops would not be a reason for me to stick my neck out.'

'Even if said cyclops was going to kill him and I can furnish him with that evidence?'

'Said cyclops has first got to cross to Macedon to accomplish that and that could prove harder than one might think; although, I suppose he could always employ the Exile-Hunter to do the deed seeing as he's on the way there anyway.'

Seleukos smiled. 'The noble Archias is working exclusively for Ptolemy at the moment.'

'Things change, old thing, things change. Anyway, I have two questions for you: why would Kassandros even be tempted to interfere in any war that did not involve Macedon and Greece directly now that he is so secure? And what would Alexandros and Polyperchon gain by antagonising Kassandros even though they have formed an alliance with Antigonos when he is engaged elsewhere?'

'The answer to the second question is that Alexandros and Polyperchon antagonise Kassandros just by being there and supporting Greek democracies. And the answer to the first is he doesn't have to get involved in the Asian theatre yet.'

'Yet?'

'Yes, yet. At the moment it is enough for him to take the fight to Polyperchon and Alexandros in the Peloponnese. You see, *old thing*, Ptolemy's strategy is to have Antigonos' superior forces stretched around Asia and Europe, until the army facing him on the Egyptian border is small enough to handle and then he will strike. You will do your bit here and in the Euxine Sea; Polycleitus and his fleet will raid along the coast of Cilicia; Menelaus holding Cyprus can use his fleet to harry the Phoenician and Palestinian coasts as well as run the blockade of Tyros with supplies thus extending the siege and tying down thousands of his troops. Kassandros fighting Antigonos' allies in Greece is a bonus because the great thing about Kassandros, as we have all been surprised to discover, is that he's good and he's lucky.'

Asander wrinkled his nose at the thought of such an ally. 'He's also thoroughly unpleasant.'

'Granted, but when did that ever be a reason for not dealing with someone? But however unpleasant he is, he will defeat Antigonos' new allies – thus making Antigonos look weak, unable to support his allies – unless Antigonos sends them more of his troops and drains his strength even further in Asia.'

Asander had a moment of clarity. 'I see, old thing: Antigonos has made a strategic mistake by courting Alexandros and his father, hasn't he? Ptolemy was always going to drive them into Antigonos' camp for that very reason. They're expendable bait to pull in Kassandros.'

Seleukos nodded, pleased that his ally had grasped the essence of the strategy. 'Precisely; whatever happens to them is irrelevant because Kassandros is a bigger prize for us than they are for Antigonos. Antigonos misread what Kassandros would do: he assumed that if he brought Alexandros and Polyperchon in on his side, Kassandros would follow to prevent Antigonos using their territory as a foothold for an invasion of Greece. The trouble is I had already predicted to Kassandros that Antigonos would try to make such an alliance with them and not with him, and that would expose his antipathy towards him and desire for Macedon. Kassandros is, even now, probably contemplating the pros and cons of a swift campaign in the south.'

'And your arrival with Artonis will be the last bit of impetus he will need to head south.'

'Kassandros finds out about Alexandros and Polyperchon's new alliance with Antigonos immediately before he hears just what Antigonos offered Eumenes in return for his life and...'

'It leaves him no option.'

'It's perfect. He's ours.'

Asander put his palms up, wincing. 'Hush, old thing. Do not tempt the gods so.'

'You're right. With the will of the gods he'll be ours. And so I shall be leaving tomorrow and spurring Kassandros into action as soon as possible.'

Asander's eyes widened. 'You'll obviously not be taking your fleet to Macedon; that would look like an aggressive move on your behalf. So might I—'

'No, Asander, you may not.'

'Is it just going to sit here and do nothing?'

'Far from it; I'm going to use it to besiege Erythrae.'

'Erythrae? Why?'

'Antigonos has given Lydia back to Menander as a reward for his service for him in the east. If I lay blockade by sea and lay siege to his main port, Antigonos will be forced to send more troops and ships to relieve his old friend's main strategic naval centre.'

'Antigonos is going to be very stretched.'

Seleukos gestured to the window and the army formed up now on the beach. 'So, *old thing*, take Myrmidon and his men inland and hit Antigonos hard. By the spring of next year the resinated cyclops won't know in which direction to point his remaining eye.'

ANTIGONOS.
THE ONE-EYED.

THE FRUSTRATION WAS mounting with the passing of each day and the wasting of each life; Antigonos cursed the wall of Tyros which had remained unyielding to all assaults. In the months since he had returned from his foray south he had attacked thrice at three different points of the wall but, at each attempt, repulsion had been his fate and his grim mood had deepened with every reverse. 'Where do they get the men from?' he growled as he and Andronicus, his commander of the siege works, surveyed the many figures manning the landward wall of Tyros; before them, in smouldering heaps, lay the wreckage of three of the great siege towers; within their mangled remains, charred and broken bodies, the dead from the last failed assault, lay festering in the sun providing a feast for the countless gulls flocking around the carnage, their endless cries of contentment echoing off the walls. 'And, more to the point, where do they get the food to feed them all? My arse! If I ever get my hands on Archias and his Thracians I'll make them pay for assassinating Monimus and his men.'

Andronicus, his eyes ringed with tiredness, looked at his commander. 'How can you be sure it was the Exile-Hunter who killed them?'

'The timing: I learned from prisoners we took from the Gaza garrison that Archias had been in the town shortly before we arrived and so, presumably, he left on the fleet that sailed north. It stopped in Tyros for the night and when I eventually came back I had Monimus' head waiting for me in a jar of oil. Of course it was Archias. And now we have to make our way over or under the walls because I haven't got anyone inside who can open the gates any more.' A series of guttural curses rumbled in his throat as he contemplated his situation. It was good but not nearly as good as it had been when he had first arrived on the coast, seven months previously.

It had been the sight of Ptolemy's great fleet in the process of embarking an army to the south of Gaza's harbour and the distinct possibility that he might catch it in the water that had been the high point of his campaign; the low point had come very soon after as he stood on the beach and watched the fleet disappear north and then had to endure being waved at by a grinning Ptolemy as he sailed back to Alexandria. He had consoled himself with the swift taking of the city and its harbour – the garrison had opened the gates to him without him even having to get his artillery up on the hill – but the triumph of completing his conquest of Palestine had been severely diluted when he saw the quality of the troops that Ptolemy had left in that final city. *He had meant for Gaza to fall. But why?* Having left Demetrios – with the steady Nearchos, old and experienced, to temper his impetuous spirit – in the south, with a substantial field army of approaching twenty thousand men, to fend off any counterattack by Ptolemy, Antigonos had come back to Tyros to find his grisly gift and his chances of taking Tyros by treachery gone.

And then the news from Cyprus had arrived and not for the first time he regretted either disaffecting Seleukos or failing to execute him when he had the chance – depending upon his mood. For Seleukos' swift campaign in Cyprus had been brutally effective and none of the petty kings were even prepared to hold secret negotiations with him any more and the island was now lost to him for the foreseeable future. But that had been only the beginning of his troubles for he had now learned Asander had sent a force north through the Hellespont to lay siege to Amisius on the northern coast of Kappadokia.

Gods, is there no end to it? I need to send troops to secure Kappadokia and prevent Asander's men from getting inland, until I have the ships to relieve Amisius; I can't afford to keep wasting lives trying to scale the walls. Antigonos gritted his teeth and swore again. *I'm going to have to do this the slow way.* 'We'll have to starve them out over the winter.'

'But they're still being supplied by Menelaus' fleet from Cyprus,' Andronicus pointed out. 'They run the blockade whenever they like because we still haven't got enough ships to prevent them. Since you went south they have done it twice, each time taking supplies to last the city a month.'

Ships; it always comes down to ships, I'll never have enough; for every three I build one gets destroyed before it even gets its hull wet. 'How many do we have in the blockade now?'

'Sixty-three.'

Antigonos had never been much of a naval man. 'And why is that not enough to seal off the harbour?'

'Menelaus comes with at least a hundred; obviously the arithmetic is simple.'

Antigonos' one eye turned on his subordinate, its infamous glare burning full as he assessed whether Andronicus was patronising him on purpose.

The siege commander felt the intensity and held up his hands. 'I meant to say: we are presently a little outnumbered at sea.'

'Hmph. I take your point. Well, keep the men not on the siege lines at their ship-building. In the meantime I should have a fleet of around fifty ships coming south very soon from the shipyards in Rhodos and Cilicia, along with six thousand recruits under the command of two old comrades of mine, Theodotus and Perilaus; that should help move things along. And I warn you, Andronicus, things do need to move along because I'm losing the initiative stuck here and I can't leave the place in Ptolemy's hands; I would never gain any respect if I were to do that.' With another growl he turned and stomped off to his tent with his hands clasped behind his back and head down deep in thought for it only to be disturbed by his nephew, Ptolemaios.

'Uncle, Aristodemus has arrived,' Ptolemaios said, looking more nervous than he should being the bearer of such tidings. 'He's brought Alexandros with him and news that I think you should hear from his own mouth.'

It was, therefore, with a mixture of emotions that Antigonos found Aristodemus and Alexandros waiting at his tent. 'You'd better come in.'

Stepping inside, Antigonos remembered his manners – what there were of them – and turned to Alexandros, clasping his forearm as Ptolemaios and Aristodemus seated themselves. 'Forgive me for being abrupt, I have much on my mind; but you are welcome nonetheless as I assume that you're here to formalise the alliance between us.'

'I'm honoured to be here, Antigonos. My father and I have always been keen supporters of yours.'

My arse, you have; had I not cut Eumenes off from crossing the sea and uniting with you and Olympias in Greece you would have been fighting with him against Kassandros and then coming over to

Asia to deal with me. 'And I have always had great respect for you and your father.' *Mediocrities though you are.*

With the pleasantries over, Antigonos invited his guests to sit and clapped his hands for a jug of resinated wine. Once they had all been served and the slave departed, he turned to his latest ally. 'Aristodemus has provided you with reinforcements?'

'Yes, eight thousand mercenary hoplites and peltasts; Greeks mainly but also some Thracians, Illyrians and Epiriots.'

'So what is your present strength?'

'Just under twenty thousand; two thousand five hundred of which is cavalry.'

'And what are your plans?'

'What would you like us to do?'

'That all depends on how Kassandros responds to our alliance.'

'Until then I suggest we remain in our position across the isthmus.'

Antigonos studied Alexandros, unimpressed by his lack of charisma or initiative. *A younger version of his father but with more hair and fewer ideas if all he can suggest is to remain dug in along his present position.* 'We'll see.' He turned to Aristodemus. 'What word is there of Kassandros? Ptolemaios here hinted that the news wasn't good.'

Aristodemus swallowed before answering. 'No, it's not good; things are getting out of hand, spreading in what seems to me to be an orchestrated manner. A clear strategy.'

'Ptolemy?'

'Who else?'

'Tell me.'

Again Aristodemus swallowed. 'Well, no sooner had Seleukos terrified all of the surviving petty kings on Cyprus into submission, than he left the island, leaving Menelaus in command, with the bulk of his army, eight to nine thousand men, and sailed to Caria to reinforce Asander.'

'Asander! My unwashed arse!' Antigonos' mind raced for a few moments, considering the weak garrison at Gaza, the strong policy on Cyprus and now the interference in Caria so soon after Asander had sent troops to Amisius and the pattern became clear. 'You're right: this has all been planned to force me to run around dealing with various incidents scattered all over the place. Asander knew he would soon receive reinforcements; it was on that condition that he sent an expedition to Amisius forcing me to send men all the way up north and now I'm going to have to reinforce Phrygia so that Asander doesn't humiliate me by taking my satrapy.'

Aristodemus swallowed again. 'It gets worse.'

'Worse?'

'I'm afraid so.'

'How much worse?'

'A lot.'

Antigonos fortified himself with a whole cup of unwatered wine. 'Go on.'

Aristodemus swallowed again. 'Seleukos has laid siege to Erythrae and left his fleet there to blockade it. Menander has neither the men nor the ships to repel him and is sending to you for help.'

'How do you know this?'

'My spies in Caria and Lydia both got messages to me on trading ships whilst we were waiting in Rhodos for a chance to sail through to you; Polycleitus is operating along the Pamphylian and Cilician coasts and is intercepting shipping.'

'So I must peel off yet more troops and ships to deal with Menander's problem, must I?' *Oh, Ptolemy, you have been busy.*

'But wait a moment: you said he's left his fleet there; where's he gone to?'

'Pella.'

'Again? Why?'

'He's taken Artonis there.'

And now Antigonos could see the magnitude of Ptolemy's strategy. 'She will tell him what I offered for Eumenes' life.'

Ptolemaios nodded. 'I'm afraid she will, Uncle. Kassandros won't now be able to be lulled into an alliance with us.'

'He'll be heading south as soon as he can,' Alexandros said with a hint of nervousness in his voice. He looked at Antigonos. 'I will need gold to bribe the Aetolians to hold Thermopylae against him again.'

'I said the news would get worse,' Aristodemus interjected before Antigonos could reply. He swallowed once more. 'Well, it does. As soon as Kassandros heard of your alliance with Alexandros and Polyperchon he made advances to the Aetolians and now they are his. He holds Thermopylae should he wish to come south, which, after he has spoken to Artonis, seems inevitable.'

Antigonos sighed and refilled his cup. 'And if Alexandros takes an army north to halt him then he faces being taken in the rear by the combined forces of Athens and the newly reconstituted Thebes. My arse, it's a fucking mess.' *And it all seemed so straightforward at the beginning of the year.* 'So, I need to send a fleet and troops to Greece now, as well?'

'Without them we can only fight on the defensive,' Alexandros said.

I suppose he does have a point. 'Very well; I'll send orders to the fleet of new ships and the six thousand recruits coming down from Pamphylia and Cilicia to be redirected to Greece.'

'I'm afraid that you can't do that, sir,' Aristodemus said, swallowing.

274

'Can't do that! My arse, I'll do what I want.'

'I meant that you are unable to do that, sir.'

'Unable?' And then he remembered that the news was going to get progressively worse. He fortified himself once more. 'Why not?' But he already knew the answer as he wiped his wet beard with the back of his hand.

'Because Polycleitus captured or sunk all the ships and took prisoner most of the recruits he didn't slaughter; we came across some survivors two days ago as we sailed along the coast. Your ships and men are now in Cyprus and Theodotus and Perilaus are both dead.'

Antigonos closed his eye and groaned. *Ptolemy, you are not only a colossal bastard, you're a lucky colossal bastard. But now you have contrived to bring Kassandros onto your side I can turn that against you.* 'Ptolemaios, I want an army assembly called for tomorrow.'

The hound had died well, its trusting eyes looking around, its tail busy, not sensing death's presence until its throat had been ripped open; with two mighty cleaves of an axe, the carcass had been cut in two and each part dragged to opposite sides of the field. Between the two halves of the dog marched the Macedonian citizens of Antigonos' army, all thirty thousand of them, to the sound of the prayers and hymns of Lustration. And thus was the army cleansed and made ready for the business of the day; formed up in great blocks before a high dais, with the besieged city of Tyros almost a league behind it and the non-citizens of the army looking on from either side, it waited to be addressed by its general.

In no mood to procrastinate, Antigonos mounted the steps, with his senior officers following, to stand on the platform, hands on hips, looking down at the largest body of Macedonian citizenry outside the country itself. And how they cheered him, for they loved their resinated cyclops as he brought them victory far more often than defeat.

Antigonos raised his hands in the air and bathed in the praise, turning this way and that to take in his full audience until he judged that they were ready for what he would ask of them. He signalled for quiet. 'Soldiers of Macedon!' he declaimed once silence was manifest. 'We are gathered here today to face a problem that is growing like a canker in our land.' He paused and waited for the heralds spaced throughout the huge crowd to relay his words so that all could hear.

'I speak of Kassandros,' he bellowed once the heralds had finished, 'and of his bloated ambition! I speak of his execution of Alexander's mother, *Queen* Olympias. The mother of Alexander is dead at Kassandros' hand! Imagine, citizens of Macedon, imagine what our Alexander would have done to the man who had killed his mother.' *Thanked him in all likelihood*, he mused as again the heralds relayed. 'And then, not satisfied with that fell deed, he takes Alexander's wife and son and imprisons them in Amphipolis; Alexander's son, our king, is a prisoner in his own land!'

This statement brought howls of outrage from the army of the man who had the boy-king's inheritance in his sights. But Antigonos was not one to let hypocrisy get in the way of a rousing speech. 'And then, with Alexander's mother murdered, his wife and son imprisoned, Kassandros still is not content, still he wants more; and so he takes more. He takes Alexander's sister and forces marriage upon her.' *Thessalonike is his half-sister and she was quite keen on the marriage by all accounts, but let's not let facts dilute the outrage*, he mused again as he waited for his words to reach the limits of the crowd.

'Mother, wife, son and sister, Kassandros has taken from Alexander and if that were not enough to convince you that he wants his crown as well, consider this: within the past couple of years he has usurped the royal prerogative thrice in that he has founded two cities, Kassandreia and Thessalonike, and he has undone what Alexander did by re-founding the city of Thebes. What more proof could we look for as evidence of Kassandros' bloated ambition?'

His audience needed no further convincing and they roared their outrage for many scores of heartbeats and Antigonos indulged them. He turned to his senior officers behind him, Ptolemaios, Dioscurides, Aristodemus, Andronicus and the veteran Telesphorus, and nodded. As one, they came forward and lifted Antigonos onto their shoulders; and there he sat with his arms punching the air as he milked the crowd for every last drop of indignation at the actions of Kassandros.

Down he jumped, as the volume began to fade, and called for calm. 'And what shall we do about this ambition, men of Macedon? We shall demand that it is crushed down, shall we not?' And the army assembly agreed. 'Kassandros, and anyone who supports him, shall be declared an enemy of Macedon unless, firstly, he releases Alexander's mother and son and hands them over into our safe custody; secondly, he destroys the three cities that he has, in his arrogance, brought into being; and thirdly, he yields to me, the established general of the empire and guardian of the throne. What do you say, soldiers of Macedon? Does the army assembly pass this decree?'

It came as no surprise that there was not one voice against and so Antigonos allowed them to cheer on, working up their frenzy until he judged that they would pass what he next proposed without thought.

'And now I have one more motion to bring before the assembly,' he continued as quiet descended. 'It is a motion that will pile even more pressure upon Kassandros for it will bring our Greek allies against him. I propose that we declare the Greek cities free: free from external influence, free to arrange their affairs as they wish. Do you, the army assembly, pass this motion?'

It was with a smile upon his face and triumph in his one eye that Antigonos raised his arms to the crowd's acclamation. *The question now is, Kassandros, whether you and Thessalonike between you have the power to resist and overturn the decree of the army assembly.*

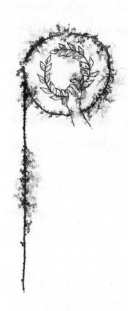

THESSALONIKE.
THE HALF-SISTER.

THE CHILD KICKED within her; Thessalonike placed both hands on her belly, caressing it, as she sat next to her husband on a throne of equal standing to his. Kassandros caught her movement in the corner of his eye and turned to her with a look of genuine love and pride in her condition. She held out a hand to her husband; he took it, squeezed it and kissed it, with no thought as to how it looked to the rest of the gathering of nobles in the audience chamber as Seleukos entered with a veiled eastern woman in tow. Beyond the new arrivals, barred from entry by the guards at the door, at the far end of the room, stood Archias and his Thracians.

Once again finding herself amazed at the growing feeling of warmth she was discovering for a man she had once loathed with all her being, Thessalonike bestowed upon Kassandros her sweetest smile and then turned back to their surprise guests. *His second visit in just over a year; Seleukos is making himself a very busy little bee.*

'Seleukos, you are welcome in Pella, once again,' Kassandros said, letting go of his wife's hand.

'I'm pleased to return, Kassandros,' Seleukos replied, stopping ten paces before the thrones. 'Ptolemy sends you his fraternal regards and the gift of timely information.'

Thessalonike looked at the veiled woman, her curiosity piqued. 'Is this Artonis, the widow of Eumenes?'

Surprise showed on Seleukos' face. 'It is.'

'We've been expecting her ever since my husband's sister Eurydike wrote, telling us of her and her sister's arrival in Egypt.' She held out her hand. 'Come forward, my dear.'

Artonis looked sidelong at Seleukos, who nodded his consent.

So, she goes by his leave; interesting. 'Artonis, we heard of the death of your sister Artakama; it was most unfortunate and you have my sympathy.'

Artonis inclined her head in acknowledgement of the sentiment. 'Unfortunate and avoidable; Ptolemy should never have sent her away.'

Ah, so it's Ptolemy's fault, is it? Excellent; that could be very useful at some point. I'll demonstrate my sympathy for her opinion. 'Indeed; a man should honour his marriage commitments.' She reached out for her husband's hand. 'I wish that all women had the same good fortune as I've had.' *That is a very interesting new view of Kassandros.* 'But you are welcome, Artonis; I hope to have the time to get better acquainted with you.'

'You are very kind, Thessalonike; I too share that desire.'

But Kassandros' new-found conviviality did not extend to women being overly polite to one another for too long. 'Why have you brought her to me, Seleukos?'

Seleukos gestured to the Macedonian nobles lining either side of the chamber. 'That is a question that I should prefer to answer in private.'

*

It amused Thessalonike just how regal she and Kassandros were gradually becoming; as they rose from their elevated seats, descended the steps and processed the length of the chamber, the nobles bowed their heads to them. *More out of fear than respect, no doubt; but neither of those is a bad motivation. They are all aware that if we can execute Olympias, keep Alexander's wife and son prisoner and have Aristonous killed, then there would be no hesitation in doing the same to them.* It was a comforting thought and one that had surprised the first time it had occurred to her; it had been at that moment when she had realised that in the same way that Kassandros was coming over to her more moderate approach to power so she was moving into his direction of thought, and that the logical conclusion was that they would meet somewhere in the middle. This, she had concluded, would be no bad thing: the excesses of Olympias and the weakness of Polyperchon were both things to be avoided. Strength and resolution without unnecessary cruelty were what would keep her and Kassandros in power so that the son she bore would succeed them; and that now had become her chief motivation. Again she stroked her belly as she walked.

Whether or not Seleukos was surprised at how the nobles of Macedon now deferred to their rulers in a manner unthinkable in Alexander's time, Thessalonike could not tell from his expression as he was far too canny to let his feelings play upon his face.

'Come,' Kassandros said, as their guests stepped aside to let them pass, 'walk with us; my wife has had a new garden planted in the east courtyard since you were last here.'

This time Seleukos could not control his thoughts; his mouth dropped open in disbelief that Kassandros, of all people, should take an interest in gardening.

Read into it what you will, Seleukos.

'You were right in what you suspected last time you were here, Seleukos,' Kassandros said as they walked out into the cool winter air of the east courtyard. 'Antigonos did make a deal with Alexandros and Polyperchon, and Alexandros has sailed to Tyros to secure the alliance in person.'

'Alexandros is in Tyros? I didn't know that.'

'He won't be back until the spring, thus leaving the old nonentity in command down on the isthmus.'

'Giving you the chance to have a lightning campaign to remove him,' Seleukos observed.

'Over the winter?'

'Early winter if you were to go now.'

'But who said we would want to declare against Antigonos,' Thessalonike asked, 'for that is what a campaign against his new allies would amount to, is it not?'

Seleukos feigned surprise. 'And you would rather ally yourself with the man who would have your husband dead and, no doubt, yourself, as soon as he could arrange it; because that is a fact.'

Thessalonike addressed Artonis. 'And is this why Seleukos has brought you here on Ptolemy's request? You can prove that to be a fact?'

Artonis had no hesitation in replying. 'Antigonos offered my husband his life should he support your union and your right to be regent of the young Alexander. He refused and went to his death instead.'

Kassandros stopped to admire the layout of a shrubbery. 'And how does that prove he would want me dead? Surely it shows the exact opposite: he wants me alive and regent of the king ruling in Macedon.'

Oh, Kassandros, you still have the ability to disappoint. 'I think that we can all speak plainly here between the four of us. Kassandros, what would happen should Alexander become king?'

Kassandros' attention was immediately taken from the horticulture. 'Ah, we are really going to speak plainly, are we?' He looked at Seleukos. 'Alexander would have to have me killed and so he can never become king.'

And now it's out in the open. Thessalonike put her hand on her husband's arm. 'The logic of it is that the boy must die before his fourteenth birthday and Antigonos knows that we are the ones who have to do it to survive. Don't you see, Kassandros, had Eumenes agreed and come to Macedon to offer his support we would have felt safe within our borders, thus leaving Antigonos free to deal with Ptolemy. Then, once Ptolemy was no longer a problem and we'd relieved him of the final obstacle in his way, in a manner that obviously had nothing to do with him, Antigonos would have come north to kill us as punishment for murdering the boy whom he wanted dead – as well – and would have had justice and the people of Macedon on his side. There you have it, Kassandros: just by giving Eumenes his life, Antigonos would have the whole empire in his hands, for Lysimachus would, without doubt, submit to him in those circumstances. Eumenes saw that and went to his death rather than support it. The sly little Greek was always a man of honour.'

Kassandros snorted. 'That's one way of putting it.'

Thessalonike shot her husband a warning look. *Now is not the time to air your hatred of the Greek. It was not his fault that Iollas died; your father should never have been waging war against him.*

Artonis blinked back welling tears. 'He wanted what was best for the true line of Alexander.'

'Do you think that we share your husband's objectives?' *You've just heard us admit that we will kill his son.*

'Macedonian politics mean nothing to me now that Eumenes is dead; all I thirst for is revenge, and an alliance against Antigonos furthers that ambition. What happens to the boy is no concern of mine; my husband didn't go to his death to protect the young Alexander; he died to prevent Antigonos taking everything for himself that should belong to the Argead royal house. The boy is just one constituent part of that house – there are more: Alexander's full sister, Kleopatra, or my half-sister Barsine's boy, Heracles, for example. The child you carry, Thessalonike, is of Alexander's blood as well; and your husband is the son of the regent who ruled Macedon in Alexander's stead.' Artonis shrugged. 'It will be a child of the Argead royal house and that would be enough for my husband; it would not have to be Alexander's own son.'

Thessalonike stroked Artonis' cheek through her veil. 'You are so right, my dear. We will help you to your revenge; Eumenes was always a good friend to me.' *Let not the fact that I did not see him from the age of eight get in the way of that statement.* 'I can see what Ptolemy is planning; I assume you go to Lysimachus after here – if you have not been there already.'

'Yes, I go to Thrace next; Archias the Exile-Hunter will escort me overland as Seleukos goes back to continue his fight against Antigonos' ally, Menander, in Lydia.'

'And we have just come from Caria,' Seleukos added. 'Asander was very receptive to the message and was grateful for the troops Ptolemy sent him.'

Kassandros now saw the strategy. 'So with Lysimachus in the north, Asander in Anatolia, you in Lydia and Ptolemy in the south, Antigonos would be hard put upon.' He smiled to himself at first and then to his wife. 'He would scarcely have the resources to reinforce Polyperchon if we were to hit him soon.'

'That is what Ptolemy would hope you would do,' Seleukos said.

Thessalonike wagged a finger at Seleukos. 'We do not do what Ptolemy wants us to, unless it serves our interests.'

'And your interests to the south of Macedon must be the domination of the Greek cities; agreed?'

Thessalonike considered the question for a moment, combing it for a trap. 'Yes, agreed. That is why we have re-founded Thebes.'

'Corinth would therefore be a fine addition to your sphere of influence.'

'It would,' Kassandros admitted. Thessalonike did not contradict him.

'But that stands in Polyperchon's and his son's territory.'

'It does.'

'And further south, Tegea is firmly for them, since they restored it to a democracy, am I right?'

'You are,' Thessalonike said with slow caution.

'So of the other main cities in the Peloponnese, Sparta is too far south and too concerned with its own fading to worry about; which leaves Argos, now that it has rebelled and thrown out the oligarchy you installed last year, and its ally, Orchomenus, as the two other major democracies opposed to you.'

'It is a large area to subdue if we can't dislodge Polyperchon from his position across the isthmus.'

'But Megalopolis and Nemea still have the oligarchies installed by your father in place and therefore could both be used as a base for operations. You could attack from them from the south and from Thebes and Athens from the north.'

Of course, he's right: take those cities and our domination of the Peloponnese would be undisputed. 'We should go, Kassandros; before Alexandros returns and there is someone of substance to hold out against us.'

'But winter's almost here. There has already been snow in the mountains.'

'But not down in the south. Not for a couple of months, maybe. And anyway, it's the same for everyone.'

'Not if you're nice and warm behind your walls and we're freezing our balls – sorry, my dear – our behinds off in frozen trenches.'

'You won't be; sieges won't be necessary if you send money in advance and prepare the ground. Some of the democracies have been in power now for almost five years since your father declared the freedom of the Greek cities; such a weak form of government is never popular after so long.'

He's correct again; the right time has come. And then a thought struck Thessalonike. *Of course; it's the right time in more ways than one.* 'We must go soon, Kassandros; this needs to be done as soon as possible.'

'I know; before Alexandros comes back.'

'No, before that even. If you want to be seen as the power in the Peloponnese then there is a great opportunity coming up to advertise the fact. Early next year is the Nemead. Nemea is just south of Corinth, right at the centre of what we'll subdue; let's take advantage of the only games held in winter and have the whole of Greece take the message of you presiding over the Nemean Games as Alexander himself once did.'

It was with promises of a lasting alliance with Ptolemy and permission to use the Athenian naval base on the island of Lemnos for operations in the northern Aegean, as well as an undertaking to give Artonis an escort of cavalry on her journey to Thrace, that Seleukos set sail from Pella the following day to return to the siege of Erythrae. From the high walls of the palace, Thessalonike watched his ship glide out through the harbour mouth, passing an arriving vessel, and then head along down the inlet that led to the sea. Artonis stood with her, with Archias in attendance; not that she felt threatened, it was just that she was so valuable to the Exile-Hunter that he would not let her stray from his sight. His Thracians, however, Thessalonike had banished from her presence on hygienic grounds.

'Tell me, Archias,' Thessalonike said as she watched the newly arrived ship dock, 'after you have taken Artonis to Lysimachus how do you plan to get her back to Egypt?'

Archias had an unconcerned air. 'It depends on the situation. "The right moment decides all things; take it and win."'

'I would prefer not to travel by sea,' Artonis stated. 'And I would also like to visit my half-sister Barsine in Pergamum, so we can mourn Artakama together.'

Archias made no reply.

Thessalonike moved her point along. 'It may be that I would have some employment for you on the way back should you not mind a diversion.'

Archias' boyish face took on an interested aspect. 'Work is always of interest to me and my men.'

'Good, then come and see me before you leave tomorrow.' With a nod, Thessalonike turned and walked away, pleased with herself. *If he's successful, it will deflect Antigonos' gaze from us when Kassandros takes Greece.*

She decided, however, not to mention to her husband her dealings with the Exile-Hunter, preferring instead for the results to come as a pleasant surprise to him.

And it was a pleasant surprise that Kassandros appeared in need of when she eventually found him in his study with his half-brother Philip; for his normally pallid face was burning with fury as he looked up at her with anger bright in his eyes.

'What is it, Husband?' Thessalonike asked, stopping still at the sight of him.

'Tell her, Philip.'

Philip shrugged. 'I just arrived from Athens; news reached us there that Antigonos has had the army assembly declare Kassandros an enemy of Macedon unless, and I quote: firstly, he releases Alexander's wife and son and hands them over into Antigonos' safe custody; secondly, he destroys the three cities that he has, in his arrogance, brought into being; and thirdly, he yields to Antigonos, the established general of the empire and guardian of the throne.'

Kassandros slammed his fist down on the desk. 'Me! An enemy of Macedon! I *am* Macedon. I'll show that drunken cyclops just who is the enemy. And it gets worse, Thessalonike: he has also proclaimed the freedom of the Greek cities, which could mean that Megalopolis and Nemea may well have thrown out the oligarchies loyal to me by the time I reach them.'

'Then you had better hurry.'

Thessalonike's pleasure at the despatch with which her husband mobilised his army was matched only by the pleasure she felt as she surveyed the new harbour at Thessalonike, the city named after her. It was to here that Kassandros had summoned his troops for he intended to sail south with as much of the army as possible to gain maximum surprise, whilst the rest of the men followed by land with Kassandros' half-brothers, Philip and Pleistarchos. And now the lucky ones who would be ferried south stood in lines along the water's edge as they boarded, under Crateuas' and Atarrhias' supervision, the huge fleet that represented the entire naval strength of Macedon; the fleet that Antigonos had lent Kassandros to take Greece and Macedon; the fleet that he had refused to return along with the army that had stayed with Crateuas and Atarrhias after Antigonos had executed Crateuas' son, Peithon. And now, commanded by Antigonos' former generals, that combined naval and land force was being used to bring the war to the allies of its previous owner.

Such was its size that it could not have been accommodated in the small harbour at Pella and thus it was to Kassandros' new city, rising from the coast along the shore from the small port of Therma, that he had summoned his strength.

Much had been achieved in the year since Thessalonike's founding: the main thoroughfares, the agora and the harbour district had all been laid out and great construction sites now sprang from their midst, clad in wooden scaffold, peopled by thousands of slaves toiling in dull rain to ensure that her name was not to be forgotten.

Thessalonike kissed the man who had ensured her immortality and looked up into his pinched, avianesque face and caressed his pockmarked cheek. 'Take care, Husband; I will travel south as soon as I'm delivered of our child and will be at your side at the Nemean Games.'

Kassandros' face contorted into what passed for a smile for his physiognomy. 'Four months will be a long time to bear without you.'

'You'll be busy, you won't notice the months, and by the time I'm with you again you will be master of Greece.'

'And Antigonos' sworn and most bitter enemy.'

Thessalonike dismissed the notion with a shake of her head. 'That'll be easily overcome: with Polyperchon and Alexandros defeated we'll be safe; Antigonos won't be able to get at us. We can withdraw from Ptolemy's alliance and perhaps do a deal with the cyclops; one of mutual recognition. I'm sure that, by then, he will be only too glad to have one less opponent to worry about. The army assembly vote can easily be overturned and we've got a few things that Antigonos would want in return for that.'

Kassandros frowned. 'Like what?'

'Perhaps I should've said: would not want in return for that.' Thessalonike was rewarded by a look of understanding that spread over her husband's face.

'He would not want us to send him Alexander and Roxanna.'

'No, Kassandros; they would be the last thing he would want to be lumbered with and just the threat of that will be enough to bend him to our will when the time comes. Now go.' And with a tender kiss she sent her husband off to war.

KASSANDROS.
THE JEALOUS.

KASSANDROS KEPT LOW, loping at the crouch, as he led his men across the open ground between his siege lines and the city walls of Corinth. Dark was the ground as the moon had already set in a sky laden with cloud. Rain fell in soft drops, adding a fresh fragrance to the vegetation they trampled over. Weapons muffled with rags beat with dulled slaps against thighs as careful footsteps took the night assault closer to its objective.

On they went, hunched and silent, breathing in steady lungfuls of night air, careful not to gasp and wary of stumbling.

Excitement welled in Kassandros' breast for this was something that he could do – and be seen to do – without great fear, for, as yet, he was in no danger. Here he was, leading his men from the front, in an action that, if all went to plan, would give him one of the great cities of Greece, and he could do it without fear of his bladder disgracing him or of his resolve failing to the point that he would become a quivering, sobbing wreck or just bolt in terror. And most importantly, should it be a success, he would be able to tell Thessalonike of his feat and impress her; his desire to shine in her eyes was great but he knew that his abject cowardice made that almost impossible. *I can't wait to see her face when I tell her that I led the mission that took the city.*

Even as their objective neared, he still felt little fear; he looked to his brother Philip, to his right, and confidence increased knowing that he had someone who cared for his safety next to him should events not pass as planned at the gate.

And it was a gate that was the goal of the mission: not one of the three main gates of the city but, rather, a lesser portal. And that was why Kassandros led only thirty men, for more would have been of little use as they would certainly have encumbered one another, and besides, that number was exactly right for what he had planned.

'Over here,' a voice said in a light-breathed whisper that carried on the breeze.

Following the sound, Kassandros veered to the left as the shadow of the great wall materialised as a darker solid against a black sky rimmed with the faintest of red glows from one of the very few torches on this section of the wall still burning so far into the night and with dawn still distant.

'Quick!' the voice said again, this time with urgency.

And this, Kassandros understood, would be the crucial stage of the plan, for it was one thing to creep up on the city in the dead of a moonless night, it was quite another to slip through a sally-port, unnoticed, whilst the city was under siege and on guard against such events. But that was what was planned, and that was what they would do, and Kassandros had enough confidence in his ability to be able to lead the operation for he knew that should they be discovered he would not fight but immediately surrender and then pay his ransom. It was a comforting thought and it gave him strength as he approached the source of the whisper.

A figure appeared in the gloom. 'Do you have it?'

'Who are you?' Kassandros demanded.

'Demochares.'

'And what have you to say to me?'

'Athena stands over me.'

'Philip,' Kassandros hissed, satisfied that he had the right man, 'bring the sacks.'

His brother came with two men weighed down by heavy loads; Kassandros turned to Demochares. 'Be quick counting it.'

The Greek judged the weight of each sack and then took a sample of the coinage within, squinting at it and placing it on the tip of his tongue. 'It seems about right. If it's not, Kassandros, I'll make sure it is widely known that you are not a man to do business with.'

That will be hard from beyond the Styx. 'It's all there. Now hurry.'

Demochares turned to a couple of men, hitherto unseen in the shadows, and handed them a sack each. 'Follow me,' he said, beckoning to Kassandros.

Within fifty paces they had reached the wall as it fell a few feet into a dell at the bottom of which was a recess. Demochares disappeared inside and gave a knocked signal on a wooden gate. Within a few heartbeats, Kassandros heard the creak of hinges lacking in usage and the scraping of wood across stone. They were in.

With haste Kassandros hurried forward, dipping his head as he entered the recess, passing through the open door, and then jogged on through a dank and odorous short tunnel.

'To the left,' Demochares whispered. 'Follow Laetes here.'

Doing as he was told, Kassandros followed a figure climbing up some steps as behind he was aware of Philip and the rest of the men tramping up after him. Up they went with just the occasional window looking out over the town to give any semblance of light; but Kassandros needed none, for by now his ears and eyes had sharpened to the high sensitivity brought on by a long time in the dark and he could judge his steps and the distance between him and the man ahead.

With his chest heaving, they came out onto the walkway running along behind the wall's parapet. Two bodies, guards, lay on the ground; dark pools had formed on the wet stone under their heads. Two more guards stood close by. 'They're ours,' Laetes said, as Kassandros paused.

Relieved, Kassandros stepped over a body, moving away from the doorway as the rest of his men came out into the open and began to form up into a column, two abreast.

Philip came up next to Kassandros. 'The men are ready; I've reiterated to them that they should act as if they have every right to be marching along the wall.'

And that was the crux of the plan: get to the wall unnoticed and then march along it not worrying about being noticed; hiding in plain sight. Off came the men's shield covers to reveal the Pegasus motif of Corinth, painted on a white background; that and their full-faced Corinthian helmets with white horse-hair plumes would be enough to deceive a curious inquisitor into thinking that a unit of the guard had been called out – especially as Laetes naturally had the flat and toneless accent of Corinth.

Off they went at the jog – a sense of urgency adding to the deception; Kassandros next to his brother in the front of the column with Laetes in the lead, ready to deflect any questions.

His pulse quickening and his stomach churning, Kassandros fought to stay calm, focusing on what Thessalonike would think of him for his leading role in the night's escapade: finally he would be able to claim that he was a general who led from the front – albeit occasionally.

'Wait where you are and identify yourselves!'

Laetes held up his hand, halting the column, and then walked forward to address the guard standing at the entrance of a tower through which they had to pass. 'Laetes with an *enomotia* of the guard called to the main gate.'

The man's face was in shadow; Kassandros could not tell how he had taken the explanation. Above the guard, on the flat roof of the tower, were stationed two more men with a bell to raise the alarm – as with all the towers around the circuit; their silhouetted forms could be seen peering down at the confrontation below. Kassandros felt his bladder strain.

'On whose orders?'

'How would I know? Demochares orders us up here and I obey; where the order came from is none of my business.'

'What's going on?'

'How the fuck should I know seeing as we haven't got to where we're meant to be yet? As soon as I know I'll write you a nice love-letter telling you all about it and how much I wish you were with me and the sooner you let us through the sooner you'll get it.'

'All right, all right, I was just asking.' The guard stepped aside; Kassandros realised he had been holding his breath and had to check himself from sighing. Through the tunnel under the tower Laetes led them, keeping their eyes to the front and their demeanour relaxed.

Two more such obstacles did they pass with the same result – such was the audacity of the move that none thought it anything but genuine. Thus they approached the gate tower; torches burned around it, speckling it with flickering light. Down a set of steps, at ground level, guards milled – at least a half dozen from what Kassandros could make out – leaning against the wall, or pacing up and down, talking in low voices to one another, evidently bored of doing the night watch on gates that had not opened for four months.

'Identify yourselves!' came the customary cry.

Again Laetes halted them and walked up to the guard. 'Laetes with an enomotia of the guard called to the main gate.'

'To do what?'

'This.'

The dull, butcher's thud, exhalation of breath and choking in the throat told the story only too well.

'Now!' Kassandros hissed, pointing to the steps.

Philip did not pause; down he led his file at the charge to hit the unsuspecting night-guards with bloody menace as Kassandros set about his task of signalling their success to the waiting assault troops by throwing as many torches over the wall as he could. Laetes, meanwhile, secured the tower with the rest of the men.

Leaving a line of torches burning on the ground before the walls, Kassandros ran down the steps to where Philip's men had formed a perimeter shield-wall in front of the arch while he and three others struggled to open the bar across the gate after so long a time in place.

Cries from within the city heralded the first of the troops rushing to the aid of their comrades on the gate – all of whom now lay in bloody heaps as obstacles beyond the shield-wall. Down the main thoroughfare they ran, towards the gate, in various states of dress, their numbers being fed all the time from side-streets.

'Harder!' Kassandros shouted at the men pushing up the bar, hurrying to lend his weight hoping that it would take his mind off the incoming clamour of voices and swords beating upon shields. A javelin hit the ground and clattered along the stones just a pace from him; he pushed at the bar with his shoulder; a creak and a groan and loose it came, dropping to the floor. Kassandros and one other were quick to drag it clear as Philip pulled back the heavy bolts, one by one. A mortal shriek caused Kassandros to turn; the shield-wall was in contact, death was being dealt. Kassandros' bladder failed him.

But that was the least of his worries for there was nowhere to run to as the gate remained closed and the shield-wall blocked his route to surrender. He had no choice. He pulled at the gate, hauling with his brother at the great rings now that the bolts were freed. Grinding and slow they moved, until fingers could be got in the gap between them and more pressure was brought to bear; by degrees they opened, revealing the flaming torches still burning on the ground outside. Kassandros peered out but could see nothing as the flames dulled all that was in darkness beyond; a glance over his shoulder told him that the shield-wall was holding and getting aid from the comrades in the tower above as javelins rained down. *I must wait; don't give in to panic.*

Again he tried to peer into the night. *Surely they saw the signal?* And then it became obvious what he could do in order to be seen to be active but staying away from the action: picking up a couple of the torches he waved them over his head, crossing them back and forth, bellowing at the top of his voice for Pleistarchos and the flying column of cavalry that would lead the assault in through the open gates.

The combat escalated, the shield-wall dwindled, pushed back into the archway, now barely ten paces away from him. Kassandros gave one last mighty set of waves, knowing that his nerves would not stand to look behind him one more time. Down he threw the torches and as he was stepping forward the dark surge of cavalry came out of the night and he managed, just, to turn the forward motion of flight into a sideways jump.

Through the flame and the gate Pleistarchos' men thundered, knocking the shield-wall aside, crashing into and then through the scrum around it; swords slashing down on heads and shoulders, cleaving arms and necks in sprays of torch-lit gore. Surging on, with the weight of those coming behind pressing upon them, the cavalry ploughed through the defence, haphazard as it was, and clattered up the main thoroughfare leading to the heart of the city, its agora. And behind came the infantry rank upon rank running to keep up the momentum of the attack now that Corinth was laid open to pillage and rape.

Relief that it was over weakened Kassandros' knees and he sank to the ground, watching his army pass by, breathing deep gulps and trying to keep down a rising tide of vomit welling within.

'We did it,' Philip said, standing in front of Kassandros and looking down at him. 'You did it. We're in.'

Kassandros nodded and then shook his head, not in disbelief at the feat achieved but, rather, in disbelief at his part in it: he had not run – just – and he had played an active role. He would be able to look Thessalonike in the eye and tell her that he had taken Corinth and had led from the front; fortunately his fearful release of his bladder had gone unnoticed by all save him and he would not be mentioning it to anyone.

Long did the cries of pain and anguish go on through the morning, for part of Demochares' price for betraying his city was the freedom to massacre his enemies, whether real or imaginary. But this was of no concern to Kassandros for his garrison was soon installed and the new oligarchy in place before the last of the screams had been stilled; the shocked citizens of Corinth ventured out of doors to find that their streets were free from foreign troops, as Kassandros had business elsewhere.

Speed had been the key to the campaign over the last few months, speed and ruthlessness. The drive south had taken Polyperchon completely by surprise and, within a moon, two of his largest defences along the isthmus line had been taken. Most of the garrison in both sets of fortifications had surrendered, willingly coming over to Kassandros, the equipment and turnout immaculate, their morale low and their opinion of their commanding officer lower still. Many of the mercenaries, newly recruited by Aristodemus, had also crossed over to Kassandros, preferring, they said, to earn their daily pay without always fearing an inspection at any moment.

And thus Polyperchon had been pushed aside, his positions now manned by troops under the command of Atarrhias, whilst Crateuas had driven south, leaving Kassandros free to engage Corinth. Now that the city had fallen, thanks to treachery that had been negotiated for three months, Kassandros could lead his army away, south and east, for news of a concerning nature had come from Crateuas.

Kassandros looked back at Corinth still writhing under the convulsions of a change in leadership, as the city faded into the distance. *Let them do what they like to one another, my garrison will keep them in line.* And with that thought he pressed on to Argos.

'They've taken Antigonos' decree to heart and thrown out the oligarchy,' Crateuas told Kassandros as they stood looking at the barred gates of what had been until just recently his main city base in the Peloponnese. 'And they've sent to Alexandros for help.'

'Alexandros?'

'Yes, he arrived back in Greece a couple of days ago. It was news of his arrival that acted as the catalyst to the rebellion.'

'Well then, we'd better do this fast; I can't preside at the Nemean Games next month if Argos is not in my hands, without looking like a fool.' *And Thessalonike will tell me so to my face.* 'What are your thoughts?'

Crateuas' lined and scarred face creased into a squint-eyed grin. 'Walk straight in.'

'Walk straight in?'

'Yes. Our garrison is still in the citadel, they couldn't dislodge them. They have hardly any decent troops, just a citizen militia that hasn't fought an engagement for a good few years; that's why they've sent to Alexandros for help.'

'And Alexandros, even if he wanted to help, couldn't afford to spare the troops.'

'No, not since Polyperchon managed to scare so many of them away with his obsessions.'

'Straight in it is then; any particular way?'

'Straight through the gates.'

It was without preamble that Kassandros sent in the attack to storm the gates once the four rams had been fashioned from mighty plane trees. Ancient, even by Greek reckoning, the walls of Argos needed much in the way of repair, but the gates were of relatively recent manufacture, no more than a hundred years old.

The four attacks, each comprising a thousand men, set off simultaneously, under the cover of light archers and slingers strafing the walls to either side of each of the objectives, keeping the return in missiles to a minimum.

Kassandros sat with his half-brothers and watched the northern and western attacks from a knoll a safe distance from the town, pleased that because he had ordered four separate assaults he could quite legitimately stand back on the pretext of having to oversee all of them – he already had his story to tell his wife and needed no more, especially as his heart still raced and he broke out in a sweat every time he recalled the final few moments before the arrival of his cavalry.

But now there was a far more pleasant memory in the making as the hollow boom of the ram's metallic head striking hardened wood echoed off the walls and over the surrounding fields; each strike slow and deliberate, receiving nothing in return for the defenders had ceased to appear on the walls above the gates. It was easy, as if taking a stable manned by children with wooden weapons. The northern gates burst, their timbers shattered by the ram, their hinges wrenched from the ancient stonework; over them the assault troops piled, their cries rising though the air, their joy at being released on yet another city, so soon after Corinth, palpable. Within a few moments the western gates too split asunder and Kassandros' victorious men surged, their hunger for soft flesh and loot yearning to be sated.

'Shall we?' Kassandros suggested to Philip and Pleistarchos, gesturing with a hand to the now burning city.

'I think we should,' Philip said with a grin. 'I'll be interested in what the democrats have to say on the subject of you sparing their lives.'

'They can say whatever they like if they choose to waste their final breaths in a futile exercise.'

And futile it was for the elders of the democratic faction of the city could not deny that they had executed the leading members of the oligarchy during their rebellion.

'And why should I not just do the same to you?' Kassandros asked, his tone reasonable and light, as he sat upon his horse outside the municipal building in which the democrats had taken refuge.

The elders looked at one another; the oldest stepped forward, his gnarled hand grasping a stick, his beard fluttering in the breeze. 'They had caused much pain during their rule and had appropriated property and goods for their own use during their time in power. The people demanded justice.'

'The *people*! What care I for the *people*? The *people* do what they are told and then they get left alone. As soon as the *people* start making demands it starts to go badly for the *people*. You executed my supporters because the *people* wanted it and so I shall make an example of what happens when the *people* have too much say in their affairs.' He pushed his horse forward into the old man, knocking him down so that the back of his head cracked on the stone ground; unconscious he lay there, blood seeping from a wound to the skull. With his eyes fixed on the other elders, Kassandros pulled back on the reins, rearing his stallion up, so that its front legs scraped the air, before forcing it down on the prostrate and unconscious man, crushing his ribcage; the elders turned and ran back into the building.

'Block up the doors and windows and then torch the place. Let's send a lesson to the whole of Greece as to just what happens if they take Antigonos' decree seriously.'

It was with the screams of the Argos democrats burning alive still ringing in his ears that Kassandros took the surrender of Orchomenus a few days later. The lesson he had sent was enough for citizens who wished for life and the town was delivered up to him by treachery without any need for military action. Kassandros had no need to punish the democratic faction that had previously held out against him as they were gratifyingly massacred to a man, over five hundred of them, by their own neighbours, as they sought refuge in the Temple of Artemis.

Thus Kassandros was able to rightly claim the honour of presiding over the Nemean Games for control of the Peloponnese was his, putting the whole of Greece in his power. It was with pride – and a deal of surprise – that he acknowledged the cheers of the crowd in the stadium as he made his entry with Thessalonike, newly arrived in the south, holding his firstborn son, Philip.

'They seem pleased to have you here despite your overturning Antigonos' decree,' Thessalonike observed as she kissed her baby and handed it to the wet-nurse for safekeeping for the remainder of the day.

With his arms in the air as if he were already a victor in the games about to commence, Kassandros milked a rare moment of popularity. 'Most of these men are from the propertied class and have much to fear from democracy where those with nothing, and therefore nothing to lose, hold a majority in the assembly. Although, I have to admit, I didn't expect this kind of welcome.' Still reaping the crowd's approbation he made his way down to the arena and the altar set at its centre.

Having performed the opening sacrifice, reciting the ritual prayers, he presided over the games throughout the day, presenting the wreaths of wild celery leaves to the winners of the foot races, boxing, equestrian – both chariot and horseback – and pentathlon events, adding, at Thessalonike's insistence, generous prizes of his own to each man.

As the final victor, the pentathlete, walked back down the steps to the track from the elevated seats, high in the middle of the western stand, Thessalonike eyed his firm-muscled buttocks dusted with arena sand. 'I hope our Philip will be as well built, Kassandros.'

'Rather than thin, spindly, ugly and pockmarked, like his father, you mean?'

Thessalonike laughed, throwing her head back. 'Is that what you think of yourself? Really?'

'It's what most others think; I know, I've heard them say it enough, behind my back and to my pinched, pockmarked face.'

'Let them say it, Husband; what harm can it do you? I admire your physique for what it is. Whatever they may say won't take Greece from you.'

'Then why do you wish for Philip to be like that athlete?'

'It's normal to wish the best for one's child and that man was very pleasing on the eye.'

'From behind, perhaps, but from the front I found him, well...'

'Yes, it was hard to know where to look; he was so very, well, well...'

'Yes, he was.' Kassandros tapped the arm on his chair and, feeling a lesser man and trying to get the image out of his mind, waited for the fanfare of horns accompanied by the beating of many drums to announce the end of the games and his departure. He gave a sidelong glance at his wife who, seeing him, pulled a face of disbelieving wonder. 'Very funny.'

Thessalonike shook her head, laying a hand on his arm. 'Oh, Kassandros, I love you for what you are.'

Kassandros turned to her, his eyes puzzled, not believing what he had just heard. 'Say that again.'

Thessalonike smiled, squeezing his arm with soft pressure. 'I love you for what you are.' She leaned over and kissed him on his astonished mouth. 'And you are right, I never thought that I would say it, let alone believe it; but I do, Kassandros, and the birth of our child has shown the truth of the matter to me. I love you.'

So overwhelmed was he that the ending of the games passed him by completely and he had to be guided to his feet by his wife. He accepted the acclaim of the crowd in a daze and then walked as if in a trance out of the stadium. Never in his life had anyone loved him unconditionally: his father had barely tolerated him, his mother had died when he was young and his step-mother had made sure that he knew her low opinion of his character; his two half-brothers were, perhaps, the closest people to him but it was hardly love that they shared. No, he now found himself in completely new territory and it had taken him totally by surprise, for he had never imagined that Thessalonike would ever have such strong feelings for him. It completed his triumph. *I have Greece and the love of the woman I adore.*

As he held his child later, its head cupped in his right hand, he looked down into its scrunched face and he could see that the boy would have his fiery red hair and, no doubt, his pinched face; but he did not care, nor did he feel sorry for the infant for if he had negotiated life so well as to be the ruler of Macedon and Greece and overlord of Thessaly and Epirus, and also have the most beautiful woman in the world at his side, then the young Philip would be able to do the same. And then it occurred to him; he looked up at his wife sitting opposite in the soft lamplight of their suite in Nemea. 'This child is born to be king.'

'That was my first thought when he was presented to me after I gave birth to him. He will be a king. And what you have achieved this winter has done much to secure his kingdom. Now you need to look to our neighbours to the north-west: King Glaucias of Illyria has been taking advantage of your absence and making raids into our territory as well as into Epirus; he needs a sharp lesson so that we can concentrate our forces on looking east. I would suggest you take the west coast route home with a show of force.'

Kassandros looked down at his child again. 'Yes, and maybe I can get Glaucias to hand over Aeacides' son, Pyrrhus, who has taken refuge in Illyria according to my spies; he could be a major threat to our Philip in the future.' He handed the baby back to the wet-nurse who, cooing, took it from the room. 'As to the kingdom, the crown, do we…?' He left the question hanging.

'No, it's still too soon; we cannot afford to be the first and, besides, we are still not strong enough to have Alexander's death on our hands. And also, I have been thinking about how to go about making our claim completely legitimate.'

Kassandros was interested. 'How?'

'We need the support of two people: my half-sister, Kleopatra, and the, arguably, legitimate regent, Polyperchon.' Thessalonike raised her hand as she saw her husband redden at the reminder that he had been passed over by his father in favour of Polyperchon. 'It may not be palatable but it is a fact that needs to be lived with and used to advantage. Now, Kleopatra I can deal with but Polyperchon has seen me witness his constant humiliations by Olympias and will be less likely to respond to my advances than he would to yours, I would judge.'

'Polyperchon come over to us so soon after he has made a pact with Antigonos?'

'Of course and why not?'

'Because… well, because he has a pact with Antigonos.'

'Who is in Asia and without enough ships to get an army to Europe, even if he had one to spare with all the trouble that Ptolemy has stirred up for him.'

'But Polyperchon would never come over to us without his son.'

'Then make advances to Alexandros. Lure the son to catch the father.'

Of course; why didn't I think of it before? At our meeting in front of the gates of Tegea, all those years ago, he said that he would always be open to serving under me. Antigonos just got there first this time but there is no reason why I shouldn't change that. 'I'll write to him, suggesting that he has chosen the wrong side but it's not too late to change.'

Thessalonike smiled as she stood to take his face in her hands. 'It never is, Kassandros.'

He leaned down and kissed her and, placing his hands beneath her buttocks, lifted her off the ground and carried her off to the bedroom, all thoughts of intriguing with Alexandros and his father banished for a good while.

POLYPERCHON.
THE GREY.

'AND YOU *WILL* go and meet him?' Polyperchon looked at his son in amazement and then snatched the scroll from his hand.

'Of course I will, Father.' Alexandros pointed to the scroll. 'He asks you to come too.'

'He's guaranteed you both your safety if you come to Corinth,' added Penelope, Alexandros' wife, walking up to her husband and taking his hand. 'I believe it's always important to hear what your enemy has to say. You may find that he's not your enemy after all.'

Polyperchon grunted as he perused the letter recently arrived from Kassandros to their base in Sikyon, seven leagues west of Corinth on the north coast of the Peloponnese.

'He makes the point that it is not too late to reconsider our alliance with Antigonos.'

Polyperchon crumpled the letter and threw it to the ground. 'You've only just got back a few days ago from sealing that alliance. And now you want to go back on your word.'

'I'm not saying that I will, Father; but as Penelope said, it's best to hear what Kassandros has to say; especially as he is now the master of Greece and we hold a few villages and Sikyon in an insignificant scrap of land with no strategic value, which is why Kassandros left us here and went to preside over the Nemean Games instead. Face it, Father, we are so irrelevant that the Nemean Games take precedence over us.'

'Antigonos won't forget his commander-in-chief in Europe; he'll send help.'

'Antigonos can only send us money,' Penelope pointed out, retrieving the letter and smoothing it out on the table. 'Aristodemus came with Alexandros bearing another five hundred talents but that will be it; there won't be any troops or ships.'

'It will only be a matter of time before he does,' Polyperchon muttered.

'No, it won't be, Father. I've just come back from Tyros and I can tell you that the city won't fall until next winter, which keeps Antigonos and a large part of his army tied down. His son Demetrios is down in Gaza with a field army of twenty-five thousand to keep Ptolemy back. Meanwhile, Ptolemaios has gone north to the Euxine Sea with a small force and the only ships that his uncle can spare to relieve Amisius and prevent the northern attack on Kappadokia, whilst Antigonos' other nephew, Dioscurides, has taken the rest of the fleet that can be spared into the Aegean to counter Seleukos' ships and the Athenian navy operating together out of the Athenian island base of Lemnos; he's to take what islands he can as well as harry the Lydian coast to distract Asander from going into Phrygia. And all the time Polycleitus is operating with his fleet – swelled by the ships he captured from Antigonos – out of Cyprus, disrupting all communication and burning new-built vessels in their yards. So no, Father, it won't be a matter of time until he sends us help; his forces are now completely at full stretch, which was Ptolemy's strategy all along. The question is: if the strategy has been so successful as to prevent Antigonos from helping us, have we chosen the wrong side in this conflict?'

'But he made me commander-in-chief in Europe.'

'And what have you done since you were elevated to such lofty heights, other than lose most of the small territory that we held in Europe? At the moment you are no more than the commander-in-chief of a few sheep fields, an olive grove and a lovely view over the Gulf of Corinth.'

Polyperchon reddened. *How dare he speak to me like that!*

'I can read your expression and I'll tell you how I dare: because you did exactly what I told you not to do whilst I was away: you broke the men's trust in us and crushed their morale by ridiculous inspections and endless fatigues. I told you not to; Penelope who was here with you pleaded for you to stop, but did you? No, you just kept going with that madness until when Kassandros came south the men were almost joyful to see him and ran to him as fast as they could with open arms, to escape your petty ways. Kassandros hardly lost a man taking our positions across the isthmus. So don't tell me that being Antigonos' commander-in-chief in Europe means anything. Now, Penelope and I are going to see Kassandros; are you coming or not?'

'Kassandros hates me.'

'This is business, Father; forget the personal.'

'I will be just another of his generals if we go over to him; he'll give me no position.'

'Father, you're a born second-in-command, not a leader; you well know that. You were a disaster for Olympias, managing to lose most of her army to Kassandros through desertions, again because of your fastidiousness about the men's appearance, and now you've been a disaster here for the same reason.'

'A well turned-out army is an efficient army.'

'No, it's not; it's a miserable army that will desert at the first opportunity as you have proven too often. Perhaps you should just forget soldiering and retire to the family estates. Now, we're going; are you coming or not?'

'Not.'

'Very well, I'll negotiate for you.'

'What would Aristodemus say if he knew you were negotiating with the enemy?'

'He won't find out, will he? Not unless you tell him. Would you betray your own son?'

Polyperchon watched his son and daughter-in-law leave the room and then slumped down into a chair, shaking his head. How had it come to this, his own son criticising his methods when everyone knew that neatness and discipline were the keys to military success? He looked across to the letter left on the table; for a few moments he struggled with his thoughts. With sudden resolution he got up, snatched up the scroll and strode from the room.

'Why are you showing me this?' Aristodemus asked, handing Kassandros' letter back to Polyperchon.

'Because Alexandros has accepted the invitation to talks.'

'Why are you telling me this?'

'Because I thought you should know.'

'What's the point in me knowing if he has already gone?'

'He only went an hour ago.'

'And you've wasted that hour finding me to tell me something that you could have prevented an hour ago. Why didn't you stop him?'

Polyperchon had no reply to that question, not even a stammered one.

'It's too late to stop him now; he's already halfway to Corinth. You will just have to hope that he will see sense and stay on what will, ultimately, be the winning side. Although, I grant you, it doesn't feel that way at the moment.' Aristodemus' dark eyes narrowed as he regarded Polyperchon. 'That's thanks in the main to you managing to alienate your son's loyal Macedonians and making the mercenaries whom I hired question whether it makes any difference getting run through with a spear whilst wearing immaculate sandal straps and then deciding that it doesn't and so going over to Kassandros in droves because with him they can get run through without having worked for hours on making their sandal straps pristine.' Aristodemus held Polyperchon's eye. 'What you've lost over the winter we will now have to regain, with or without your son. And to start with I'm banning the holding of any form of inspection for the men.'

'But the men must be inspected regularly—'

'No, they must not; nor must they be put on fatigues if they fail to look smart when you walk through the camp whilst they're off-duty and eating their evening meal.' Aristodemus stared Polyperchon down. 'This must stop; the men are here to win a war, not to look decorative. Do I make myself clear? Because if you don't I shall recommend to Antigonos that he finds himself a new commander-in-chief in Europe.' He did not wait for a reply.

With misery Polyperchon looked back on the happy days when he was Krateros' second-in-command on the journey back from Babylon with the Silver Shields and other veterans who had been discharged by Alexander. *That was soldiering; supporting a man like Krateros who had such an easy way with the troops; they wanted to look smart just to please him. I just had to relay his orders and keep the supplies coming in. Perhaps Alexandros is right and I should just retire into obscurity.* But the thought of never having a position of respect again hardened his mind against the notion. At a loss as to how best to proceed, he went in search of the reports detailing the strength of each unit so that he could at least immerse himself in sick lists and combat strengths if he was not going to be allowed to hold inspections.

It was as he was going through the last of the reports detailing the strengths of the few mercenary units newly arrived overland from the recruiting centres in the south, soon after midnight, that he heard a noise outside his study door; he looked up, the door opened and his son sneaked in, checking the corridor behind him before closing the door with a quiet click.

'What are you doing here?' Polyperchon asked, putting down his lists.

'Being a loyal son, Father. I've come to warn you that Sikyon is about to be surrounded and that you should get out before it is.'

'Surrounded? By whom?'

'By me, Father; by me with the troops that Kassandros has put under my command.'

'What?' Polyperchon jumped to his feet, incredulous. 'You've turned traitor and are now coming to attack me and you say that you're being a loyal son? How much did Kassandros pay you?'

'Nothing, he doesn't have to pay me. He's given me all my old territory back, provided I hold it in his name, and he's given me back all my Macedonian troops who went over to him because they couldn't stand your regime, as well as all our mercenaries who deserted and another ten thousand of his men. He's also named me his commander-in-chief of the Peloponnese. He's heading north-west to secure Epirus against attack from Illyria; I'm left here charged with mopping up Cyllene, Dyme and, of course, here. Now you've two choices: join me or slip away before the army arrives a couple of hours after dawn.'

Polyperchon slumped back down in his chair; he looked down at the lists he had been working on and then swept them from the desk in a show of petulance. 'There is, of course, a third option.'

'I know; but neither of us wants that.'

'But if I choose it?'

'Then I will lay siege to Sikyon with you inside and I won't be able to guarantee your safety when it falls. Whereas if you leave now or join me there won't be a siege as I shall offer Aristodemus free passage back to Asia.'

'He's got five hundred talents to play with.'

'I know, Father; it was me who told you that. And he can keep it all if he just leaves Greece. Now make up your mind as I've already taken a big risk in coming here as I presume you told Aristodemus where I was going.'

'What makes you say that?'

'Oh, Father, I know you too well. As soon as I said "not unless you tell him", I knew that is exactly what you would do, as you hazarded that if you didn't and I joined Kassandros anyway, Aristodemus would suspect your loyalty and have Antigonos remove your title. Am I correct?'

Polyperchon's expression was enough.

'Now what is your decision?'

He leaves me no choice: if I go over to him I lose my position, and if I abandon the city the same will happen. He looked up from the desk. 'Do your worst; I stay.'

Alexandros nodded, understanding Polyperchon's motives. 'Very well, Father; I hope this isn't the last time we see each other alive. I'll always be willing to take your surrender once you feel enough has been done in the defence for honour's sake.'

And then he was gone.

Polyperchon sat looking at where his son had stood, trying to take in the fact that he was now at war with his own blood.

And it was true, everything that Alexandros had said. Two hours after dawn an army appeared on the eastern horizon with the sun at its back; dark was its shadow and long was its tail as it brought the instruments of siege warfare with it. Polyperchon stood on the ramparts of Sikyon and stared at the oncoming foe with a growing sense of foreboding.

'Is that who I think it is?' Aristodemus asked, coming to stand next to him.

A glum nod was all that Polyperchon could muster.

'And what do you plan to do?'

'Resist him.'

'Father against son?' Aristodemus looked at the oncoming army for a few moments and then burst out in laughter. 'As a Greek I find that hilarious,' he managed to say eventually. 'Macedonians fighting one another is a thing to be celebrated, but this takes it to another level. If only the great Alexander could have seen this.' He paused for a thought. 'However, thinking about it, I rather believe it's what he intended; why else did he not name an heir?' He turned away. 'Well, good luck, Polyperchon; I think you'll need it.'

Panic rose in Polyperchon's belly. 'Where are you going?'

'Well, I'm not staying here.'

'Why not?'

'Why not? I wouldn't want to intrude; this is a family affair after all. There's no place for a Greek from Miletus getting in the way whilst father and son fight it out. Besides, Antigonos has work for me elsewhere. No, Polyperchon, you are on your own. You've got almost six thousand men in the town, enough to man the walls, and the supplies are very well stocked up. If I were you, I'd kick the bulk of the citizens out; at least those with no practical use, the old and sick and, of course, the poor. Hold out for as long as you can and, you never know, Antigonos might not think so badly of you.'

With that he was gone, leaving Polyperchon wondering how it came to be that he had chosen to fight against his own son for Antigonos.

ANTIGONOS.
THE ONE-EYED.

F INALLY, A YEAR and four months
after arriving back in the west – two
and a half years since Eumenes'
defeat – things seemed to be coming
together. Antigonos surveyed the fleet at
anchor in the harbour of Berytus with a great deal of satisfaction. *At last I'll be able to starve Tyros into submission and be free
to head north to deal with Asander and Kassandros.*

And those were his priorities for Asander had been more than
a nuisance since receiving Ptolemy's troops and Kassandros had
proven himself to be a formidable opponent in Greece – the
subverting of Alexandros' loyalty back in the spring being the
catalyst that had spurred him into making the defeat of
Kassandros his top priority, over even Ptolemy. And besides,
Ptolemy was busy and of no threat for the remainder of the year:
for, in a bid to ensure that Antigonos was not seen to be the only
voice of Macedon, he had issued his own proclamation, voted
for by the army assembly of Egypt, supporting the freedom of
the Greek cities. Antigonos smiled to himself as he recalled the
joy and amusement he had felt when he heard that the Greek
cities in Cyrenaica had taking the proclamation seriously and
had thrown out many of the Ptolemaic garrisons, forcing

Ptolemy to spend the year bringing order to the rebels. *Let him find out what it feels like to be deflected from your objectives by manufactured events. And gold is a great manufacturer.* He rubbed his hands together at the thought of his agents' good work in stoking the uprising, although he had also had reports – unconfirmed – that he had not been the only party with an interest in destabilising Cyrenaica; but who the other was he could not say. *The more people working against Ptolemy, the better.* Safe in the knowledge that his southern borders were secure for the near future he would now take the war to Kassandros in Macedon and to do that he needed to defeat Asander in Caria to ensure that his supply lines would not be threatened and to divert Lysimachus' attention in Thrace, to which end he had sent Aristodemus to the Scythians with much gold and promises of more should they wish to cross the Danubus. The Thracian king Seuthes, who yearned to be free of the Macedonian yoke, was also to receive a visit from Aristodemus. *But first Tyros must fall, and this is the fleet that will ensure that.*

With Ptolemaios' return from relieving the siege of Amistus, Antigonos' main fleet, reinforced by many newly built vessels from shipyards in many ports, was now of a size to challenge for supremacy along the coast of Phoenicia and Anatolia thus ensuring Tyros' complete isolation. *Seleukos won't get so much as a stale loaf into the city.* He slapped his nephew Dioscurides on the shoulder. 'Well, my boy, get the fleet to sea and let us catch up with long overdue business.'

It was never a pretty sight, a city starved into surrender, for those who had survived were made almost feral by the struggle to keep alive. Filth and decay lay everywhere and sunken-eyed, emaciated survivors regarded Antigonos with little interest as he rode in through the gates of Tyros at the head of Demetrios and the two-thousand-strong garrison that he was imposing on the defeated city. Piles of rubbish lined the route – occasionally one would twitch indicating that it was a human in death throes and not discarded waste – and the stench of death enveloped it, but that was not going to detract from Antigonos' enjoyment of the day for he had taken Tyros – although it had taken him more than twice as long as Alexander. The one thing that irked him was that he had been forced to guarantee the Ptolemaic garrison free passage home in return for their opening the gates; seeing the commander who had frustrated him for so long still alive was a matter of great annoyance to him. *But an agreement is an agreement.*

He pulled up his mount, swung from the saddle and then saluted the ragged man before the defeated commander offered his sword, hilt first, in surrender.

Taking the weapon, Antigonos felt its weight and fought back the urge to slice it through the man's neck.

'We have done all that honour decrees in defence of the city and do now surrender it to you, Antigonos,' Timaeus, the commander, said in a low voice, almost a whisper.

'You had done all that honour decreed a year ago, Timaeus,' Antigonos replied, handing the sword to Demetrios.

'We were still being supplied a year ago; four months of a complete blockade is enough for honour's sake.' He looked up at the overcast sky. 'And winter is not far off; many will die unless they get nourishment.'

'And who says that I'm going to supply them with any?'

'That's down to you, Antigonos. If you want to share Kassandros' reputation for killing the citizens of the places he captures then so be it; it'll just make it harder for you to take cities in future.'

Antigonos' fists clenched and unclenched as his one eye burned with anger at being so patronised by a vanquished foe.

'Don't tempt me into killing an unarmed man, Timaeus; keep your mouth shut and leave before I change my mind.'

With a shrug, Timaeus turned back to the ragged column behind him and beckoned them to follow him out through the gate and commence the long walk back to Egypt.

Few will survive, which I suppose is some consolation. And with that pleasant thought he led his garrison through the streets to the citadel whilst Demetrios led a party down to the harbour to lower the great boom that had kept Dioscurides and his fleet at sea and the port secure.

It was now time for swift action for with winter but a month away, Antigonos had much to achieve before the snows came to the high interior of Anatolia; with the garrison installed and the fleet controlling the sea to the north and south of Tyros, he mustered his army on the wasted fields to the east of the city.

'Take another three thousand cavalry with you when you go back south, Demetrios,' Antigonos said once he had received the final count. 'That'll bring you up to five thousand; they'll be more use to you there on the flat desert around Gaza than they will be to me crossing the Taurus Mountains.'

'I could use them to mount a flying raid on Pelusium whilst Ptolemy is tied up over in Cyrenaica.'

'No, Son; don't provoke him into early action. We will fight him, yes, but on my terms. Once I've secured the north then we'll face him with the entire army; then and not before.'

Thus, leaving twenty-eight thousand men, under the command of Demetrios, in the south, Antigonos took the balance and headed north.

'Asander's planning a swift winter campaign,' Ptolemaios informed Antigonos as they met in Celaenae, the chief city of Phrygia. 'My spies tell me that Kassandros has sent reinforcements to him commanded by Prepelaus; I heard whilst I was burying my father and rushed back.'

'Your father's dead? I'm sorry to hear it.'

'No you're not, Uncle; you never thought him good enough for your sister as you proved by always overlooking him when it came to distributing commands.'

'Well, I'm still sorry for you; he was your father, after all, no matter what I thought of him personally.'

'Thank you. But enough of family sentiment; I've work to do.'

'*We* have work to do, you mean?'

'No, Uncle; you're arriving too late. Your army won't be here for at least another four days, as you said, and by that time Asander will be either dead or captured. It's all planned and ready. I leave in the morning.'

Antigonos looked astounded at his nephew, his mouth gaping. 'Are you giving me orders, you young pup?'

'No; I'm just telling you that if you want Asander beaten, I will do it tomorrow. If you want me to wait for your army then it will be too late.'

'But you've barely ten thousand men here.'

'And Asander now has at least sixteen thousand, I know. But I have to go now in order to catch him as he moves forward in a place where the numbers don't signify. If you want to come without your army then please do, Uncle, but...' His look was significant.

'I see. But you're in command, you mean.'

'Yes. I've planned it; it will be my glory.'

'My arse, you're a cocky puppy; you could rival Demetrios for arrogance.'

'Uncle, this year, with a very small fleet, I relieved Amistus, and then on the way back to Tyros, I lifted Seleukos' siege of Erythrae, forcing him back to the Athenian base on Lemnos;

and what has Demetrios done? Pleasured a few camels between drinking bouts in Gaza. I have the right to be pleased with myself and, what is more, I have the right to independent command.'

Antigonos looked at the earnest expression upon his nephew's face and burst into mirth, mock-punching his chest. 'You remind me of myself at your age. All right, my boy; I'll come along and watch your plan without saying a word.' *Unless, of course, it stinks like my arse.*

But it was a perfect location that Ptolemaios had chosen; Antigonos had to concede that, albeit grudgingly: on the road that followed the course of the Maeander River as it curled and wiggled along the borders of Caria, Lydia and Phrygia, he had selected a bottleneck where a steep cliff pushed in towards the southern bank of the river, whereas on the northern bank the ground was flat and gravelly and wide enough, before it started climbing up a wooded slope, to offer hope of escape to any ambushed force on the opposite bank: all they would need to do was cross the fast-flowing but shallow river not more than twenty paces wide at this point. It would be too tempting to refuse, even if the enemy did note the thickness of the wood on the rising slope, a thousand paces away.

And it was this thickness that gave Ptolemaios' position its great advantage for it hid completely the two thousand cavalry and the three thousand peltasts and light infantry that he had positioned within it.

'Up there, Uncle,' Ptolemaios said, pointing to the top of the cliff that constricted the road.

Antigonos looked up. 'What about it?'

'That's where you can watch from.'

'What! My arse, I will.'

'This is my ambush; trust me. You can enjoy yourself with the archers and slingers up there, hurling stuff down on Asander's head.'

It's not worth the argument; I lost Seleukos by not trusting him enough and giving him more independence. 'Very well. Make this good.'

Ptolemaios grinned. 'Naturally.'

By the time Antigonos had joined the thousand light infantry lining the clifftop high above the road the first mounted scouts pelted in, heralding the arrival of the enemy column; down ducked all awaiting it in ambush, down behind cover, sheltering in the shadows of rocks and trees so that from below nothing could be seen to give any hint of the trap. Looking over to the wood opposite, Antigonos saw nothing suspicious and nor did Asander's scouts as they ranged wide over the broken ground to the north.

And then came the steady sound of marching feet, thousands of them, distant at first but soon growing in volume. To his left and right, Antigonos watched the light infantry ready long poles and, keeping low, place them beneath large boulders, which, judging by their varying hues, had been brought up the cliff from elsewhere. *He's planned this very carefully. Gods, this could be good.*

Soon the crunch of massed footsteps resounded off the cliff below; Antigonos, resisting the temptation to crane his neck and look down, felt his heart quicken at the thought of such slaughter dealt from on high: it would stop Asander in his tracks, making one less problem to deflect him, Antigonos, from his true purpose.

And then the horn sounded, shrill and clear.

With bending backs, the men heaved on their poles, dislodging boulder after boulder, all along the clifftop, to tumble down its face, shattering stone in sudden explosions as they ricocheted off protrusions and cannoned off each other, falling with ever gaining speed along with showers of splinters and scree onto the hapless below. Crushed, heads burst open, issuing flying globules of noxious fluid and matter, as the leading units struggled to get their shields, slung over their backs, up above their heads; but a shield is of little use against a falling boulder and down men went with shattered arms and ribs to die in slow agony rather than enjoy the mercy of immediate oblivion of the more fortunate. And then, with the boulders spent, the archery and slingshot commenced as, to the front of the ambushed column, a phalanx rushed from concealment to form up, double deep, blocking the way forward; small in number it was but that was all it needed to be, for twenty-four men wide and thirty-two deep it was enough to halt any forward move by sixteen thousand spread out in column along a narrow road.

Leaning out and looking back, Antigonos could see that all along the line, until it passed out of sight a good half league off, the same story was being played out as Asander's men suffered grievously from a deadly hail pounding down on them. And it did not take more than a few score heartbeats until the first of them turned and fled to the river, splashing into its icy current to wade its breadth.

It was but a matter of moments before the trickle of flight broke into a surge; encouraged by missiles from above, the column lost all cohesion as each individual sought only to save himself and not partake in a joint defence, for there was no defending to be done against such an aerial onslaught. Into the river they fled, many tripping in their haste on large stones submerged beneath the now frothing surface, to be trampled underfoot and drowned in water that reached just above their knees. And still shaft and shot pounded into their backs bringing down many more, multiplying the chaos fivefold, tenfold, turning headlong flight into mortal panic as the rules of camaraderie were ripped down and replaced with bestial instinct.

Such was the terror and so much did it feed upon itself that sight was dimmed as those struggling for life focused on getting through the next ten paces without mishap, and thus Ptolemaios and his cavalry were more than halfway across the open ground from the wood before the screams of the dying were overlaid by the despairing shouts of the living. On came the cavalry with the peltasts and light troops running behind on either flank. And then the trap closed with the arrival of more heavy infantry forming up on the far bank, in line with the phalanx on the road, to prevent a breakthrough eastwards. There was now only one way of escape and that was back whence they came, west; but what lay in that direction none could tell.

Those who thought they stood a chance of saving themselves fled, but hundreds more, now beyond despair, knelt or sat upon the ground in submission. It was then that Ptolemaios and his Companions fanned out to protect the captives from the exuberance of the victors for, in the main, they were all Macedonians, either from Ptolemy or Kassandros and thus eminently employable.

'Over eight thousand,' Ptolemaios told Antigonos once the count was over. 'And none have refused to sign up with me.'

'Me, you mean,' Antigonos reminded him.

'Indeed, Uncle.'

'How many escaped?'

'About four thousand.'

Antigonos looked along the length of the river; the banks were lined with bodies. 'So, around four thousand dead then?'

Ptolemaios shrugged. 'They should have chosen the right side in the first place instead of fighting for that has-been who's coming this way.' He pointed over his uncle's shoulder.

Antigonos turned to see Asander, bruised and soaked, being escorted towards him. 'Now this, Ptolemaios, whatever you might think, is my business. Bring him before me when I'm ready.'

It was always a great pleasure to look down, from an elevated seat, upon a vanquished foe, chained and humiliated, and none was sweeter than this; Eumenes' defeat had not felt nearly so good, as Antigonos had once liked the sly little Greek, but Asander he had never much respected as he had refused all entreaties to help in the subjugation of central Anatolia whilst Alexander was campaigning in the south and east. *I shall make you regret your lack of cooperation.* 'Look at me,' he ordered the kneeling captive as hundreds of Ptolemaios' men looked on, encircling the two satraps.

Asander lifted his head and shook it with disappointment written on his face; he raised his chained and manacled wrists and rattled them. 'That you should treat a fellow Macedonian thus says more about your character than it does about the threat I pose. Eumenes sent Artonis to warn us of your ambition.'

So Artonis did spread her poison and the sly little Greek is still meddling from beyond the grave. 'Speak when you've been addressed and not before,' Antigonos snarled. 'Again the lack of respect says more about you than it does about the threat I pose to you. Artonis was right.'

Antigonos opened his mouth to shout abuse at Asander but quickly shut it, remembering Demetrios' words to him soon after he had executed Peithon: 'Don't execute any more officers or men who served with Alexander. Otherwise, it will be deemed that you have a jealous vendetta against them or a sense of inadequacy.' When he had insisted that he was not inadequate his son had replied: 'I didn't say you were; I just said that's how it might look.' *As much as I'd like to humiliate and then execute him, I can't do it, even though, like me, he stayed behind and didn't go on the conquest. The trouble is, Asander's right: my treatment of him says more about me than it does about him.* He looked around at the faces of the Macedonian soldiery watching. *Many of them were serving Asander just an hour or so ago. How willing will they be to fight for me if I kill him when they can see no reason to? I at least have to give him the chance to serve me as I did to his men.* 'Can you think of any reason why I shouldn't have you executed, Asander?'

'Many; not least of which it would be thoroughly bad manners, but that didn't hold you back with Peithon or Eumenes, did it?'

'They were traitors.'

'Eumenes a traitor? Really? To whom? Don't be ridiculous; he was fighting for the royal house against you. Think about that carefully and then decide who the traitor really was – is.'

Antigonos' knuckles whitened as he gripped the arms of his chair. *Don't let him provoke you.* 'Your men that I captured have all agreed to fight for me rather than face execution; do you wish to have the same choice?'

Asander laughed, sudden and loud. 'I'd be a pretty fool if I didn't. Do you want to give that choice to me?'

'I offer you your life and your satrapy back in return for swearing your loyalty to me, handing over the rest of your men who escaped to serve in my army and providing a hostage to ensure your continuing loyalty.'

'Ha! So my oath is not enough?'

'Those are my terms. Take them or leave them.'

'I take them, of course. Who do you wish as a hostage?'

'Your brother, Agathon.'

'Very well; however, he's back in Halicarnassus holding it for me since his return from Amistus.'

'I'm heading north; Peucestas will escort you back to Halicarnassus and then bring Agathon to me on the Hellespont. His life will be forfeit if I so much as suspect that you have had contact with either Seleukos or Ptolemy.'

Asander shook his head with regret. 'It's worse than Artonis made out.'

Antigonos' eye glared with anger at Asander. 'Artonis had better hope that I don't find her.'

ARTONIS.
THE WIDOW.

WITH HER FIRST sight of Pergamum, Artonis knew she would find it a hard place to leave; any desire to return to Alexandria had already withered. Its acropolis and upper town, vibrant with colour in late afternoon sun, perched on a huge hill thrusting, precipitous, out of the plain, to the height of two hundred men; it dominated the environment for leagues around. Sheer drops on the northern, eastern and western sides gave it a virtually impregnable position as it could only be approached from the southern slope that rose in three natural terraces, each one a line of defence, rising to the top.

'What do you know of the city?' she asked Archias, riding next to the covered wagon that had been her conveyance ever since crossing to Asia from Lysimachus' Thrace.

'I've never had a commission here, if that's what you're asking.'

'So you've not been here?'

'No, I was here as an actor twenty years ago. The theatre is a marvel; playing up there is like playing to the gods on Olympus. It feels as if one is in the sky.'

Artonis looked sidelong at the assassin, surprised to hear him talk thus. A look of nostalgia played on his face. 'Do you miss being an actor?'

Archias considered the question for a few moments as they rode in silence with just the muttered conversation of Sitalces and his Thracians, up ahead, drifting back on the warm breeze. 'I miss the beauty of the language and, as Aristotle said, beauty is the gift of God.'

'I did not have you down as a reader of philosophy.'

'Plays are philosophy; at least, tragic plays are. Besides, I studied in Athens under Anaximenes of Lampsacus before becoming an actor and he was a great friend of Aristotle. It was Aristotle who persuaded Philip to ask Anaximenes to come to Macedon to help him with Alexander's education.'

'So there is more to you than just being a killer for hire?'

Archias' boyish face was made even more so by the wideness of his grin. '"Matters do not have the same appearance when viewed from far or near." And that is the nearest I shall allow you to get.'

Artonis smiled to herself as the Exile-Hunter kicked his horse into a trot, moving away: it had been the first time on their journey that he had opened up to her in any way. Even during the long wait in Thrace for Lysimachus to return from his latest border war in the north – this time against a Scythian incursion supported by the Thracian king Seuthes – when she had little company to amuse her, he had kept his distance; she had assumed him to be no more than a failed actor who had found a more prosperous living with the blade. That he had studied rhetoric and philosophy in Athens and in such high circles had not occurred to her. *Matters definitely do not have the same appearance when viewed from far and near.*

The sun was westering as Artonis dismounted from her wagon and transferred to a litter to begin the arduous journey to the upper town where, they had been informed by one of the officers of the Lysimachid garrison, Berenice resided in what had been the palace of Orontes, the Persian satrap of Mysia. Pergamum had been his capital during his short-lived rebellion against Artaxerxes, twenty-two years before the coming of Alexander – a rebellion that Artonis' father, Artabazos, had joined as satrap of Hellespontine Phrygia when Barsine was a young child of eleven. Artonis herself had been born towards the end of her father's ten-year exile in Pella after the rebellion failed; Artakama had followed soon after his pardon and return to Persia.

Now, however, Mysia was no more and Pergamum was considered a part of Hellespontine Phrygia and thus was claimed by Lysimachus as a constituent of his realm – at least for the present, for who knew when, or if, Antigonos would come north? But that would be Lysimachus' affair and it was down to him just how strong a garrison he kept in the city. She felt little sympathy for Lysimachus; once he had returned from defeating Seuthes in the Succi Pass, high in the Haemus Mountains, he was barely civil to her and it had been left to his wife, Nicaea, pregnant with their first child, to entertain Artonis. It had therefore been to Nicaea that Artonis had delivered the warning of Antigonos' ambition and told of the offer he had made to Eumenes. Whether it would be acted upon or left to wither in fallow ground, Artonis knew not but she had done her duty, obedient to her husband's will, and now it was in the hands of the gods. And so, the task complete, she was come to Pergamum to see her half-sister, twenty years her senior and the mother to Alexander's first child, the illegitimate Heracles.

Now in her late forties, Barsine had visibly aged and fattened, Artonis was shocked to see, as she waddled down the palace steps to help her half-sister from her litter and fold Artonis in her well-padded arms.

'They sent a message up from the gate that you were come,' Barsine said, planting a kiss on Artonis' lips and then holding her at arm's length the better to study her. 'You look no different from when I saw you last, Sister. And don't you try to lie and say the same thing about me; I look old and bloated and I know it, but I don't care, for what man would dare to come near me? No, Sister, I'm afraid that is all over for me now since Alexander died.'

Artonis smiled, stroking Barsine's plump checks. 'You still look the same to me; there's just a little bit more of you, that's all.'

Barsine laughed and looked down at her portly form. 'Who would have thought that the beauty that stole Alexander's eye could have sagged into this? But apart from educating my son I have little to do but read, eat and drink.'

Artonis' expression saddened. 'Did you hear of Artakama's death?'

'I did, Sister, and it upset me greatly; she was on her way here, I believe.'

'Yes, Ptolemy thought he could use her as a spy in your house; he's developing an interest in your son. But she would never have compromised you, I'm sure of it.'

'And I too. Ptolemy has a lot to answer for.'

'And he shall, one day, I've sworn it.'

'And so will I.' Barsine looked over Artonis' shoulder at Archias and his Thracians; if she was surprised by the company that her sister kept she did not show it. 'I have made arrangements for your escort to be accommodated.'

Artonis indicated to the Exile-Hunter. 'Sister, this is Archias; he and his men have kept me safe throughout our journey.'

Barsine inclined her head. 'You and your men are welcome, Archias the Exile-Hunter; your fame – if that is the right word – goes before you.'

Archias gave a theatrical bow. '"No one has acquired fame through indulging in pleasures."'

'I should warn you, Sister, he's a philosopher,' Artonis said.

'And a student of Euripides,' Barsine observed. 'But we have met before, have we not, Archias?'

'It is good of you to remember.'

'Of course I remember your part in the siege of Tyros; your actions saved many Macedonian lives and shortened the siege.'

'Sitalces and his comrades had much to do with the affair.'

'And Alexander showed his gratitude.'

'Yes, he spared my life for a second time and told me that there would not be a third, but "these things we will let be as past and done with".'

'I understand. We'll speak no more of it. I hope your stay here will be both comfortable and relaxing.'

'"Whosoever is overactive when he could relax is foolish."'

'We are all indebted to Euripides for his many wise words. Come, Sister.' Barsine linked her arm through Artonis' and led her up the steps to the palace.

'What won't you speak more of?' Artonis asked, fascinated to learn yet another piece of Archias' past.

'Archias and Alexander had a difficult relationship.'

'Really? Tell me.'

'No, Sister, I can't; I don't know all the facts. If you want to know then it's Archias whom you should ask.'

Artonis looked over her shoulder at the Exile-Hunter, who was supervising the unpacking of their luggage from the wagon. 'Perhaps I will.'

'I doubt he will tell you. But enough of hired assassins. Come, you must be hungry, let's go to eat and you can see how Heracles has grown; and not in the same way as his mother.'

*

Tall for his fourteen years and fair like his father, Heracles caused Artonis' breath to catch in her throat so much like Alexander did he look. But it was more than mere looks or the similarity in the cut of his hair – long over his ears and down his neck and flicked back either side from his forehead – it was his presence. The boy had the same ability to draw all eyes to him by just walking into a room. Perhaps it was the sweetness of a subtle scent that – like Alexander – he emanated, or perhaps it was the intensity of his gaze, his eyes, one deep brown, the other blue, like his father's, mesmerising; but, whatever it was, Artonis felt herself awaiting his command and willingly obeying.

'I'm pleased to meet you, Aunt,' Heracles said, coming forward and placing a kiss on both her cheeks, 'although I am conscious that we have met before, but I was too young to remember.'

'Indeed we have, Heracles; I held you in my arms as a babe.'

Heracles smiled, his face lit up, and Artonis could not help but smile herself. 'I trust I did not disgrace myself as I lay there.'

'No, Heracles, you grinned and cooed, and I loved you.'

'I'm pleased to hear it; I wouldn't want you to have a bad memory of me.'

Barsine stroked her son's hair. 'No one can have a bad memory of a baby, especially the offspring of a sister.' She indicated to Artonis to take her place at the low table.

Sitting on a couch, Artonis was surprised to see Heracles recline, as a man.

'I killed my first boar last month,' the boy said as he read the puzzlement on his aunt's face.

'You are truly your father's son, to have achieved that feat so young.'

Heracles looked at her in earnest. 'I intend to be my father's son in all things or none.'

It was the warning look that Barsine gave Heracles that alerted Artonis to the very nature of what was meant by this. *He intends to claim his right or die in the process and Barsine supports him.* 'You have started well by having his looks,' she said, deflecting the direction the conversation was taking.

It was the arrival of Archias that completely changed the subject. 'Artonis, you should come and see this.'

'What?'

'Just come outside.'

With a shrug to her sister at the abruptness of the order, Artonis rose and followed the Exile-Hunter to a south-facing terrace.

High over the surrounding country she stood as dusk enveloped it; a cool wind tugged at her hair.

'Look there, along the road to Sardis, in the far distance,' Archias said, pointing south-east over the plain.

She squinted, wondering what she was meant to see; and then as her eyes got used to the growing gloom she realised that not all light was fading: deep in the distance there were tiny spots of light growing and, as dusk deepened, so did they wax and multiply until it seemed that she was looking over an entire city – a city that should not have been there. And she knew what she observed. 'Antigonos?'

Archias nodded. 'I don't know who else it could be with an army that big; he'll be here tomorrow. We should leave at once. Antigonos will be no friend of yours, Artonis; he will have heard the story that you've been spreading.'

Artonis looked at her sister, who had joined them. 'What do you think Antigonos will do to Heracles and you if you were to fall into his hands?'

'He's had plenty of opportunity in the past few years; he's been here, or close by, often, but not since he came back from the east. He doesn't see Heracles as a threat as he's illegitimate. Besides, we are under the protection of Lysimachus' garrison.'

'I won't run from him,' Heracles announced.

'But it might be wise to hide,' Artonis replied. 'He hasn't seen you for four years when you were still a boy; now that you look so much like your father, he might have other ideas about letting you live.'

'We won't leave,' Barsine insisted. 'Antigonos dare not touch us.'

'But *we* should go, Artonis,' Archias repeated.

'Go where? Back to Egypt?'

'Yes, that's what Ptolemy has paid me for.'

'And if I don't want to go?'

Archias frowned as if the notion had never occurred to him.

Artonis looked again at the myriad points of light, so far distant, like a part of the firmament fallen to earth. 'I don't want to go, Archias. In fact, I won't go; I shall stay here with my sister and nephew. They need me and Ptolemy doesn't, so why should I leave?'

'Ptolemy won't pay me if I turn up without you.'

'Yes, he will; I shall give you a letter for him explaining my reasons and also laying the blame for Artakama's death at his feet. He'll pay you; especially if you act as a decoy for us.'

'In what way?'

'By leaving now; ride swiftly, with your men, taking the wagon, in full view of the guards on the gate so that they will swear that we are all gone, thinking me inside.'

Archias looked doubtful.

'You're a philosophical man, Archias. You can't force me to go with you against my will because between here and Egypt I will find a way of escaping or even killing myself, and so you might as well take this very good option which at least gives you a very fair chance of receiving what you are owed.'

'"As a second-best course, take the least of two evils."'

'Aristotle was right on that account; now go and get ready; I shall be back out shortly with your letter.'

'Very well, I have business in Sardis anyway; it will cover my losses if your letter doesn't work.'

'Why are you doing this, Sister?' Barsine asked as the Exile-Hunter stalked from the terrace.

'Doing what?'

'Risking yourself by staying here with us.'

'Because, Barsine, I see what you and Heracles plan and I wish to help you in any way I can, for, if we are successful and if we can raise Heracles to the throne then I would have honoured my husband by ensuring the continuation of the Argead line and also we may be in a position to avenge our sister.'

It was not the following day but the day after that Antigonos appeared at the gates of Pergamum demanding to be let in with a small bodyguard under a branch of truce, as his army streamed by, north, towards the Hellespont.

'Why do you need a branch of truce when we are not at war?' Barsine asked as she received him in the galleried audience chamber with Artonis listening from behind a screen above in the gallery.

'Don't play games with me, Barsine. Not at war? My arse! Why are you sheltering your half-sister who has been going around the empire trying to build an alliance against me?'

'I am not sheltering her, she left yesterday at sundown.'

Antigonos sneered. 'Don't lie to me, Barsine. One of my patrols intercepted the Exile-Hunter and his empty wagon, whilst he was trying to skirt around my army and get to Sardis. He couldn't deny that Artonis is still here. Where is she?'

'I'm above you, Antigonos,' Artonis said, stepping from behind the screen and looking down over the balustrade. 'What do you want with me?'

'I want you to cease spreading your slanders,' he said, pointing directly at her, 'or I'll forget that I don't make war on women.'

'And what have you done with Archias?'

Antigonos looked momentarily confused. 'Archias? Why do you care?'

'He has become a friend of sorts over the last year or so.'

'He's not dead.'

'I'm pleased to hear it.'

'He's just in very close confinement.'

'Then I would ask you to release him.'

'Why should I?'

'In return I will do as you ask; I'll stop my agitation against you and will remain here and keep silent.'

Antigonos considered the proposition for a few moments. 'Very well. He and his men can prove of use to me: they can buy their lives by taking a difficult commission for no charge.'

'In that case I give you my oath.'

The eye glared up at her. 'So be it. But if it's broken, the fact that there is Lysimachus' garrison here won't stop me from tearing down the gates and dragging you out by your hair.' He grunted a farewell at Barsine and, turning on his heel, stormed out with his bodyguard close behind.

'Will you keep your oath?' Barsine asked as they stood on the terrace watching Antigonos and his bodyguard, far below, riding back to join the endless stream of men and wagons trudging north.

'Of course,' Artonis replied. 'I've done my part; it's now down to Ptolemy to act upon the seeds I have sown and bring the coalition together and defeat Antigonos.' She nodded, pursing

338

her lips in satisfaction as she looked down upon the army she would see destroyed; and then an even more pleasant thought occurred to her. Artonis gave her sister a knowing look. 'Perhaps we could consider what we can do for Heracles; although illegitimate, he is, after all, Alexander's son.'

'Indeed we could,' Barsine said, smiling at the notion.

'And then, Sister, you and I will avenge Artakama with Ptolemy's blood.'

PTOLEMY.
THE BASTARD.

IT HAD BEEN a tiresome few months; a hot and exhausting time. Ptolemy cursed his luck: just when this strategy was playing out so well and Antigonos' forces were at full stretch his province of Cyrenaica took his declaration of freedom for Greek cities far too literally and considered that it applied to them. *Fools! Surely they must have realised that it applied to Greek cities solely in Antigonos' sphere of influence.* But they clearly had not and rebellion had flared up throughout the province; it had only been the former Punic towns like Barca that had remained passive; all the Greek colonies had either expelled their garrisons or besieged them in the citadels. It was when the Cyreneans had executed the emissaries he had sent to negotiate a peace that Ptolemy had felt it necessary to intervene himself. And thus, instead of striking east at Demetrios' relatively small force around Gaza whilst Antigonos headed north to deal with Anatolia, Ptolemy had been forced to come west to fight a civil uprising. He was not in the best of moods and his mood had worsened since rescuing his governor from a siege by his own citizens in the citadel of the main city of the province, Cyrene.

'How did you let it come to this, Ophellas?' Ptolemy asked the governor in a voice that, although quiet, betrayed seething anger. 'How can it be that you and your garrison get surprised, and then locked in the citadel, by a bunch of provincials, who rarely rouse themselves from their boys' arses, waving sticks and shouting nasty names at you? I mean, you must have known that something was afoot; don't you have spies? Informers?'

'Yes, yes, lord.' Ophellas looked around the audience chamber in his official residence in Cyrene with a face full of misery; all the leading Macedonian dignitaries who had survived the uprising were there and each had a Greek rebel kneeling at his feet with a knife to the throat. 'But none of them heard a thing beforehand.'

Ptolemy leaned forward in his chair, incredulous. 'Not a thing? Come on. Wasn't there even a delegation from the Greek elders asking whether this proclamation applied to them?'

'No, nothing like that. But I had made it clear to each of the city councils that your proclamation was meant to apply only to Greek cities, and Cyrenaica, being an Egyptian province, was therefore not subject to its terms. I thought nothing of it when no delegation came; I just assumed that they understood the terms as I had explained them.'

'Assumed? Didn't you even try asking one of your informants what the mood in the province was?'

'Yes; and I was given no cause for alarm.' Ophellas' eyes drifted to a middle-aged man amongst the prisoners.

Catching the look, Ptolemy signalled the man holding him to raise the prisoner to his feet. 'Was it this man who gave you no reason to be alarmed, Ophellas?'

'It was.'

'Well, I think that we can see that he gave you no warning because he was already a part of the conspiracy.'

'It would seem that way.'

Ptolemy gestured with his finger across his throat; the man fell, spouting blood and twitching. A moan issued from the remainder of the prisoners as his life left him.

Ptolemy turned back to Ophellas. 'There; that should focus everyone's minds. I suggest that we find out just who was behind this, as such a coordinated uprising doesn't just happen by itself and I have a shrewd idea who the culprit might be. Ophellas, who here is the most influential of the prisoners?'

The governor looked around the room at the forty or so captives. 'Him – Galenos. He's the sufetes of Cyrene.'

'Good; is his son with us by any happy chance?'

Galenos' choked cry told Ptolemy that he was in luck; he clapped his hands together. 'Excellent; bring him here.'

A young man with the oiled, shoulder-length hair and clipped beard of a dandy was hauled to his feet and dragged before Ptolemy. Ptolemy studied the captive for a while, making a show of contemplating how to deal with him. His face suddenly brightened. 'I know; take the fingers from his right hand.'

'No!' his father shouted, struggling to get free of the Macedonian standing over him.

The young man clenched his fist, looking with terror first behind him at his captor and then at Ptolemy.

Ptolemy looked at Galenos in exaggerated surprise. 'No? Why not?'

'There is no need, lord; I will tell you what you need to know.'

'Very well. Tell your son to spread his fingers out on the floor. If he clenches his fist then we'll just have to take the whole hand off, if you don't satisfy me. Tell him!'

'Do as he says, Iason.' Galenos nodded at his son in encouragement.

Trembling, the fingers were spread on the floor; a sword hovered over them.

'Good,' Ptolemy said, turning to Galenos. 'What do I need to know?'

Still upon his knees with a knife at his throat, Galenos closed his eyes. 'After we heard of Antigonos' proclamation of Tyros we debated upon what it meant for us and decided that it would be foolish to act as if it applied to us, cut off, as we are, from any hope of support, such is the province's isolation. We decided that it would be best to stay under your protection, lord.' He paused and, opening his eyes, looked at Ptolemy.

Ptolemy gave no indication of his feelings.

'Then, after you made a similar decree, backed by the army assembly of Egypt, we still did nothing as Ophellas made it clear that again it did not apply to us. And then Antigonos sent us an envoy, promising his support should we shake off the Egyptian yoke and rise against the garrisons.'

'Who was this envoy?'

Galenos hesitated but a glance at the sword over his son's fingers loosened his tongue. 'His name was Agesilaos.'

'Agesilaos!' Ptolemy knew at once the sufetes was speaking the truth. *So this is where he came to after giving us the slip in Cyprus.* 'What did he offer?'

'Money for mercenaries, the promise that Antigonos would draw your attention away to the east and that once he had defeated you we would still be independent.'

'And you believed him?'

'Who doesn't wish to be free?'

'You are free.'

Galenos' look towards Ophellas was very articulate.

Good, it seems I have the right man in position here. 'And so you gave assurances to Ophellas and then rebelled.' Ptolemy shook his head, disappointed. 'And I suppose Agesilaos scuttled back to Antigonos as soon as you passed the point of no return?'

'No, lord; he's still here.'

Now that's the first piece of good news I've had since arriving here. 'Where?'

'He went west to Barca.'

Having always considered himself a forgiving man, to the point of leniency, Ptolemy deemed his restraint in only having five men from each of the rebel Greek municipalities executed as a sign of his goodwill and wish to make a settled peace in the province. That and the fact that he had given them the quick death of decapitation rather than nailing them up or perching them on a sharpened stake was also, he felt, giving the signal of a benevolent lord aggrieved rather than a tyrant seeking revenge.

Leaving the Greek cities to the east of the province back under the control of the chastened Ophellas, Ptolemy led his expeditionary force west, through the silphium farms – whence the province gained much of its wealth – to the former Carthaginian city of Barca. Set on high ground, five leagues from the sea, looking north-west towards distant Sicily, it had a foreign feeling to it with an architecture far more curved and rounded than the more angular Greek and Macedonian style; and more than that, most of its buildings were no more than whitewashed, rather than painted in the rich colours so favoured by the Greeks.

Glowing brilliant before him, Barca stood with its gates open and with a reception committee standing in front of them, as Ptolemy led his column up the hill, through the silphium fields towards it. As he drew near he saw that the men waiting for him were dressed in the Greek style and not the more flamboyant

Carthaginian attire that he had witnessed when an embassy from that city had come to Alexandria a few years previously.

'Lord Ptolemy,' the leader of the grey-bearded elders declaimed in a reedy voice, 'we welcome you to Barca and are honoured by your first visit to our city. I, Bostar, Sufetes of Barca, ask you to enter as our guest and accept our gifts.'

As your ruler, but we'll let that go for the time being. Feeling no need to be polite in return because of the diplomatic slip, Ptolemy inclined his head and kicked his horse forward, forcing Bostar and his fellow elders out of the way. With the grey-beards trailing behind him he made his way up the hill, his bodyguards surrounding him, towards what had once been the residence of the Carthaginian governor. Subdued, the citizens of the town, again, all clad in chitons or tunics, watched with murmured curiosity as he passed. On and up he climbed, feeling the heat of the day lessen as the breeze from the not-too-distant sea strengthened towards the top of the town. And it was here, in the agora, at the western end of which the residence was located, that the gift that Bostar had referred to awaited Ptolemy.

Inwardly he cursed, for, if he guessed rightly, it was not at all what he would have wished for. He swung his leg over his mount's rump, jumped from the saddle and then approached the three bodies, their hands tied behind their backs and with the bloodied points of stakes protruding from their shoulders – or, in one case, his mouth.

'Agesilaos?' Ptolemy asked, pointing to the central corpse, as Bostar came huffing up behind him.

The sufetes had a look of pride written over his lined face. 'Indeed, lord; he tried to buy our loyalty away from you.'

'And you said no, I take it?'

A moment of confusion passed over Bostar's eyes until he realised that Ptolemy was offering levity. 'As you can see, my lord.'

'What did he offer you?'

'Not nearly as much as the two either side of him.'

Ptolemy glanced at the two; their eyes had been put out and their ears and nostrils slit. 'And who are they, his confederates?'

'No, lord; they are nothing to do with Antigonos.'

'They don't look like Carthaginians.'

'They are not. They're Greeks from Sicilia; they were the agents of the Tyrant of Syracuse, Agathocles. They offered us his protection should we rise against you, pointing out that Syracuse is just as close to Barca as Alexandria is.'

Why am I not surprised? The Carthaginian embassy did warn me that Agathocles would be starting to meddle along the African coast. And so it begins. 'Did you get them to say anything before you helped them onto their stakes? Who their contacts are here? Anything at all?'

'We tortured them for three days and they would say nothing, except that, were they to tell us anything and Agathocles found out, then—'

'I know: all of their family and extended family and friends would be killed. Agathocles punishes his enemies by killing all they love and leaving them alive. It's rather effective, as you can imagine.' He looked across at the sea sparkling bright in the distance and the truth of what the agents had said came home to him: Syracuse really was as close as Alexandria to this arse-end of his domain. 'Are there any harbours along this stretch of the coast? There are none of note or I would know about them.'

'There are a few fishing villages, lord, but nothing that can take more than a small trading ship.'

'Then that's something I'll need to change; it's time to found another couple of cities.' *I need a fleet stationed this far west if Agathocles has started sticking his nose in where it's not wanted.* 'I thank you for your gifts and congratulate you on your loyalty,

Bostar; your reward will be suspension of all taxes due by Barca for this year and next.'

Bostar bowed. 'You are most generous, lord.'

'I also expect recognition of my generosity. I would also ask you to send surveyors along the coast to locate the sites of possible ports facing towards Sicilia. I would like to read your conclusions in Alexandria as soon as may be allowed. We are already behind.'

'It will be done, lord.'

'See that it is. I shall spend one night here and then I need to head back east.' *Now that matters are settled here in the province, it's time to take the war to Antigonos. I need to recall Seleukos and consolidate my forces as soon as I may.*

SELEUKOS.
THE BULL-ELEPHANT.

ALWAYS ONE TO dwell on the positive aspect of a situation, Seleukos would normally be struggling to see anything good in the predicament he found himself currently in; but that, perversely, from his point of view, was a very fine thing indeed: for it was time for him to withdraw from the north in a way that looked like enforced retreat. His grip on the Aegean Sea was being broken, bit by bit, as Antigonos' nephew Dioscurides, with his new and superior fleet, had taken many of his island bases in the Kyklades as well as prevented him from working in tandem with Kassandros in his new military venture. Freed by his new ally Alexandros taking over the struggle against Telesphorus, Aristodemus' replacement, and Polyperchon in the Peloponnese, Kassandros was now campaigning in Epirus, subduing a newly resurgent Aeacides whilst his half-brothers Philip and Pleistarchos had been entrusted with bringing the cities of Chalcis and Oreus, on the island of Euboea, under his sway thus securing the sea-route from Macedon to the south. However, Dioscurides' brother Ptolemaios, released from duty on land now that Asander had been defeated, had brought a fleet and army across the sea to retake the gains that Kassandros had made in the Peloponnese and Boeotia. Gradually cities were coming back to the Antigonid cause, and, good to his word, Antigonos was allowing them to run their own affairs without too much interference. However, Alexandros had shown much initiative in the north and west of the Peloponnese, taking Cyllene and Dyme and still besieging his father in Sikyon; with help he could still resist Antigonos' forces. But Seleukos could do nothing to help matters in Greece – nor, indeed, did he have any interest in doing so other than be seen to try but fail – for a pivotal point in the war at sea had been reached as Dioscurides was now in a position to directly threaten the Athenian island base of Lemnos.

And Seleukos could do little to avert the disaster, for disaster it would be for Athens and Kassandros should Lemnos fall into Antigonos' hands as it was the key to the Hellespont: it controlled the traffic coming in and out of that vital stretch of water dividing Europe and Asia and thus protected the Pontic grain fleets that were the life-blood of Athens and so many other Greek cities; it also would open the way for Antigonos to make a deal with Lysimachus in Thrace and cross with his army into Europe, threatening Kassandros' powerbase of Macedon.

That would be such a shame for Kassandros. Standing on the deck of his flagship, looking towards the huge fleet that was assembling to the east of Lemnos less than a league distant, he smiled to himself at the thought of just how desperate things were and how that suited his purpose perfectly. For now had come the time to begin losing the war in the north so as to keep Antigonos occupied up here with most of his army and navy. And it was the navy that Seleukos had drawn this far up the coast, tempting it with the prize of Lemnos by leaving the Athenian fleet unsupported as he took his ships south on a fool's errand to the waters off the Peloponnesian coast, showing his face but doing very little until he judged it was time to turn back east. *Fool's errand it may have seemed, but it has worked perfectly in that it has allowed Dioscurides to get past me and cut me off from my unfortunate Athenian allies.*

Blockaded in Lemnos' harbour the Athenian fleet could do nothing against the might of the force awaiting it, nor could it prevent the landing of hundreds of marines come to storm the landward walls of the harbour. Unable to put to sea to either escape or brave an engagement, it was but a matter of time before they would do what Seleukos knew to be inevitable; but first he had to put on a reasonable display of attempting to relieve his allies. He turned to the triarchos at his post between the two steering oars. 'Ready?'

'Yes, sir. All the other ships have acknowledged the orders.' He pointed to a couple of sailors standing by at the main mast. 'And they know to watch for your signal.'

'Then let's get on with it.'

With a couple of commands bellowed down to the oar deck the great Five edged forward as the first pulls of the oars tore at the water to either side to the slow beat of the stroke-master's flute. With the pace of the stroke and the groans of the oarsmen steadily increasing, the huge beast of the sea got under way as the rest of the fleet followed, heading towards a superior force that Seleukos had no intention of engaging at its full strength.

'Keep it to cruising speed for the time being,' he called back to the triarchos; the order was followed by another shout down into the oar deck.

Seleukos looked to either side: his ninety-eight surviving ships were doing a good job in keeping their station, a few with him in the centre of the formation but the great majority of them on either flank. *The irony is that, had I joined with the Athenians, between us we would have had a fair chance of defeating Dioscurides.*

But that had never been an option, for Seleukos' strategy had been firstly to slow the building of Antigonos' navy over the last couple of years and then, when the fleet had finally been launched, draw it as far north as possible; once done, that would be the time to make his move.

Now it was obvious that Seleukos was bringing his fleet forward, threatening Dioscurides' flank as he blockaded the harbour entrance and landed his marines to either side of it, a good half of his more than two hundred vessels manoeuvred to face the oncoming threat. And that was fine with Seleukos; indeed, he had gambled on it for he had rightly assumed that Dioscurides would not wish to abort the landings and could not afford to withdraw the ships from before the harbour mouth for fear of the Athenians escaping the trap they had been enmeshed in. And thus Seleukos had prevailed in narrowing the odds for he was now only outnumbered by a mere twenty or thirty ships rather than over a hundred.

But still, it was an engagement that he could not hope to win for within a short period of time the enemy would be reinforced by the ships currently disgorging their marines onto the shore. And so, therefore, the affair would require very careful timing.

Seleukos squinted against the glare of the sea and the spray, raised by the bow and ram ploughing through the waves, blowing the length of the deck. The two fleets were now less than a third of a league apart; the time to make the manoeuvre was approaching. 'Attack speed!'

The triarchos relayed the order and the ship moved into a new gear. Seleukos looked about to check that the fleet was acting in concert; satisfied, he turned his attention back to the oncoming enemy. *Not long now.* He counted backwards from fifty in his head. 'Ramming speed!' he shouted once the fleets were two hundred paces apart. And now the flute was marking the time of a heartbeat, a pace that the rowers would only be able to keep up for a hundred of theirs. 'Now!' Seleukos cried to the sailors standing by at the mainmast.

With a couple of yanks on a rope a red flag unfurled at the masthead; Seleukos felt his ship veering to starboard and then turned to watch the fleet make the pre-agreed manoeuvre. It was almost instantaneous: the fleet split down the middle; his ship was on the left flank of the half making for starboard as the other half headed to larboard, catching the foe by surprise and throwing them into confusion as their ships, now unopposed in the centre, scrambled to adjust their course, some to the left, others to the right. Oars fouled and collisions ensued; in moments, chaos abounded. Seleukos laughed out loud as he watched the formation of the enemy centre collapse and then the hurried course adjustment of the ships on the opposition's left and right as they realised that they were now greatly outnumbered, for Seleukos had weighted his flanks to begin with and the manoeuvre had strengthened them by, in effect, refusing his centre.

On they ploughed for the final few score strokes; and then the first booming reports, sudden cracking and splintering of wood, resounded over the massed groans of exertion of almost spent rowers and waves crashing against hulls. Into the enemy they tore, some thrusting their great rams into the bellies of ships caught almost side-on by the speed of the turn, others raking down their sides, splintering oars and causing mortal carnage amongst the oarsmen. But this was to be no full-on engagement, for that, Seleukos knew, he would surely lose as already many of the ships landing their marines had completed the task and were now backing oars to head into the fray. No, this was to be a hit and run operation and now they were hitting and hitting hard; soon it would be time to run and run hard.

The order to ship larboard oars was roared; Seleukos, along with the marines and deck crew, braced for impact as the flagship bore down on a slender trireme. Too late did the enemy vessel respond and the cries of the oarsmen who had been catapulted backwards, chests cracked and broken, drowned out the matchwood splintering of the oars as they were raked at full power. Marines thumped arrows into their opposite numbers who were sprawling on the deck in the wake of the collision, and sailors hurled fire-pots to smash upon dry wood.

Grinding down the length of the stricken foe, Seleukos felt the very being of the great Five vibrating as it mangled its prey, felling its mainmast with the weight of its impact, reducing it to a smoking, drifting hulk, crewed by the broken and pierced wailing their misery to the stiff sea breeze. And so the flagship left its victim wallowing and aflame, to bear away with the rest of Seleukos' right wing, leaving the burning wreckage of more than a quarter of their opponents helpless in the water and obstructing their fellows, thus forming a protective barrier from Seleukos' now running fleet.

Well, I did my best by attacking a force more than twice my strength, Seleukos mused as he looked back, through the carnage he had just dealt out, to the real issue unfolding before the harbour of Lemnos. *But I'm really sorry, Kassandros, I just couldn't get through. We really could have done with your navy in support but you were busy at Chalcis. I can't blame you for not coming to our aid; but the harsh reality of the situation is that Antigonos now controls access to the Hellespont.* And so, with varying versions of that conversation playing in his head, he led his fleet south, back towards Cyprus, leaving the north in Antigonos' hands. *And hopefully he'll be busy there for long enough for Ptolemy to defeat Demetrios in the south and then for me to get back to Babylon.*

Halicarnassus held nothing for Seleukos; Asander had become an irrelevance since his surrender to Antigonos and his delivery of his brother Agathon to him as a hostage. He did not intend to call in on his way south; it therefore came as a surprise to Seleukos to have a ship intercept his fleet as it sailed down the coast of Caria with a message from the satrap delivered by none other than Agathon, inviting him to dine with Asander and discuss how to take the war against Antigonos in Anatolia forward.

'How did you get released?' Seleukos asked Agathon, astounded, after he had delivered his brother's message.

'Asander had a change of heart: seeing as Antigonos left immediately for Hellespontine Phrygia and he sent Ptolemaios over to Greece to bolster Aristodemus' forces there; and then as soon as they had gone, Menander, to the north in Lydia, was found dead in mysterious circumstances.'

'What happened?'

'No one knows; he was found dead in bed with a stiletto wound in his chest. The woman he had been sleeping with knew nothing, even under torture. It's a mystery.'

'Not really. He was murdered.'

'Yes, and my brother wants to thank whoever did it because with Menander gone he feels he can take Sardis and control Lydia and so he decided to go back on his arrangement with Antigonos. Effectively there was no one other than Peucestas and his small escort to keep him in check.'

Seleukos smiled; he could see what had happened. 'Ah, poor Peucestas; he's not going to be very welcome with Antigonos when he has to report that he had his hostage stolen from him.'

Agathon shared the amusement. 'He should be used to it by now, it was some time ago after all.'

'How did it happen?'

'Peucestas decided to go overland and pick up the Royal Road at Ephesus; before we got that far my brother had sent a strong force of cavalry to intercept us. Peucestas had no choice but to hand me over; you should have seen his face.'

'I can imagine it: all outraged conceit and undermined arrogance.' Seleukos indulged in the mental image for a moment. 'He's fallen a long way from impersonating the King of Kings as the satrap of Persis. Perhaps there's a lesson to some of us there?' *For some of the less talented, at least.* 'Very well, I'll come in. You won't be offended if I bring a large bodyguard, will you?'

'Of course not,' Agathon replied, understanding from Seleukos' tone the correct answer.

'I thought not.'

The royal residence was all astir as Seleukos, surrounded by his bodyguards, entered the main hallway with Agathon: soldiers ran this way and that, shouting, with no obvious sense of purpose, and the few officials that could be seen were huddled in small groups talking; a couple of slaves lay dead on the stairs, the blood trickling all the way to the bottom.

Seleukos looked at Agathon.

'I don't know,' Agathon said. 'Everything was fine when I left this morning when we spotted your fleet.'

'Draw your swords,' Seleukos ordered his men as a couple of armed soldiers approached.

'Well?' Agathon asked the men. 'What's happened?'

The two soldiers looked at each other and took deep breaths. 'Your brother's dead, sir,' one of them told Agathon. 'He's been assassinated.'

'Assassinated?' Agathon stepped back, blinking, digesting the news for a few moments. 'How?'

'That's just it, we don't know. We found him dead in his study at midday. It was bolted from the inside; we had to break it down. The only other way in is through the window and no one could have climbed up to it without being seen from the ground. It's a mystery.'

Agathon's shoulders and head sagged as he exhaled; his fists clenched.

Seleukos could see exactly what had happened and even had a suspicion as to who had carried out the assassination; but he kept that to himself as he put a hand on Agathon's shoulder. 'I'm sorry for you and for your brother's life. My guess is that Antigonos ordered his death for going back on his word; that being the case I would say that you aren't safe here either. You'd do better to come with me back to Cyprus and then on to Egypt.'

Agathon shook his head. 'No, there's nothing for me in the south; I'll take my chances here. I'll bury my brother and then think to my vengeance. I'll go to Sardis; Kleopatra is still there and she's a friend.'

'As you wish; good luck to you.' Seleukos gripped Agathon's forearm and then left him to his grief to make his way back to his ship for it was pointless staying.

'Now, why am I not surprised?' Seleukos said as he saw a familiar group waiting at the foot of the gangway.

'Because you are heading to Egypt and we need to go there.' Archias' boyish grin beamed; his eyes were all innocence. 'Artonis has decided to stay with her half-sister, Barsine, in Pergamum and I can't persuade her home to Alexandria. So that we can claim our reward,' he tapped a pouch hanging from his belt, 'she's written to Ptolemy explaining her reasons for not coming back and asks that he will pay us just the same.'

'But just in case he doesn't, you decided to do a little job or two on the way?'

'"Seek your fortunes by hard work."'

'I should just have you killed here and now.'

'I don't think Ptolemy would take too kindly to that, do you?'

'He won't know. But I think I'll just leave it to him to decide what to do with the man who assassinated Asander, one of his allies, at the behest of Antigonos his enemy.'

'You just do that, Seleukos; I'll be pleased to hear his thoughts on something that I'll deny and cannot be proven.' He looked at the ship. 'May I?' Without waiting for an answer he mounted the gangplank.

Seleukos watched him go, finding it impossible to dislike the man. *No doubt it was him and his Thracians who did for Menander as well, on the way here; I wonder who ordered that – Lysimachus or Kassandros?* And then another thought occurred to him. *What about Kleopatra or Thessalonike? Archias will never say, so forget about it.* And then, pleased to have done the job expected of him over the last three years, he followed the Exile-Hunter aboard to leave the north to be fought over by Antigonos, Kassandros, Alexandros and Polyperchon, and leaving him one step closer to Babylon.

POLYPERCHON.
THE GREY.

POLYPERCHON LOOKED EAST from the walls of Sikyon, as the sun set over the siege lines, towards the road that led to Corinth, the road along which an army, coming to relieve the town, must come; and still none came, and still the siege endured. Besieged by his son and forgotten by his supposed allies, Polyperchon cursed Antigonos, regretting his decision not to follow Alexandros over to Kassandros.

But it should not have been this way: as the war had widened and Antigonos' forces under Ptolemaios and the newly arrived Telesphorus had taken advantage of Kassandros' troubles with King Glaucias of Illyria and the re-emergence of Aeacides threatening his puppet on the throne of Epirus, Polyperchon had expected to be relieved after Ptolemaios regained Attica. Instead, however, Antigonos' nephew had secured a non-aggression pact with Demetrius of Phaleron, the Tyrant of Athens, and then, with his rear secure, he had turned the other way and gone north into Boeotia, ousting Kassandros' garrisons, and then forging an alliance with the Aetolians. This done, he took his fleet and army to Euboea, directly threatening Philip and Pleistarchos' attempts to take the island for Kassandros. Aristodemus, meanwhile, had concerned himself with keeping Attica subdued and taking the odd town in the eastern Peloponnese. There had been no mention of help for Polyperchon, not even a response to his letters, smuggled through the siege lines, asking for assistance – nothing.

Thus, Polyperchon had come to a decision: what pride that remained to him must be swallowed; he would flee the city and join with Aristodemus in Attica and resume his position as commander-in-chief in Europe.

His mind made up, he went to enact the plan that he had standing by for his escape; if his letters could get through then, surely, so could he.

It made perfect sense to Polyperchon that he should travel with one of the couriers that he had used for his futile correspondence; the man along with the garrison commander awaited him and a companion, shortly after midnight, by the sally-port he always used for his clandestine work.

'Are we set, Diokles?' Polyperchon asked, pulling a hooded cloak over his shoulders and fastening it with his golden brooch.

'We are, sir,' Diokles, a short, compact little man capable of great turns of speed, replied, kneeling down to tighten his sandal straps.

Polyperchon turned to his companion, his beard the only feature visible under his hood. 'I'm leaving you in overall command, Sykirion. I hope to be back with an army by the full moon; hold out until then and don't let my son tempt you into negotiations.'

'Trust me, that traitorous bastard will never take this city.'

'Let's hope we can tempt him back onto our side once I've broken the siege now that Ptolemaios has regained so much territory.'

The garrison commander spat his disgust. 'I would never trust Alexandros again.'

'Kyros is right,' Sykirion agreed. 'The bastard can never be trusted again.'

Polyperchon pulled Sykirion's hood down to better see his eyes. 'That bastard happens to be my son and don't you forget it.'

'I won't forget it, but *you* should; it's contrary to the natural order of things a son going against his father.'

Kyros spat again. 'Any man who does that loses the right to be acknowledged as a son.'

'That may be your view, Kyros, but I am a little more forgiving and still hope to be reconciled with Alexandros.'

'Then you're more of a fool than I thought.'

Polyperchon stepped up to Kyros. 'Be careful.'

'You know I'm right: your son changes sides too easily.'

'My son is still my son.' He turned to Sykirion and squeezed his shoulder. 'Now, I should be going. Take care, my friend.'

'And you, sir,' Sykirion replied.

'I'll send Diokles back at midnight in eight days with a message telling you how I'm doing.' He turned to the garrison commander. 'Have this door ready to open when he arrives, Kyros; the password will be what, Diokles?'

'Paris.'

'I'll be here myself.' Kyros took a key from around his neck and, fitting it into the lock, he twisted it and, with a click, the sally-port opened.

Diokles moved to the door, pausing for a moment to listen and then sniff the air; satisfied they were unobserved he cocked his head to Polyperchon and slipped out of the city. Polyperchon drew a breath and then followed, keeping low as they traversed the rocky ground leading down from the walls.

Moonless, the passage to the siege lines was gloom-ridden,

and the footing, treacherous. Trying to follow the nimble Diokles, who had the advantage of previous knowledge of the route, Polyperchon stumbled from rock to furrow in his efforts to match his pace. With hands and knees torn from arresting his falls and stubbed toes bleeding, Polyperchon slowed as Diokles came to a halt just twenty paces from the first of the trenches marking the siege lines, illumined by the occasional flickering torch. The odd muttered snippet of conversation drifted out from the trench.

Indicating complete silence with a finger and then motioning him to remain where he was, Diokles crawled forward on his belly, half the distance to the lines, towards where the light was at its dimmest; he paused. After a few moments he turned and waved Polyperchon on; with his breath held he scrambled forward, his scratches and cuts receiving yet more ill-treatment. Coming level with Diokles, Polyperchon let go his breath and inhaled deep of the fresh air.

'Shhh!' Diokles put his finger to his mouth, his teeth clenched. He indicated with a down-turned palm that they should remain motionless.

Polyperchon tried to breathe as quietly as possible, but each breath he took sounded like a gale within his head; he strained his hearing but the soft whisper of conversation had vanished. An ominous hush lay over the immediate area.

Long they stayed immobile; nothing moved within the trench, apart from the flickering glow of the torches playing on the shadows some distance away, both to the right and left. Ahead it was almost dark; just a faint glimmer reached that far.

Diokles tapped Polyperchon's shoulder and then, with no other warning, leaped to his feet and sprinted, hunched over, towards the trench to disappear into its gloomy depths; a few moments later his dark form could just be made out scrambling up the other side. A wave of panic rushed through Polyperchon. *I was meant to go with him!* He had no hesitation. He jumped to his feet and ran.

'Get him!' a voice barked in the night.

Polyperchon's old man's legs pushed him forward but the speed was not enough; as he jumped down into the trench two men grabbed him before he could scramble up the other side. Down he was punched; an iron-hard fist gripped his wrist; his arms were pulled back and expert hands slipped a noose around them securing them in a heartbeat.

Trussed up and breathless he was rolled onto his back.

'Where do you think you're going?' a silhouetted figure asked, bending down and ripping off his golden brooch. 'Wherever it is you shouldn't be wearing this; it reflects torch-light, you know; you might have escaped our notice without it.' He looked to his mate. 'Come, let's take him to the general.'

'What am I meant to do with you, Father?' Alexandros looked at his father and then to his wife, Penelope, and then back to Polyperchon; he was at a genuine loss. 'I can't ransom you back to your family because I *am* your family. I doubt very much whether Antigonos would be interested in purchasing you – I know for a fact that Aristodemus would pay not to have you back – so that leaves keeping you as my prisoner. What do you say to that?'

Polyperchon could not meet his son's eyes. 'Do what you will, Alexandros; I'm done. I'm done with it all.'

'Oh, come, Father; show a little more resilience than that.'

'You can always give us Sikyon and then be free to either go or join us,' Penelope suggested. 'Now we have you it makes no sense for the city to hold out.' She glanced at her husband and, seeing no objection to the plan, pressed on with the idea. 'There must be enough men within the walls who would wish for this to be over by now. Tell them that we won't foist a garrison upon them and they will be free to choose their own form of government. I can't see how they could refuse such an offer. Can you?'

Polyperchon shook his lowered head, looking as miserable as he felt. 'No, I can't.'

'Come on, Father; cheer up,' Alexandros said, slapping Polyperchon on the upper arm. 'Make the arrangements and then you're free to join with us or to leave as you will.'

It was futile to resist; he was at the end of his journey as the commander-in-chief in Europe, and he knew it. And with no position, just who was he? 'Very well; I'll make the arrangements.'

The arrangements were surprisingly easy as Alexandros already had a line of communication to the faction sympathetic to him within the city led by the deputy commander of the garrison. Polyperchon had only to use the same method and was astonished by how many of the leading citizens sympathised with Alexandros.

'Of course, they are only interested in power for themselves,' Alexandros said as they waited with the assault troops for the deputy commander's men to open the gates at the time specified. 'They like the idea that I won't make them accept a garrison; they'll re-form the oligarchy and, no doubt, massacre anyone who tries to prevent them.'

Polyperchon knew that to be the truth but cared not and offered no opinion on the subject as shouts and the clash of weapons erupted from behind the city gates.

Short was the fight, sharp was its end and swift was the outcome: the gates creaked open to reveal a group of armed men, backs towards them, holding at bay a mob with their shields locked together.

'Now!' Alexandros cried and broke into a jog; behind him, a column of men, eight abreast and countless deep, crunched after him. Polyperchon stepped aside to let them pass; he wanted to be no part of this betrayal. *Although none can deny that it was I who arranged it, I would rather not be there at the end.*

It was, therefore, a while later that he entered the city and, to his relief, found that his son had controlled his troops: none of the tell-tale signs of a violent sacking littered the streets: no bodies sprawled in puddles of their own blood; no women weeping, clutching dead children to their breast, or screaming as they endured rape after rape, and no soldiers running through the streets blind drunk and taking what they will. It was into a peaceful town that Polyperchon walked, or so he thought, until he reached the agora. It was here that the leading citizens of the town were gathered along with Alexandros with his wife and senior officers; before them stood Kyros, the commander of the garrison, restrained by two men; at his feet his deputy lay dead, laid out with his hands crossed over his breast.

'What's this?' Polyperchon demanded, running up to his son. 'The agreement was that the garrison can march out bearing their arms and standards.'

'It was,' Alexandros agreed. 'It was until this man,' he pointed to Kyros, 'killed his second-in-command.'

'He betrayed us,' Kyros shouted and then spat at the corpse on the ground.

'I ordered him to,' Polyperchon countered. 'I organised the opening of the gates. He was following my instructions.'

'You! You couldn't organise anything more complex than an arsehole inspection; you're a martinet not a planner and couldn't give reliable instructions on how to pick your nose.'

It had been a long time building up within him, this sense of failure and inadequacy, but when his faults were laid bare, so clear and obvious, before him, Polyperchon could take it no more. His sword was in his hand quicker than at any time in his life, even than in his glory days as a phalanx commander in the east. 'I am the commander-in-chief in Europe and I demand respect! I demand respect!' As he finished the final word he looked into Kyros' eyes; they were wide open in shock. Polyperchon tried his grip on his sword; it was stuck fast. He looked down to see the blade wedged under the man's breast-plate, deep in his groin. He twisted it, felt the suction give and then wrenched it out. 'I demand respect,' he whispered to the dying garrison commander. 'And I will have it.'

The soldiers restraining the man let go their grips; he slith-ered to the ground.

Polyperchon looked down at the blood dripping from his blade and then at Kyros, twitching in the last throes of death. He felt peace seep through his mind: he had shown he was not to be laughed at or humiliated any more and all in the agora had witnessed it. He wiped his sword on Kyros' tunic and then held his head up for the first time since he had been captured. 'I demand respect!' Turning to his son and his daughter-in-law, Polyperchon sheathed his weapon. 'Now make good your promise and leave the city with your men; I shall come with you, but I won't stay.'

'Where will you go?'

Polyperchon's smile was thin. 'If Aristodemus would pay not to have me back then I shall go south; I'll take what men remain to me to Messene, out of everyone's way, and wait to see how things play out.'

Alexandros got to his feet and embraced his father. 'As you wish, Father; but please, be at my side as I lead my army out of the city and then take your men and head south with your honour intact.'

Polyperchon took his son's face in both hands, looking him in the eye. 'You have turned out to be a better man than I, Alexandros; for that, at least, I am proud.'

It came as little surprise that the people of Sikyon turned out in their hundreds to see the army and the defeated garrison march out of their city and leave them to resolve their own affairs. At the head of the column Polyperchon rode next to his son and Penelope; feeling better about himself since killing a man who had so grievously insulted him in public, he even waved at the crowd in acknowledgement of their cheers.

'Will you take on Ptolemaios?' Polyperchon asked Alexandros as they neared the main gates.

'No, Father. I shall keep Corinth and the other cities I hold in the Peloponnese in Kassandros' name and, like you, wait to see who emerges as the stronger party.' He gave his father a sly smile. 'I've already changed sides once; I can easily do it again.'

'People will cease trusting you should you try to.'

'Oh, I won't try to; I'll just wait to be asked like the last time.'

'And what if Antigonos beats Kassandros and doesn't ask you to join him again?'

But if Alexandros had an answer to that question he did not have the chance to give it for he jerked back in his saddle, grasping at an arrow buried deep in his chest, punching clean through his cuirass. With a shocked glance at his father, he slid from his mount; he was dead before he clattered to the paved road.

'So dies a traitor,' a voice shouted from high on the gate tower.

Polyperchon raised his eyes to see Sykirion loose another arrow; he had no time: it too struck him on the chest, but a fraction to the left, and slid off his breastplate, furrowing its bloody way under his arm to strike the paving with an explosion of sparks. Sykirion fell with two javelins in him before he could release a third time. As the body broke below the tower, Polyperchon was aware of a high bestial wail, grief and anger combined in full measures. He looked down to see Penelope cradling the body of her husband – his son. And then the truth of what had happened struck through his shocked mind and he saw with clarity his son lying dead beneath him. He jumped from his horse and joined his daughter-in-law, clutching at the body of his son. But clutch and shake as they might, Alexandros did not return from his path to the Ferryman.

How long he and Penelope wept, Polyperchon knew not nor cared for his grief was deeper than he had ever known and made more bitter by the closeness he had so recently shared with Alexandros. With eyes red and flowing he stroked his son's face. 'Round them all up!' he heard Penelope screaming. 'All of them who supported or who are suspected of supporting Antigonos. I want them all!'

He looked up to see a woman afire with hatred, more terrifying even than Olympias in full rant: a woman released to bring death to her enemies and despair to those who would not bend to her will.

'Take back the citadel!' Penelope screeched at her men. 'We remain here now; my husband's death ends any agreement we might have had with this accursed place. I will hold it in his name against any who'll come against me.'

Polyperchon got to his feet, tears still flooding. 'We'll bury him here, Penelope.' And as he said those words he realised that he was now alone in the world. It did not matter where he went, he would always be a loner, for it now mattered not who he served; Alexandros would no longer be at his side, whether it was Ptolemy, Antigonos or Kassandros who paid for his loyalty.

KASSANDROS. THE JEALOUS.

IT HAD COME as quite a surprise to Kassandros that he should have acquired the reputation as a martial man but his campaigns over the past few years had all been successful. The most recent in Illyria had been the most successful of all for he had defeated King Glaucias, whose territory bordered on both Epirus and western Macedon, so decisively that the terms of the peace treaty were almost all he could have wished for: Glaucias had undertaken not only to refrain from raids across the border into the uplands of Macedon but had also undertaken not to attack Epirus.

But what Kassandros had not been able to secure was the transfer of custody to him of Aeacides' six-year-old son, Pyrrhus, currently in exile in Illyria; the Illyrian king maintained that Phthia, the boy's mother, had fled with the child – where, he did not know – once she heard of Kassandros' coming. Glaucias' promise to hand the boy over to him should he come into his possession was only half believed. However, Pyrrhus' father, Aeacides, was now no longer a threat as he had been killed in battle by Philip, Kassandros' half-brother, in a lightning campaign in Aetolia and southern Epirus after the former king had challenged once again for his throne. Thus, with Glaucias neutralised, Aeacides gone and replaced by his puppet, Alcetas, the unstable, murderous elder brother of Aeacides – originally passed over for his excessive cruelty – Kassandros had secured his western border in preparation for what he knew could be an existential conflict with Antigonos, now consolidating his hold on the Anatolian coast with a view to taking his army north to the Hellespont. Kassandros was under no illusions that the resinated cyclops would attempt to cross into Europe if he had the right set of circumstances.

And it was to the Hellespont that he and Thessalonike were now headed for Antigonos had invited him and Lysimachus to sit down and talk to find a way of avoiding war; Kardia, whose tyrant, Hecataeus' policy of equal friendship to all parties made it the ideal venue.

'It will be impossible, of course,' Thessalonike had said when he arrived back in Pella to pick her up on his way through to the conference, 'because he will insist that you recognise him as your superior and agree that you hold Macedon in his name.'

Kassandros had been realistic about the chances of finding a solution since receiving the diplomatic invitation but still held out a little hope as they set out on the journey. 'He knows that neither I nor Lysimachus would ever accept that, so perhaps he will suggest some form of a compromise.'

'Why should he?' Thessalonike asked as they boarded the ship, in the port named after her, that would take them to Kardia. 'With Alexandros dead and Aristodemus' replacement, Telesphorus, evicting all the garrisons that he put in place—'

'Apart from Sikyon and Corinth.'

'Indeed, apart from what Penelope holds, nominally in your name; although, now she seems to have made an alliance with her father-in-law, it's hard to say just whose side she is on.'

Kassandros shrugged. 'She has no love for Antigonos; it was one of his men who killed her husband. His remaining supporters tried to stage a coup; she put it down and crucified thirty of the rebels in the agora. They're now calling her the Conqueror of the City.'

'Cratesipolis? That's a rare honour for a woman.'

Kassandros looked down at his wife. 'Do I detect jealousy?'

Thessalonike smiled and took her husband's hand and indicated around her to the fine city still rising around the harbour. 'She may have conquered a city, but I have one named after me; an honour that will last through the ages. And I have you for company whereas she only has the old nonentity, Polyperchon. What have I to be jealous of?'

Once more Kassandros found himself unable to believe his good fortune in having the love of this woman. *I'll not risk losing her; Antigonos won't wrest one bit of what I have away from me.*

And so it was in that frame of mind that he sailed into the grand harbour of the ancient port city of Kardia. Nominally it was a part of Lysimachus' realm of Thrace but in practice it was a law unto itself: rich from the tolls it charged for passage through its waters and strong within its tall defences, Lysimachus allowed it to keep its autonomy, finding it a useful tool.

'I know you've bribed the cities along your coast to remain neutral, Lysimachus,' Antigonos said almost as soon as the three leaders had sat down around a table in the Temple of Artemis, having taken sacred oaths respecting one another's safety. 'They're refusing to enter into an alliance with me.' The single eye burned with outrage. 'What do you say to that?'

Lysimachus, much weathered since the last time Kassandros had seen him, when he fled Pella shortly after his dying father had named Polyperchon as his heir, scratched at his thick black beard, holding the great eye's gaze. 'I have no control over what the cities decide as their policy. That they have chosen to favour none of us is as much of a hindrance to my ambitions as it is to yours.'

'My arse, it is!'

Lysimachus slammed his palm onto the table, his temper already broken so soon into the meeting. 'I will not take this shit from you, old man. You talk of me bribing cities when you have bribed an entire nation into revolt. For the last year I have been taking back the Greek cities around the Euxine Sea that took your declaration of Greek freedom to heart and expelled my garrisons. I still have Callantia under siege.'

'None of that was my doing.'

'No? And I suppose it wasn't your gold that encouraged the Scythians to cross over the Danubus and had the Thracian king Seuthes join them in rebellion?'

'I know nothing of that.'

Kassandros found he was rather enjoying himself.

'Well, who was Aristodemus working for then? I know he's been up here with a lot of gold, although I've yet to catch him. But I've thwarted his nasty work; I repelled the Scythians and chased Seuthes all the way up to the Succi Pass in the Haemus Mountains, where I have recently completed the construction of a fortress.'

'Good for you.'

'And bad for you because I defeated him and captured most of his army; the Thracians I executed to a man but the Macedonians I incorporated into my army.'

'Macedonians?' Kassandros asked, leaning forward.

Lysimachus' smile was grim within his beard. 'Yes, surprising, isn't it? Macedonians, fighting for a Thracian! Who would have thought it, eh, Antigonos?'

Antigonos made no reply.

'No, I didn't think you would have much to say. You can't really deny it, can you, seeing as I have thirty-two of your officers waiting outside to be ransomed.' He indicated to the door. 'Shall we?'

Antigonos did not get to his feet. 'What proof do you have that they are my men?'

'Apart from the commanding officer Pausanias' confession before I executed him, you mean? Not much, other than every one of the men outside has admitted to being loyal to you and that Aristodemus was the paymaster of the rebellion. Now, will you pay their ransom or must I execute every one of them and then let it be known that you don't care for your followers enough to be bothered saving their lives? Your choice!'

Kassandros really was enjoying himself now. 'That *is* an unfortunate position to find yourself in, Antigonos.'

Antigonos did not take his glare away from Lysimachus. 'Keep out of this, you pockmarked little toad.'

'Yes, you're right: you instigating and then supporting rebellions in Thrace is none of my concern; nor does it affect me when you get caught doing it.' This time he was rewarded with a look that would have cut him to the bone had he not been in a sacred precinct and covered by an oath. *That's enough baiting of the cyclops.*

'Well, Antigonos?' Lysimachus asked, allowing a smile to play freely on his face at his enemy's discomfiture. 'What's it to be? Shall I take your men outside the city walls, away from our oath, and kill them? Or will you pay a ransom of, say, ten talents a man?'

'Ten talents?'

Lysimachus examined the back of his hand. 'Yes, I think that is only fair seeing all the expense you have put me to; especially as I use my gold to build fortresses to keep our world safe from the threat in the north. So, three hundred and twenty talents and you can have your men back. Take it or leave it.'

With a feeling not far short of glee, Kassandros watched the hatred curdle Antigonos' expression.

Antigonos jumped to his feet. 'I'll take it; but there will be no further negotiation. You submit to me or there is war between us.'

'I didn't even notice us negotiating in the first place,' Lysimachus replied. 'Did you, Kassandros?'

Kassandros shook his head. 'I can't say I did. But seeing as I'm not prepared to submit to him and nor, I suppose, are you, then negotiation could only have involved Antigonos agreeing to stay in Asia and take his troops out of Greece and Thrace and then, I believe, we would have a deal and not war.'

'My arse, I will! Ptolemaios and Telesphorus stay in Greece until you submit to me.'

Kassandros pushed his chair back and stood. 'In that case I'm wasting my time here.' He inclined his head to Lysimachus. 'I'm sorry to leave so soon, but it sounds to me as if I've got yet more work to do in Greece, so I'd better be getting on with it. Gentlemen.' He turned and walked to the doors knowing that it had been, in part, a successful, if short, conference: Lysimachus had humiliated Antigonos in such a way as to draw the old man's anger towards him, giving him, Kassandros, some time to campaign against his nephews in Greece.

'At least the world will see that you were ready to talk peace,' Thessalonike said as their ship rowed out of Kardia. 'There can be no doubt as to who is the aggressor now. You hold the Great Ring of Macedon; you are the regent to the rightful king and yet you are the one who is told that he has to submit to a man with no official position within the empire whatsoever.'

'And I am married to Alexander's half-sister.'

'That has nothing to do with it.' Thessalonike gave him an arch look. 'Yet.'

'But until that time we have to defend ourselves against his aggression and the best way of doing that is by keeping his nephews and their fleets busy delaying his now inevitable invasion of Europe.'

'Yes; and then pray that, in the meantime, Ptolemy does something to draw his attention back to the south.'

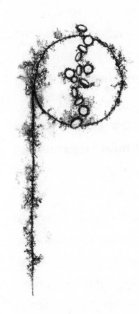

PTOLEMY.
THE BASTARD.

'IT'S BEEN A long time, Babrak,' Ptolemy said, as always, for some unaccountable reason, feeling genuinely pleased to see the Pathak merchant. 'Four years at least, I would say. Did you have a successful trip?'

Babrak touched his forehead with the tips of his fingers and inclined his head. 'The great lord is too kind in enquiring after my welfare. But yes, I impregnated my wives and had such a deal of business to do in the east that I was there for the births – only two were boys, sadly – and was able to leave them all impregnated again when I left.'

'I'm very pleased to hear it.'

Babrak displayed his red-stained teeth. 'As am I; they should have enough to keep them occupied for a while. I need a rest; I hope I shan't be called upon to do my duty again for a few more years yet.'

Ptolemy put on his most sympathetic expression. 'So do I, Babrak; so do I.'

'A boy may lose his charms with age but a wife loses hers with opinions and when one has many wives, well...'

Ptolemy understood only too well. 'You don't need to tell me, old friend. Now, come and sit with me and tell me all you have seen of interest on your way here.'

'So, Nearchos and Andronicus are advising Demetrios,' Ptolemy said, looking out over the Great Harbour of Alexandria to the military harbour on the far side of the now-completed mole; a fleet was arriving. *Seleukos at last, I hope.* 'Neither are outstanding military tacticians: Andronicus can handle a siege and Nearchos is more at home on the sea; what strange choices.'

'Ah, but noble lord, a boy who is good in all things is expert in none,' Babrak pointed out, eyeing the purse on the table between them. 'That is why Antigonos has also summoned Pythan from Babylon with two thousand cavalry and a thousand foot-archers. They arrived whilst I was in Demetrios' camp at Gaza. Pythan is a general of some repute.'

'And he is also the satrap of Babylonia, here with his body-guard.' *Leaving Babylon less than fully protected. That will be of real interest to Seleukos. What a motivation he'll have in the coming battle.*

'A thought that struck me also, when I saw him arrive.'

'What?'

'Nothing, noble lord; far be it from me to read your thoughts.'

Ptolemy looked at the merchant, studying him. *What he doesn't grasp or guess about the politics of this world is not worth knowing. I suppose that's why no one executes him.*

'There were also a couple of other arrivals whilst I was at Gaza.'

'Oh yes?'

'Yes. Envoys from Cyprus: one from King Pygmalion of Kition and the other from members of the new oligarchy in Marion. I'm told that they feel that, with Antigonos' nephews' success in Greece and Asander's strange assassination, it is time to switch chariots and back Antigonos.'

'Do they? Well, that is the final time that either of them shall have that luxury.' He weighed the purse in his hand and then tossed it over to Babrak. 'Thank you, my friend; you have been most useful.'

'I only live to please you, noble lord.'

'Me and anyone else with a weighty purse. Is there anything I can do for you?'

'Yes, lord, there is. I am told that silphium grows in abundance in your province of Cyrenaica.'

'Indeed, it does; it grows nowhere else.'

'Then perhaps I may be allowed to have access to the market. With all the Greek colonists out in the east I believe it would be a profitable business to export it there.'

'And I shall be a very willing business partner.'

'And I would be honoured, noble lord.'

'Lycortas, my steward, will make the arrangements.'

Ptolemy's pleasure at Seleukos' return was tempered by what he had learned from Babrak. 'I can't risk losing Cyprus; I need to act fast.'

'Do you want me to resupply the fleet and then leave immediately?' Seleukos asked, unable to keep the reluctance out of his voice or his expression.

'No, I'll go myself and I'll take Lagus with me, it'll be good experience for him. I want the world to see what happens when people take advantage of my forgiving nature.'

'What do you want from me?'

Ptolemy considered the question for a few moments. 'This could be turned to our advantage. Pythan has just arrived with Demetrios from Babylon, bringing two thousand cavalry and a thousand archers with him, which gives Demetrios a slight mounted advantage.'

'Pythan?' Seleukos' eyes lit up.

'Yes, I thought that would interest you. I imagine you would like to bring Demetrios to battle as soon as is feasible?'

'I'd like to kill Pythan as soon as is feasible.'

'Let's hope that it comes to the same thing. You muster the army at Pelusium, ready to invade Palestine, whilst I take the fleet to Cyprus, join up with Menelaus and destroy Marion and then execute Pygmalion.'

'I brought the Exile-Hunter back with me; I'm sure he could help with the latter. He assassinated Asander, you know, although he'll deny it all the way to the Ferryman.'

'Antigonos paid him, I assume.'

'I assume so too; although, who paid him to kill Menander, I don't know.'

'He killed Menander too?'

Seleukos shrugged. 'He was in the area when Menander died in curious circumstances.'

'I wonder if our old friend Archias is getting a bit too dangerous?'

'That's what I've been wondering.'

'Did he bring Artonis back?'

'He did not; she decided to stay in Pergamum with Barsine.'

'Really now? That makes my arrangement with Archias very interesting: the deal was that he brings her back here.'

'She's given Archias a letter asking you to honour your agreement even so.'

'It's not up to her. Still, I'm not surprised she didn't come back; I expect she blames me for her sister's death.' Ptolemy waved the thought away. 'But she's done what I needed: Kassandros and Lysimachus are both keeping Antigonos busy in the north;

378

giving me the opportunity to strike in the south. When I've done in Cyprus, I'll raid Cilicia and the northern Syrian coast; Demetrios will, I hope, take a flying column north to repel me.' Ptolemy raised his eyebrows, inviting Seleukos to continue.

'Cavalry! It'll have to be cavalry.'

'Yes, and to have a chance of catching me they'll have to travel very fast.'

'But your fleet will be faster.'

'All the way back to Pelusium; then we attack and Demetrios will have to decide whether to fall back, endure a siege in Gaza or face us with either a few mounted troops or, if he's back in time, a full complement of exhausted cavalry.'

Seleukos nodded his agreement to the plan. 'And I get to kill the man who replaced me.'

'And then we shall see, Seleukos.'

SELEUKOS.
THE BULL-ELEPHANT.

WE SHALL SEE *indeed.* Seleukos felt his spirits lift for the first time since his flight from Babylon; now, at last, he could see the real possibility for the realisation of his dream and the key to it had been provided by Antigonos himself. *Ordering Pythan west with his best troops is an act of arrogant folly; one I'm very happy to benefit from.* Thus it was in a very positive state of mind that he was reunited with Apama and introduced to his new daughter, named after her mother, after many months away at sea. 'You and the children will come with the army when we march,' he told his wife as they lay entwined, their skin slick with sweat. 'If we win the battle, speed will be of the essence.'

'Then won't we slow you down?' Apama asked, kissing her husband's cheek.

'Antiochus is almost twelve, he can ride his own horse. Archaeus can go in front of me and little Apama can be strapped to your back. I'm not going to risk leaving you here stuck in Egypt because the first thing that will happen—'

'If you win,' Apama cautioned, holding her thumb between her fingers to ward off the evil eye.

'If we win,' Seleukos agreed. 'The first thing that will happen if we win is that Antigonos will abandon whatever he's doing in the north and come south to punish Ptolemy; I don't want my family marooned in Egypt.'

'To be captured should Antigonos prevail.'

'Quite.'

'Then we'll come. What about our baggage?'

'What about it?'

'Well, how will we get it to Babylon?'

Seleukos took his wife's face in both hands and kissed her. 'Apama, when we have Babylon, we'll have everything we want. Now, tell me: are you really worried about our baggage?'

Apama returned his kiss. 'What baggage?'

With the waning of summer, the dry heat of Egypt became more bearable and Pelusium, on the Pelugic branch of the Nile delta where it flows into the sea, was almost pleasant. And it was a blessing from the gods for there was much work to be done mustering the army that would march east and then north, following the coast, to Gaza. Seleukos sat in the relative cool of the shade of an awning with a faint sea breeze keeping the sweat from forming on his forehead, studying muster lists. 'This predicts that we should have a phalanx in the region of eighteen thousand heavy infantry,' he said, looking up at Lycortas who was mopping his bald pate with a fragrant cloth.

'Does it? That is good,' Ptolemy's steward replied.

'What do you mean, "does it?"? You compiled the lists.'

'I must correct you on that point, sir: I had others compile the lists for me; there is a difference. The people who compiled the lists told me only how much the whole thing would cost; that is all I am interested in. How many men you have in your phalanx is a matter of indifference to me – so long as you win, of course – as I have no understanding of, and little interest in, military matters; it's for that very reason that we have people like you in Egypt.'

'Well, I can tell you that if we do indeed have that many heavy infantry then we shall outnumber Demetrios' phalanx by seven thousand, if the reports of your little birds are correct.'

'I think you can rely on my spies, Seleukos.' Lycortas dipped his cloth into a basin of scented water and then applied it to the back of his neck.

Seleukos studied the lists again and then looked at the reports received from agents in Gaza. 'If that's the case, we will be outnumbered by his elephants seeing as we have none.' He prodded a list with his forefinger. 'That's where the battle will be won or lost: his elephants. We are going to have to do something about them; it's pointless having the larger phalanx if half of it is mush on the ground.'

'That, sir, is a military maxim that I can understand.'

'I'm pleased to hear it.' Seleukos looked once more at the elephant numbers, chewing on his bottom lip, before coming to a decision. 'Now, tell me, Lycortas, how is your understanding of carpentry?'

'To be generous to myself: rudimentary.'

'Well, here is an opportunity to expand your knowledge: get me ten wagon-loads of planks, a couple of thousand long nails, plenty of hammers and as much chain as you can lay your hands on.'

Named after Seleukos' father, his eldest son, Antiochus, had grown in body and mind in the four years of their exile in Egypt and was now an interesting companion. Taking after his father in build and his mother in looks with a fine-featured face with large, almond eyes and skin of the same hue, Antiochus was at the same time both athletic and intelligent. During the muster of the army, Seleukos had taken to having the boy accompany him in most of his duties, and when he was not accompanying his father Antiochus trained with the fifty Companion Cavalry that Seleukos had brought with him from Babylon. Having witnessed the pride that Ptolemy had shown in the development of Lagus, his eldest son by Thais, Seleukos was enjoying the same feelings as he and Apama watched Antiochus jump from his horse, run alongside it for a few quick strides, and then swing back up into the saddle cloth to repeat the action on the other side of the beast. Around and around the training ground Antiochus and the Companion Cavalry half rode and half ran, accelerating with every circuit, until keeping pace with their mounts was impossible and elongated hops and skips, hanging onto the reins, were all they could do along the ground.

'He's doing well to keep up with the others,' Apama said, 'even though his horse is slightly smaller.'

'I don't think I could have gone that fast at his age,' Seleukos admitted. 'Alexander and Hephaestion were always the best at this – well, Alexander was always the best at everything – but they struggled to keep up with the Companions. Peucestas, Perdikkas, Peithon, Leonnatus and I would all fall once we got to a brisk canter.' He smiled at the memory. 'Strangely enough, the only one of us who could also do this well was Kassandros; probably because it didn't involve having to be brave.'

'How was Ptolemy at it?'

'Ptolemy was older than Alexander and us pages; he was already one of Philip's Companions; we used to look up to him.'

'And you still do.'

Seleukos considered that notion. 'Yes, I suppose if I'm completely honest, I do. I admire him because he has the great ability to think ahead and plan for almost all eventualities. It was he who first made me realise that what we are embarking on will have implications that will last for generations; he made me understand that it will be a dynasty that we will found, you and I. It's not just me becoming satrap of Babylonia again, just another one in the empire; no, it's breaking the empire apart and taking a chunk of it for our family to hold forever.' He pointed to their son. 'That boy will be a king one day and then his son, and his son, and his son and so on. That's why I look up to Ptolemy, because he understood that concept the moment Alexander died without naming an heir; he knew that if he were to take Egypt, no one would be able to get him out and he would be independent.'

'Babylonia is going to be far harder to defend than Egypt is; there are two great rivers that lead into the very heart of it for a start.'

'We'll expand to the east and to the west; it won't just be Babylonia that Antiochus will be king of and his mixed-race blood will stand him in good stead in the east. Antigonos and Eumenes both showed how easy it is to take the east, but neither of them showed a great interest in keeping it; that's where I'll improve on them.'

'And the west?'

'Ah, the west? Well, Ptolemy has already suggested that I will need a port and suggested that I should build one around where the Orontes flows into the sea.'

'And he keeps all of Syria to the south of that?'

'Yes.'

Apama looked up at her husband and smiled. 'He is clever, you're right. He'll give you that port because that will mean that anyone who wants to take Egypt has to come through you first, making you Ptolemy's shield.'

Seleukos nodded. 'Yes, I saw that too, but what does it matter? I would rather be Ptolemy's independent shield than just a general in Ptolemy's army.'

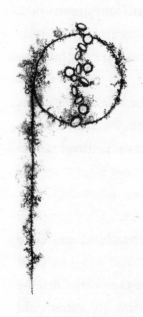

PTOLEMY.
THE BASTARD.

PTOLEMY WAS NOW a man in a hurry once again for he had much to do before he could return to Egypt and he wished to do it before winter made the seas even more treacherous. He stood before the walls of Marion, with his son Lagus and Menelaus, surveying the rows of armed men along their length; the gates were firmly shut. 'What amazes me is that, having watched Seleukos execute the entire royal family in the agora and make it an oligarchy, the city should risk intriguing with Antigonos again.'

Menelaus was in no doubt of the reason. 'They believe that Antigonos will be the eventual winner and so when Pygmalion went back on all his oaths they took advantage of me using my army and fleet to blockade him in Kition and called on Antigonos to come and relieve them.'

'Only Antigonos' fleets are busy in Greece and Lemnos. What about the Rhodians?'

'There's been no sign of them this year. Perhaps they've decided to take a more cautious course than Marion.'

Ptolemy shrugged. 'They're not here so I won't worry about them.'

'What are you going to do, Father?' Lagus asked, removing his helmet and running his fingers through his wavy hair.

'What would you do?'

'I would destroy it and either remove or sell the population depending upon how hard they resisted me.'

Ptolemy put his arm around his son's shoulders. 'That is exactly right, my boy: a second chance rebuffed means a harsh response. It was my forgiving nature to just have the royal family punished last time; now the people will find out what it means to take advantage of my generosity.'

'So, shall we prepare for a siege?'

'No, there is no time for that; I want to be back and marching on Demetrios soon after the winter solstice, just when he's not expecting it and, hopefully, whilst he's still in the north with his cavalry responding to our raids. No, in situations like this, gold is the most effective weapon.'

'But how will you know where to spend it?'

'That is where the Exile-Hunter comes in useful. If anyone can sneak into a locked city and find a disgruntled faction who would rather live in luxury than spend the rest of the lives as slaves, he can.'

'They say they want a talent of gold apiece and that all five of them should have a residence in Alexandria next to each other, and they want their entire families removed to there as well,' Archias reported to Ptolemy at dawn the following morning.

Ptolemy yawned but was pleasantly surprised. 'Is that all?'

Archias lifted his forefinger and widened his eyes as if he had just remembered. 'Ah, yes, and they want the right to decide who of the population dies, who is sold into slavery and who gets to live.'

Ptolemy splashed water from a bowl over his face and the back of his neck. 'That seems reasonable enough: no doubt they have a few scores to settle. I'd better get some pens constructed so we can sort them all out.'

'That would seem to be the best way of doing it.'

'Yes. All right, so long as they open the gates at midnight tonight, I'm willing to grant them everything they want.'

'It won't be tonight.'

'Why not?'

'I need to get back in with your written agreement; they won't move without it.'

Ptolemy sighed as he rubbed his hair with a linen towel. 'And you can't get in in daylight?'

'"Night hides the deeds the day can see."'

'I thought not.'

'I left two of my men inside the town; we have an arrangement for the third hour of the night tonight to get me back in.'

'How *do* you get in?'

Archias' face lit up with boyish glee and he wagged his finger at Ptolemy. 'If only I could tell you, but as you know, I never reveal my methods or my clients.'

I just can't help but like the man, but I still need to bring him down a level or two. 'Very well; make the arrangements for tomorrow at midnight.'

'"Attention to planning brings best results."'

'Indeed. And, oh, Archias,' Ptolemy said as the Exile-Hunter turned to leave. 'You and your men will obviously not be paid for this.'

'But you agreed—'

'To pay you what I owed you even though you failed in the letter of our deal by not bringing Artonis back, yes. But that was before I found out that you killed my old friend Asander.'

Archias' face was all shocked innocence. 'I did not.'

'I'm not going to waste time arguing the point. You were in Halicarnassus when he was murdered, that's enough for me; I'm not stupid. Now, if you work for me, you can't just go around killing my friends at Antigonos' behest.'

'I'm a free agent.'

'Whose wealth happens to be banked in Alexandria; so you work for me. Do we understand one another?'

Archias said nothing, his face neutral.

'I'm a very forgiving person, Archias, and I'm willing to overlook Asander's death and allow you access to everything you own in Alexandria, once you have delivered Marion to me and the head of King Pygmalion in Kition.'

'Oh? Is that all? Anything else?'

'I would be interested to know who paid you to kill Menander.'

'Now I really don't know what you're talking about.'

'My guess would be Kleopatra or Thessalonike.'

'Your guess is your own to have.'

'Indeed; and your wealth is your own to have once you have done those two things. But never kill one of my friends again unless I pay you to. Do we have a deal?'

'We do, so long as you understand that I'm free to leave Alexandria whenever I wish.'

'I do, and should you do that, you would never be allowed back.'

'"Blessed is the man who stays happily at home."'

'Good. It's always a pleasure to reach an understanding with an old friend. So midnight tomorrow, yes?'

'The gates will be opened.'

One of the most pleasing attributes of the Exile-Hunter was that he always kept his word – unless someone paid him more not to

– and this was no exception. At midnight the gates opened and Ptolemy unleashed his men, most of whom had already been drinking in anticipation of the sacking, into the town to extract his vengeance upon it.

All night did the screams rise from within the walls of Marion but none came to the aid of the suffering; as the dawn broke it was into a scene of horror that Ptolemy took his son so that he could see for himself the brutality that accompanies the fall of a city. But this lesson was going to be more than usually harsh, for as they went around the corpse-strewn streets Ptolemy's men were already hard at work: into groups they herded the survivors, and out of the gates they were pushed; each house was searched so that none would escape.

Before the gates sat the men who had betrayed their city and past them the captives were led; each man, woman and child was examined and the fates of their erstwhile neighbours were decided. Into one of three great pens the citizens of Marion were led: one for the fortunate given the sentence of exile; another for the less fortunate sentenced to death; and then the third for those who were doomed to suffer the living death of slavery and be sold in the markets of Delos. Only a few were set free to go where they will, but where that would be none knew for they could not remain in Marion as the demolition had already begun.

'I don't want to see one stone still standing when I return,' Ptolemy said to his brother as he readied himself to leave with his fleet. 'And bring the elders from each of the kingdoms here to witness the fact that Marion no longer exists.'

'It will be done. What about Pygmalion?'

'I think you'll find he will come here himself in a few days to see what happens to disloyal cities; well, his head at least will come, I'm not sure about the rest of his body.'

Menelaus took his brother's proffered forearm. 'How long will you be?'

'Just long enough to make Demetrios and Antigonos think I'm going for the treasury at Cyinda.'

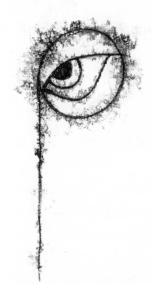

ANTIGONOS.
THE ONE-EYED.

NOW WAS THE time to make his move. If he went now, now that Asander was dead, Caria suppressed and all of Anatolia under his control and with Kassandros distracted by his nephews in Euboea, he could get across the Bosporus and winter in Pella as the Lord of Macedon. But if this were to happen, Antigonos knew that he would have to move with the speed that Alexander used to display in order to catch Lysimachus – currently fending off another Scythian raid over the Danubus, paid for, again, by his spies – off-guard so as to cross the Bosporus unopposed. But still he needed the cooperation of Byzantium to be able to ferry an army across that narrow stretch of water in safety without him recalling one of his fleets from Greece. '*You* can make a deal with them, Hieronymus, if anyone can,' Antigonos said to the man he thought would be the best emissary to the city. 'You're eloquent and can explain the advantages of an alliance with me over neutrality which manages to annoy everyone and please no one.'

'They won't see it that way.'

'Well, make them. I need to get across the Bosporus and it has to be there. If I cross the Hellespont, I land on a peninsula on the

European side; I can't risk getting trapped on it so a pontoon bridge across the Bosporus it must be.'

'And the Byzantines know that so will charge a heavy price for their cooperation, especially as Lysimachus is paying them handsomely to remain neutral.'

'Pay whatever they ask; if it's too outrageous they will suffer for their insolence at a later date. But, for now, I need them.'

'I'll do my best,' the Greek historian and erstwhile friend of Eumenes said as he took his leave.

'Do better than that. Peucestas will have the army ready to march tomorrow, I'll be there with it in twenty days, perhaps less, and I want to see that bridge being constructed.'

'As I said: I'll do my best.'

Antigonos watched Hieronymus board the ship that would take him on his mission from Miletus. 'He's right not to be too optimistic,' Antigonos said to Aristodemus as they watched the ship leave the harbour, 'but it has to be tried. I dare not bring Dioscurides and his fleet away from Tyros and leave Demetrios with no naval support in the south, and if I were to recall a fleet from Europe, Kassandros would realise immediately what's going on and race north to oppose me.'

'Which will have the advantage of leaving Greece open for the taking.'

'True to a certain extent but he will leave his half-brothers there with enough men to make things difficult for Ptolemaios and Telesphorus; and now that neither Epirus nor Illyria are any longer a threat to him he'll have the numbers to force me into a fight that I might well be wise to avoid.'

'Then Hieronymus had better succeed despite not being optimistic.'

*

And so the race began: in a series of forced marches Antigonos led his army, of almost thirty thousand men, up through Caria into Lydia where he picked up the old Persian Royal Road at Ephesus. Travelling ahead of the baggage train he managed a steady ten leagues a day, passing through Sardis and then Ipsus before arriving at Gordium just twelve days after he had set out. It was here, as he was about to leave the road and turn north to follow the line of the Sangarius River into Bithynia and then onto Chalcedon on the southern coast of the Bosporus, that the messenger from Dioscurides caught up with him.

'When did he write this?' Antigonos asked the messenger, his face grim as he looked again at the letter and then handed it to Aristodemus.

'I sailed from Tyros ten days ago,' the man replied.

'I assume my nephew also sent a message to Demetrios.'

'He did, sir; we left Tyros at the same time.'

Antigonos dismissed him with a wave and turned to Aristodemus. 'Well?'

'Well, there is not much that you can do about it; if King Pygmalion has been executed and Kition and Marion are back under Ptolemy's rule then Cyprus is temporarily lost to us.'

'And the Cilician coast is open to Ptolemy.'

'Cyinda!'

Antigonos nodded. 'That was my first thought too. I can't turn around now that I have the chance of getting an army to Europe but, equally, if Ptolemy gets the contents of the treasury at Cyinda it could cripple me; there are over ten thousand talents in there. You go; I need you to coordinate the response should Ptolemy make a move for the treasury. Get a message to Demetrios that it's his responsibility to see that Cyinda is safe. Winter's coming; Ptolemy won't try anything this late in the year so the lad will be safe enough taking a force north.'

'I'll leave right away and won't stop until I'm on a ship at Ephesus.'

'Do that, my friend, and you will be well rewarded.'

With the threat of disaster in the south it became even more imperative for Antigonos to succeed in the north and so on he drove his men through the rough terrain between the Royal Road and the coast, keeping the Sangarius River to his right as he followed it along its course north-west until it made a dogleg, heading back north-east to the sea. It was here he left it, four days after Aristodemus had set out from Gordium, to make the final approach to the Bosporus. To reach the divide between Asia and Europe it took the thirty thousand men of his army three days out of a journey of nineteen days in total and on each of those they had covered at least ten leagues. Thus it was an exhausted army that stood and looked across the narrow stretch of water over to the walls of Byzantium, barely a quarter of a league away; an exhausted army and a thoroughly demoralised one for instead of a pontoon bridge awaiting them, there, on the glittering blue water, stood a fleet and it was facing them, preventing them from crossing.

'My arse!' Antigonos growled as his one eye surveyed this most unwelcome sight. 'My pox-ridden, fetid arse! Where's my fucking bridge? Find Hieronymus and get him here, now!'

'They refused,' Hieronymus told Antigonos as they watched the squadrons patrol the Bosporus below from the high walls of Chalcedon. 'No matter how much I offered they kept on saying no.'

'Why?'

'Because those are Lysimachus' ships down there, not Byzantine ones; they sailed in from the Euxine Sea the day before I arrived and have blockaded Byzantium's harbour. Lysimachus is paying them at the same time to remain neutral as well as threatening to put them under siege.'

'But he's meant to be busy up on the Danubus.'

Hieronymus gestured to the ships below. 'Well, he's busy here now. He told me that he realised that the Scythian raid must have been your doing in preparation for a move across to Europe so he paid the Getae, a Thracian tribe, to hold his northern border for him.'

Antigonos was astounded. 'You've spoken to him?'

'Yes; actually I've had a couple of dinners with him. He's been telling me of his northern wars; I've been taking notes for my history as it's definitely worth a couple of chapters.'

'Fuck your history! I sent you to Byzantium to organise me a bridge across the Bosporus, not to fill out your book with what Lysimachus has been doing to hairy-arsed savages from the north.'

'The reason I had dinner with him was because, seeing as he intends to prevent you from crossing as he fears what you may do to him, I thought it prudent to try to arrange an alliance with him against Kassandros whereby he gives you free passage through Thrace.'

Antigonos' eye lit up.

'And?'

'And he wasn't at all keen on the idea. In fact he said, and I quote, that I "could go and fuck Antigonos' pox-ridden, fetid arse that he's always going on about". I think that makes his views quite clear.'

'And then you stayed to chat about his campaigns?'

'I'm a historian, Antigonos; it was too good an opportunity to miss; and besides, the food and wine were excellent.'

'But a waste of time from my point of view as I'm still stuck here in Asia; meanwhile, you are hobnobbing with my enemy with a view to glorifying his deeds.'

'Antigonos, when I entered your service after you defeated and killed my friend Eumenes, you said that I would be free to write whatever I wanted in my history; and that is what I will do. And no, it wasn't a waste of time from your point of view because I did manage to extract this from Lysimachus: he would be prepared to recognise your rule over the whole of Asia provided you do not cross to Europe.'

This was too much for Antigonos. 'Oh, will he now! How very kind of him. I'll show the bastard what comes of trying to dictate terms to me. I'll get across this piss-streak of a channel and see if Lysimachus is prepared to recognise my cock up his arse. I'll get Ptolemaios to send his fleet to get me across, even if it means abandoning Euboea to Kassandros.'

KASSANDROS.
THE JEALOUS.

OREUS, ON THE north coast of Euboea, was the most strategically important town on the island after Chalcis; it controlled the Mallian Gulf along which any navy sailing in close support of an army marching north or south via the Pass of Thermopylae must travel. And this was Kassandros' second attempt at taking it. But nothing had gone right for him, indeed he had had no luck in his first siege which he had been forced to abandon after Aristodemus' replacement, Telesphorus, had surprised his brother Pleistarchos' fleet with a superior force and burned four ships before forcing the rest to retire. Kassandros had, soon after, caught the enemy fleet on the beach and managed to destroy a couple of vessels and take three as prizes. This act had only drawn Ptolemaios north, from the isthmus, into the conflict and now he was encamped outside Chalcis, the chief city of Euboea and loyal to Kassandros, intriguing with a faction within to open the gates for him.

'If he gets into Chalcis, Oreus is worthless to me,' Kassandros said to his twin half-brothers Philip and Pleistarchos as they digested the news from the south on his flagship, cruising the waters off Oreus. 'So I'll leave you two here to conduct the siege and keep up the naval blockade and force-march the fifteen leagues to Chalcis and surprise Ptolemaios in his camp.'

'If he hasn't been let into Chalcis by the time you arrived,' Pleistarchos cautioned.

'Of course, if he hasn't been let in by the time I arrive. Why do you always have to point out the obvious, Pleistarchos? It's not helpful. I need a bit of luck and being negative won't encourage the gods to look kindly upon me. In fact, I'm beginning to wonder whether it isn't you who whose luck is cursed.'

'Me?' Pleistarchos looked at his twin appealing for help; Philip averted his gaze.

'Yes, you; you seem to lurch from one mishap to another, whereas Philip manages to corner and kill King Aeacides in Epirus and then come south and secure Aetolia whilst you just drift around Thessaly losing ships and men, not to mention being late coming with the assault force after I had opened the gates at Corinth.'

'That is not fair, Kassandros,' Pleistarchos said, getting to his feet, 'you're always going on about that. I do everything you ask of me. Had you asked me to go to Aetolia instead of Philip then I'm sure I would have done just as good a job.'

He's not sure, is he? One look in his eyes tells me that. 'Then prove it to me: get me Oreus whilst I'm gone. And Philip, don't you dare lift a finger to help him unless he's going to lose the whole campaign with another blunder.'

'I do not make blunders,' Pleistarchos shouted.

'No? Good. I'm pleased to hear it. Let's hope that is still true when I return. Philip, keep an eye on him. Oh, and send a message to Demetrius of Phaleron that I need him to send as many Athenian ships as he can spare to meet me at Chalcis.'

*

It was to be the last time, Kassandros swore to himself as he headed south at the head of his small field army, the last time that he would personally lead on a campaign rather than stay in the comfort of the royal palace at Pella. Now that Philip had proven himself to be a talented and trustworthy general he would leave the fighting to him and his subordinate, Prepelaus, who had shown himself capable of independent command in the recent war against Aeacides. With Atarrhias commanding the small garrisons on the Epiriot border, Crateuas guarding the king and his mother in Amphipolis as well as looking after the Thracian border and Philip doing the work in the south, Kassandros could, he hoped, spend more time securing his position in Macedon. But first he needed to push Ptolemaios and Telephorus out of Greece and then, by linking up with Athens, Thebes and the redoubtable Penelope, or Cratesipolis as her people now referred to her, on the isthmus, perhaps Greece would finally be his again; the past three years of campaigning would not prove to be as futile as it now looked from his current position. *It was Antigonos acquiring so many fleets and Ptolemy being unconcerned about any of the cyclops' ships operating further north than Rhodos that has proved the turning point in this war. I should have known that he would abandon me once I'd served my purpose.*

Through the narrow valleys of the interior of Euboea, Kassandros led his men, shielded from the coast by Mounts Telethrius and Macistus so that on the evening on the second day they navigated the pass between Macistus and Mount Dirphys to approach Chalcis from the north-east. And it was with speed that Kassandros sent his Companion Cavalry down scrub-bearing foothills to the city that controlled the Euripus Strait, the narrowest point between the island and the mainland. And it was speed that caused them to sweep through Ptolemaios' camp, catching many by surprise and leaving a trail of dead in their wake. By the time Kassandros had brought the infantry down – a far less hazardous task, and better suited to his temperament – Ptolemaios' forces had retreated to their beached ships and were struggling to refloat them whilst fending off repeated mounted attacks.

Seeing the work almost done, with the enemy in such disarray, Kassandros had no hesitation in leading his infantry, mainly peltasts and archers, into the fray, for surely he would be safe pitted against a crumbling perimeter. Headlong they ran down to the beach, passing through their own cavalry, to slam their shields into those of the defenders trying with increasing desperation to keep their comrades launching the ships from danger. And it was just before his shield crunched into an adversary's, bearing a grotesque caricature of the snake-haired Medusa, that Kassandros' courage failed him. Try as he might, he still could not thrust himself into the line of danger, even with vigorous support on either shoulder. Down he went in a manufactured slip, to fall short of his target as the man behind him cleared his prostrate body in one bound to fling himself at the Gorgon-faced shield, hurling his javelin as he did with a cry of fury cut short by the spear-blade ripping into his exposed throat. Blood spurted from the wound, sloshing down onto Kassandros' outstretched arms and increasing his panic with its cloying smell and viscous nature. With a great concentration of the will, Kassandros managed to keep himself rigid upon the ground, resisting the urge to jump up and rush away, bladder draining, as far as possible from the stench of death. And thus did he remain until the fight had moved four or five paces forward, away from him; only then did he dare to get to his feet, rubbing the blood onto his face for good effect. Forward he staggered, his sword extended before him, as if he were about to leap into the melee. But Ptolemaios' men had no reason to continue the fight as their ships were now afloat and the marines and rowers aboard. Back the troops went as the marines, now higher on the decks, covered their retreat with short-range volleys of arrows. Down onto their knees the attackers went, to hunker down behind their shields, too small for complete protection. With their tormentors immobilised, Ptolemaios' men turned and fled into the churning sea, dark and heavy with the sand dredged up by the passing of many hulls, and waded out to their vessels as their comrades kept up the strafing of the beach. Almost in tears with fear, Kassandros hunched behind his shield, the sand between his feet moist with urine, struggling to restrain the tide of panic that surged with each shaft juddering into his meagre protection. How long he remained immobile, he knew not, but slowly his mind registered a change in the atmosphere; no longer did projectiles hiss by or thump into his shield. With care he peered over its rim to see the ships, oarsmen at full stretch, heading away to Aulis on the far side of the strait, taking the marine archers out of range.

The danger past, his confidence and authority soon returned; he stood and strode forward to the water's edge and, holding his sword aloft, shook it at the retreating enemy. 'Cowards! Come back and face me!' It was an idle invitation and he knew it but his men were impressed and many joined him in his taunting, ridiculing the masculinity of the foe, for none knew the truth of Kassandros' behaviour, none save the man behind him when he had purposely thrown himself down, and that man now lay on the strand with an open throat and glazed eyes.

The sight of the Athenian fleet, two days later, sailing up the Euripus Strait, gave Kassandros and his men heart for they had been dreading a counterattack from Aulis which, with but few ships in Chalcis' port, they would be at pains to repel. On they came, fifty triremes, majestic with their sails full and their oars spread like wings beating soft on the water. One by one they tacked, gliding into the port, furling their sails and shipping their oars as they slowed; all except one: the very last ship turned the opposite way and docked at Aulis.

'He must have been a messenger for Ptolemaios,' the commander of the Athenian fleet said when questioned about the matter. 'He just attached himself to our formation and then split off when we passed Aulis. No one would have questioned him being with us.'

Kassandros took the explanation as being most likely and thought no more about it until, within an hour of the messenger's arrival, Ptolemaios' fleet, over a hundred and fifty vessels in all, pulled out of the harbour and headed north. But as he strained his eyes across the strait, Kassandros could see that the military camp was still fully manned: the fleet had not taken the army with it. That Ptolemaios remained on the mainland with his men was for sure, thus he was not trying to relieve the siege of Oreus; and with that realisation, Kassandros knew the only possible use for a fleet that carried no men was to head to the north. *Antigonos has sent for them to take his army across to Europe. He's coming for me, and if Lysimachus doesn't stop him, I'm on my own, because Ptolemy has abandoned the north as he must always have meant to do.*

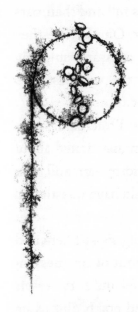

PTOLEMY.
THE BASTARD.

AGAIN AND AGAIN Ptolemy had brought his fleet into ports under Antigonos' control, capturing or burning any shipping within, attacking the garrison and taking off anything of value, so that the coast of Cilicia was left smouldering, its populations crying out for protection from Antigonos to whom they owed their allegiance. But no help had come – thus far.

With Cyprus now, once again, secured with Pygmalion's head on a spike above the main gates of Kition, and Marion but a memory in a flattened field, any of the petty kings on the island who might have been entertaining thoughts of intriguing with Antigonos had been taught the error of their ways and now acquiesced, without a whimper, to Ptolemy's rule on the island through his brother Menelaus, backed by a considerable army.

And now Ptolemy sailed up the Cydnus River with the walls of Tarsus in sight. On either bank, east and west, units of marines and archers had been landed; they now ran ahead as Ptolemy's pace slowed for there was no breaking into Tarsus without lowering the boom that spanned the river. Coming to a halt within missile range of the defences, the bolt-shooters mounted on the decks opened up, aiming at the men on the walls as the marines approached, scaling ladders to the fore, under covering volleys from the comrades on land and ship. Straight to the walls they ran as their protective missile storm raged over them, keeping the heads of the garrison down; up the ladders went, to be scaled by the fleetest of foot as, from either bank, a score of specially trained men dived into the river to swim around the walls.

Ptolemy could have laughed at the simplicity of the thing: within moments the marines had a foothold on the walls and were clearing them of the garrison troops; and this was an easy business for they were not frontline combat soldiers but, rather, local militia stiffened by a handful of older mercenaries more used to taking their ease in the shade of a tavern awning keeping a skin of wine company. With no one now resisting, the swimmers heaved themselves out beyond the walls and soon had the boom mechanism under their control; the rattle of chain unwinding, scraping the quay's stone edge as it loosened and fell to the river bed, was the sound that Ptolemy had waited for. With a shouted command he ordered the squadron forward; one at a time they passed over the boom and entered the river harbour, their artillery and archers alert for any perceived threat; but there were none within with the heart to resist and all had now fled the scene to lock themselves away in as much safety as could be contrived.

It was, therefore, onto a deserted quay that Ptolemy disembarked with his son. 'Send some men to requisition a couple of dozen horses, Lagus, I've a quick trip I need to make. Whilst I'm away, get busy going through all the warehouses; leave whatever is obviously merchants' private property alone and just take anything military: weapons, armour and all the rest of it. I don't want to make enemies of the wealthy citizens of a town I intend, one day, to make into Egypt's possession.'

'Yes, Father,' Lagus replied, the expression on his face making it clear that he relished the chance to be of use to his father.

'Oh, and Lagus, no more killing.' Smiling to himself, Ptolemy watched his son issuing orders to a couple of marine officers and was pleased to see how naturally it came to the lad. *Thais was right; but then again, she always is: the boy's got a lot of potential.*

And that was proven very quickly with the arrival in the harbour of two score horses complete with tack. It was not long before Ptolemy was riding north, with an escort, towards Cynda. 'Not that we'll be able to break into the treasury,' he explained to the escort commander, 'there's a garrison of a thousand troops guarding it and I haven't got the time or the right troops to take them on. I'm just interested in speaking with their commander to find out exactly where he stands on the subject of a nice, fat, healthy bribe.'

'I'm not interested,' Philotas, the garrison commander of Cynda, said, having been offered ten talents to open the gates for Ptolemy. 'If I wanted, I could take a hundred talents from the treasury and run off with a few mates and set up on my own somewhere nice and quiet.'

'Why don't you?' Ptolemy asked, looking up at the middle-aged man standing above the treasury complex gate.

'Because my father was Antigonos' life-long friend until he was executed by Eumenes. My loyalty is to my father's friend; I have all I need, and besides, I've been to Egypt and it's too hot for me and that's where I'll have to live if I were to accept your offer.'

Ptolemy could see that there was little point in arguing with the man or upping his offer; Cynda would have to wait for another time. But he was unsurprised. He turned his mount.

'Ptolemy,' Philotas called. 'Just to show that there are no hard feelings, let me give you a warning.'

Ptolemy looked over his shoulder. 'I'm always grateful if the warning is well founded.'

'Oh, yes, this one is: a messenger arrived this morning from Demetrios; he's coming north with four thousand cavalry and is due here tomorrow so I'd get out of here if I were you.'

'Philotas, my friend, that is the best news that I've had for some time. If you ever overcome your aversion to the heat, you will find a warm welcome in Alexandria.' He did not wait for the response but kicked his horse forward, for, with Demetrios one hundred and fifty leagues away from his army, now was the time to attack. And once again, Ptolemy was a man in a hurry.

The arithmetic was simple: with his army mustering in Pelusium, thirty leagues from Gaza, or five days' march with a baggage and siege train and then with him being five days' sailing – with good weather – from Pelusium, even if the army were ready to march as soon as he arrived, Ptolemy could not expect to be at Gaza in less than ten days. *Ten days...* but there was nothing he could do to change that so it was pointless cursing. He had achieved what he had set out to do and drawn Demetrios away to the north but with one flaw: Demetrios would see his fleet heading back south and, if he was anything as wily as his father, would guess that he, Ptolemy, planned a winter campaign and would rush south again. Yes, Demetrios would beat him to Gaza and have his cavalry there when Ptolemy's army arrived but in what state would they be? Two hundred and fifty leagues in ten days at the beginning of winter? *I wouldn't like it to be me, that's for sure.*

And so on he raced, transferring to a Five at Salamis on Cyprus, better able to plough through the choppy seas, bringing with him a complete change of oarsmen so that not a moment may be lost. Leaving the rest of the fleet to embark a couple of thousand mercenaries that could be spared form Menelaus' army, and then to follow as best they could, the great Five surged south under leaden skies, raising its sails when possible and pausing only when absolutely necessary. Across from Cyprus and then down the coast they went, risking passing within sight of Tyros, but nothing came out to challenge the beast of the sea. In a huge gamble, Ptolemy ordered the vessel away from the coast, cutting the corner as Asia turns west to meld into Africa, to head directly for Pelusium; and to Pelusium it came just five days after Ptolemy had sat outside the walls of Cyinda.

'Are you ready?' Ptolemy shouted at Seleukos as the ship docked.

Seleukos smiled back from the quayside. 'Oh yes indeed, very. I've had the lads standing by to march ever since the reports came in of Demetrios leading most of his cavalry away north.'

'We leave at dawn tomorrow if the reports are favourable; all right?'

'No problem.'

'Who's out scouting?' Ptolemy asked as he disembarked.

'My Sogdians.'

'*Your* Sogdians? I thought they were in *my* service, especially now as Artonis stayed up in Pergamum.'

'They want to go back east with me. They've also taken Apama to their heart as a fellow countrywoman, and I know they'll prove to be faithful bodyguards for her and me on the way back to Babylon.'

Ptolemy was not going to argue; he would have to give Seleukos some men to retake Babylon. *Better that they be volunteers.* 'Let me know as soon as they come back in.'

'They're due in an hour before sunset.'

*

'There is no one between here and Gaza,' Azanes, the commander of the Sogdian light horse-archers, stated with confidence as he reported to Ptolemy and Seleukos.

'That's because he took most of his cavalry away up north,' Ptolemy said with a grin. 'Silly boy; he's got nothing to harry us with as we advance.' A thought occurred to him. 'Unless he's paid the Nabateans to make life difficult for us on the march.'

Azanes shook his head. 'I don't think so; I sent a few men down to The Stone where they congregate in the desert; there was no one between there and the coast so they must have gone deep into the desert for the winter.'

Ptolemy clapped his hands together. 'Excellent; it sounds like there is nothing between us and Demetrios.'

DEMETRIOS.
THE BESIEGER.

F ATHER WILL HAVE *my balls and wash them down with resinated wine if I don't get there in time.* For five days now, since Philotas had told him of Ptolemy's rushed departure from Cyinda, Demetrios had led his cavalry back south, losing more than a few mounts in early snowfalls as they traversed the foothills of the Taurus Mountains and then more each day as the withering pace took its toll. But Demetrios cared not for the losses: all that mattered was that he should be at Gaza when Ptolemy's army came into view; if he lost a few hundred cavalry then so be it for he had elephants and Ptolemy did not. That's where the difference would be between the two armies.

But if he did not arrive in time, forty-three elephants would not save his unprotected phalanx without cavalry. Again he cursed himself and his father: himself for not taking Pythan, Andronicus and Nearchos' advice and sending Pythan, with a couple of thousand cavalry, north to repel Ptolemy's raids instead of going himself; but Demetrios had wanted to claim the glory and had laughed at the thought that Ptolemy would raid in the north as a diversion for a winter campaign in the south, and so he had overruled his advisors. And he cursed his father for the pressure that the man had always put him under to succeed and live up to his warlike standards; in writing to him to say that he expected Demetrios to ensure the safety of the treasury at Cyinda, Antigonos had made it virtually impossible for Demetrios not to go in person. Had he sent another in his place and his choice had not been successful then his father would not forgive him for failing in his duty; and if the other man were successful then Antigonos would accuse him of shirking his responsibilities and failing to lead by example. It had been ever thus in his relationship with his father: constant pressure, constant fear of failing to live up to his expectations and only muted praise when he succeeded in a task.

For this reason Demetrios had an insatiable desire for glory: if he could only shine but dimly in his father's eyes he would make sure that he would glow like the brightest star in the eyes of the world: he would be the Alexander of his generation. And he would prove that by beating Ptolemy.

But first he had to get his cavalry to Gaza.

Down the coast they sped, shedding men and mounts along the way; past the site of Alexander's victory at Issus, a little over twenty-one years previously, and then on to Phoenicia, past Tripolis, Berytus, Sidon and now Tyros where Demetrios had called a brief halt to allow the men to rest their raw thighs and to change the worst affected horses with fresh blood from the supply of Median mounts, acknowledged to be the finest cavalry breed in the world, newly arrived from the east.

'You say that Ptolemy passed here two days ago?' Demetrios said, shocked.

'Yes, lord,' Eutychios, Andronicus' replacement at Tyros, confirmed. 'At least we assume it was Ptolemy; the ship was a huge Five and the triarchos wasn't sparing the oarsmen.'

'Why didn't you send ships out to intercept the vessel? You could have captured him.'

'Winter's here; we were starting the annual refits.'

'But you knew that I had gone north to fight off Ptolemy's naval raids! His ships weren't laid up for their winter refits so why were yours?'

'With respect, lord, we thought his ships were four hundred leagues away and unlikely to come any further south this year than Cyprus. I mean...' he held his hands out in disbelief. 'I mean, who raids in the winter?'

'The same man who is just about to launch a winter ground attack against Gaza. You have to move with the times, Eutychios: did my father stop to worry about winter when he was chasing Eumenes around in the east? Did he? Did he my arse! As he would say. I want you to always keep a squadron of at least twelve ships ready for sea at all times; the way we do things is changing; we...' Demetrios' voice trailed off as he was distracted by a sight out to sea in the distance: sails; many sails. He shaded his eyes, squinting in the pale winter sun. 'That's the rest of Ptolemy's fleet sailing back to Egypt.' He manhandled Eutychios around to better see for himself. 'Look, man! There! That's a fleet in winter and can you do anything about it? My arse, you can! In fact, that's about all you can do: show your arse to them and what's the good of that?'

Knowing that if he were to spend another moment in the man's company he would rip out his throat with his bare teeth, Demetrios pushed Eutychios away and, turning on his heel, left him to contemplate his obvious inadequacies.

By the time he reached Gaza, after another two days of hard riding, his mood had not improved and the news he received, upon his arrival, from his three advisors waiting outside his harbour-front quarters – far cooler than the city, a third of a league inland – soured it still further. 'You let them disembark two thousand mercenaries just ten leagues south from here, and did nothing about it, Pythan?'

Pythan, a steady hand who had served his time as a cavalry officer under Alexander and then Perdikkas before transferring his allegiance to Eumenes, was in no mood to be treated like a raw recruit by the son of his new master since Eumenes' demise. 'You took the cavalry north against all advice, so what could I do? They were ashore and dug in before I could have got the infantry down there to hinder their disembarkation; so don't talk to me in that tone of voice... sir.'

Demetrios looked at the expressions of Nearchos and Andronicus but detected no sympathy there. *I can't lose face in front of my senior officers; whatever I do is reported straight to my father.* 'I left five hundred troopers with you; they would have done the job. They would have caught the infantry in the sea.'

Demetrios burned within as he saw Pythan struggling to mask a smile.

'Had I taken our last five hundred *light* cavalry south to face two thousand mercenaries whilst they were disembarking, then, yes, I could have caused them a slight inconvenience but not as much inconvenience as their archers and deck-mounted bolt-shooters would have caused me. I need to remind you of your arithmetic, sir; five hundred goes into two thousand four times and when the enemy comprises a thousand mercenary hoplites, supported by eight hundred Cretan archers and two hundred Tarantine light cavalry, those are not good odds at all.' He turned to Nearchos and Andronicus. 'Or am I much mistaken in my reckoning?'

Neither of the advisors left by Antigonos to guide his impetuous but inexperienced son met Pythan's eye; but nor did they contradict his analysis.

And this was the problem. For although Demetrios was now twenty-five and although he had already fought in the two largest battles since Alexander's time, at Paraetacene and Gabene out in the east, as well as many smaller engagements and countless skirmishes, and although he had begun to master the art of siege-craft at the siege of Susa and then again in the opening phases of the second siege of Tyros, Demetrios was still untried as an independent commander as his father had very rarely taken him into his counsel, preferring just to give him orders with no explanation. Yes, Antigonos had made sure that the lad had understood the workings of an army from all angles but he had not instilled judgement into him, and for one born impetuous, as was Demetrios, judgement is not something that can easily be instilled except by patient teaching and leading by example. Antigonos had not been that sort of father.

Demetrios stared at Pythan and, despite his ire at being so condescended to, knew that the man was right and to argue the matter would be to compound his loss of face even more. He grunted and walked up the steps into the grand building, signalling for his advisors to follow him to his suite.

Dipping his hands in a bowl of cool water held by a slave, Demetrios rubbed the dust of travel from his face, arms and hands, before drying himself with a linen towel. 'So, Pythan,' he said in a tone that did not imply any previous ill-temper, 'what do our spies say about the readiness of Ptolemy's army?'

Pythan was also very happy to pretend that the previous disagreement had not occurred. 'Seleukos has had it ready to march since about two days after you left for...' His voice trailed off as he realised that this led them right back into the previous conversation.

'After I left for the north with the cavalry, yes.' Demetrios paused for a moment's thought. 'So, assuming that it will march as soon as Ptolemy arrives in Pelusium, we can safely say that it marched two days ago and so should be in sight of our long-range scouts round about now. Indeed, the first reports of its advance should reach us by dawn tomorrow.'

And it was at dawn that the first scouts came in to confirm what Demetrios had guessed and thus Ptolemy's advance was no surprise. What was a surprise, however, was the scale of the army he brought with him.

'A phalanx eighteen thousand strong?' Demetrios questioned. 'Where did he get those numbers from? Surely the garrisons in Cyrenaica and Cyprus have drained his resources, not to mention the troops he lost when Asander was defeated; so where have these all come from?'

Pythan cleared his throat. 'Our spies reported a couple of years ago that he was training Egyptians to fight in the phalanx, if you remember.'

'Yes, but that was just an experiment, wasn't it? Indigenous Egyptians aren't suited for the phalanx, no more than the Persians were in Alexander's misguided attempts to integrate east and west.'

'The numbers he's bringing east would indicate otherwise,' Nearchos said, 'so let's stop asking how it happened and get on to deciding what we're going to do about it.'

Demetrios was in no doubt. 'Fight them, of course.'

'Even though our phalanx amounts to a mere eleven thousand?' Andronicus pointed out. 'Two thousand Macedonian pikemen, one thousand mixed Lycian and Pamphylian pikemen and eight thousand mercenaries, mainly hoplites but some light peltasts.'

'And three thousand archers and light javelin men,' Demetrios added. 'And we have forty-three elephants whereas he has precisely none.'

'Yes, but *he* is Ptolemy and *he* is backed up by Seleukos,' Pythan said. 'We are facing two of Alexander's best commanders with a superior army behind them and you say we should stand and fight them. It's winter; we could just withdraw before them, pay the Nabatean Arabs to harry their supply lines and use the Tyros fleet to prevent them from resupplying by sea. Let's see how long they last if we do that.'

'And if we do that, how much territory we will cede. And besides, the Tyros fleet is being refitted.'

'We can put a halt to that and have them at sea within half a moon,' Nearchos asserted.

'No, we stay here and fight.'

'And what about the cavalry?' Andronicus asked. 'At least fifteen hundred of them are barely fit for action.'

'We'll use them to do my father's trick of refusing on one flank and you can command them, Andronicus; but we'll use the right flank for that, not the left, which will give us superiority on our left with three thousand cavalry backed by the elephants and their light infantry escorts. If we win the fight there, his infantry superiority in the centre won't matter except in that the more there are, the more satisfying it will be rolling them up.' He looked around the faces of his advisors. 'That is my plan, gentlemen; let's put it into action. I'll not give Ptolemy one foot of our land.'

Pythan looked grim. 'In which case you might find that Ptolemy ends up giving you six feet of his newly won territory to lie in.'

Demetrios waved away the notion. 'It'll take more than Ptolemy outnumbering me by a few thousand to kill me, Pythan; it's you who should be worried. I imagine Seleukos would be very interested in getting to grips with you in the coming battle.'

'That's the one thing that keeps me from arguing further against your rash decision,' Pythan said, 'the chance to finish Seleukos.'

SELEUKOS.
THE BULL-ELEPHANT.

LIFE WAS GOOD, there could be no denying it; being a part of a large army marching to a victory that would pave the way to reclaiming what was his filled his heart with joy. Seleukos sucked in deep of the sea air and then looked over to his son, Antiochus, riding next to him at the head of the fifty Companion Cavalry he had brought from Babylon four years previously. 'Take some deep breaths of that, my boy, and savour it for it's the last time we'll smell the sea for a long while.'

Antiochus grinned and gestured to the water, azure and sparkling in the late-afternoon winter sun. 'It's blue and beautiful, Father, but not as blue or as beautiful as the walls of Babylon.'

Seleukos laughed. 'Perhaps you have literary ambitions, Son; but don't worry, I won't let them get in the way of your martial development.'

Antiochus shared his father's mirth. 'Nor will I.'

Seleukos took another couple of breaths, contemplating the beauty and vastness of the sea. 'We'll be back, Antiochus; it'll take a few years but we'll be back to claim a harbour somewhere up this coast.'

On the fourth evening of the march, as the army made its rendezvous with the two thousand mercenaries shipped from Cyprus, the scouts came back in; bearded, barbarous and be-trousered, the Sogdians ululated their way into the camp as the tents were being pitched, drawing a cheer from the rest of the army who had come to respect these riders from the east for their extraordinary feats of horsemanship.

'He's standing to face us,' Azanes reported to Ptolemy and Seleukos as they ate fish grilled over an open fire of driftwood on the beach packed with soldiers all doing the same.

'I thought he would.' Ptolemy threw a fishbone into the fire and licked his fingers. 'Demetrios is too rash and impetuous to do the sensible thing and withdraw before us. I wonder if anyone has pointed out that it's winter and forage will be hard to come by, especially for an army this size.' He indicated to the countless fires along the strand and the men sitting around them, their faces half seen in flickering light.

'So much the better if they have and he's ignored them,' Seleukos said, handing Ptolemy another fish, balanced on his sword blade. 'It means that he thinks he can win because he has elephants and we don't.'

Ptolemy glanced at his subordinate in a conspiratorial manner as he took the grilled offering. 'But your little trick will deprive him of that advantage, won't it?'

'I should hope so.'

Ptolemy juggled the hot fish between his hands. 'Did you get a good look at his numbers, Azanes?'

'Ten to twelve thousand infantry mainly spear armed; only about three thousand pikes; between four and five thousand cavalry—'

'Of which a good deal will be barely fit for action,' Seleukos commented.

Azanes hunched his shoulders and spread his hands. 'We could not judge their fitness from a distance.'

'He'll brigade his unfit cavalry together and refuse a wing,' Seleukos said with certainty. 'That's what his father did at Paraetacene and again at Gabene.'

Ptolemy finally won his battle with the fish and took a bite, contemplating Seleukos' theory. 'I think you're right; it's what I would do too, in his position. I'd put my knackered cavalry on the left and then draw my opponent's right with it, negating his best troops in a pointless game of chase. Meanwhile, I'd bolster my right with as much quality cavalry as possible, with a screen of elephants, and smash through the enemy's weaker cavalry wing and get behind the phalanx. Job done.'

Seleukos turned the remaining fish on the grill. 'Yes. That sounds about right. Did you manage to count the elephants, Azanes?'

'Forty-three with fifty or more light infantry escorts each.'

'That's over two thousand at least; that's a lot of missile power.'

'They won't all be with the cavalry,' Ptolemy said. 'He'll screen his weaker centre with some, a third of them in all probability, so that leaves thirty or so with the cavalry; your traps will manage that. Thank you, Azanes; go and see to your men.' He tossed another bone onto the fire and put his hand out for more fish. 'So, my friend, it seems that you and I will be on the left wing facing his cavalry and elephants whilst we'll put a token force on our right to play catch with his knackered refusers. I'll give that command to Lagus with a couple of sound lads to look after him; it'll be good experience for him. And then we send the centre forward once we've won the fight on our left.'

Seleukos lobbed him a fish. 'I can almost smell the Euphrates.'
And see Babylon.

With haste, Ptolemy led his army towards Demetrios' position in the morning; haste so that he would catch him where he stood before good counsel had the chance to prevail and he began a fighting retreat.

Seleukos led the vanguard with his Sogdians fanned out before him, to spring any ambushes, and his Companions in a short column behind, followed by the rest of his command of mercenary cavalry, both heavy and light, with their accompanying archers and slingers. To his right the desert stretched away in a shimmering haze of midday heat, despite the winter season, as the sea, to the left, crashed onto a rocky beach, its waves whipped up by a stiffening wind. But it was to his front that he was focused, for in the distance, possibly two leagues off, was the unmistakable shadow of an army of considerable size. Leaving orders that the advance should proceed at the same pace and sending a message to Ptolemy as to his present intentions, Seleukos kicked his horse into a canter, with his son and Companions following.

Using the Sogdians as a screen, Seleukos came to within half a league of the enemy drawn up a couple of thousand paces to the south of the city of Gaza; Alexander's siege hill rose in the distance, north of the town. 'You see, Antiochus,' he said after he had studied the situation for a while, 'he's not showing us anything: he has his infantry in a block but his cavalry and elephants he keeps hidden behind so we can't see what his intentions might be. He's just going to stand there as we advance and wait to see if we give him any hints as to what we plan before he makes his final dispositions. My guess is that Pythan, Nearchos and Andronicus are holding Demetrios back, preventing him from being too rash. Well, let's hope the young pup gets fed up with their restraining hands very soon.'

'What will you do, Father?' Antiochus asked as they turned to gallop back to the vanguard.

'Report to Ptolemy what we have seen and then form from column to line of battle.'

'I'll still wager he'll refuse on his left,' Ptolemy said over the shouts, jangle and foot-stamps of the eighteen thousand men of his phalanx deploying, fanning out, at a jog, left and right, to create a solid block of infantry almost a third of a league wide; the same distance, in fact, as they were from the enemy. 'So let's be ready for when he makes his final deployment.'

Seleukos pointed to a procession of four carts heading for the left of the field escorted by some cavalry. 'I've sent the elephant traps over there already with my Sogdians to screen them; the lads are ready to unload them and lay them as soon as the phalanx moves up into position.' Ptolemy glanced to the left and then surveyed the featureless field upon which they would fight just a little further south from where he had embarked the army headed for Cyprus, three years previously. Seeing nothing that could be of advantage to either side in all the flatness, he made up his mind. 'All right, we deploy the cavalry as if he's refusing the left.'

That was the order that Seleukos had been waiting for; he gestured to his signaller amongst his Companions. Three clear calls of the horn were sounded and the cavalry, all four thousand of them, bestirred themselves to a chorus of equine excitement.

The orders had already been issued and each officer knew his place in the line; dust rose as thousands of hooves pounded the dry ground with Lagus leading his command of a thousand mercenaries, mostly Thessalians and Thracians, over to the right wing and Seleukos and Ptolemy taking their combined three thousand cavalry and thousand infantry to the left, ready to counter Demetrios' main attack – or so they thought.

It was not until all was set, in the mid-afternoon, and the dust began to settle that the positions became clear. Seleukos' heart froze as he peered ahead of him; and it froze not because of what he saw but because of what he did not. *Where are the elephants?* He looked along the line to the right and could make out a dozen or so of the lumbering beasts, at intervals, in front of the heavy infantry, but there were none in sight before him. He looked closer and to his horror could see very little cavalry at all, and the few that were visible were formed up at an angle, sloping away from him, on the phalanx's flank. *He's swopped sides and is refusing with the right, the little bastard.* It was then that he real-ised that his chances of regaining Babylon now depended on the coming race. 'Get the traps back onto the carts!' he shouted at the officer commanding the light infantry and the anti-elephant devices. 'And then get over to the right flank, but shield your movement by going behind the phalanx. And do it faster than you think possible.'

Satisfied that the most time-consuming part of the race was under way, he turned his mount and galloped over to Ptolemy.

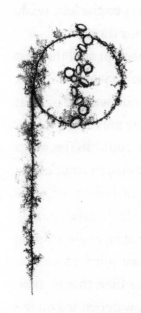

PTOLEMY.
THE BASTARD.

P TOLEMY DID NOT need to hear what Seleukos had to say as he could see the situation, quite plainly, for himself. 'We've been duped. Duped by a boy.' *A clever little boy who's showing some talent.*

'I've started work on moving the traps,' Seleukos said, pulling his horse up next to Ptolemy's command post.

'Good. How long will it take, do you think?'

'Half an hour, at least.'

'You concentrate on that. We've got to delay their attack for as long as possible; send over your Sogdians to skirmish with any cavalry Demetrios tries to move forward and I'll give orders to the phalanx to advance as soon as it is formed – that should help to cover our redeployment; and tell the commanders that the signal to halt will be three rising notes repeated again and again. Once it's moving forward, I'll bring the rest of the cavalry over. Lagus can stay where he is until we're almost there and then he can replace us here on the left.' He pointed to the distant enemy cavalry set up to refuse. 'We won't worry about them just now; I don't think they're in a position to be a threat as we sort this mess out.'

With the briefest of nods, Seleukos turned and galloped off. *This will be close.* Turning to his aides, four young scions of the new nobility of Egypt, Ptolemy pointed to the eldest. 'Cleon, ride to the Greek mercenaries and the Tarantines, and tell them to take up the exact same position on the right flank. Aristides, the same message to the Thessalians on this flank, and Bion, you go and tell the heavy lancers. Hypatos, you ride like the furies are after your arse, across to Lagus, and tell him to be ready to swop sides and not to get in the way of the cavalry I'm sending over. Understand, all of you?'

The 'yes' was unanimous and in unison.

As his aides split in several directions, driving their mounts on with the urgency required of the situation, Ptolemy signalled to his three hundred Companion Cavalry bodyguard, their bronze helmets glowing in the afternoon sun; he raised his voice: 'Follow me!' He accelerated away towards the right flank with his Companions, cloaks billowing in the wind and lances held aloft, following in loose order. He had known many tight situations in Alexander's battles and had watched the great man deal with them, using speed as a weapon; the question now was: had Demetrios yet learned that invaluable lesson or was he still too inexperienced and would therefore miss the chance to send his elephants into the phalanx's right flank as it formed up? *Don't think about it and don't look; you're doing all you can as fast as you can. Don't distract yourself with things you can't control.* But then he was distracted, but it was a distraction that he had hoped for: trumpets blared all along the line and the phalanx edged forward. Sixteen pike-armed men deep for two thirds of its width, the rest eight-man files of long thrusting-spear wielding hoplites or looser peltasts, the great beast of many parts roared with one voice as it surged into life. Forward it went at a rhythmic trudge so as to keep the line and not break into its constituent pieces. The sight and sound of it gave Ptolemy heart, for, with over one thousand five hundred paces between the two sides, there would be time for its sheer magnitude to strike fear into the enemy as it drew nearer with every thunderous step.

On Ptolemy led his Companions, on along the rear of the beast, on until its far end was visible through the dust it kicked up; there he saw his son riding to meet him.

'What's happening, Father?' Lagus asked as he turned his mount to speed alongside Ptolemy, keeping pace. 'I've had a message telling me to be ready to move to the left flank.'

'And are you?'

Lagus looked over to his cavalry command, a couple of hundred paces away. 'Yes.'

'Good, then get going. He's refusing with his right. There are about fifteen hundred cavalry set back from the flank of his phalanx. If all goes well on this side, get the bastards before they can reach the safety of the city; understand?'

'Yes, Father.'

'Then go.'

Lagus veered off, back towards his men.

'And don't get yourself killed in your first battle,' Ptolemy shouted after him, doubting he would hear, as he too veered, but in the opposite direction, to bring his men onto the unprotected right flank of his phalanx, still travelling at a steady pace.

Around his troopers came, wheeling so as to form three ranks of a hundred, as the infantry, grizzled veterans in the main in the place of honour, the unshielded right, cheered their mounted comrades with grinning irony, asking what had kept them and whether they would like to have a nice little rest now as their arses must be sore after such a long ride from the left flank.

And as Lagus' men disappeared into the rising dust so did the Greek and Tarantine mercenaries appear, causing Ptolemy to pull his Companions further to the right allowing the Greek heavy cavalry in between them and the infantry. Out in front, Ptolemy could now see the Sogdians flowing back and forth towards the line of elephants shielding the opposing cavalry, releasing volleys as they came into range.

It was as the last of the cavalry arrived from the left flank that the carts bearing the elephant traps appeared, their mules, cruelly abused by the whip, snorting in protest; but Ptolemy cared not for the animals' welfare for their arrival along with the light infantry and finally Seleukos and his Companions meant that the army was at least in the correct formation, if not in the right position. That would come next, but to achieve that he had to bring eighteen thousand men to a halt without risking the integrity of their formation. He turned to his signaller. 'Three rising notes and keep repeating them, until the bastards stop.'

The call was clear, shrill and recurring.

'Ride closer to the phalanx!' Ptolemy yelled as the great formation pressed on oblivious.

The signaller, red-cheeked but still blowing for all he was worth, urged his mount on, keeping his instrument always to his lips.

Come on, you bastards, hear the order. Stop.

Still the infantry marched on and still the signaller blew.

And then a call rose from within the great formation, to be echoed by another and then a third and a fourth as the signal spread down the line; and the shouts of the officers in the front and rear ranks echoed over the sea of helmets. With remarkable unity, eighteen thousand men ground to a halt just five hundred paces from the enemy.

Ptolemy breathed deep, realising that he had not taken a breath for many of his racing heartbeats.

Ptolemy's cavalry command, all three thousand of them, advanced at the walk to take up position on the shoulder of the phalanx as the light infantry ran forward, spreading out to screen them and mask the laying of the elephant traps. The planks, a dozen feet long and studded with nails half a foot in length, were offloaded from the carts and laid on the ground behind the light infantry screen. Chained together in lines of ten, they were dragged into position, and then unhooked from one another, three rows deep, hidden lines of pain lying in wait for the great pachyderms of war. But the elephants did not advance despite the Sogdians retiring before them to tempt them into attack. With the Sogdians skirting around the line of traps to take position on the far right of the cavalry line, all movement ceased and the two sides stood and looked at one another, neither seeming willing to make the first move. Silence descended and the men stood still, sweat running from under their helmets down their faces; here and there a horse stamped or snorted.

Come on, you young pup; live up to your reputation of being impetuous. And still there was no movement as the sea breeze blew away the dust, leaving the field of battle under clear skies as the afternoon slipped by.

Ptolemy, at the centre of his cavalry, directly opposite eight hundred Companion Cavalry lancers, could feel the tension all around him as the men had time to contemplate what fate awaited them in the coming hours. *It's never good to let the lads mull for too long on the dangers they're going to be facing. Perhaps I should order the advance and try to move the traps forward.* Wrestling with the problem in his mind, he looked along Demetrios' cavalry line. Fifteen hundred mixed mercenary cavalry stood next to the phalanx, then came the Companions; next to them was Demetrios himself with two hundred bodyguards and on the extreme left stood one hundred mercenary Tarantines, a new form of shielded cavalry from southern Italia; to the front of them were a further three hundred troopers and between them and the phalanx stood the elephants and their escorts. *If I go, I need to avoid the elephants and hit him hard on the wing.* He had almost come to a decision when a distant horn sounded; banners were raised. The Tarantines on the extreme left of Demetrios' line pulled back leaving a gap between them and the three hundred troopers in front of them. Into this gap Demetrios led his bodyguard followed by the eight hundred lancers and then the fifteen hundred mixed mercenaries. Moving fast, streaming around the left wing, came Demetrios and his cavalry.

He's trying to outflank me; who'd have thought he had it in him?

DEMETRIOS.
THE BESIEGER.

T HE POWER WAS intoxicating: leading an army into battle was what his whole life until now had been working up to. Now, finally, it was down to him to decide when and where to attack and not do everything according to the whim of his father without knowing the reasons behind the decisions. And it was around the flank that he intended to go and once he had turned it, pulling Ptolemy's cavalry out of position, Nearchos would unleash the elephants into the exposed right of Ptolemy's phalanx.

It was a good plan for it meant he could win the battle without the paucity of his infantry becoming an issue. But first he had to win the cavalry battle on the flank. He had not minded that Ptolemy had reinforced his right when he had seen his disposition; Demetrios had expected a strong cavalry presence against him and, indeed, he relied upon it so that he could deal with much of Ptolemy's cavalry in one action. And so, with wind in his face and joy in his heart, Demetrios led his bodyguards diagonally to his left, behind the three hundred troopers that he had placed to the fore in order to shield his move. As they passed by the Tarantines on the end of their line, Demetrios veered to the right, aiming for the flank of the Sogdian horse-archers who had so tormented his elephants; punching his lance in the air thrice, he gave the order for the charge; the signaller's horn shrilled and Demetrios kicked his horse into a full gallop. Behind him his men did the same, but gradually; first his two cover-men, followed by another four troopers and then eight more and so on, so that the formation changed from a block to a wedge with Demetrios at its head.

Demetrios did not look behind him; he did not need to – he could feel the power of the men following him; on towards the easterners he led them, as bows were drawn and arrows nocked. But there was naught he could do about the coming volleys; they just had to soak them up as best they could. It was in the hands of the gods who would fall and who would crash into the enemy's line.

Like a sudden squall of hail the first volley hit, clattering off metal and thumping into flesh of both man and beast. Down many went, skidding along the dry ground in a confusion of limbs and dust, issuing equine shrieks and human wails as those behind the wrecks strove to leap them or swerve around, ricocheting off the riders next to them. But still the charge kept on, its formation steady, even as the next two volleys swept through it. Head low, lance in his right hand and reins in the left, Demetrios urged his mount on as arrows flicked and hissed by him and massed hoof-beats thundered in his ears. With a final shot over their horses' rumps as they fled, the Sogdians cleared to reveal what he had wanted to see: Ptolemy's cavalry heading straight towards him; their equipment and formation the same as his men's: Companion Cavalry lancers both, former brothers in arms under Alexander, but now mortal foes to whom no pity could be shown.

'At them!' he cried, although it came out as an inchoate scream, such was his excitement. Forward he thrust his lance, its sleek point glinting in the sun, forward towards the chest of the man hurtling at him. And then they hit, the two units, head on; with blurs of movement, sprays of gore and a rush of bodies to either side, Demetrios crashed through the first couple of ranks of the enemy, the end of his shattered lance left in the shoulder of his opponent whose blood smeared his face and covered the wild grin written upon it. It took but a moment to reverse what was left of his weapon so that he could bring the heavy counter-weighting butt-spike to bear. Down he crunched it onto the arm of a raging foe, trying to pull his sword free of the scabbard; unheard in the din the limb snapped into an obscene angle, the hand losing all grip; up Demetrios brought his improvised weapon, up under the man's jaw, to slam his mouth shut, taking off the tip of his tongue with the suddenness of the enforced bite. Taking no heed of his victim now that he was of no threat, Demetrios whirled his gored club around his head to crunch into the helm of the next man in line; but the blow was of little use as his cover-man, to the right, skewered his target a moment later, taking out his throat and stilling his cries.

Thighs gripping tight around his mount he pressed on into a rapidly compressing area as the opposing units slowed each other's forward ranks; and now it became a scrimmage of extreme violence with little skill involved for there was no time for anything other than instinctive self-preservation. Transferring his butt-spike to his left hand he drew his sword with his right, slicing it into the thigh of a man attempting to wrench the lance from his right-side cover-man; with a scream he clutched the newly carved wound and again Demetrios struck, severing half the hand so that only the thumb remained. A crunching punch on the nose from the cover-man felled the maimed trooper, sending him arching back off his mount, spraying blood, to disappear under the maelstrom of stamping hooves.

And now it was a matter of hacking and thrusting with both weapons for with no shield there was no respite. On he worked his arms as the blood flew, half-blinding him as it mingled with his sweat. What was happening to the left and right of his bubble of brutality he had no way of telling for all his senses had merged into one cruel depiction of violence and were unable to focus on anything beyond.

How long he struggled wading through the ebb and flow of death's tide, he could not tell, but with a suddenness that shocked, the way before him opened up. They were through, their opponents either in flight or overtaken. To his left, he saw Pythan leading the eight hundred heavy lancers against Ptolemy's main force. Into each other they surged to repeat on a larger scale the fight that Demetrios had just come through and, as they closed, Demetrios saw the sight he had been waiting for: Ptolemy. Fighting in the front rank, Ptolemy punched his lance head through the cuirass of one of Pythan's Companions, exploding it out through the man's shoulder. For the briefest moment, Demetrios tried to turn his horse towards his foe but he was swallowed by the flow of combat; and as he searched for the distinctive, high-plumed helmet amongst the carnage, or a sight of Seleukos, a new danger thumped in from the opposite direction as his left-side cover-man crumpled off his mount with an arrow juddering in his temple: the Sogdians came swarming back in picking off targets now that they were disengaged from the enemy.

'To me! To me!' he roared, waving his sword above his head as he pulled his horse up into a thrashing high-hoofed rear. 'To me!'

And his men did rally to him even as the easterners pounded them with another couple of volleys; with the joy of battle raging through their veins, Demetrios and his cavalry charged the horse-archers, knowing that they would never catch their fleet steppe horses but wishing for no more than to be rid of them. Away the Sogdians turned, releasing one parting shot as they did, and then to their right they veered, for Demetrios' Tarantines had now made their move around the flank and had come to do exactly what these javelin-armed, shielded light cavalry had been designed to do: protect their heavier comrades from troops such as the Sogdians. In amongst the easterners they hurled their javelins, bringing down a dozen or so as they fled, leaving Demetrios and his men free to press their advantage in the cavalry action. Again he raised his sword and pulled his mount up into a heroic pose and urged his men to follow him for he was now going to decide the matter once and for all; he was now going to kill one of the opposing generals in hand to hand combat. He was now hunting for Ptolemy or Seleukos.

SELEUKOS.
THE BULL-ELEPHANT.

SAVAGE WAS THE pressure bearing down on Seleukos' command on the left of Ptolemy's cavalry wing; savage for Demetrios' move was gaining momentum and thus had to be halted or they would roll up the wing and threaten the rear of the phalanx. And still the elephants did not move; visible three hundred paces to his left in front of the fifteen hundred mercenary cavalry not yet committed by Demetrios, they had not charged and fallen into the trap set for them, and soon, if the pressure continued to grow, a portion of Ptolemy's cavalry would be pushed onto the very devices set to disable the enemy. Now was no time for caution, Seleukos fully understood; now he must throw the dice and pray that fortune would favour him for as the pressure mounted so did Babylon recede.

With a mighty roar he called his Companions, not already engaged with the enemy, to him as he backed off fifty paces from the fight; tight they formed a wedge behind him and, with another roar, back into the fray he led them, riding hard, increasing momentum. It was into the eight hundred heavy lancers, already in combat with Ptolemy's Companions, that he thundered with his men; a small unit of fifty they might have been but the shock of impact of weight and speed drove a hole deep into the foe. And it was into Pythan's command that he had driven, for it was Pythan he sought as his death would demoralise his men and open the way to Babylon.

Punching his lance forward, his arm at full stretch, Seleukos provided the sharp point of the wedge as it ploughed on, driving all before it as his men thrust left and right, reaping lives and limbs and sowing terror with the ferocity of their charge and the heat of their rage. As their momentum was slowed by the mass of foes, Seleukos rammed his lance ahead, into what he knew not, and whipped out his sword for bloody, close-quarter work. Raising it into a ringing parry, he became engaged in a battle of strength with the man whose weapon he had blocked; grabbing his shoulder with his left hand, Seleukos grappled with him, heaving, to unhorse him. Their eyes met as their exertion increased, but still none could better the other. It was then, as he struggled, that Seleukos realised that he was fighting not a Macedonian lancer, but an easterner dressed in Macedonian uniform. *Pythan's been training up Babylonians as cavalry.* The urgency to win was now such that his strength, already considerable, increased; down he forced his blade, pushing at the easterner's weapon, edging it towards him. The man's eyes squeezed shut with the effort of resistance and his left hand grasped his right wrist to add to its inertia; but it was not enough; his will snapped and his guard was broken through. Swift was the swipe that opened his throat and down he slithered from his horse. Seleukos pushed on and then halted as the cry that he had wanted reached him: 'Seleukos! Seleukos! Fight me!'

Seleukos wanted nothing more.

He turned to face Pythan.

By common consent when witnessing a challenge to single combat between two generals, those around them pulled back to reveal Pythan on his stallion walking towards Seleukos, his lance lowered and the sun hitting his bronze helm with a tall white feather rising on each side of its red, horsetail plume. 'You're mine, Seleukos.' His smile was grim, his eyes malevolent. 'I came all the way from Babylon for this.'

'And I'll go all the way to Babylon after this.' Seleukos signalled to one of his Companions who lobbed him his lance. 'On horseback first.'

'Agreed.'

Although the din of battle raged all around, Seleukos felt his mind calm as he hefted the lance, feeling its weight. But Pythan did not wait; with a bellow of intent he kicked the beast beneath him into action, his lance high, overarm, pointing down at an angle. Reacting fast, Seleukos urged his mount on, keeping his lance underarm; but with so short a distance between the two combatants, Pythan's speed was much the greater as they clashed. Down his spear thrust, down towards Seleukos' groin; with a whip of his wrist, Seleukos brought his weapon flicking up to hit Pythan's, diverting it as it slid down its length, grazing his knuckles as it scraped over them; keeping his wrist firm, Seleukos raised his arm, pushing his opponent's lance away, to smash his fist squarely on his jaw. With a grunt of pain, Pythan passed by; Seleukos turned his horse, his slower speed hastening the manoeuvre, and was halfway to his enemy before he managed to bring about his mount. Leaning forward along his horse's neck, Seleukos extended his right arm, the lance head waving, towards Pythan's chest; with a yank on the reins, Pythan brought his stallion's head up and to its right. The shriek of the beast as the blade slit through its tongue and up into its palate grated on Seleukos' ears and yet still he thrust, pushing the blade ever on up into the brute's brain as he simultaneously grabbed Pythan's flashing lance with his left hand. Up the stricken stallion went, up onto its back legs, ripping the weapon from Seleukos' grasp as it went; at the perpendicular it did not stop but carried on, roaring like Prometheus as the eagle ate his liver daily. With a desperate leap, Pythan cleared the dying animal just as it crashed onto its back, its hooves thrashing the air. As Pythan struggled to his knees Seleukos brought the tip of his weapon onto the nape of his neck.

Pythan froze.

'I should kill you now,' Seleukos shouted over the dying bestial screams. 'But what fun would that be with you grovelling in the dirt and me sitting proud on my horse?' He dropped the lance and, kicking his leg over his mount's rump, jumped to the ground. 'Stand up and face me.'

Pythan turned his head and snarled: 'I'll make you regret your honour.'

'That is for the gods to decide.' Seleukos stepped back, drawing his sword with his right hand and his dagger with his left. 'This will be fun.' His smile was mirthless and his eyes dark as he waited for Pythan to rise.

And rise he did, in a fleet blur of motion, twisting to his feet and launching a weighted throwing-knife at Seleukos' heart with such speed that it juddered into his breastplate as he tried to dodge it. He felt the tip of the blade pierce his skin, a thumb-nail's length, just below his ribcage, but had no time to extract it as Pythan came hurtling at him, sword slashing down.

With sparks flying from metallic contact, up he pushed his blade to check the downward cut, wincing as the movement pulled at the blade gouging him. With his left hand Seleukos stabbed low with his dagger, only for Pythan to spin to his left, avoiding the strike and taking him clear of the parry.

Now both men had their swords free; at a crouch they circled each other, sweat trickling lines down their dust-smeared faces.

With each breath Seleukos took, the knife wedged in his cuirass tore at a little more flesh; to wrench it out would mean dropping one of his weapons, so he could but endure the biting pain.

Again Pythan came at him and again he parried with the clang of honed and tempered iron. With lightning reflex, Pythan swept his sword down to Seleukos' thigh; his reaction was swift: he countered with the dagger, but, as his attention was drawn, Pythan slammed the palm of his left hand onto the handle of the impaling blade; in it thrust another thumbnail's length, shooting pain up his side and into his head as he brought his sword down to cleave into the base of Pythan's neck with the dull thud of a butcher's cleaver and releasing a welter of blood. Wedged it was in flesh and in the rim of his bronze breastplate; Pythan's eyes looked down at the blade, blood pumped out in regular heart-beats; his arms went limp.

Seleukos stepped back, leaving his weapon embedded, and gripped the handle of the dagger tormenting him; as Pythan's knees buckled, Seleukos jerked the blade free, stepped forward and rammed it through bronze into Pythan's heart. 'That's where this belongs.'

Pythan gasped and looked up into his killer's eyes; he tried to speak but only frothing spume emerged from his throat.

Seleukos shook his head in distaste and kicked the dying satrap of Babylonia in the chest; he fell back, his legs underneath him, dead, vacant eyes to the sky. There came a collective moan from his men watching on, one that soon turned into a cry of fear as their foes, no longer transfixed by the single combat of their general, set on them with the fury of those determined to match his deed. In they slammed into Pythan's wavering men, hewing at them as they turned and fled in the face of their wrath.

It was then that the first bestial trumpets sounded, faint above the cacophony of battle. Seleukos turned towards the noise to see the great beasts of war rumbling forward. 'Find Ptolemy!' he shouted to his right-hand cover-man. 'Tell him the elephants are charging; now is when we have to push all their cavalry back!'

PTOLEMY.
THE BASTARD.

B UT PTOLEMY HAD already stemmed the flood; the line was holding and, if anything, the pressure was easing as, over to his left, much of Pythan's cavalry seemed to be suddenly in flight. On to victory, he urged his Companions around him as they hacked and stabbed their way through the chaos of close-quarter combat; and slow, before them, did the knot of horses and riders begin to unravel. But it was not through flight that the numbers in front of Ptolemy lessened, it was through withdrawal. *He's pulling back; what's he up to?* And then he too heard the sound that they had been waiting for. *He's taking his cavalry back round to support his elephants seeing as he's failed to break through on this flank.* 'Let them go! Let them go! Don't follow them up!' he roared as more than a few of his men kicked their horses forward in pursuit. *We don't want to get any nearer to those elephants than we have to.*

Shouting orders to his staff to rally the cavalry where they were and await his decision to move forward, Ptolemy rode with a small escort a short distance forward to see the elephants in the last stages of their charge, accelerating from a walk to a lumbering trot as they followed their light infantry escorts forward against the archers, slinger and javelin men waiting for them. Clouds of arrows hissed up from both sides as slingshot whizzed invisible until it stove in some unfortunate's face. On the great beasts came, their turbaned mahouts guiding them with their goads; astride each was an armoured man with a long pike, his legs entwined in a rope around the animal's body.

Ptolemy once more held his breath as they approached the line of traps; with no more than fifty paces to go, the escort infantry slowed to allow their charges through as the light infantry opposite them retired, with care, through the unseen hazard. To the right of the beasts, Pythan's beaten cavalry rallied as Demetrios brought his Companions around behind the elephants in readiness to follow up on the carnage that he believed they would cause as they hit the phalanx's flank. *You're going to be greatly disappointed, my young friend.*

And as that thought flicked across Ptolemy's mind, the first great bellow of pain, so high and loud it was almost a physical thing, issued from within the herd. Up on back legs, trunk aloft, a great creature rose, a plank skewered to the tender underside of a flaying front foot, chains dangling down. And then another rose in its torment, and another. But as more were transfixed on the nails those already suffering came back down only to hop forward on three legs and step on another of the spiked planks. Up again they went, maddened now with pain and uncomprehending of what was its cause. As if it were not enough for them to suffer on the nails, the enemy light infantry now turned and strafed the beasts, aiming mainly at the mahouts; as they died so did any slim hope of controlling their mounts. Those that still could turned and bolted, many of them with planks still nailed to their feet until the weight of the chains pulled them free. Some went straight back towards Demetrios' cavalry, some to the right into the unsteady newly rallied Companions, and a few more veered to the front of the phalanx causing the mahouts of the elephants screening it to steer their animals away from the madness, leaving the infantry exposed. On they crashed, trumpeting and bellowing, shedding planks as they left bloody footprints in their wake, scattering the cavalry as every man and mount struggled to get out of the way of their erratic flight.

Back the cavalry fled, Pythan's men, Demetrios' Companions, with Demetrios himself unable to prevent them fleeing in the face of such untrammelled rampage.

'Now!' Ptolemy yelled towards the phalanx. 'Now you go!' His voice lost amid the anguished cries, Ptolemy kicked his horse towards his infantry whilst shouting orders to three of his escort to ride back and tell the cavalry to follow up the rout. Over the churned ground he raced as the first of the routers passed into the fifteen hundred unused mercenary cavalry still standing their ground. But they would not stand for long as letting a fleeing cavalryman through the ranks is one thing, but being faced with maddened beasts with bloodied tusks and some with planks nailed to a foot proved to be a quite different affair. As if by common consent the entire unit turned to race from the field.

'Forward! Forward!' Ptolemy cried as he closed on the phalanx. This time his voice was heard and, seeing who had issued the order, the nearest officer relayed it. The horns sounded, blending with the agonised bellowing from across the field; with a chorus of shouts from the file-leaders and -closers, eighteen thousand men set off to seal the victory. At a jog they went, so keen were they to finish the matter as, to their left, Lagus led his cavalry against Andronicus' command; but, unlike the phalanx, Andronicus did not wait; in good order he led his men from the field and raced north towards Gaza. The phalanx, however, did not have the luxury of a swift escape, and nor did they now have the elephant screen to deter attack, and, as the greater mass of infantry approached them, to a man, they sat on the ground in surrender.

Ptolemy surveyed the field: in all quarters the enemy were in flight and now it was time to capitalise on his victory; now it was time to expand his army. 'Take your men and get after those elephants,' he ordered the officer commanding his escort, pointing away towards the uninjured beasts that had been screening the phalanx. 'Offer the mahouts gold to change sides and then use them to calm the injured animals down; I want as many elephants out of this as possible.' *And Demetrios' gold will pay for them.*

'Yes, but sir—'

'Don't worry about me; I've got eighteen thousand infantry to protect me. Now go.'

The commander saluted and, shouting at his men to follow him, sped away on his mission. Looking over the cavalry, Ptolemy saw that all were now in flight pursued by the bolting elephants and then followed up by his men. *Seleukos will take care of that for the time being.* Pleased with the day's work so far he cantered between the two phalanxes. His men cheered him as he rode by whilst Demetrios' men, sitting or squatting, looked on with fear for they knew that with just one word from him most of them could be dead.

Pulling his mount up at the central point of the formation, he turned it to face the captured soldiers. 'Soldiers of Macedon, Greece and Asia, hear what I say.' He waited a few moments and then repeated himself as self-appointed heralds stood up to relay his words. Once satisfied that he was reaching all points of the enormous formation, he continued. 'I hold nothing against you personally and you are free to go. I would only ask that, should you decide to leave, you will swear an oath never to take up arms against me or Seleukos again.' He paused as his words were relayed and was rewarded with a hum of approval. 'However, I am not only merciful but also generous and I offer this to those who want it: employment in my service at the same rate as I pay my men, which, as I'm sure you have heard, is more than generous. Those who have them may bring their women, and for those who don't, women will be provided. What say you? Who will join me?'

It did not take long for the first men to stand and cheer and by the time the message had run through the entire formation almost all the men were hailing Ptolemy as their lord.

Eleven thousand men, Antigonos: I'd love to be present when Demetrios comes to explain that to you.

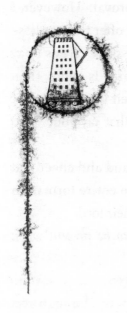

DEMETRIOS.
THE BESIEGER.

NONE WOULD STOP, no matter how much he shouted or implored, not one of his men would stop and rally on him. Only his Companions remained steady, as well as Nearchos and his bodyguard. Demetrios wept tears of shame and frustration as his authority was so flagrantly ignored. And then he looked about him, as his army sped by, and the scale of the disaster gradually dawned upon him: his whole cavalry were in flight and the infantry had sat down in surrender. As to the elephants, the arm of his army that was meant to have delivered the crushing blow, they were now trampling his own men. Nothing of his army remained. *How can I tell my father? What can I say that will make up for such a disaster?* The sight of an elephant, mad with pain, bringing down a fleeing Greek cavalryman with a sweep of his tusks just twenty paces away brought home the precariousness of his situation; giving up all thought of rallying, he turned and, with his bodyguard remaining in good order, joined the rest of his men in flight.

With gathering fear, Demetrios fled, for, although the elephants were soon outpaced, falling away, faint with pain, the pursuing cavalry was relentless; it was now a race to Gaza. Past his camp he raced, abandoning his tent and all the luxuries contained therein, but they meant nothing to him now as he had a far more urgent errand: his wife, Phila, and their two children were in Gaza Harbour; should they fall into Ptolemy's hands the shame would be unendurable.

As they approached Gaza, Demetrios could see the gates to both the city and the harbour were already crammed with people both trying to escape and attempting to get in to retrieve their possessions. 'Take the men, Nearchus, and wait on the beach by the walls on the north side of the port. I'll see you there as soon as possible.'

'Be quick,' the old Cretan warned, 'they're right on our heels.'

'Find four more horses; I don't care how.' Taking two men with him, Demetrios headed for the Harbour's main gates. With the flats of their swords and the soles of their boots, his men beat a passage through the panicking crush. Defeated soldiers ran here and there desperate to collect their baggage from their billets before it fell into enemy hands; but away from the gate the rest of the port became remarkably quiet as the citizens awaited the next event, behind shuttered windows. Clattering through the streets to his harbour-front residence he saw virtually no one as he passed, until, that was, he came to the quay; here it was full of men trying to escape by ship, but of these he took no notice for he had seen on the top of the steps, standing with an arm around each of their two children, his wife.

'I won't ask what happened,' Phila said as he drew near, 'for I can see the result and it's not good. As I stood here with our children, I was prepared for either you or Ptolemy to come and get me. I'm surprised it was you, Husband, but I'm glad of it.'

Not wishing to rise to this double-edged compliment, Demetrios jumped from his horse and ran up the steps, and swept up his three-year-old daughter Stratonice – named after his mother – into his arms. 'Quick, Phila, we've hardly any time.' He looked down at his son. 'Antigonos, be brave and do as I say.'

The boy nodded, dumb.

'Take your mother's hand and follow me.' Without looking to see if he was obeyed, Demetrios set off back down the steps and along the quay as the two escorts protected the party from being buffeted in the crowd. On they went towards where the quay met the port's northern wall; here, Demetrios led them up a set of steps onto the beginning of the harbour mole. Along he went until the wall fell away and there was nothing between the mole and the sea, ten feet below. 'You'll need to throw her down to me, understand?' He looked at his wife, deep into her eyes, as he unstrapped his breastplate; it clanged onto the stone ground. His greaves soon followed.

'Yes, Demetrios; I can do that.'

He had no doubt that she could, being the daughter of Antipatros. In he jumped, feeling the shock of the winter sea as it submerged him. With a couple of kicks he resurfaced. He raised his arms up towards his wife. 'Now!'

She did not hesitate; Stratonice screamed as she was hurled to the sea. As the little body hit the water Demetrios grabbed her around the waist, preventing her from going under. 'Come on,' he shouted over his daughter's screams. 'Jump and swim.'

The young Antigonos jumped, holding his mother's hand; the two bodyguards, stripped of their armour, followed.

Spluttering on the seawater, Demetrios pulled towards the shore with one hand, kicking with his feet, as he clutched his daughter in the other. On he struggled through the waves but with good heart for, just fifty paces away, on the water's edge, stood Nearchos with his Companions. Stratonice's cries had subsided now, whether through cold or from an understanding of the danger they were in, Demetrios knew not, nor cared; his daughter was safe and that was all that mattered. He glanced behind him to see Phila and Antigonos both pulling strong breaststrokes through the waves, with one of the bodyguards to either side should they get into difficulty.

At last he came to the surf and felt the power of the sea wash him to the beach, fighting not to be drawn by the undertow, he pushed himself on until his feet hit the sand and he could walk from the sea. Falling to his knees on the beach he held Stratonice's face between his hands and kissed her. 'Good girl; brave girl.' He then looked up at Nearchos. 'Ready?'

'We've got the horses, if that's what you mean?'

'It is.' He turned to help his wife and son out of the water. 'You take Stratonice and I'll have Antigonos,' Demetrios said, kissing Phila out of pure relief for having had one success in the day. He hauled his son up onto the horse Nearchos proffered whilst the two bodyguards saw to Phila and Stratonice before mounting their own stallions.

'Where to?' Nearchos asked as Demetrios swung up into the saddle.

'North to Azotus; we should be safe there and it's close enough.'

'Close enough for what?'

'Close enough to enter into negotiations with Ptolemy about the burial of our dead. It's my duty.'

Nearchos looked at Demetrios with approval in his eyes. 'I'm pleased to hear it; your father will be proud of you.'

Demetrios' smile was grim. 'No, he won't; he won't be proud of me until I avenge myself on both Ptolemy and Seleukos.'

Seleukos.
The Bull-Elephant.

HARD THEY RODE in pursuit of Pythan's cavalry, with each stride of his horse causing Seleukos much discomfort. The wadding he had wedged between his wound and the pierced cuirass was sticky with blood but it had stemmed the flow. But he did not have time to stop to have it tended to by a physician, there was too much at stake and haste was of the essence. With their fleeter horses, Azanes and his Sogdians were gaining on their quarry; Seleukos and his Companions and other heavy cavalry units who had joined in the chase pressed on as fast as their tired mounts could go. But if they were tiring, so too were the routing cavalry after all they had suffered and the Sogdians began to draw level with them; no arrows did they send into their midst for the objective was not to destroy but to capture.

With teeth gritted and sweat oozing from beneath his helmet, Seleukos endured the ordeal, for he knew that he had to as there was no one but him who could deliver the speech required after Pythan's cavalry had been brought to a halt. And soon they would be for, already, individual riders were drawing up now that the Sogdians were outpacing them.

As Azanes led his leading comrades across their line of flight, the fleeing cavalry saw no alternative but to throw themselves at the mercy of the horse-archers; with a lack of coordination they pulled up, piecemeal, many colliding such was their disorder. Within moments, Azanes had them surrounded, his men with arrows nocked but bows undrawn so as not to instil more fear than necessary.

Seleukos came to a halt next to the Sogdians' commander. 'Well, done, my friend; I shall remember this when we are back in Babylon.'

Azanes grinned. 'There is a long way to go before we get there.'

'Yes; but this is now the beginning of the journey.' He swung his leg over his horse and dismounted, wincing as his wound smarted with the jump, and looked at the captives. *Judging by their looks, most of them are easterners, I can see hardly any Macedonians. Four or five hundred of them in total, I should think; along with the three hundred Sogdians, that should be enough.* He walked forward, his arms spread wide to show that he meant no harm. 'Men of Babylon, we are not enemies, you and I. Indeed, I believe that we are friends, for I am Seleukos, the rightful satrap of Babylonia.' He raised his arms in the air, extending them to his audience. 'Many of you will know me; many of you will remember how I was forced to flee Babylon. Antigonos then put Pythan in my place and look what he has done to you: he has involved you in a war in the west which is none of your concern; many of your brothers in arms are lying dead next to a sea that few of you had ever seen before.' He paused to let his words resonate and was rewarded with more than a few nods of agreement and murmured conversation. 'But Pythan is dead; I killed him with my own hands.' A small cheer greeted this statement. 'And now I intend to take back what is rightfully mine. I intend to take back Babylon and Babylonia and I will leave tomorrow. What say you, men of Babylonia? Will you accompany me home? Share with me in my struggle and, when I am successful, I swear to you that I will never lead you west against your will, for our interests will remain in the east; together we shall forge an empire out there and you shall be handsomely rewarded for your services. So what say you, men of Babylonia? What say you?'

They said yes. They broke into a spontaneous chant of his name, punching their fists in the air, their weariness forgotten. Seleukos indulged them for a while, until he remembered his wound and the necessity of getting treatment before setting out on the long road to Babylon; he signalled for silence. 'Tonight we camp outside the walls of Gaza; we will bind our wounds and sharpen our swords and then leave at first light.'

'Will that be enough?' Ptolemy asked as he watched Apama bathe Seleukos' wound. 'Eight hundred men to take a satrapy doesn't sound overly generous.'

Seleukos sucked the breath through his teeth as Apama applied a cloth soaked in vinegar. 'It'll be enough provided that the preparations that I put in place just before I left have been completed.'

'And if they haven't?'

'Then I'll have to improvise.'

Ptolemy shrugged. 'Well, you improvised well enough with those elephant traps so I suppose I shouldn't worry. We got all of them, you know; all forty-three elephants. They should all be fine according to the surviving mahouts; what I will be short of, though, are mahouts, we killed more than half of them, so...'

'I'll send you some as a thank you, yes, of course I will. I owe you a lot, Ptolemy, and I shall not forget it. I shall always remain your friend. Let's hope our descendants can maintain that friendship.'

'Oh, I doubt they will; things change, alliances shift and all that sort of thing.' He leaned forward and slapped Seleukos on the shoulder. 'When Apama has finished patching you up, I expect you both in my tent for dinner.'

And thus it was with a heavy head that Seleukos rose before dawn the following morning to find his wife and children already up and breakfasting on bread, cheese and olive oil. With a groan he slipped out of his campbed and, rubbing his temples, dipped his face into a bowl of cold water, sloshing it over his neck and ears.

'Ptolemy sent a message asking you to come to his tent as soon as you were awake,' Apama said, smiling at the look of pain on her husband's face.

'Did he say why?' Seleukos coughed, his throat dry; the action hurt his wound. He cursed and rubbed it under the bandage wrapped around his midriff.

'No; perhaps he thought you could do with a drink before we leave.'

Seleukos grunted and slipped on his tunic and sandals, fighting to keep down his intake from the night before. Taking a hunk of bread to help him in that endeavour, he walked out of the tent into the cold pre-dawn, winter air.

'You don't look well,' Ptolemy said with unreasonable cheer.

'What do you expect? I got skewered yesterday and then I drank enough to fell one of your newly acquired elephants.'

'Sit down, join us.' Ptolemy indicated to a spare chair opposite him.

It was then that Seleukos noticed another figure sitting at the table. 'Good morning, Nearchos.'

The Cretan smiled. 'Seleukos.'

'Nearchos is here to negotiate,' Ptolemy said. 'I thought it only polite to invite you to listen in.'

'Very thoughtful.' Seleukos sat down and poured himself a mug of water.

'The trouble is we have already concluded our business.'

Seleukos was unconcerned; he downed his water.

'Demetrios may take his dead, all five thousand of them, and give them the rites due to fallen soldiers.'

'Fair enough.'

'I'm also returning his tent and all his possessions therein, as well as any of his captured officers who wish to go back to them on the proviso that they swear never to take up arms against you or me again.'

'Generous and sensible.' Seleukos succumbed to temptation and reached for the wine pitcher.

Ptolemy inclined his head in agreement. 'Yes, I thought so too. However, that is as far as I'm willing to accommodate our young buck.' He turned to Nearchos. 'I'm afraid, old friend, that I will not comply with Demetrios' request for me to with-draw back to Egypt and I find the request quite puzzling seeing as I beat him on the battlefield yesterday. Quite the opposite, actually, as I shall be moving north, reclaiming everything that Antigonos took from me. No doubt he'll come back and retake the towns and then I shall once again take them back from him. This can carry on indefinitely, and be a constant drain on our resources, or we can come to an agree-ment. Say that to Antigonos when you see him next; I will always be happy to sit down and talk with him. We need to agree upon our areas of influence. Me, Antigonos, Lysimachus, Kassandros and Seleukos.'

Nearchos looked confused. 'Seleukos? Why him?'

Seleukos knocked back his wine in one. 'Because, Nearchos, I'm going to retake Babylonia and this time I'm going to keep it whatever Antigonos tries to do.'

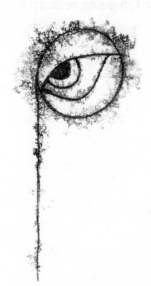

ANTIGONOS.
THE ONE-EYED.

I T HAD BEEN frustration followed by frustration ever since Ptolemaios had arrived with his fleet from Greece the previous month. Nothing had gone right and Antigonos still sat in Calchedon, on the southern shore of the Bosporus, unable to make the crossing due to terrible weather that made a pontoon bridge of boats lashed together unfeasible. However, even had the weather been fine, Byzantium was still proving to be a problem and had refused all financial incentives to allow him to cross. But now that the weather had cleared the winter had come; snow fell in the high hills and mountains opposite in Thrace and would soon come to the passes of central Anatolia. And he had decided to make one last attempt at crossing into Europe and wintering in Macedon after a hard forced march across Lysimachus' territory.

But first he needed to know whether his latest, outrageously large, bribe had been sufficient to secure the goodwill of the city standing on the northern shore, not even a third of a league away. Ancient, wealthy and mighty, Byzantium was the key to his crossing. He could blockade its harbour with his fleet but what use was that when he could not get the troops across to seal off its land walls? The only weapon he could utilise was, therefore, gold and it was to this end that he watched the ship that had taken Hieronymus across the narrow stretch of water to negotiate with the city fathers make its return journey.

'Well?' Antigonos asked as the vessel docked in Calchedon's port. 'Did they accept this time?'

Hieronymus waited as the gangplank was rigged and then descended onto the quay. 'Yes and no.'

'Yes and no? My arse!' Antigonos was in no mood for riddles. 'It's either yes or no, surely?'

'Not in this case.' Hieronymus paused and collected his thoughts. 'How shall I put this?'

'Just tell me what they said; I'm not interested in a historian's flourish. Get on with it or I'll be wondering how I shall put you.'

'Well, they said that they would be only too happy to accept your money in return for allowing you to build your bridge and getting your army across unmolested. In fact, nothing could delight them more. And that was the very word they used: delight. And the ten talents a man for the council was more than adequate to secure their goodwill and they thank you very much for your generosity.'

Antigonos' one eye narrowed in confusion. 'So what's the problem?'

Hieronymus scratched the back of his neck. 'Well.'

'Well, what? Get on with it.'

'Well, in a spirit of fair play and even-handedness and because they wish to remain on good terms with everybody as they are a peace-loving people, they feel it only right that, should they accept your offer and allow you onto their territory, they should extend the same courtesy to Lysimachus and invite him too so that no one can be said to have been treated with undue favour over another.'

'But I'm offering them a fortune!'

'And Lysimachus is evidently matching it.'

'But he can't afford it; he's forever pleading poverty and asking for extra money for those forts of his. Where's the gold come from?'

'Ah, that's just it. It's come from you.'

'Me? My arse, it has! I haven't given Lysimachus anything of value since I last farted in his direction.'

'Well, not directly, no; but indirectly, yes. You see, Antigonos, when you paid the Scythians to invade from the north and the Thracian king Seuthes to rebel in support, Aristodemus paid them in gold and silver coinage. Unfortunately—'

Antigonos groaned, putting his hand to his forehead. 'Unfortunately, Lysimachus defeated them both and captured my payment.'

'And a lot more besides: the Scythians came across the Danubus fully intending to stay.'

Antigonos groaned again, deeper. 'So they brought all their wealth with them.'

'I'm afraid so, and they didn't take nearly so much back with them after Lysimachus gave them a good hiding; and as for King Seuthes, he lost the lot when Lysimachus defeated him in the Succi Pass. No, I'm afraid our gallant satrap of the north finds himself in funds and—'

'I have no one to blame but myself.'

'I wasn't going to say that; but yes, it would seem that way.'

Antigonos cast his eye over the fleet berthed in the harbour. *It might as well stay here for the winter now; I'll see what the spring brings, but I'll get across somehow.* He turned to Hieronymus. 'I've had enough for one year. I'm taking the army back to Phrygia before the passes are closed; we'll winter in Celaenae; the fleet winters here and then in the spring we'll even a few scores.'

It was with relief that Antigonos approached the walls of the chief town of his satrapy four days later. He had ridden ahead of the army, leaving his nephews to bring it south once the oarsmen, sailors and marines of the fleet had been billeted around Calchedon, in order that he could spend some quiet time in Celaenae with his wife Stratonice and his younger son Philippos, who was now coming of age and becoming interesting; having not seen the boy for almost two years, Antigonos' curiosity was piqued.

Stratonice greeted him with the tired eyes of one who has been weeping. 'What's the matter?' Antigonos asked as he placed an affectionate kiss on her cheek; over her shoulder he espied Philippos, now a striking youth of fifteen, a smirk flickering on his face. 'What is it, boy?'

Stratonice pulled back and held her husband by the shoulders at arm's length. 'Get out, Philippos!' she shouted over her shoulder. Stung by the vehemence of the order, the boy scuttled out with the smirk still lingering on his face.

'What is it, woman? What's happened?'

'Nearchos is here, he arrived this morning.'

Antigonos' stomach did not feel quite as good as it had a few moments before when he first saw his wife. 'Nearchos? What reason has he got to be coming all this way in winter?'

'I think it's best that he tells you himself.'

Antigonos' stomach lurched and dread seized him as Stratonice took him by the hand and led him from the room.

Nearchos waited out on the terrace wrapped in a woollen cloak against the cold. The look in his eyes made Antigonos wish to be anywhere else but here. 'I heard you were close so I thought it best to wait here to give you the news rather than you receive it on the road.'

Antigonos felt Stratonice's grip on his hand tighten; a lump formed in his throat as he prepared himself. 'Tell me, it's Demetrios, isn't it?'

The Cretan nodded. 'Yes, I'm afraid so.'

Antigonos felt a pit opening up before him into which he would be cast with no hope of return. 'Oh my sacred arse, tell me.'

'He's been defeated by Ptolemy.'

'And?'

'And he is now in northern Syria rounding up what he can salvage from his army and putting them into winter quarters.'

Antigonos' heart leaped. 'What?'

'I know, Antigonos; it's shameful.'

'Shameful? Shameful, my arse!' He grabbed Nearchos and embraced him, kissing him on both cheeks. 'I thought the boy was dead; that I couldn't have borne. But suffering a defeat, pah! It's just what the cocky little puppy needs. I should probably write to Ptolemy and thank him. The boy oozes overconfidence and perhaps this will knock some sense into him. No wonder Philippos was smirking, nothing would please him more than his big brother getting trounced. And I'll bet Ptolemy is gloating, although I would say that he can't claim much credit for defeating a beardless boy.'

'He's twenty-five.'

'Half Ptolemy's age. What happened?'

Antigonos shook his head as the tale came to an end. 'Pythan, eh? That was a blow. But we still hold Tyros thanks to Andronicus getting his cavalry back there safely; mounted troops threatening his supply lines will prevent Ptolemy from advancing too far north. But losing all the elephants – that will have to be remedied. We'll send to the east in the spring for replacements.'

'That might be difficult, Antigonos.'

'Difficult? What makes you say that?'

'Well, when I left Gaza six days ago, Seleukos was also departing for the east with about a thousand men.'

Antigonos laughed. 'He thinks that he can take Babylon with just a thousand men? My arse, he can! He had ten thousand when he first took it.'

'Well, just say for a moment that he does.'

Antigonos paused for thought and then laughed again, long and full. 'All right, say he does, well, I'll be buggered if I'm going to march all the way east again, the food's terrible. No, there is only one person responsible should we, in the unlikely event, lose Babylon: I'll go south and clean up Demetrios' mess in Syria and push Ptolemy back into Egypt, but it will be up to Demetrios to get Babylon back from Seleukos.'

SELEUKOS.
THE BULL-ELEPHANT.

I T HAD BEEN a gamble that had paid off and had cut a four hundred league journey down to two hundred and fifty; but it had only been possible because of the season. Yes, the desert had been freezing at night, but that could be endured; it was the unrelenting heat of the day that could not be and at this time of year, winter, that was not an issue. With haste being imperative so as to come to Babylon before news of Pythan's death reached the garrison commanded by Teutamus, Seleukos had decided to risk crossing the desert rather than going north and then south around it; thus he had headed south-east from Gaza to the place the Nabatean Arabs call The Stone, or Petra in Greek. Here he hired guides who knew the oases and wells, and with them they brought pack-camels whose loads were nothing but skins of water; and thus he had been able to arrive on the Euphrates, two leagues to the south of Babylon, after a journey of just fifteen days. And here, as their horses and camels drank deep of the slow-flowing river, did he make his plans. At dawn the following day, leaving most of his men, with silver and orders to purchase as many boats as possible, in their camp – which, with the presence of the camels, looked nothing more than a caravan resting up – he left to put those plans in motion.

And to this end he now stood, dressed in the long robes and headdress of a Nabatean, in the New Town on the west bank of the river watching his wife and son walk across the stone bridge over to the Old City, one hundred and fifty paces away, its blue walls in shadow from the rising of the sun. With her face veiled, her hair covered and her skirts long, Apama would draw no attention, as she was escorted by Antiochus and would seem to be the model of decorum; the basket of grain that she balanced on her head added to her anonymity as did the two live chickens that Antiochus clutched under his arms. Seleukos glanced around to see Azanes and a half dozen of his men strolling in ones and twos close to Apama, there as a backup should something go wrong as she passed through the gates and on into the city. But nothing would go wrong, Seleukos was sure about that, for what was more natural than a woman and her son taking a gift to the priests of Bel Marduk?

All Seleukos had to do now was wait, for the success of his venture now depended on his wife and the messages she carried. He sat down on a stone next to the bridge and watched the river fishermen land their catch and haggle with the market traders for the best price. Behind the fish market were the costermongers, plying the fruit and vegetables grown in the huge areas of fertile, well-irrigated ground along both banks of the river to the north and south of the city; colourful, varied and plentiful was their produce and the sight of it gave Seleukos a feeling of comfort: his people were well fed and content. He noted all the various different costumes of the populace, from the rich Babylonian merchant surrounded by flatterers and hangers-on and trailed by a small army of slaves, to the almost naked holy men from the east or the Greek mercenaries, Persian travellers,

Cretans in their flat, broad-rimmed hats, Bactrians in leather tunics and quilted trousers. Here were all manner of people, and all would soon come under his rule – Bel Marduk willing.

The houses around the riverside market seemed to be well kept up and the public buildings too had good coats of bright paint adorning them. All in all, from where he sat, Babylon looked to Seleukos as though it was prospering under Macedonian rule and he would make certain that its fortunes would rise even further once he had come back into his own.

For most of the day did he sit there, moving only to buy some grilled fish and a flat, unleavened bread which he ate gazing towards the gates at the far end of the bridge. It was not until he was beginning to get concerned, as the sun was westering and the markets packed away, did he finally see his wife and son making their way through the crowds back across from the Old City; he rose and, rubbing his sore behind, fell in next to Apama as she came off the bridge. South they walked for a while waiting until the crowds thinned out before talking.

'Well?' Seleukos asked.

'Well, the repairs to the Ziggurat of Bel Marduk have been completed and it looks fantastic; Naramsin is very pleased with it.'

'You know perfectly well what I'm asking about. Well?'

'Naramsin did build the tunnel; the entrance is below the eastern end of the bridge.'

'Good man; that makes things so much simpler.'

'I was wondering how you were going to manage if he hadn't; the priests of Bel Marduk must be fed up with you burning down their apartments.'

'It was only once and we all decided that it was the god's doing as the timing was so fortuitous; anyway, I rebuilt them far grander than they were. So, will Naramsin do as I ask?'

'He will be at the entrance at midnight tomorrow to let you in.'

'And will he get a message to Temenos?'

'Ah, that's the only problem; Temenos disappeared soon after we left. Naramsin assumes that he was either executed or thrown in prison; either way you're going have to find a different way into the two citadels.'

'Then I'll have to improvise getting through the second gate as well. And then how to take the citadels without betrayal? Well, once we have the city under control and the people in our hands, which, if the priests of Bel Marduk play their part, should be possible, then we'll worry about the garrison. It all depends upon tomorrow night.'

At dusk the following evening his men embarked on the small fleet of ninety boats that they had assembled; the couple of hundred for whom there was no room had been despatched earlier to wait close by the southern gate along with Apama and the children. For secrecy's sake, he had not risked sending men into the city in advance for they were all known in Babylon, and Seleukos knew only too well the dangers of men with their tongues loosened by wine as they passed the nervous time with an old acquaintance before a combat that could well claim their lives. And, besides, if Naramsin played his part it was not necessary to have anyone on the inside.

The moon, but a narrow crescent, gave enough light with which to navigate as they rowed upstream towards the glow of a quarter of a million people's lamps and cooking fires; bright did the city shine and from it, as they drew near, emanated the continual buzz and hum of human existence. As they came to where the river entered the city, Seleukos signalled for the main body of boats to wait whilst he went on with his fifty Companions in five small craft. Keeping close under the walls along the eastern bank, hiding in their shadow, the little flotilla edged its way towards the bridge, delineated by flaming torches along its body. Seleukos checked his sword was loose in his scabbard as he sat in the prow of the lead boat hardly daring to breathe in his excitement.

When they had parted earlier, Apama had sensed his mood and squeezed his arm. 'Not long now and we shall have all we wish for.'

And it would not be long – should all go to plan.

Under the bridge, Seleukos' boat was rowed until it nudged the stonework beneath it. He looked up in the gloom: he could see no indent in the stone or change of texture to indicate a door of any kind; he stood, balancing himself as the boat rocked. 'Pass me an oar,' he whispered. Again taking care not to topple, he held the oar in two hands and tapped the stonework above his head; the *tak tak* of wood against stone frustrated him for he knew that the door was there – somewhere. And then the hollow knocking of wood on wood cheered his heart and he tapped the door for a second time, louder, before passing the oar back into the darkness.

Above him, a shadow moved and three ropes came into view. 'They're secure,' a disembodied voice hissed.

First tugging one of the ropes out of habit, Seleukos committed his full body weight to it and shinned up, his shield slung across his back.

'Welcome back, lord,' Naramsin said as he hauled him into the tunnel. 'I rejoice at your coming, as will my brethren when they see you, for Pythan was no respecter of Bel Marduk.'

I'm pleased to hear it. 'I'm sorry to hear that, Naramsin. I will certainly be making my appreciation of the god and his priests known when this is over.'

'I'm pleased to hear it, lord.'

I'm sure you are. Seleukos turned around and looked back down into the boat. 'Come, as fast as you can, leaving one man in the boat to row it to the opposite bank to help pick up the others.'

And as his men scaled the ropes behind him, Seleukos followed Naramsin along the tunnel in which torches burned every ten paces along its brick walls: it was exactly as he had specified, wide enough for three men and high enough for most men to be able to stand. Dank it smelled and wet was its stone floor but Seleukos cared not for it led into the heart of Babylon. 'How long did it take to build?'

'We finished it last year,' Naramsin replied. 'Although it was serviceable a year before that, but we hadn't bricked up the walls to make it safer.'

Seleukos counted thirty torches before they emerged into a room dominated by a large desk.

'This is my study,' Naramsin said. 'I thought it the safest place to have the entrance.' He crossed the room and opened the door at the far side out into a corridor. 'Come, lord; this leads to the precinct of the temple; as you know, the gates are just behind it. You can gather your men there to make the assault.'

Along the corridor and then out into the night Seleukos went with a trail of men behind him. Just the fifty he needed for this part of the operation; the rest waiting in the boats on the river or on the western bank; they would come into their own once he had the gates by the bridge opened. And that would be the difficult part.

In the shadow of the Esagila, the Temple of Bel Marduk, he counted his men; they were all present, swords and shields at the ready and a coil of rope each, with a grappling iron attached, over their shoulders.

With his men two abreast behind him, Seleukos joined Naramsin at the wooden door that led out of the temple precinct and into a wide road running along the length of the river wall. Right they turned, and into a marching column four abreast they formed, for Seleukos had decided that the best way to approach the gate was not through stealth but openly as if they had every right to be there. And thus they marched, in step, along the road the two hundred paces to the gate, making no attempt to hide their coming. The gate commander, curious, came out of the guardroom to enquire as to their business. It was the last enquiry he ever made. As his body fell to the floor, Seleukos' men broke and formed a shield-wall facing the dozen shocked guards, now quite outnumbered.

Seleukos pointed to the man whose throat he had slit lying at his feet. 'Lads, you can either end up like him or you can join me.' He stepped into the light of a torch. 'Most of you know me: I am Seleukos, son of Antiochus, friend to Alexander and rightful satrap of Babylonia, and I have come to take back what is mine. Which do you want: me to give you your death or you to give me your loyalty and open the gate?'

The answer did not take long to come; the gates swung open on a mechanism of great antiquity. Seleukos' men ran through and began to attach their ropes to the bridge with the grappling irons so they dangled down to the water level whilst he took a couple of torches from their brackets and waved them above his head from side to side.

With the ropes in place, Seleukos led his men back through the gates and on to those in the second wall. 'What's the password tonight?' Seleukos asked one of the erstwhile guards.

'Antigonos and Marduk,' came the reply.

'Pythan's deputy sounds to be a very loyal and religious man.'

'Teutamus? No, he's a bastard.'

'That's a rather generous description of the man.'

'A complete and utter bastard, then.'

'That's him. Where is he?'

'He has his headquarters in the Main Citadel.'

'Good. Come with me. I'll tell you what to do to get this gate open.'

Seleukos hung back as the man, fully briefed, banged on the second gate.

'Antigonos and Marduk!' the guard shouted.

'What is it?' came a voice from the other side.

'It's Menanthios from the first gate; Pelagios sent me with an urgent letter for Teutamus just arrived by river.'

'What? At this time of night?'

'Look, Brother, I'm just the poor bastard that gets sent on the errands; how and why are not up to me. Now, do you want to take this letter or would you prefer explaining to Teutamus, as he has your balls crushed, why you chose to delay an urgent missive?'

'All right; just a moment. Wait by the postern door.'

As the small door in the gate began to swing open on goose-fatted hinges, Seleukos dashed forward, with his men trailing him, to ram his shield into the guard coming through to receive the fictitious letter. Down the man went and over him Seleukos ran, sword drawn, shield up with support flooding through, quickly forming up on each of his shoulders as he advanced on the surprised guards. 'The city will be mine by dawn, lads,' Seleukos said as the guards went for their weapons. 'Either you put those down or we'll put you down; what's it to be?'

The guards looked at one another, nervous and tense, as yet more men came through the little postern gate.

'We'll put them down,' the eldest of the guards, a grey-haired veteran, said, dropping his sword; his mates followed.

'A good choice; now open the gates.'

And as the gates swung open a fine sight greeted Seleukos when he looked back: the Babylonian cavalrymen and the

Sogdians were now swarming up the ropes, onto the bridge and running towards him. 'Menanthios, are there any more troops in this area?'

'Not at night, sir; just a dozen on each gate. The nearest are the guards on the Ishtar Gate and then the garrison in the Southern Citadel next to it.'

'Good; that's where we're heading.'

As the last of his troops arrived so did Apama with Antiochus, Archaeus and the little Apama cradled in her arms, surrounded by an escort of eight guards.

'We're almost there,' Seleukos said, kissing his wife. 'It's just a matter of the two citadels now.'

'And just how are you going to manage them without Temenos?'

'I improvised for this gate; I shall improvise again. Now, you stay here in the guardroom with your guards and I'll send for you when we have our prize.' He kissed her once more and then turned to look at his men. 'Azanes! Come here.'

The Sogdian chieftain waddled over, his gait unsteady after so many years in the saddle.

'We'll need fire arrows, get what you need.'

With a grin of anticipation in the torchlight, Azanes went on his way shouting at his men in their strange language.

Seleukos turned to his Companions. 'Go and fetch the ropes from the bridge; we'll be needing all of them.'

With all set, Seleukos led his small invasion force out left onto the Processional Way, heading north to the Ishtar Gate. The sight of over three hundred Sogdian archers aiming at them was more than sufficient for the guards to join in Seleukos' endeavour and his attention was now focused on the Southern Citadel. 'I need to speak to your commander,' he shouted up at the walls.

'Who's asking?' came a reply.

'Seleukos, son of Antiochus, the rightful satrap of Babylonia.'

'Who?' The tone was incredulous.

'You heard; now go and drag him off his boy and get him out here.'

It was a tired-sounding voice that shouted down from the wall a little time later. 'Is that really you, Seleukos?'

'Yes, it is; who's that?'

'Phoibos; I served with you in the Hypaspists. I was just a ranker then so you probably won't remember me.'

Seleukos had a vague memory of the man but could not be sure. 'Look, Phoibos; I've taken the main gates and control the bridge and the New Town as well as the Ishtar Gate. Now, I'm going to have a chat with Teutamus and I would appreciate it if you were standing next to me when I do.'

'I'm sorry, I can't do that, Seleukos, much as I'd like to; I'm sworn to Pythan.'

'Pythan's dead; I killed him in a battle at Gaza seventeen days ago.'

'Impossible; how could you have got here in that time?'

'I came across the desert with Nabatean guides.'

Phoibos digested this information. 'I still can't give you the citadel; but I'll do this for you: if Teutamus surrenders then so will I.'

'Let's hope for your sake that I'm still in a good mood after he surrenders.' He turned on his heel and walked away. 'Azanes, have you got your fire ready?'

'Yes, lord.'

'Good; it's time to warm up Teutamus.'

The Main Citadel, its walls the height of six men, stood outside the Ishtar Gate. Its western and northern walls formed a part of the river wall and its southern wall was hard up against its sister citadel; it had only one weak point: the eastern wall. Seleukos decided that negotiation would be a waste of time and would simply mean that the defence had more time in which to organise itself.

'Azanes, count to a hundred in your head and then light your torches, run through the gate and start pumping fire into the citadel; spread it around, I need a big diversion; just keep your aim away from the eastern wall and the gates. When they open come and join me.'

Azanes' grin showed just how much he was enjoying himself.

'Bring your boys through the gate after the Sogdians,' he ordered the commander of the Babylonian cavalry, 'and follow us.' He turned to his Companions. 'With me, lads, and have your grappling hooks ready.' He held out a hand. 'Pass me one.' A coil of rope was tossed to him; he turned and ran.

Through the gate he pelted with his fifty comrades behind him; along under the eastern wall he went as fast as possible at a crouch. At the far end he stopped and hefted the rope, swinging the grappling iron around. 'Wait for it, boys.'

And it soon came; three hundred streaks of fire roared through the night sky; up and up they went until, reaching their apex, as a second and then a third volley followed, they fell, flaring to earth, slamming into all parts of the Main Citadel. As one, Seleukos and his men hurled their grappling hooks skyward; as each man's was secured either on the first or second attempt, occasionally the third, he started up the wall. Seleukos tugged on the rope and then hauled himself up, getting his feet onto the stonework to walk up it, pulling himself on, hand over fist, his shield hanging behind him. Up he went as fire continued to fall from the sky and the Babylonian cavalrymen ran to await their turn on the ropes. Onto the wall he swung his leg, rolling over the parapet onto the walkway as heavy footsteps and harsh cries hurtled towards him. With a jump he regained his feet, sweeping his blade free and ducking beneath a savage swipe at his neck.

With a jab he punched the tip of his sword into the midriff of the youngster charging him as more of his Companions made the summit, hurling down any defenders still with a mind to resist.

Along the walkway Seleukos hurried, crunching back a screaming man with his shield as he came up the steps from the courtyard. Down the steps he ran, two at a time, his men close behind as newly wakened garrison troops tumbled out of the barracks, some in tunics but many still naked, only to stop and turn away, back into shelter as the flaming rain continued to fall all around them. But now the first of the fires had caught on the old buildings and they multiplied with speed as Seleukos reached the main gate. Unmanned it was, for all had fled or rushed to stem the attack over the walls. 'Get that open,' he shouted to the closest men following him as he turned and stood, four square, with his shield firm and sword poised, for the rest of his men to form up on him. And the gates swung open and Seleukos advanced to let the Sogdians come in behind him. In the middle of the courtyard he stopped; the shield-wall, a single line of fifty men across, stood with the Sogdian archers behind ready to shoot at anyone who charged out of the steadily building flames. But none charged; they just walked at pace quick enough to escape the growing heat but not so quick as to draw an archer's attention.

'Teutamus!' Seleukos shouted. 'Teutamus, come out; Babylon is mine!'

'Over my dead body it is.' Teutamus appeared through the smoke, helmet on and shield and sword ready. Onward he came, swiping his sword left and right. 'We'll settle this man to man!'

Seleukos sighed, lowering his head and shaking it at the futility of the gesture. 'Azanes, would you mind?'

One shout was all that it took for three hundred arrows to pepper the advancing Teutamus; shield, legs, sword arm and face were all hit instantaneously, punching the man back as if he had been struck by a Titan's fist.

Through the smoke Seleukos walked, the flames glinting on his blade as the garrison sat down in surrender. He looked down at the riddled body of Teutamus, his face unrecognisable under the mass of burning shafts. He drew a deep breath, spread his arms and tilted his head up to the sky, his eyes closed, and roared his thanks to Bel Marduk.

And tears rolled down his cheeks, for he had Babylon.

Author's Note

Once again this work of fiction is based upon the writings of Diodorus, Plutarch and fragments of Arrian, all of whom used the lost history of Hieronymus as their primary source. I have kept mainly to what are the accepted facts – if any historical detail can be considered factual, as there is so much that is uncertain over such a period of time and the primary sources were written after the events. Again, I have blurred things in the timeline as the High and Low timelines differ by a year, so I have created an amalgamation of the two to best suit the narrative. The actual timeframe of the book is almost four and a half years, so – much as in *The Three Paradises* which has a similar timescale – I felt that some obfuscation of the passing of time was necessary to avoid continually saying how much time has passed. This necessarily led to a few little round-ups of what had been occurring elsewhere, for which I hope you will forgive me as they saved probably in the region of half a book!

Crateuas was Peithon's father, which explains why he deserted to Kassandros on hearing of the execution of his son. Why Antigonos made such a politically inept move seems at first sight to be puzzling; however, I believe that it is a good insight into the way he was thinking: once he had defeated Eumenes and the east was in his hands he believed that nothing and nobody would stop him and could therefore treat his allies with disdain. Pythan, Antigonos' satrap of Babylonia, was really another Peithon so I had to change the spelling to avoid confusion. There are, indeed, quite a few similar-sounding names and even some duplications, for which I can only apologise but hide behind the defence of historical accuracy.

Dioscurides, his brother Ptolemaios and their cousin Telesphorus were all Antigonos' nephews, though whose sons they were is not clear.

Some sources say that it was Kassandros who demanded Kappadokia and attacked Amistus but that makes little sense considering what his objectives were at the time. It is therefore more likely that Kassandros has been transposed from Asandros who, in order to avoid confusion with Kassandros, I refer to as Asander.

The demands made to Antigonos by the satraps are a matter of record and were, I believe, purposely designed to be unacceptable and force him into war. Artonis being the tool that Ptolemy uses to bring the alliance together with Eumenes' message from beyond the grave is my fiction – but I missed Eumenes so I wanted to keep the sly little Greek involved!

Kassandros did preside over the Nemean Games as had Alexander before him. This, in conjunction with his using the royal prerogative of founding a city, Thessalonike and Kassandreia as well as re-founding Thebes – razed by Alexander – along with burying King Philip III, leaves little to the imagination as to what was going on in his mind – and probably in Thessalonike's also. That Thessalonike was the main force behind the couple is my fiction, but, with the way that things played out historically – to be seen in later books – I find it perfectly feasible. Demochares was allowed to massacre his opponents in Corinth as thanks for his treachery, and it was considered by many to be a normal way of showing gratitude.

The democrats were burned alive in Argos and slaughtered in the Temple of Artemis in Orchomenus.

Finally, the battle of Gaza happened very much as I've described. Ptolemy did draw Demetrios north by threatening Cilicia thus exhausting much of his cavalry before they arrived back at Gaza. Nearchos, Pythan and Andronicus were left by Antigonos to advise the young Demetrios but he did not take much heed of them; but it was the elephant traps that won the day for Ptolemy as much as Demetrios' impetuousness. Seleukos did fight Pythan hand to hand and then went immediately back east to claim his prize. How he took Babylon is not clear but I enjoyed having my take on it. Teutamus being the commander of the garrison is my fiction but I so wanted to give him a nasty ending after what he did to Eumenes.

I am indebted to many modern histories of the time, especially the compelling *Ghost on the Throne* by James Romm, *Dividing the Spoils* by Robin Waterfield, *Antigonos the One-Eyed* by Jeff Champion, *Antigonos the One-Eyed and the Creation of the Hellenistic State* by Richard A. Billows, *The Rise of the Seleukid Empire* and *Antipater's Dynasty* by John D. Granger, both volumes of *The Wars of Alexander's Successors* by Bob Bennett and Mike Roberts, *The Rise of the Hellenistic Kingdoms* by Philip Matyszak and *The Macedonian War Machine* by David Karunanithy.

My thanks, as always, go to my agent, Ian Drury at Shiel Land Associates, and Gaia Banks and Alba Arnau in the foreign rights department.

My thanks also to my new editor, Sarah de Souza, for her insight and making the book better; and also thanks to Tamsin Shelton for her attention to detail during the copy-edit.

My love and thanks go to my wife Anja whose map and chapter symbols add so much to the feel of the book.

Finally, my thanks to you, dear reader, for joining me thus far.

Alexander's Legacy continues with *Forging Kingdoms*.

LIST OF CHARACTERS

(Those in italics are fictional.)

Adea	Deceased daughter of Cynnane and Alexander's cousin Amyntas. Wife of Philip III, formerly Arrhidaeus.
Aeacides	The young king of Epirus.
Agathocles	Tyrant of Syracuse.
Agathon	Brother of Asander.
Agesilaos	Antigonos' agent in Cyprus and Cyrenaica.
Alexander	The cause of all the trouble.
Alexander	Alexander's posthumously born son by Roxanna.
Alexandros	Polyperchon's son.
Antigenes	Veteran commander of the Silver Shields. Now deceased.
Antigonos	Satrap of Phrygia appointed by Alexander.
Antiochus	Son of Seleukos and Apama.
Antipatros	Regent of Macedon in Alexander's absence. Father of Kassandros and Philip. Now deceased.
Apama	Seleukos' Persian wife.
Archias	A one-time tragic actor turned bounty-hunter.
Aristodemus	Antigonos' chief agent
Aristonous	The oldest of Alexander's seven bodyguards.
Artakama	Ptolemy's first wife, from Persia. Sister of Artonis and half-sister of Barsine.
Artonis	Eumenes' Persian widow. Sister of Artakama and half-sister of Barsine.
Asander	Satrap of Caria.
Atarrhias	A Macedonian general.

Azanes	*A Sogdian chieftain.*
Babrak	*A Pathak merchant.*
Barsine	Alexander's Persian mistress and mother of his bastard, Heracles. Half-sister of Artakama and Artonis.
Berenice	Antipatros' niece and cousin to Eurydike. Ptolemy's third wife.
Crateuas	A Macedonian general. Father of Peithon.
Demetrios	Son of Antigonos.
Demetrius of Phaleron	De facto Tyrant of Athens.
Dioscurides	Antigonos' nephew and brother of Ptolemaios.
Eudamos	Alexander's satrap of India. Now deceased.
Eumenes	First Philip's and then Alexander's secretary, a Greek from Kardia. Now deceased.
Eurydike	One of Antipatros' daughters, married to Ptolemy.
Heracles	Alexander's bastard by Barsine.
Hieronymus	A soldier turned historian; a compatriot of Eumenes.
Kassandros	Antipatros' eldest son.
Kleopatra	Daughter of Philip II and Olympias, Alexander's full sister.
Krateros	The great Macedonian general killed in battle with Eumenes.
Lagus	Eldest son of Ptolemy and his mistress Thais.
Lycortas	*Steward to Ptolemy.*
Lysimachus	One of Alexander's seven bodyguards. Satrap of Thrace.
Matthias	*Jewish garrison commander of Joppa.*
Menelaus	Governor of Cyprus. Brother of Ptolemy.
Monimus	Commander of Pella. Now deceased.
Myrmidon	*Athenian mercenary general in Ptolemy's pay.*
Naramsin	*Priest of Bel Marduk and Seleukos' architect.*
Nearchos	A Cretan, Alexander's chief admiral, now in Antigonos' pay.
Olympias	One of Philip II's wives, mother to Alexander and Kleopatra. Now deceased.
Oxyartes	Satrap of Paropamisadae. Father of Roxanna.

Peithon	One of Alexander's seven bodyguards, son of Crateuas. Satrap of Media.
Penelope	Alexandros' wife.
Perdikkas	One of Alexander's seven bodyguards. Now deceased.
Peucestas	One of Alexander's seven bodyguards. Satrap of Persis.
Phila	Antipatros' daughter, widow of Krateros, now married to Demetrios.
Philip	Son of Antipatros and Hyperia, twin brother of Pleistarchos, half-brother of Kassandros.
Philip – formerly Arrhidaeus	The mentally challenged and deceased half-brother of Alexander.
Philippos	Younger son of Antigonos
Philotas	Friend of Antigonos. Executed by Eumenes.
Phthia	Wife of Aeacides, King of Epirus. Mother to Pyrrhus.
Pleistarchos	Son of Antipatros and Hyperia, twin brother of Philip, half-brother of Kassandros.
Polycleitus	*Ptolemy's garrison commander of Gaza.*
Polyperchon	Former regent of Macedon. Father of Alexandros.
Prepelaus	Commander of the Pella garrison.
Ptolemaios	Antigonos' nephew and brother of Dioscurides.
Ptolemy	One of Alexander's seven bodyguards, perhaps Philip II's bastard.
Pyrrhus	Son of Aeacides, King of Epirus.
Pythan	Antigonos' nominee as Seleukos' replacement as satrap of Babylonia.
Roxanna	A Bactrian princess, widow of Alexander and mother to his son Alexander.
Seleukos	Satrap of Babylonia.
Stasoikos	King of Marion on Cyprus.
Stratonice	Daughter of Demetrios and Phila, grand-daughter of Antigonos and Stratonice.
Stratonice	Wife of Antigonos and mother to Demetrios.
Telesphorus	One of Antigonos' senior officers.
Temenos	*Macedonian officer loyal to Seleukos, commander of the Babylon garrison.*

Teutamus	A Macedonian officer loyal to Antigonos, commander of the Babylon garrison.
Thais	Long-time mistress of Ptolemy.
Thessalonike	Alexander's half-sister and wife of Kassandros.
Xenophilus	*Warden of the royal treasury in Susa.*